HEARTLESS DEVIL

CHARITY FERRELL

HEARTLESS DEVIL

USA TODAY & WALL STREET JOURNAL BESTSELLING AUTHOR
CHARITY FERRELL

*Oh, you want a morally gray hero who says he'll
burn the world down for the heroine?
Meet Enzo Marchetti.*

"Hell is empty and all the devils are here."
- William Shakespeare

ONE

ENZO

I sat on the edge of the cloister wall as rain cleansed the blood from my hands.

Look at me, conserving water and using natural resources. Someone award me a fucking Nobel Prize.

Thunder rumbled through the night, and I inhaled the cool, damp smell of aged stone as my legs dangled over the wall's ledge.

I'd started coming here during my first year at Saint Vale University. Now, four years later, I'd made it a ritual to return after I took a life.

A cruel smirk spread over my face as my mind drifted back to Marv and how he'd pleaded for his life in the warehouse. The agony in his screams was a symphony to my ears as I severed his fingers cleanly at the knuckles. Each lie he told me cost him another digit. When I ran out of fingers, I took his entire hand.

Mental note: Have Nico mail the hand to Marv's family tomorrow. That way, Marv can always be there to lend a helping hand.

Bright headlights cutting through the storm stole my attention. I brushed raindrops from my face as a Rolls-Royce drove around the fountain at the university's entrance. The car screeched to a halt at the limestone steps that led to the entrance doors.

Saint Vale University was difficult to access. You had a better chance of gaining clearance to the White House. The university restricted public access and prohibited students from going out after curfew. Headmaster Arisono was strict about that shit.

Strict about it with other students, that was.

The rules never applied to me. Never applied to us.

Annoyed by the late-night visitor disturbing my peace, I drew my knife from my pocket. I had come here for silence, and they'd ruined that.

A scrawny man sporting an ivy cap exited the car, popped the trunk, and hauled out a suitcase. He dumped the luggage on the bottom step like trash, ignoring the downpour.

I spun the knife in my hand when the car's back door opened. A foot emerged, then another, and seconds passed.

She stepped out into the open, and I stopped spinning my knife. I tightened my grip on the handle, wanting to slit the moon apart so all its light would fall on her.

I blinked, mentally scanning through the faces I knew here. She wasn't one of them.

When I'd first arrived at Saint Vale, I'd learned everything about the students. Blood types. Social Security numbers. Every skeleton hidden in their closets.

She adjusted her skirt, and I dragged the blade across my palm when she slammed the door shut. Pathetic thing just stood there, all wet, but the rain didn't seem to affect her.

She looked so innocent.

So lost, like a stray animal.

Lifting my knife, I lined it up with her head but held back. I bit into my lower lip, and a new thrill replaced the echo of Marv's screams in my head.

Hunting her like a Fawn.

I flashed a smile like the devil I was.

She stepped toward the man, but he walked past her as if she were a ghost. My smile deepened when her shoulders drooped at his rejection. He climbed into the Rolls-Royce and sped off. The tires ripped through a puddle, sending a sheet of water over her.

With a shriek, she stumbled back.

I scoffed and lowered the knife. I'd gut a rat bastard if he ever tried that shit on me.

My gaze stayed locked on her as she grabbed the luggage handle and lifted it, looking utterly pitiful.

If I were a gentleman, I'd help her.

I wasn't.

Like mercy, good manners were overrated.

I pulled out my phone and snapped a photo of her humiliation. It was just my luck that when I did, she glanced straight at me, giving me the perfect shot.

After I got it, I slipped back into the shadows, where I preferred to stay.

She shook her head, as if she'd imagined my stare, and hauled her suitcase up the steps. After a few steps, she stopped to shake out the ache from her hand. She had a good twenty more steps to go before reaching the vestibule.

I opened the photo and increased the screen's brightness. Her features were grainy and pixelated. Dark hair clung to her wet cheeks, and a loose blazer hid her shape.

The night and my phone's shitty resolution blurred everything else about her.

I sent the photo to Nico before texting him, my fingers moving across the screen furiously.

Me: New girl.

Me: Find out who she is.

Me: NOW.

It took him less than thirty seconds to reply.

Faster than it took her to climb the next step.

Nico: That's a shit picture, Zo.

Me: I don't give two fucks if it's a stick figure. Find out who she is.

Nico: I'm in the middle of something.

Me: I'm about to be in the middle of slitting your fucking throat.

Nico: 👍

I pocketed my phone, knowing he'd do as I instructed.

I wasn't a rescuer of strays, and I enjoyed kicking people when they were down. If I were honest, which I rarely was, I liked kicking them until they were six feet under.

I decided right then that she was it.

My Fawn.

My chosen for the year.

She was almost at the top step when my phone buzzed again.

Nico: Blair Dupont.

Me: How'd you figure that out so fast?

Nico: The chick sucking my cock told me.

I blinked raindrops from my eyelashes.

Nico: I can tell you're interested ...

Since he didn't know how to complete fucking sentences, I didn't reply.

Like a stage-five cling-on, he texted me again.

Nico: You won't believe why she got kicked out of her last university. If she's your chosen, I fully support it.

Me: I don't care about your support. I'm not running for fucking mayor.

I hopped off the wall and walked along the stone path bordering the university that led to my private dorm wing. With each step, I plotted the ways I'd make Blair Dupont wish she'd never been born.

God help her fucking soul.

Two

Blair

I was climbing the stairway to hell.

All that was missing was funeral music.

Water soaked through my clothes as I walked up the slick steps. Each one felt like a warning that I didn't belong here.

When I looked up, Saint Vale University towered above like a cathedral. It resembled a castle with its stone walls more than a university. Darkness wrapped around it like a cloak as it reached toward the sky. Stained glass windows glowed from each floor.

There wasn't another soul outside.

At least not one I could *see*.

What I felt was a different story.

A prickle curled up my spine like smoke as I scanned the darkness.

Someone was watching me. I felt it.

Like a predator, waiting for the perfect moment to strike.

I shook off the thought of getting murdered and kept climbing. The closer I got to the top, the tighter my stomach knotted.

Once I reached the vestibule, it'd be official. I'd be a student at Saint Vale University. My third university in four years.

My stepfather had made it clear: Saint Vale was my last chance. If I screwed up here, I was done.

Since I'd never heard of the university, I'd immediately pulled out my phone and researched it, doing a deep dive into its history and rumors.

Royalty, politicians, drug lords, and tech gods all sent their heirs to Saint Vale for its security and privacy. Private donors and tuition fully funded the university. It took nothing from the government, which meant no government eyes were allowed in. The last official who had pushed for oversight vanished.

Saint Vale sat on the edge of Westchester, New York, surrounded by dense forests and towering stone walls that looked centuries old. The kind of walls meant to keep people out or trap them inside. The trees were so thick that they nearly swallowed the entire campus.

The entire place screamed isolation, money, and secrets.

I'd already witnessed how seriously they took security measures when we arrived. Guards carrying rifles stood beneath the black wrought-iron entrance, engraved with the university's crest. They checked our IDs, scanned our fingerprints, and searched every inch of my luggage before even allowing us entry.

When we made it through the gate, it was like I'd crossed into another world.

How my stepfather had gotten me accepted here was beyond me. I was sure his checkbook helped, but I was far from a model student. My academic record had more negative comments than a politician's Facebook profile.

By the time I reached the arched entrance, I was drenched, and my thighs ached. I stepped beneath the stone shelter, and my vision blurred from the rainwater running down my face.

Black iron sconces glowed on each side of the doorway, supplying me with enough light to admire the baroque carvings etched into the stone. I ran my finger over the winding vines, roses, serpents, and gargoyles.

The university crest was on the iron double doors. A shield framed a raven, tangled with two serpents. One serpent's jaw hung open, fangs bared, while the raven's beak and wings were stained dark with carved streaks of blood.

"That's not creepy at all," I muttered before pushing them open.

They groaned as I entered and slowly shut behind me. My jaw dropped as I took in the empty expanse in front of me. The interior matched the exterior's Gothic style.

It radiated wealth from every angle. Marble floors and tall ceilings. Ornate moldings climbed the walls like ivy. It bled with old money. New money. *All* money.

A massive staircase loomed at the center of the hall, splitting into two sweeping wings as it reached the second floor and repeated with the third. Thick stone columns held up the vaulted ceilings high above me. Shadowy archways stretched down the corridors that disappeared into darkness.

Saint Vale was beautiful but felt almost dead inside.

Water dripped from me as I looked around. I froze when I heard the click of heels against the floor.

My gaze lifted to a woman in a black pantsuit—very Hilary Banks—walking toward me. As she grew closer, I noticed the university's crest pinned neatly to her blazer.

She stopped in front of me and didn't smile or frown. Her face remained completely still.

"Hi, I'm Blair." I awkwardly smiled. "I'm new." I peered down, noticing a small puddle forming around my black loafers.

"Yes, Blair Dupont," she said, irritation clear in her tone. "I'm Headmaster Arisono."

I smiled again. This one just as awkward and strained.

She clutched a folder with the university crest pressed against her chest. "I'll escort you to your dorm. You're in a double."

I dragged my luggage behind me, groaning as we headed toward more stairs. My arms and legs throbbed as I forced myself up the next flight.

"All classes start at seven sharp," she said as we climbed the steps, handing me a folder and staring at me sternly. "Your schedule and a campus map are inside. I run this school by the *three strikes* rule and have very little tolerance for unruliness. I consider it a headache. A source of wrinkles I won't risk."

I nodded, shifting my suitcase to the other hand to hold the folder.

Fortunately for my arms, we stopped on the second floor and turned right. I followed her down a narrow corridor. No harsh overhead lighting here. That was at least a plus for my migraines.

Arisono stopped at a door inscribed with *Poenas Dare Hall.*

My Latin wasn't perfect, but I understood enough.

To pay the penalty.

Just lovely. My dorm's theme was apparently retribution.

Arisono pushed the door open, revealing a quiet hall lined with six doors, evenly spaced along the walls. We passed one before stopping at room 205, and my palms turned clammy.

The door was completely bare.

No posters, pictures, or decorations, like the dorms at my other schools.

I gripped my luggage tight as Arisono knocked.

Seconds passed before the door swung open, brightening the hall. A skinny blond girl stood there, wearing a black satin night-gown and fluffy pink slippers. Her green eyes darted nervously between Arisono and me.

"Headmaster?" she asked, trying to hide her irritation.

"Daphne, this is your new roommate, Blair." Arisono nudged me forward.

Without another word, she turned and left us.

The smile I gave Daphne felt just as stiff and forced as the ones I'd given Arisono.

Now that Arisono was gone, Daphne looked less annoyed and waved me inside. I rolled my suitcase behind me and shut the door. The room smelled strongly of sage, as if we'd interrupted an exorcism.

I wrinkled my nose at the smell while taking in the room.

I'd never seen such a lavish dorm. Though the spawn of the elite probably didn't sleep in standard dorms.

I never saw myself as part of the elite. Nor would anyone else.

Maybe that was because I never had money growing up. It was my mother's husband, who she didn't become involved with until I was older, who paid for everything now.

Also, most people didn't even know I existed. I was the secret she kept hidden. The one who threatened to expose her past.

The beds sat on opposite sides of the room, nestled into cherrywood alcoves beneath sculpted archways. Each alcove had its own window and chandelier above the bed. Maroon curtains draped in front of the alcoves, the option to draw them across the opening for privacy, and floor-to-ceiling bookshelves framed each side.

The room also had two long desks, two dressers, a vanity, and a private bathroom.

It didn't take long to figure out which side belonged to Daphne. Except for the pile of clothes dumped on my bed, my side was empty.

The space felt just as dark as the rest of the university.

But there was a sense of comfort, like I could be *me* here.

Could lose myself in books and my studies in that alcove.

"I swear, I'm not a bitch," Daphne blurted.

Her upbeat voice made me flinch, and I looked toward her.

"Arisono's late-night dorm visits usually mean someone's about to get expelled." She grabbed the bundle of sage and blew it out. "I was a tad freaked because my mom would literally kill me if I got kicked out. I'm already on Arisono's shit list."

She tossed the sage in an ashtray and padded across the room. "She could've at least given me a heads-up that I was getting a new roommate. I would've taken my things off your bed."

I shuffled aside as she swept the clothes off my bed and dumped them into a basket.

"And excuse the mess," she rambled. "I've had the room to myself since Clarissa fell out of that stupid window."

My gaze moved from the window to the bed. "She fell out of the window?"

Daphne dropped the basket on the Persian rug, kicking it away with her slipper, and muttered, "Technically, yes."

"How does one *technically* fall out of a window?" I tossed my suitcase onto the bed, hoping *I* wasn't the one coming off like a bitch.

I clutched my stomach; the thought of sleeping in a dead girl's bed sounded as appealing as being burned alive. That new piece of information just made this place even creepier.

"Ugh, blame it on Enzo's crazy ass." She collapsed onto her bed and hung upside down while digging through a drawer beneath it. When she resurfaced, she held a bottle of tequila. She released a breath while untwisting the cap and took a long swallow without even flinching.

I dragged my fingers through the wet knots in my hair. "Who's Enzo?"

"He's ..." She frowned, searching for the right word. Failing to find one, she took another drink. "Just to let you know, I didn't push Clarissa. I'm a great roommate." She pointed the bottle at me. "I was voted Best Roommate at my boarding school." A proud smile hit her lips. "You're in good hands."

Her need to clarify that didn't calm me.

If anything, it did the opposite.

She took another swig, capped the bottle, and shoved it back inside the drawer. "The sheets are new, and we checked the mattress for blood. You're all good!" Sitting upright on her bed, she fluffed her pillow and made herself comfortable. "What year are you?"

"Senior," I replied. "You?"

"Sophomore."

I'd never shared a room with someone in a different year before.

But right now, that was the least of my worries.

My gaze skimmed back to the window.

"Why would there be blood if she fell out of the window?" I asked slowly.

"There wasn't. We checked for it, just in case." Daphne grabbed an eye mask and stretched it over her head. "I'll let you get settled. We can chat about it tomorrow. Nice to meet you, Blair." She blew me a kiss, lowered the mask over her face, and pulled her curtain shut.

All righty, I mouthed.

My heart didn't relax as I started unpacking my suitcase. Dread accompanied it like a new friend as I folded my clothes into the drawers and hung the rest in my closet. It worsened as I dressed in my pajamas, brushed my teeth, and finally climbed into bed.

Into the dead girl's bed.

I pulled the curtain closed and scooted toward the window to check the lock. The window opened and closed with a crank and was too narrow for something to simply *fall out.*

You'd have to squeeze through. Jump. Or someone would have to push you.

I carefully peeked outside and stifled a scream when my eyes landed on someone wearing a mask, standing below the window, staring straight up at me. My breath caught as I jerked it back closed, then pressed my hand against my chest.

I forced myself to look again.

My pulse raced as I slowly peeled the curtain aside, scanning the darkness outside. The person was gone, but that didn't make me feel any more relaxed.

"You're seeing shit, Blair," I tried to tell myself, yanking the curtain shut.

I repeated the same mantra as I collapsed onto my back and pulled the quilt up to my chin. It felt like a lifetime had passed as I struggled to get comfortable.

Something wicked hung in the air. No matter how many times I shut my eyes, sleep wouldn't come to me. Even in the safety of this room, I still felt watched, just like I had outside on those steps.

When I finally drifted off, another nightmare found me.

In the same bellowed voice, he said the words he always did. *"Admit it, Blair. Admit it's your fault!"*

I shot upright in bed as I gasped for air.

I hadn't dreamed of that in years.

But the nightmare was back now that I was here.

Something dark and evil crept through the halls of Saint Vale.

I'd only been here an hour, and I could already feel it.

I'd willingly walked straight into hell.

How far would I allow the devil to drag me in?

The bright morning sun filtered through the window when I woke, warming my comfortable alcove. For a moment, I just lay there, staring up at the crystal chandelier above my bed, counting the crystals.

The memories of last night didn't take long to rush through me.

The rain. Arisono. Sleeping in a dead girl's bed. The masked figure outside my window.

I groaned as I rolled toward the window and peeked outside.

My mind could've been playing tricks on me last night. I had been stressed and tired. It could've been a shadow of something moving in the storm.

I frowned when all I found was a stone wall below. Thick ivy climbed its surface. No trees or anything else for me to mistake for a person's shadow.

Yawning, I pushed back my curtain. Soft music drifted through the room, and I had to hold myself back from covering my ears.

Daphne sat at the vanity curling her hair.

The warmth of the alcove and the quilt slipped away as I slid out of my bed.

"Morning!" Daphne chirped, sounding way too chipper for a girl who had chugged tequila last night. "You ready for your first day?" She dropped the pink curling iron to swivel in the stool and look at me. "You seriously started at the perfect time. The professors aren't being as annoying as they are at the beginning of the school year."

"Morning," I grumbled, politely smiling while shuffling toward the vanity.

I grimaced at my reflection in the vanity mirror from behind her, taking in the puffy, dark circles beneath my eyes, and swallowed down the urge to tell her I wasn't ready at all.

Not ready for classes, for Saint Vale, and definitely not for whatever had lurked outside my window last night.

Daphne glanced down at the watch on her wrist, settled between gold Cartier bracelets. "We have twenty minutes before classes start. If we're late, the professor emails Arisono. She considers it one of her *strikes*." She rolled her eyes while unplugging the curling iron.

I gave her a small, appreciative smile for the heads-up.

The last thing I needed was a strike on my first day.

While Daphne might've been a roommate killer, so far, I liked her.

I shuffled to the bathroom, wishing I'd set my alarm last night, and took the fastest shower of my life.

When I returned to our room, Daphne was finished with her makeup. We switched places at the vanity.

Her crisp white Oxford shirt, with the Saint Vale crest neatly embroidered over the left breast pocket, matched mine. So did her gray pleated skirt and white socks. Saint Vale's uniform. Though they did give us the option of the socks or black tights. I chose tights today.

Not having the time to dry my hair, I pulled it into a ponytail, smoothing the strands down. Scooting closer, I drew a sharp line of black winged eyeliner across each lid before applying mascara. For the final touch, I tied a red ribbon around my ponytail, pulling the knot tight.

"Any words of advice?" I asked Daphne.

"About what?" she asked.

I stood and zipped my skirt. "Surviving Saint Vale."

"Honestly? Most students don't leave this place with their sanity fully intact." She grabbed her black Mary Jane pumps from the floor and slid them on. "This place can be the best time of your life or the absolute worst."

"How do I make it not the worst?"

"Lie low and mind your business. It's boring but safe."

"I'm okay with boring."

"Suit yourself." She flashed a smile. "I hate boring."

We grabbed our bags and left the room.

Other students were already walking out of the corridor toward the steps.

"Definitely follow Arisono's curfew," Daphne added as we walked. "She's strict as fuck about it. And trust me, don't test her. Just because she can't move her face doesn't mean she's not crazy. Only a few students are exempt from her rules, and no offense, but if you were on that list, you wouldn't have me as a roommate." She motioned toward the third floor. "You'd have your own wing."

I nodded in understanding, filing everything she told me into my brain.

She smiled and waved at a girl as we passed, clicking her tongue against the roof of her mouth as she thought about what else to tell me. "Oh! Don't go outside campus after dark. *And* don't make fun of me for this ridiculous idiom, but there *are* things that go bump in the night here."

There was no stopping my snort. "What, like the bogeyman?"

"I'd say bogey*men*."

I slowed, remembering the figure outside my window last night.

Daphne kept her pace. "Since we're on the subject of bogeymen, if you see a guy wearing a mask, turn around and walk in the other direction. Do. Not. Run."

"Why don't I run?"

"They'll see it as a game."

"Who's *they*?"

She skipped down the stairs, all peppy, but nothing was lighthearted about the way she'd told me not to run.

She'd said it like it was the law, and breaking it would send you straight to prison.

No, straight to the death penalty.

"Are masked men ... a regular thing here?" I asked.

She didn't answer me.

"Daphne," I pressed, *"are they?"*

She shrugged, adjusting the strap of her Hermès bag on her shoulder. "Look, we're in the middle of bumfuck nowhere. Most of us grew up in cities with clubs, private yachts, places to always have fun and party. Saint Vale doesn't have any of that."

"What does it have?"

"Nothing, so we find ways to entertain ourselves. Since I'd prefer not to have another dead roommate, especially after my mom had to hire an attorney *and* the assholes here called me the Roommate Killer for a freaking month"—she stopped talking and turned to look at me—"remember, lie low, okay?"

"Lie low," I repeated with a nod when we reached the last step.

That was always my strategy at every new university.

Stay quiet, invisible, and out of trouble.

But somehow, I always messed up.

"Oh! Let me add another piece of advice: if his last name is Marchetti, stay the hell away from him. If he's hot here, he's psycho." She pressed a peck on my cheek, as if boundaries didn't exist to her. "Have a good first day."

I stood there, rubbing my cheek in confusion, as she skipped across the vestibule toward a group of girls waiting near a door.

All four of them turned to look at me.

None of them smiled. Their expressions ranged from curious to unimpressed. They were beautiful in that untouchable, intimidating way that made you feel like you'd wandered into the cool kids' party that you were never invited to.

They were definitely not the welcoming committee.

New Girl Syndrome was never fun.

I turned away from them and checked my schedule before searching the campus map for my first class, American Gothic Literature.

A few students bumped my shoulder as I followed the corridor toward the lecture room. The room was already half full when I arrived. I handed the professor my paperwork and slipped into the seat in the third row beside two empty desks.

A minute later, two guys dropped into the seats next to me.

One winked. The other jerked his chin up.

I reminded myself of Daphne's advice. *Lie low.*

But just like every university before this one, I messed up.

During my first class at Saint Vale, I caught the devil's attention.

THREE

ENZO

Punctuality was as important to me as a pussy to a eunuch.

The only man whose time I respected was my father's.

Nobody disrespected his schedule. Not me. Not the president. Not the richest man on earth.

Which was why I gave no fucks that I was going to be thirty minutes late to American Gothic Lit. While I had zero interest in pursuing a career in literature or any profession that required a degree, my parents expected one thing from me while I was here: an acceptable GPA.

My father viewed failure as a weakness.

He despised weakness.

He'd never attended college. Nor did my older brother, Benny.

College had never been in the cards for me either until President Byron approached my father four years ago. He gave him an offer that led to lucrative deals, contracts with high-powered officials, and further opportunities for our family's illegal ventures. It was a deal too good for my father to refuse. It'd also introduced me to a world that changed my life.

Most people feared the Marchetti name. Saint Vale made us even more untouchable. I was here to expand our influence, not for some shitty-ass, overpriced piece of paper. Running a criminal empire didn't require a degree.

Cristian Marchetti—my father, who was also known as Monster Marchetti—was the boss of the Marchetti Mafia family. Benny served as his underboss. Our name sat on the top of every Fed's wish list, but no matter how hard they tried to pin our crimes on us, we were always two steps ahead of them.

I aspired to be as sinister as my father.

As brutal and merciless.

Every day, I got closer.

Professor Nelson glanced up from the whiteboard when the lecture room door opened. Instinctively, he parted his lips, prepared to scold the tardy student. He slammed them shut when he found me.

I gave him a lazy salute, adding a flip of the bird for fun. His glare followed me down the aisle as I walked to the back row.

I had no respect for a man who wore a man bun and had once claimed Melville was superior to Poe. I'd take a lunatic hiding corpses beneath his floorboards over the idiot chasing a whale any day.

Last night, after leaving the wall, I had called Nico and told him to tell me everything he'd found on Blair. Judging from the slapping sounds in the background and the chick whining his name, he was mid-fuck but still managed to explain why she'd been expelled from her last university.

It confirmed what I'd already suspected. I'd chosen well, and she deserved everything coming to her.

I told Nico to hack into Saint Vale's system and send me her class schedule. After that, I spent the rest of the night stalking everything I could find out about her, though I found very little.

She wasn't on social media.

If you weren't on social media, you were hiding something.

That was why I wasn't on it.

American Gothic Lit had turned out to be the only class we shared, which was unfortunate.

I scanned the lecture hall and spotted her quickly. She sat at a desk in the third row between two morons.

Her back was straight, shoulders square, posture perfect. As Nelson droned about symbolism, she tapped her pen against her temple in sync with his words.

Unlike our classmates, she hadn't looked at me when I arrived late.

That got under my skin.

I slid into the chair behind her, two seats away from Cedric. He glanced up from his phone, flipped me off, and resumed his texting.

Cedric and I were the only ones without laptops. We never took notes and still aced every exam.

Blair's MacBook sat open on her desk, and the screen was dark. A notebook rested across the keyboard while she wrote in it with her left hand.

I licked my lips, imagining all the things I'd make that hand do.

Her dark brown hair was pulled into a tight ponytail and tied with a red ribbon. Six freckles dotted the nape of her neck. I wanted to take my knife and play connect the dots with it.

Resting my arms on the desk, I leaned in closer, inhaling her perfume and frowning in disappointment at the cheap scent.

Did she buy that shit at the gas station?

Anyone who willingly wanted to smell like raspberry candy deserved death row.

She'd need to fix that.

Her Saint Vale button-up was crooked at the collar, which annoyed me even more. While she matched the rest of the students in their white shirts, mine was black. So was Cedric's. White wasn't good for bloodstains.

Sunlight poured through the tall windows, striking her right cheek. I peered over her head, appreciating the mural of a demon sacrificing angels above the whiteboard.

Aside from the loser professor, this was my favorite class,

thanks to that painting. I respected any form of art that involved slaughter.

I cracked my neck and clicked my tongue to get Blair's attention.

Her neighbor glanced back, but not her.

I cleared my throat. Same result.

Tension knotted in my neck. I flexed my fingers, debating if she was ignoring me intentionally or just too absorbed in that notebook of hers. I made a mental note to burn that fucking thing if it became a habit.

Blair was about to learn her first lesson at Saint Vale: nobody ignored me.

If I coughed, if I so much as breathed in her direction, she needed to give me her undivided attention.

While Nelson prattled on, I stretched forward and clamped my hand around her ponytail. I pulled on it, but she didn't react.

Heat rushed to my cock when I tugged it again. Harder this time.

Her head snapped back, and she whipped around to glare at me over her shoulder.

I settled back in my chair, keeping a straight face, waiting for her to confront me.

But all she did was narrow those green doe eyes at me.

Disappointment settled over me like dust when she spun back around. Her ponytail whipped through the air with the movement.

When she started writing again, I yanked her ponytail harder. So hard that I nearly dragged her out of the seat.

Cedric snorted beside me.

She dropped her pen, swinging entirely around to stare at me in horror. "Why are you pulling my hair?" Her voice dripped with attitude but was still soft-spoken. Like sugar laced with poison.

I smiled wickedly, now fully able to see every feature on her face.

Up close, she was prettier than I'd expected, more attractive than her school photos. Smooth skin with no blemishes. Her short bangs parted over her forehead, framing her heart-shaped face. Cheeks a subtle pink, like she'd been out in the sun for too long.

Her lips were glossy and full, and I wondered how hard I'd have to bite to make them bleed. Then I imagined them bloody while my cock made them open wider.

When I didn't answer because I was too busy brainstorming all the ways I wanted to ruin that pretty face, she waved her hand in front of my face.

"I asked why you pulled my hair, jackass," she snapped.

I curled my lip at her interruption.

Another nail in her coffin.

She rubbed at her scalp, waiting for my response, as if I'd waste my breath giving her one. I never answered for my violence.

"What's your name?" I questioned.

I already knew it, obviously.

But I wanted to hear it leave her mouth. Hear how it sounded in her voice.

That way, I'd have something I could replay while planning all the things I'd do to her.

She reared back, as if I'd asked her for a lung. "Excuse me?"

I leaned in as close as I could to the desk. "Your. Name."

Her attitude sharpened. "That's none of your concern."

"It's fully my concern."

Her thick brows furrowed. "My first name is Fuck Off. And my last? It's I'm Reporting You to Arisono If You Pull My Hair Again." She looked smug, clearly proud of her lame answer.

I kicked my feet up on the desk, appreciating her smart mouth. I'd punish her for it later, though.

I stared at her with pure satisfaction. "Your parents should be shot for giving you that name. Provide me with their address, and I'll do you that favor."

She gaped at me, her mouth falling open.

I half expected her to give me some sob story about a dead parent. Not that I'd care if she did.

Instead of arguing, she huffed and spun back around.

I chuckled. Joke was on her.

Cedric stared at me as I rolled my shoulders and pulled my knife from my pocket. I ran my finger over the blade, checking for any trace of Marv's blood. I'd cleaned it well last night.

Cedric's attention shifted from me to Blair.

Of course, it'd take violence to pry his attention away from texting whatever poor girl he was fucking over. Last time I had stolen his phone, I'd noticed he sent a chick's nudes to her priest. The fucker loved violence and cruelty as much as I did.

It made sense, given we were both Marchettis. Cruelty came naturally.

I leaned forward, and my fingers twitched as I wrapped them back around Blair's ponytail. This time, I yanked it hard enough that I knew her scalp would hurt for days.

A loud gasp rattled from her lungs. Smirking, I wrapped her hair around my wrist, holding it like a leash as she shrieked, struggling to escape my grip.

Nelson paused his lecture.

I was providing better entertainment than his mediocre teachings anyway.

I steadied my hand and cut her hair cleanly as the chair rocked underneath her.

All eyes were on us, witnessing her humiliation.

A bonus I hadn't planned.

Before her chair tipped over, I swiftly released her.

No reason for my Fawn to get a brain injury. Not yet, at least.

I needed to have my fun first.

A shrill gasp left her when she lurched forward. She slammed her hands onto the desk to catch herself. I slipped the clump of severed hair and my knife into my pocket.

She stood, clutching her ruined and now shorter ponytail, and parted her lips in disbelief while taking in the damage I'd done. I kicked my feet up on the desk again, acting bored, and crossed my arms.

It took the poor girl a few stunned seconds to find words.

"Did you just fucking cut my hair, you asshole?" were the ones she found.

Her attitude impressed me.

I uncrossed my arms to pop my knuckles, matching her glare. "I have no idea what you're talking about."

She inched closer, holding up her hair.

I rolled my eyes. She was lucky I was too lazy to snatch my knife and take off a few more inches.

At my lack of answer, she held her ponytail in front of my face. "You cut my hair, you psycho."

I swatted the ponytail away. "I'd rather not get lice, thanks."

She spun toward Nelson. "You all just saw that, right?" She lifted her ponytail as proof.

I loved that her voice trembled and cracked. Her being on the brink of crying made my cock hard.

It was laughable that she believed anyone would come to her rescue or stick up for her. She was at the wrong university if she thought she mattered to any student or professor here.

Like the pussy he was, Professor Nelson stared at the whiteboard and started writing nonsense about homework. The rest of the class pretended to focus on their laptops.

So many fucking cowards here.

"Seriously?" she screeched, flinging her arms toward our worthless professor. "He assaulted me!"

Nelson's beady eyes lifted to me, squinting in my direction.

I cocked my head, daring him to challenge me.

His warning look was entertaining. I'd seen Marchetti toddlers look more threatening.

My evil smirk grew as I watched him gulp.

The glare he wanted to give me shifted to Blair. "Ms. Dupont," he said stiffly, "do not interrupt my lecture again."

"But—" she tried.

Nelson cut her off. "I understand you're new here, but you are to keep all *personal disputes* out of lecture halls. If you have an issue with him, take it up after class. Now, face forward and pay attention."

"Yeah, *Blair*," I drawled from behind her. "We can handle this *after class*."

Her mouth opened, as if to argue more, then closed. The pink in her cheeks brightened, and she whirled around, dropping back into her seat.

I slipped my hand into my pocket and touched the strands of her hair.

Shame I hadn't cut more.

But then what would I pull when she misbehaved?

My sister Seraphina had once asked me why we had Fawns. Her voice carried a tone of curiosity and disapproval, reminding me too much of our mother. Seraphina didn't share our father's appetite for cruelty like me. She had too much of our mother inside her. Too much conscience.

Still, she was a Marchetti, and that blood ran too deep to erase it all.

When something she cared about was threatened, that defiant spark came out. We all had our triggers. Hers was injustice. Mine was pretty much everything.

My answer to her question had been because it was fun.

After class finally ended, the room emptied quickly. Classmates poured out like rats scurrying from a sinking ship. Even Nelson packed up faster than usual, most likely not wanting to witness whatever hell I planned to put Blair through.

I stayed where I was, eyes on Blair, who remained in her seat.

She was waiting for me to leave first. Smart girl.

It was just the two of us, and from the way she kept fidgeting in her chair, I knew she was uncomfortable with that.

Good. That was exactly how I wanted it.

I tapped my fingers slowly against my desk.

Tap. Tap. Tap.

Then I leaned back in my chair and hummed a Nine Inch Nails song, whispering her name every few seconds, as if I were a demon breathing down her neck.

"*Blair.*" *Tap, tap, tap.* "*Blair.*" *Tap, tap, tap.*

"Asshole," she muttered while standing, shoving her MacBook into a cheap leather bag without sparing me a glance.

A chill rolled through the room as I palmed my knife, slipped it free, and reached across the desk. I sliced her tights in one clean motion. She recoiled instantly, stumbling back a step as the fabric tore. The rip spread along the thin black material, exposing her pale skin beneath. For a moment, I thought she might fall.

I frowned when she caught herself.

My attention dropped to the tear, the exposed strip of her skin, and a slow smirk curled across my face. The urge to kneel in front of her, to inspect my damage and see if the blade had drawn blood, ran hot through my veins.

But that would have to wait.

Like so many other things with her would.

Her eyes turned glossy. She was so close to crying that I could practically taste the tears.

I pushed back my chair and stood slowly. "*Alla prossima, ratta.*"

Her stare was a mixture of horror and disbelief.

I twirled the knife between my fingers, let out a slow whistle, and left.

She was a rat who'd pay for her sins.

Starting tonight.

Four
Blair

The rest of my classes that day passed in a blur.

Words from professors drifted past me like fog. All I could think about was *him* and the sting of his knife nicking my skin. The way my tights had torn and that stupid, callous smirk of his that promised more carnage.

My jaw clenched every time I replayed his arrogant look in my head.

Everyone, including the professor, had witnessed what he did, but no one defended me. Instead, they'd cowered, as if he were an untouchable god they feared and worshipped.

But didn't they know that all gods eventually fell?

Prometheus had been chained. Atlas condemned to carry the heavens on his back. Ares shamed.

Even the divine eventually answered for their sins.

What was worse, was that the asshole who'd cut my hair looked like a Greek god. One who belonged in a painting that'd sell at auction for millions.

I hated how symmetrical his face was. It was almost unnatural, too perfect for a living, breathing person. Frowning, I resented how I found such a horrid man attractive. But beauty wasn't the only thing I saw when looking at him.

Something dark and predatory lurked behind his brown eyes.

He was a devil dressed up as the man of your dreams.

During my next lecture, while the professor rambled, I pulled my phone out and searched what he'd said to me before leaving the lecture hall.

"Alla prossima, ratta."

Until next time, rat.

A chill crawled down my spine.

The way he'd said those words to me wasn't friendly.

They'd left his lips like a threat. A promise.

I debated closing out of the search results and booking an Uber to get the hell out of here.

For the rest of the day, people avoided me, and I knew it was because of the gossip around my new haircut.

Classmates looked away from me or turned in the opposite direction. No one sat beside me in class. I heard whispers behind my back.

I tried asking a few classmates his name, but no one answered.

One girl pretended she hadn't heard me and scurried away. Another guy literally trembled, as if saying his name would summon a demon.

When lunch finally came, I brought my food to the library to avoid another run-in with him.

And by food, I meant a stale, half-crushed granola bar.

A gold plate labeled *Somnus Library* was on the wall before I walked in. As I moved deeper into the library, I looked around in awe. Sunlight streamed through the arched windows. The space was breathtaking with two stories of carved wooden bookshelves that stretched to the ceiling. There were hundreds of books— newer titles, along with some with spines so worn that you couldn't make out their titles.

It felt more like a fairy-tale castle than a library in a weird-ass university.

I climbed the staircase to the second floor and found a small study table tucked in a corner. The farthest away from anyone.

After setting down my bag, I pulled out my notebook and unwrapped my granola bar. The bar instantly crumbled in my fingers, making a mess.

I'd just taken a bite when a voice spoke from across the table.

"They call them the Night Sons."

My hand flew to my throat as I coughed, choking on my bite, and crumbs scratched my throat.

A short guy, wearing the same crisp Saint Vale uniform, sat across from me.

His blond hair was swept back, perfectly styled, like he'd just stepped off Wall Street. For some reason, he reminded me of crooked wealth, like the kind that'd eventually run for office, then get a felony for insider trading.

He gave me a bright, calculated smile.

"Excuse me?" I croaked, grabbing my water bottle and taking a sip.

"The guy who cut your hair," he said. "He's a Night Son."

I wrinkled my nose at him. "And what does that mean exactly?"

"The Night Sons are the secret society that runs Saint Vale."

"Okay," I drawled slowly. "Is that supposed to scare me?"

Honestly, it kind of did.

Men like the one who cut my hair fed on fear. Thrived on it. Devoured it like it was their favorite carb.

And the fact that he belonged to some secret society that supposedly ran the university made things even scarier.

The guy scratched his clean-shaven cheek, though I noticed there was a fresh nick, like he'd cut himself this morning. "It should scare you more than anything."

I scoffed, faking indifference. "I've attended enough universities to know exactly who the guy who cut my hair is. That prep-school jerk will peak early. Give him a few more years, and he'll have a receding hairline and erectile dysfunction before he hits thirty. Men like him aren't a rarity, particularly in *this* tax bracket."

He shook his head violently. "Enzo Marchetti *is* a rarity."

Enzo. The name of my tormentor.

His name hit me like a warning label of poison after you took a drink of it.

"He's not some prep-school jerk," he continued. "He's fucking crazy." His voice lowered a notch. "Your haircut? Child's play compared to what he has planned for you. You need to watch your back here."

Fear shot through me.

He adjusted the cuff of his blazer, deliberately showing off his gold diamond watch.

I forced a polite smile, thankful he'd at least had the guts to provide a name. "Thank you for the warning. Is this a club they just started? Do they meet on Thursdays?"

He unfortunately didn't share my sense of humor or return the smile. "The Night Sons existed before the university. They created the society to protect the university's secrets. To keep powerful families safe from outsiders. Every year, new members are recruited." He cleared his throat. "And every generation becomes more ruthless than the last. Now, it's nothing but sadistic rituals, like who can be the most brutal."

The more he explained, the more his tone changed.

It sounded like envy, like he desperately wanted to be one, but had never been invited.

"How does one join the Night Sons?" I asked, tapping my nails against the wooden table.

He drew his shoulders back. "Only the Sons know that. What I *do* know is that all of them come from bloodlines of powerful families. Royalty, politicians, drug lords, and the Mafia."

"Mafia?" I snorted. "Didn't they wipe out the mob, like, decades ago?"

He scoffed. "The Mafia never died. They just got better at hiding. They pay the right people to pretend they disappeared and then sent their heirs here."

The crumbs of the granola bar threatened to make their way up.

"Which powerful bloodline is Enzo?" I asked, taking another drink of water. "Royalty? Mafia? Drug lord?"

"His father is one of the most feared Mafia bosses alive. And believe me, Enzo inherited every ounce of his father's viciousness. He makes the devil look like a saint."

I slowly capped my water. "Why are you telling me this, then? If he and this ... society are as dangerous as you say, shouldn't you be too afraid to warn me?"

He paused, scanned the library, and crept closer. I wrinkled my nose at his strong aftershave. It smelled like he'd bathed in it.

"Every year, the Night Sons select a Fawn—their *prey*, if you will," he explained, then nodded in my direction. "It looks like Enzo chose you this year."

A shiver ran through me, and I wrapped my arms around myself.

With a low voice and zero sarcasm, I asked, "What do they do to these *Fawns*?"

"They wear them down until they break. They manipulate, isolate, and torment them. Break them piece by piece until nothing is left." He closed his eyes, his voice lowering as he reopened them. "Last year, Enzo chose my sister, Clarissa, as his Fawn."

That fact hit me like ice water.

"I'm doing this because I wish someone had warned her." He rubbed his palms over his eyes. "Consequences or not."

"Clarissa?" I repeated slowly. "Daphne's old roommate?"

He pulled back and nodded. "Enzo caused her death. But no one will do anything about it. Not Arisono. Not the administration. Not even the police."

My thoughts flashed back to him cutting my hair and how no one had stood up for me. Yep, it checked out to none of them having spines.

Before I could ask another question, a book fell from a shelf. I shot upright, shoving my chair back, ready for Enzo to arrive, knife in hand.

The guy jumped to his feet, looking in every direction. "Be careful, Blair." His gaze held mine. "No one at Saint Vale is who they pretend to be."

After my last class, I gave myself a small tour of the university.

Students passed me and again acted as if I didn't exist, but I didn't mind. I wanted the quiet and space to breathe and think.

I needed to process the fact that some random guy in a secret society had cut my hair in front of an entire classroom and chosen me as *his*.

Saint Vale was old but meticulously cared for. The stone walls carried nearly a century of history, but there wasn't a speck of dust anywhere. No cobwebs in the corners. The tall windows shone, smudge-free.

Whoever had built the university didn't make education their main goal. It had been built to impress and lure in the wealthy. And apparently, the psychotic.

The first floor housed the library, administrative offices, and lecture halls. A gym and pool took up the rest of the space on the opposite side.

The second floor was quieter with dorms that extended from the staircase, branching into corridors like webs. The east wing's dorms were all accessible, but when I wandered toward the west wing, I found tall, locked wrought-iron gates blocking the corridor. It was the same on the third floor.

That reminded me of what Daphne had said about some students having their own wings.

Every hall had a Latin name, like mine.

All dark, morbid phrases that promised gloom.

Sunshine didn't exist in this place.

I was also learning that predators ran these halls, not the administrators.

So far, Daphne was the nicest person I'd met, which was a plus. I'd spend more time with her than anyone else here, given that we shared a room.

When I returned to my dorm, it was around eight. Almost curfew.

Daphne sat at the vanity again, curling her hair while music drifted through her phone speaker. I winced, shook my head, and took a calming breath.

She'd changed out of her uniform into a pink sweater and a short, black skirt.

"Hey, you," she greeted cheerfully, gazing at me in the mirror. "How was your first day?"

I smiled, a thousand questions about the Night Sons trying to climb their way up my throat, but I swallowed them down.

"It sucked," I admitted honestly, stepping closer to the vanity to show Daphne my hair. "Some asshole cut my ponytail in class." I ran my fingers through the jagged strands. "Do you have scissors by chance?"

Her face immediately paled, and she set the curling iron down.

"Shit," she muttered. "I was worried that was you." She opened the drawer, rummaged around, and handed me scissors.

"Thanks." I stood behind her, trimming the uneven pieces while catching fallen strays in my free hand.

Enzo had taken more than I realized. At least a few inches.

My hair no longer brushed the middle of my back. Now, it fell a little past my shoulders.

"Is cutting girls' hair a common practice here?" I asked, snipping another uneven lock. "Like some kind of hazing thing?"

Daphne chose her words carefully. "I wouldn't say ... *common*."

"What would you say, then?" I discarded my hair in the trash.

"Enzo ... he enjoys reactions."

I snorted. "He's a fucking weirdo."

"Remember when I said to avoid the Marchettis?"

I nodded.

"*He's* a Marchetti. And it seems you caught his attention."

"I didn't do anything to catch his attention!" I shrieked, throwing my arms up and pacing behind her. "I was minding my own business in class. He came in late, sat behind me, and"—I stopped my pacing to hold up my hair—"cut my ponytail out of nowhere, like he was bored and decided to play craft time."

She returned to curling her hair, not saying a word, but I could tell she was holding back laughter at my *craft time* comment.

"Has he done that before?" I asked, already dreading her answer.

I thought back to what the guy at the library had told me.

The Night Sons. Clarissa. That stupid freaking window.

"Cut a girl's hair?" Daphne cocked her head, thinking. "Not that I'm aware of." Her shoulders slumped. "Look, just ignore him. Make Enzo think you're not worth his time. If he cuts your hair again, don't react."

"If he cuts my hair again, I'm shaving those preppy-boy strands right off his demon head."

She cracked a smile. "I'm serious. Even if he cuts your hair, your clothes, or, hell, burns down your family home, *ignore him.*"

My jaw dropped. "He burns down homes?"

"He did Clarissa's, and I told her to tell him she'd hated that house and to thank him for it. You have to recognize their games and beat them at it." She shrugged and went back to curling her hair.

"He *burned down* her home?"

At this point, I was positive Enzo was the one who had pushed Clarissa out the window. Hell, I was positive that he'd committed every crime in the Westchester area. It all seemed in his wheelhouse.

She flicked her curling wand in the air. "They had insurance, and he waited until the family dog was at the groomer." She dropped the curling iron and grabbed a lip gloss tube.

I slumped on the edge of her bed, next to a pile of stuffed animals. "Some guy in the library said Enzo chose me as his *Fawn*."

Daphne froze.

"What the hell is a Fawn, Daphne?"

"Well, Bambi was one," she replied, trying to maintain her chipper tone.

I shot her an annoyed look.

Her silence was the answer I'd feared.

She didn't hate the Night Sons like the guy from the library.

It seemed like she wanted to protect them more than anything.

Before I could keep questioning her, someone knocked on the door.

I frowned.

The person on the other side didn't wait for us to respond. A tall red-haired girl slipped inside like she owned the room. She was gorgeous, like a supermodel.

The moment she came into full focus, my jaw dropped as I stuttered, "You're—"

"Adelina Byron," she said with a smile, like she was used to people reacting the way I just had. "Hi, Daphne's new roomie, Blair."

She knew my name.

If I wasn't freaked out that I was someone's human version of Bambi, I'd probably have been grinning like an idiot that the president's daughter knew my name.

Adelina Byron was the most famous first daughter in modern history. I'd seen her face a thousand times online on the news, social media, and magazine covers. In person, she looked even prettier.

Glossy curls spilled over her shoulders in perfect waves, a few strands pulled away from her face and tied with white ribbons. Her outfit was nothing like the polished outfits you saw her wearing at political events.

The baby-blue crop top and pleated skirt didn't match her public style.

"You ready, babe?" she asked Daphne, stealing the lip gloss from her.

Daphne shook her head. "Five minutes."

Adelina uncapped the gloss, looking in the mirror as she smeared it over her lips. When she finished, she smacked her lips together and glanced over her shoulder at me. "Do you want to come with us, Blair?"

"Bad idea," Daphne said quickly with a touch of nervousness. She fluffed her curls and unplugged the curling iron before gesturing toward my uneven ponytail. "Enzo gave her a haircut in class today." She mimicked snipping with her fingers.

"Shit." Adelina shot me an apologetic look. "I thought he was skipping that this year?"

"We had high hopes," Daphne said with a sigh. "But apparently, my new roommate managed to change that."

From the expressions on their faces, it was clear that my invite had been revoked.

Did that mean Enzo would be wherever they were going?

The guy at the library had said the Night Sons all came from powerful families. No one was more powerful than the president. Adelina's older brother had to be close to Enzo's age, and if she was here, I was positive he was too.

Is he also a Night Son?

Daphne stood and forced a smile in my direction. "We'll be back soon. There's a movie night in the commons. You should go and meet some of the girls."

"Okay," I said while nodding.

But I already knew I wasn't doing that.

A deep instinct told me these two were my best chance at learning more about the Night Sons.

To learn about Enzo and make sure I didn't end up a Fawn.

If I couldn't join them, I'd follow them.

FIVE

BLAIR

I grabbed my sweater and waited a few seconds before cracking the dorm room door open.

The student handbook Arisono had given me last night stated that students could study in the library or commons after curfew, but leaving the building was prohibited.

Daphne and Adelina were ignoring curfew, which meant they weren't afraid of Arisono's *three strikes* policy. Daphne had warned me to lie low, acting like sharing a room with me meant she wasn't immune to Arisono's expulsion threats, but maybe she felt safe being with Adelina.

Peeking out, I heard their voices echo in the hallway. My pulse raced when I saw two men in dark suits trailing them.

Probably Secret Service, making this even riskier.

Not only was I sneaking out, but I was also following the president's daughter. They could shoot me just for that.

Once they were far enough ahead, I slipped into the corridor, pulled on my sweater, and stayed in the shadows. They walked quickly, making it hard for me to keep up. The halls grew darker as I followed them toward the west wing.

Frustration crawled through me when I peered around the corner and saw them unlock a metal gate blocking off a corridor.

They slipped through it, and the second suited man secured the padlock behind them. He gave it a firm shake and turned back toward Daphne and Adelina.

Beyond the gate, I saw them stop outside a room. Another girl joined them. I blinked, recognizing her as one of Daphne's friends from this morning.

They didn't come back through the gate. Instead, they went in the opposite direction and vanished down the hall.

I crept to the gate and tried to open it.

It didn't budge.

I tried to squeeze through the bars.

Nope.

Never one to quit, I looked for another way.

I glanced out the window, which faced the side courtyard, and remembered that earlier, I'd noticed an exit door in the library that said it led outside. If I moved fast enough, I could circle the courtyard and reach the other side before they got too far.

I sprinted in that direction, keeping my head down as I slipped into the quiet library and moved between the towering shelves. Ducking low, I pushed open the back door and prayed no alarms would blare when I did.

I gave myself a mental fist bump when it didn't.

Muggy air smacked me in the face. The sky above me was black, illuminated by a thin crescent moon peeking through the clouds. Fog swallowed the campus as I searched for the girls. I pulled my sweater tighter around myself and stepped onto the stone walkway bordering the courtyard.

The world felt unnervingly quiet. Only the sound of the wind and my footsteps followed me as I passed the greenhouse, tennis courts, and another dark building. The farther I walked toward the woods, the heavier my chest felt.

My stomach sank with every step, and I gulped down shallow breaths as I took in the trees around me.

There was no laughter or clicking of heels. I'd been stupid, thinking I'd catch up with them.

I froze when a branch snapped somewhere behind me.

The sound was small, but in the silence here, it felt like a firework.

My stomach turned to stone as I shrank back, every muscle in my body tightening.

I spun around, taking in my surroundings, but didn't see anyone.

Just the wind whispering through the leaves.

"Hello?" I called out before immediately regretting it.

Really, Blair?

You've seen every scary movie.

The person who says hello in the darkness is always the first to die.

My body trembled as I gave up and turned on my heel, ready to sprint back to the safety of my dorm. I had no idea how I was going to sneak back inside without Arisono catching me, but that was tomorrow's problem.

I wasn't staying in these woods for a second longer.

I barely made it two steps before someone snatched my arm and spun me around. A shriek ripped from my throat as my back slammed into a hard chest.

My heart rattled as I screamed at the top of my lungs.

The sound barely escaped me, and a hand clamped over my mouth. Large fingers crushed into my cheeks so tight that I felt them against my teeth. I struggled to break free, choking back air, as my feet scraped against the ground.

But it was no use.

His arm locked around my throat, holding me firm against him, and my breaths hit his palm.

I knew I'd made a mistake when cold lips brushed my ear and said, "Gotcha."

Six

Blair

"*G*otcha."

That one word lacerated me with a thousand cuts.

Cold terror ripped through my body as the hairs along the back of my neck rose. His leather glove sealed over my mouth, trapping my air like a hostage.

My lungs burned as I struggled to breathe against his palm, my vision blurring at the edges. The trees began to smear together, melting into shapes I couldn't make out.

This is it.

Today was the day I'd die. I was sure of it.

All because some rich assholes had decided to torture playthings like me for their twisted entertainment. I'd fallen into a disturbing, privileged world I wanted no part of.

Whatever happened to reading a book? Playing a sport? Fucking studying?

Regret poisoned me for not staying in my dorm and minding my business. I'd wandered into the dark woods alone like an idiot, knowing I'd caught the attention of the devil.

My stepfather's voice echoed in my mind. *"Your problem, Blair, is that you fly too close to danger,"* he'd told me after I was expelled from my last university. He'd called me Icarus, saying he'd given me wings, but I refused to listen when people warned me how to use them.

He blamed it on overconfidence. I blamed it on my upbringing.

As I gasped against the hand crushing my mouth, I thought about the guy in the library again.

His warning about Enzo and his cult buddies.

About how that same murderous psychopath had turned his attention on me.

But why me?

Because I have choppable hair?

Because I'm the new girl?

And speaking of the lunatic ...

I was sure he was the one restraining me.

Trembling, I drew shaky breaths through my nose, his masculine scent flooding my lungs. It reeked of insanity with hints of spiciness, gunpowder, and pine.

His forearm pressed harder against my jaw, forcing my head back as he pulled me flush against his chest. The sudden movement jolted me back into the present.

His body was solid behind me, my spine pinned against him.

I felt his heartbeat. It was so slow that you'd think he was knocking on death's door.

My heart? Quite the contrary.

It violently slammed against my ribs, desperate and frantic, like it was trying to escape my chest entirely and abandon my body to fend for itself.

A strangled gasp tore from my lungs when he slid his hand from my mouth to my throat, tapping his fingers to the frantic pulse beneath my skin.

He was counting my pulse.

Fucking asshole.

I screamed the moment his forearm loosened slightly around my neck.

Screamed so loud that my throat went raw.

That scream was short-lived.

He clenched his hand around my throat to silence me, so hard that I waited for my windpipe to crush. My vision grew hazy as I clawed at his arm, my breaths turning into ragged gasps.

He loosened his hold *just barely* to allow me a sliver of air, like he wasn't ready to kill me *yet*.

He still wanted to have his fun.

That was one thing we had in common: I wasn't ready to die yet.

While he could silence my screams, I wouldn't go down without a fight. The harsh wind stung my face as I thrashed against him.

I kicked wildly, drove my elbows into his stomach, dug my nails into his sweatshirt, and twisted and jerked in his hold like a deer fighting to break free against a hunter's snare.

But he didn't flinch.

My blows didn't even affect him.

He outpowered me in every way.

Physically. Mentally. Strategically.

He laughed wickedly, as if reading my mind. A chill ran down my back.

That laugh promised nothing but destruction. He had planned my ruin and couldn't wait to watch it unfold.

He was the hunter, and I was the prey.

But hunting was never a sport if both parties didn't consent to play. And I sure as hell hadn't signed up for this game.

I took in my surroundings frantically. Nothing but the fog, trees, and silence. No one was coming to save me.

The lion had smelled the fawn in the forest, and he'd come for her blood.

"Oh, sweet Blair," he taunted. "You shouldn't wander into the dark, looking for trouble." He didn't speak in my ear this time. He said the words loudly and dominantly, like a judge delivering a death sentence. "You never know what's hiding, waiting to *snatch you* right up."

I ground my teeth as saliva pooled in the back of my throat, hating the way my name rolled off his tongue. He said it like a word he blessed and damned.

He whipped me around to face him and slid his fingers beneath my chin, forcing my head upward while keeping his other hand clasped around my neck like a leash. I attempted to shrink away, to twist free, but failed.

Dread seeped into my bones like a malignancy. Predators only showed themselves if they planned for their prey not to make it out alive.

My eyes locked with the narrow slits of menacing ones.

His eyes were a violent storm, his irises burning like embers in the darkness. They were the only part of his face I could see. The rest was hidden behind a skull mask.

It wasn't one of those cheap Halloween masks. The white part —*the bones*—glowed eerily in the dark, like a neon sign in an empty diner window. The hollow eye sockets cast shadows across his face, making him look less like a person and more like a killer.

A dark hoodie covered most of his hair, though a few messy strands had escaped, falling across his forehead.

I gawked at him, lost for words, lost for screams. His long fingers wrapped around the nape of my neck again, squeezing hard, like it was his favorite fucking hobby. I winced as he pushed them so deep into the muscle that it hurt.

Bile bubbled violently inside my stomach as I cried out in desperation.

"But you're in luck," he said callously. "I'm here to show you the way." He clicked his tongue against the roof of his mouth. "Though don't get your hopes up. I'm not showing you to safety." His glowing mask tilted slightly. "I'm about to show you exactly what you came out here looking for."

I didn't want him to show me *anything*. I wanted him to let me go.

My fight mode returned, and I swung my elbows in every direction, trying to hit anything I could. *Anyone* I could.

"Please," I pleaded. "Let me go."

His shoulders shook as he laughed. "I love it when they fight. You have no idea what kind of monster it brings out in me." His voice lowered. "How hard my cock gets when you try to escape me."

I'd never heard a voice so sinister.

I stilled, not wanting to provide him with anything he *loved*.

At that, he released my throat. I took in a mouthful of air.

But the relief didn't last long. He lifted one hand and slowly shoved a finger into his mouth, pulling off the leather glove with his teeth. His bare hand returned to my throat, gripping it tighter, showing me how much control he had.

My breath scraped out of my lungs like gravel.

"I'll break that fight out of you, sweet Blair," he continued with the tone of a thousand demons. "And the more you resist, the more fun I have." He ran the tip of his cold finger along my jawline before making a slicing motion across my neck. "Fight me. Curse me. Hit me. I feed on it like a starved man."

"Let me go," I pleaded.

"Let you go?"

"Please," I whimpered, hating how weak I sounded. But I was fucking terrified.

This man had killed Clarissa. I was sure of it. He'd have no problem doing the same to me.

"Since you asked so politely."

I almost lost my balance when he shoved me forward. I stumbled, nearly losing my footing as I crashed into another body.

Another solid chest that belonged to a Greek god, not a college kid.

My head spun, and I now realized we had never been alone.

This man's mask blazed neon red, and horns crowned the top of it.

He caught my arms, holding me at arm's length.

"Please," I begged, lowering my voice to a whisper, as if this man would be my savior.

Stupid, stupid Blair.

He tilted his head, like my plea amused him.

I was certain that behind the mask, he was smiling.

This man was just as ready to sign my death sentence.

My words were as meaningless as the dead branches littering the forest floor under our feet. Rotting. Useless. Something you could easily break.

He dug his gloved hands into my shoulders. "I don't know," he said, as if thinking. "Do you think she'll look better crying or begging?"

His chilling words weren't directed at me. They were for the man now crowding my back again. My initial terrorizer.

The masked man in front of me dragged his hands slowly down my shoulders, over my collarbone, until his palm rested against my chest, right over my racing heart. "You have nowhere to run here, Blair. Nowhere to hide from us."

He held me in place as I tried to jerk away from him. I slammed my eyes shut, accepting defeat.

The man behind me pulled my hands to my back. Dread knotted in my stomach when zip ties sliced into my skin.

At the same time, the man in front of me forced my mouth open. I struggled, whipping my head relentlessly, but his grip tightened. He reached into his pocket and pulled something free. I gagged when he shoved a rag inside my mouth. Before I could spit it out, tape sealed over my lips.

I retched at the pungent taste of chemicals, and vomit swept up my throat. I quickly forced it down, still tasting the remnants of the concoction.

Everything went black when they pulled a cloth over my head.

The man behind me patted my cheek through the cloth. "Time to have some fun." He shoved me forward.

My head spun as they dragged me deeper into the woods. I dug my heels into the ground, pressing the soles of my sneakers into the dirt in a desperate attempt to stop them.

One of the men sighed in annoyance.

I sucked in a breath, tasting something rancid, when the other pulled me back. He ripped my shoes and socks off.

My feet pressed into the moss-covered ground. Twigs and needles stabbed into the bottom of my feet like thorns.

The men guided me in unpredictable directions.

Left. Right. Forward. Backward.

Never warning me or giving me time to adjust.

They were trying to disorient me to make sure I couldn't track where we were going.

"Hush, little Fawn," one whispered. "You can't hide now that you've caught our eyes."

He didn't recite it like a chant.

It sounded more like the Devil himself reciting a nursery rhyme with a sinister twist.

"This isn't just a game," he continued. "We've laid our claim." A pause. "Now, let the fun arise."

Goose bumps prickled my skin as he repeated the rhyme.

During our walk, they played games.

They'd trip me, then let my body pitch forward, only to yank me back before I smacked into the ground.

Their every word and move was meant to torment me.

To show me I had no control over anything.

They cupped me under my armpits and lifted me off the ground entirely. My feet no longer felt dirt. Instead, something cold and hard met my skin.

It had to be stone or concrete.

The vomit started to make its way back up, and I struggled to swallow it down.

I was being dragged straight into hell.

The Devil didn't rule the underworld.

The Night Sons did.

The bitter taste of chemicals coated my mouth, numbing me like a drug and making me dizzy.

We took more steps.

Made more twists and turns.

They continued their taunting as they forced me forward, leading me down what felt like a set of narrow steps. Their hands stayed on my arms, but their assistance wasn't out of concern for my safety.

It was all about control. Nothing more.

When my forehead slammed into what felt like a concrete wall, neither man apologized. They only laughed.

It grew colder with every step, and a draft swept through the fabric covering my head.

Somewhere ahead, a door creaked open.

The energy turned even more sinister. Colder. Suffocating.

Lights blurred through the cloth, just faintly, not bright enough for me to see anything clearly.

I grew lightheaded. Their voices echoed as they spoke, but I couldn't make out their words.

When we stopped, I dramatically choked on the rag stuffed in my mouth, hoping it'd convince them to remove it. My tongue felt thick and swollen from whatever they'd soaked it in.

They shoved me down, my knees slamming into the cold floor as they forced me onto them. One man shoved my head forward. The other yanked the cloth from my head, and I blinked, adjusting my eyes to the sudden light. I winced when he ripped the tape off my mouth. I gagged, spitting the rag onto the floor and coughing from the chemical taste.

I looked around, seeing the man in the white mask in front of me.

No, *Enzo*.

"Welcome to the show, Blair," he said smoothly. "You're about to get an Oscar-worthy performance." He waited a second, tilting his head, as if wanting to taunt me. "And guess who's the star of the show?"

He stepped aside, moving out of my line of sight, and my blood turned cold.

I suddenly wished the chemically soaked rag had killed me.

SEVEN
BLAIR

Still on my knees, I stared at the man tied to a chair. Blood covered him, smeared across his skin, soaking his clothes, and dripping slowly from his fingers to the floor.

It wasn't until he raised his head that I realized who he was.

The guy from the library who'd warned me about the Night Sons.

A single spotlight shone above him, revealing his every injury, like he was on display in some morbid museum.

His eyes were swollen shut, bruised and purple. Dried blood streaked across his face, cracked in the cuts carved into his skin. Fresh blood trickled from his crooked nose onto his shirt.

The white button-up he'd worn earlier was torn and stained with blood and dirt. It looked like they'd brought him here the same way they brought me, except they didn't give him the dignity of walking.

Instead, they had *dragged* him.

As if my appearance lit a fuse inside him, he fought against his restraints. His screams were muffled beneath the tape stretched across his lips. He threw his weight around, trying to tip the chair, but it didn't move. The metal legs were bolted to the concrete floor.

A rancid taste filled my mouth.

I'd been so wrong about the Night Sons.

They weren't some entitled frat boys who hazed, bullied, and committed petty crimes to pass their time. They were darker than that. Crueler than that.

They inflicted pain not for their survival but because it made them feel alive. Because watching suffering made them feel powerful.

And worst of all, they knew no one could stop them.

With their stature and money, they were untouchable.

The windowless room's air was damp and reeked of blood and sweat. We hadn't walked far enough to leave campus, but this place wasn't on the map in Arisono's welcome packet. That was the kind of information they should include.

Not curfews or dress codes.

But places where you could be taken hostage.

Since we walked *down* steps, not up, my guess was that we were underground.

Breaking my gaze away from the chair, I desperately scanned my surroundings. A metal table stood beside the chair, with a variety of instruments—pliers, knives, hammers—meant for tearing into flesh and causing pain.

Rusted nails littered the floor, some of them nicking my feet.

I fought back the tears stinging my eyes when my gaze landed on something a few inches from the table.

Is that a ... finger?

It was most definitely a finger.

Severed clean at the knuckle with the nail still intact.

My heart spasmed, exhausted from tonight's endless plot twists.

I gulped as Enzo appeared at my side like death itself.

The urge to swat him away like a gnat swept through me. He loomed over me, like a guillotine ready to fall. I lifted my chin, glowering at him in defiance.

I refused to beg or plead.

I'd rather choose decapitation.

Lower the guillotine, asshole.

I wouldn't die as someone's Fawn.

Wouldn't die a helpless creature.

Red Mask stepped beside the chair. Like Enzo, he wore all black. A hoodie hid his hair. He was tall, leaner than Enzo, with a long, narrow frame. Nothing about him was recognizable, which was the point.

I clenched my teeth as Enzo stroked my hair.

It wasn't gentle. It was *possessive* in the way he did it.

He gestured toward the chair, jerking his chin toward Red Mask.

Red Mask ripped the tape off the guy's mouth. His busted lip split further with the motion.

Without wasting a second, the guy tried to scream, "You fucking assholes," but his words came out in tiny gasps. One of his front teeth was gone, and the other hung cracked and crooked in his mouth.

Red Mask dragged a hand slowly down the front of his mask before suddenly driving his elbow into the guy's face. The crack echoed through the room.

The guy's head snapped back, barely missing the concrete wall behind him. When it lurched forward again, more blood poured from his nose like a faucet.

Enzo stopped his creepy petting to advance toward the chair. I chewed the inside of my cheek as he drew back and spat in the guy's face.

The guy cried out words I couldn't understand.

Enzo grabbed his face with both hands, then slammed his forehead into the guy's. I winced when I heard bones crack.

While Enzo focused on him, my gaze drifted to the door.

The unguarded door.

Still on my knees, I carefully inched toward it while Enzo punched the guy.

A dark laugh ripped from Enzo's chest. A roar so dark that it could snuff out every star in the sky.

I froze, my head slowly turning to look at him over my shoulder.

"Now, Blair," he said with a soft *tsk*, "why would you leave before the fun starts?"

He crossed the distance between us in two long strides.

I screamed when his hand dug into my hair, jerking me to my feet. Pain ripped through my scalp. He released me, shoving me forward, and my body crashed into the chair.

I stumbled into the guy's knees before collapsing at his feet.

Enzo's hand twisted into my hair again, wrenching my head backward. "Blair, meet Jett."

I didn't say a word.

His grip tightened. "Apologies. I forgot that an introduction isn't necessary. You two were spotted getting cozy in the library, gossiping like two bitches in a locker room." He sounded pleased, all sadism, at the thought of Jett telling me his secrets.

My throat still burned from the rag as I glared up at him.

Enzo reached down and grabbed my jaw, pinching my lip painfully between his fingers. "Don't worry, Blair. I really am a feminist at heart." He pressed a hand dramatically to his chest, right where I was certain no organ existed.

I couldn't stop the scoff that slipped from my lips.

Jett jerked violently against his restraints. His arms strained against the ropes as broken words bubbled through the blood in his mouth. "Let me ... fucker ..." The rest dissolved into a hoarse choke.

Enzo savored Jett's agonized pleading as he stroked my cheek with a disturbing tenderness. "What did you and Jett talk about in the library?"

I kept my eyes forward, hating that his touch warmed my insides. "He asked me what book I was reading."

Enzo chuckled softly. "She makes jokes." He clamped his hand around the back of my neck and shoved my face down until my nose nearly brushed the bloodstained tarp lying under Jett's shoes.

I gagged at the smell and the sight.

"I'll ask you *one more time*," Enzo snarled, tugging my head up from the plastic, and I inhaled a deep breath as I came up for air.

My jaw, face, *everything* ached.

My plan for not fighting fell apart with every second.

But I'd try *one more* thing. I shoved my elbows back, blindly aiming for his groin. Every miss earned chuckles from him and Red Mask.

"He didn't tell me anything I hadn't already known," I spat. "That you're a fucking psychopath."

"Psychopath?" he scoffed, sounding almost amused. "Surely, you can be more creative than that."

I curled my hands into fists as he reached into his pocket and pulled out scissors. My heart lurched, and I prepared myself for another haircut.

Why did he carry scissors around like I did my favorite lip gloss?

I made a mental note to brainstorm insults worse than *psychopath*.

But right now, I had bigger problems, like being trapped in a murder room, a severed finger lying inches from my knee, and a lunatic twirling scissors like someone would show off a luxury bag.

He stepped around me and drove the scissors into Jett's hand. The metal punching through his flesh made a wet sound.

Jett wailed in agony.

"Stop it!" I shouted, my voice cracking. "Just fucking stop it!"

Enzo ignored me, but his eyes never left mine as he forced the scissors deeper into Jett's hand, like he wanted to hit every nerve ending.

"Do you know what I hate, Blair?" he asked casually.

I didn't hesitate to reply, "Sanity. Empathy. Being a decent human being?"

He laughed under his breath and flicked the scissors handle. "Liars." He pushed the blade deeper into Jett's hand. "I despise liars."

"He didn't lie." I rubbed at my wrists, the zip ties making my skin raw every time I moved. "You killed his sister."

"Ah." Enzo made a light-bulb-moment gesture. "You believe I gave Clarissa the window treatment." Not one scrap of empathy was in his tone, only humor. He whipped his venomous stare to Jett. "Is that what you told her, fuckface?"

Jett struggled to suck in air and speak through the blood clogging his throat.

"Blair, do you believe Jett is a victim?" Enzo asked me.

"You murdered his sister and also have him tied to a chair," I shot back. "Pretty clear who the victim here is." My voice grew colder. "He's the victim, and *you're* the tormentor."

Deep down, I hated that I couldn't see Enzo's face.

I wanted to see his changing expressions as he spoke.

The shapes of his smirks and frowns.

That stupid mask hid too much.

"You believe Jett is an innocent man, then?" He circled me slowly.

Red Mask scoffed.

"More innocent than you," I bit back.

He shrugged. "I won't dispute that."

"Then let us go," I said around a sigh of exhaustion.

"Unfortunately, I'm not in the business of catch and release."

He mimicked casting a fishing line into the air, flicking his wrist, as if sending it flying over water. Then he pretended to reel it back in. When the imaginary line returned to him, he slammed his hand down onto the scissors embedded in Jett's hand.

The blades sank in deeper—so deep that I was certain they'd pierced the chair.

Enzo stood tall before slowly pulling the scissors out. Blood burst from the wound.

Jett tried to scream, but it came out wet and broken. His jaw trembled as blood spilled from every corner of his mouth. He attempted to clamp his jaw shut in a useless effort to stop it.

He spat blood. The only words that made it out were a garbled, "Who ... my father ... is." His neck veins bulged as he struggled to speak.

Enzo turned back toward me.

I swallowed when he slid the scissors beneath my chin, lifting it, and I had no choice but to meet his scolding stare.

"I find that unethical," he said. "Inflicting trauma and then expecting someone to return to normal." He lifted my chin a fraction higher. "How." *Higher.* "Fucking." *Higher.* "Cruel."

"How fucking boring," Red Mask commented.

Enzo didn't even glance at him.

"We're all monsters here, Blair." Enzo dragged the scissors from beneath my chin to my jawline, smearing Jett's warm blood on my skin. "Some of us are just better at hiding it."

"I guess that fits you, the man *hiding* behind a mask," I said with a sneer.

The words barely left my mouth when Enzo hurled the scissors across the room. They hit the wall before clattering to the floor.

I held my breath when he slowly removed his mask and pulled down his hoodie. The sight of his face hit me harder than any blow he'd delivered to Jett.

I hated how my body reacted to it.

How I clenched my thighs. And how heat rushed low in my stomach, pooling between my legs like a river, and how my clit suddenly throbbed.

Hated how, for a moment, desire replaced my fear.

The villain of my story was devastatingly beautiful.

Beautiful in the way that a shark was before it bit you.

In the way a storm smelled before it blew through a home.

He was mesmerizing yet catastrophic, all at once.

Sweat gleamed along the sharp angles of his tawny face. His skin looked flawless, smooth, as if nothing would ever dare to mark it in fear of consequences.

Dark hair swept back in careless disarray. Untamed and wild, like him. His jaw was clean-shaven, his cheekbones sharp and deep, unmistakably Italian.

All features that made Jett's claim about his family ruling the Italian Mafia feel even more believable.

His dark and wicked eyes were the sort that promised to take your world and never give it back.

He ran his tongue over his lips, then across his teeth, giving me my moment to stare. Then his mouth curled, his expression turning vicious like a triggered animal.

I glanced at Red Mask. He didn't remove his mask.

Only Enzo had revealed himself. Only the one who deemed me *his*.

"Mask is off," Enzo said, lifting the mask in one hand and spreading out his arms. "Do you see a monster, Blair?"

Reality swept into my bloodstream.

I couldn't run or hide from him. No one would save me.

"Please," Jett rasped, his voice breaking the silence. Blood cut his plea short as his head sagged forward.

Enzo raised Jett's head to backhand him across the face. "I only enjoy pleading when it comes from my Fawns. Not from my victims."

I stopped myself from correcting that his Fawns were also his victims.

Enzo's attention shifted back to me. "Blair, do you want me to kill Jett?"

I snorted humorlessly, staring up at him until the strain made my neck hurt. "That can't be a serious question."

He smirked harshly. "What would you do for me to *not* kill him?"

I pressed my lips into a thin line, refusing to answer him.

I shuddered when Enzo reached out and tucked a strand of hair behind my ear, his fingers brushing along my skin. "Would you bow at my feet and suck my cock in exchange for his release?"

"Fuck you," I spat.

His mouth twitched; he was not offended at all. "Don't worry. I won't choke you with my cock *yet*. Fortunately for you, I don't provide free shows." His palm slid over my cheek. "Jett isn't worthy to see those pretty little lips wrapped around my dick."

"Why?" I fired back. "Because you're embarrassed by your small cock?"

His lips spread into a cold, predatory smirk.

He pulled a knife from his pocket, flipping it in his hand, and ignored the sounds coming from Jett.

Jesus. Does he have an arsenal in his coat?

Does he think he's John freaking Wick?

"Keep running your mouth," Enzo told me, stepping toward Jett and digging the tip into the hollow of his throat, right against his Adam's apple. "And I'll make *you* slit the douchebag's throat."

Jett froze.

"Why are you doing this?" I asked.

"I thought this was what you wanted, little Fawn." He pressed the tip deeper into Jett's neck. "Answers to your questions."

"I'm not your fucking Fawn."

"*Yet.*" He pulled the knife away from Jett's throat, then lowered himself to his knees until we were at eye level, and ran the blade along my cheek.

His scent filled my lungs, nearly intoxicating me.

I studied his face up close—a masterpiece, like something rare and untouchable.

For a heartbeat, I considered crossing that line.

Enzo's words cut through that thought.

"But soon, you'll be mine," he stated with absolute certainty.

My panting stalled when the blade lowered to the zip ties around my wrist. The plastic snapped when he sliced them. Blood rushed back into my hands, and my arms ached.

Enzo peeled off his glove the same way he had in the woods. He lifted his bare hand toward me, palm up, presenting it like a prize. I flinched, readying myself for the sting of his palm hitting my cheek.

It never came.

He had no intention to do that.

Instead, he dragged the blade across his own palm, carving a deep *X* into his skin. Blood welled around the open flesh.

I didn't fight when his bloodied hand caught mine. He turned it over, exposing my palm. I hissed between my teeth when he carved the same mark across my palm. The pain seared through my hand.

The rest of the room ceased to exist at that moment.

Warm blood seeped from my cut. I watched, transfixed, as he pressed our palms together. He lowered the knife and covered our joined hands with his other palm.

An oath sealed with blood.

A holy vow.

A vow I never agreed to, but somehow couldn't refuse.

Yet, as sinister as this moment was, intimacy bled through.

Enzo was a poison I knew would slowly kill me.

His softness was brief, as if Enzo's sanity had a daily cap, and his cold voice broke through my trance.

His grip on my hand became painfully tight. "Breathe a word of this to anyone, and I'll kill your entire family." He pulled me to my feet, still gripping my hand, and grabbed my chin.

He inched so close that we were nose to nose. Breath to breath. Mouth to mouth.

"I'll gut your stepfather first, right in his New York office," he explained. "Your mother will be next. The mother who hides more secrets than just the hideous tramp stamp she got when she was nineteen."

I shuddered, chills tormenting me.

"I'll make you watch me torture and kill them." He snaked out his tongue, running it along the seam of my lips. "And once

I've finished slaughtering them, I'll force you to bathe in their blood before I drown you in it."

I tried to bite his tongue, but he stopped me, shoving his hand into my mouth. He pressed his bloody palm against my jaw so hard that I waited for it to break. He released his grip just before it did.

He skimmed his nose against mine before his mouth grazed my ear.

His voice was only a whisper, yet it inflicted the fear of a thousand screams. "By the time I'm done with you, my little Fawn, you won't remember who you were before me. I'll own you, every inch of you, until the day you take your last breath."

EIGHT

ENZO

"That was fun," Cassian said with a crooked smile. "Jett will die as he lived—annoying as fuck." He bounced on the balls of his feet as adrenaline vibrated through him.

All of us had our rituals after violence. Our own little quirks.

Cassian's resembled someone who'd just done an irresponsible amount of cocaine and needed to burn the power in his veins before it electrocuted him.

Cassian carried both Marchetti and Lombardi blood in his veins. Two of the most powerful Mafia families in the world. His ruthlessness was inherited.

My gaze drifted to my palm. "The asshole won't be missed."

Blair's blood was still smeared across the cut I'd carved into my skin. Dark, sticky, slowly drying between the lines of my hand.

I stared down at it, fascinated by how her blood looked mingled with mine. Something about it felt intoxicating. I couldn't wait for the next time.

Black iron sconces burned along the concrete walls while we walked through the underground passageway. Our boots echoed through the tunnel. The sound echoed off the walls in hollow vibrations.

The symbols carved into the stone always felt like they were following me as we passed them.

They were marks no outsider would ever understand.

The First Benefactors—the original Night Sons who had founded Saint Vale—had built these tunnels long before the university rose above them.

Miles of hidden passageways stretched beneath campus, splitting into chambers, corridors, and rooms that only we knew how to navigate.

Despite being a century old, the tunnels were in immaculate condition. Every generation of Night Sons maintained them. They were regular visitors here, whether they still attended the university or had graduated years ago.

Blood had been spilled here for decades. Enemies killed. Deals made.

The Night Sons weren't just a secret society whispered about as rumors. This was a lifetime commitment. We took an oath for life, and in return, we were granted power, access, and control.

Every one of us was destined to rule something—governments, bloodlines, corporations, or criminal empires.

My father had taught me early that real power wasn't owning land or money. The real power was owning people across every tier of society. We made sure power never slipped through our fingers.

For us, Saint Vale wasn't just a university. It was a hunting ground.

A recruitment tool to advance our agendas.

It opened doors for us to further rule the world.

When we reached Locker Hall, Cassian and I stepped to the steel door and scanned our fingerprints against the black panel. Two sharp beeps, and the lock released.

Inside, iron lockers stretched along both walls, but they weren't lockers in the traditional way. Behind them lay more hidden rooms. Armories and storage vaults. This was where we kept our weapons, tools, and anything else we didn't leave lying around.

Every locker had a symbol. Not a name.

Emeri sat on a stool in front of his locker, his long legs stretched out as he methodically sharpened his favorite knife with obsessed precision.

The blade had been custom-made in Italy by a famous weaponsmith. His father—Emilio Lastro, a Lombardi Mafia capo—had purchased it for him there. It was Emeri's most prized possession.

The overhead light above him caught the pale scars that cut across his face. Some thin, some thick, and some faded.

Emeri raised his chin when he noticed us. That was always his version of a greeting. Of the Night Sons, he was the quietest. He wasn't shy, just always uninterested in conversation.

Cassian and I dumped our masks and weapons on the steel table in the center of the room. I wiped the blood clean from my scissors and knife with a cloth before tossing both into the disposal bin.

The launderer would come in the morning to collect the items and dispose of them properly. He'd also scrub the place spotless.

"You good?" I asked Emeri as I pulled my hoodie over my head and tossed it into the bin beside the weapons.

He gave me a simple thumbs-up without looking at me before testing the sharpness of his blade by dragging it lightly across his forearm. A cut opened on his skin, blood seeping through it. He frowned, displeased, and returned to his sharpening.

Cassian and I changed into clean hoodies and pants from our lockers.

I crouched to tighten my shoelaces and gave Emeri a mock salute. "Later, asshole. Try not to hit bone when you're playing with that knife. You're already a walking scar magazine."

The knife took the place of his finger when he flipped us off.

Cassian laughed. "You're a fucking asshole."

I tapped the doorframe twice and left Locker Hall with Cassian behind me.

We turned right and walked thirty feet before cutting a left. At the end of the corridor, a neon *Lair* sign glowed above a steel door.

The Devil's Lair was the only place beneath Saint Vale where the Night Sons allowed themselves to relax. It was where we partied and unwound, free from prying eyes or loose lips.

Saint Vale itself was intentionally remote, isolated, miles from the city, and dull as fuck. We had to create our own entertainment here. That was what Fawns and the Devil's Lair were for.

Unlike the rest of the tunnels, the Devil's Lair was also the only space outsiders were permitted to enter. But even then, we were selective. *Very selective.*

The people allowed were all women connected to us—sisters, cousins, those we trusted. Or sometimes, we'd allow former Fawns who'd survived their time with us without losing their sanity.

The rest of the tunnels were off-limits. They had only one entrance and exit for non–Night Sons. It was a hidden passage in the greenhouse on campus.

Me? I had access to everything above and below ground.

I controlled Saint Vale.

I could piss in the fucking headmaster's bed if I wanted.

Could slit a professor's throat between lectures.

Rip the drywall off the library walls and turn the place into a strip club.

Linkin Park's "Numb" thundered through the Devil's Lair when we stepped inside. The sound wasn't nearly as satisfying as Jett's screams or Blair's desperate pleading, but it'd suffice.

The sharp scent of furniture polish and citrus lingered in the air.

Cassian and I walked beneath stone arches and aged vaulted ceilings. The rich oak floors stretched beneath the amber lights.

Oxblood leather couches and barstools were scattered

throughout the space. Every piece of furniture had belonged to the First Benefactors.

"Piss break," Cassian muttered, veering right toward the hallway that led to the restroom.

I headed straight to the bar. Behind it, brass shelves lined the wall, and the light made the liquor bottles almost glow.

The First Benefactors' tastes were tacky, very speakeasy in style, with dark woods and brass fixtures. But I wasn't going to waste my time remodeling. I had a Fawn to break.

I poured a shot of vodka and downed it in one swallow. Then I poured three fingers of bourbon into a crystal tumbler before moving farther into the room.

I passed the group of girls crowded on one of the leather couches. They were laughing, talking, and drinking.

They were the ones allowed down here.

The ones we protected.

I dropped onto the couch beside Brooks. His black tux was wrinkled, the collar of his shirt open, and he stared at me with dark, tired eyes.

We were the only ones who saw Brooks like this.

Outside, in the world above the tunnels, he was the perfect son of the president. He had been bred for the cameras with his polished smile and perfect blond hair. They called him America's Golden Boy. His entire life had been created for him to become president one day and take after his father.

But down here? He was just Brooks.

He and I ran the Night Sons.

Every year, two seniors were chosen to lead the society, and this year, the crown had fallen on us.

Across from us, Nico sat on a leather couch with his MacBook balanced on his lap and his feet propped on the cedar coffee table. He was typing fast, probably hacking into something.

"How's our buddy Jett?" Brooks asked, rolling a joint between his fingers.

I glanced at my Rolex. "Fingers crossed he's dead by now."

"Hey, assholes," Cassian announced as he returned, zipping his fly and strolling toward us. His gaze landed on me. "You couldn't even get me a drink? Ungrateful prick. You're welcome for the help tonight."

I lifted my crystal tumbler in a fake toast. "You should be thanking me. You enjoy violence." I drained the rest of the bourbon and extended the empty glass toward him. "Pour me another while you're at it."

He answered with a smirk and a quick flick of his middle finger before heading for the bar. "Go fuck yourself."

I launched the glass across the room. It shattered against the back of his head with a loud crack.

Cassian didn't even slow down, just laughed and flipped me off over his shoulder again as he kept walking.

"Did you send the video to Jett's dad?" Nico asked without looking up from his MacBook.

"Sure did." I shifted on the leather couch and pulled my phone from my pocket. The screen lit up when I unlocked it.

Reginald's reply waited for me.

One word: *OK.*

I held up the phone so the others could see. "Nothing like fatherly love."

Before tracking down Blair earlier tonight, I'd sent Reginald the video Nico had pulled from the library cameras. The video showed Jett spilling his mouth about the Night Sons like a drunk idiot begging to be killed.

Reginald, an Elder Night Son, understood the rules.

The rules had existed long before he was even born. Either we punished him or Jett. Bloodlines didn't matter when rules were broken. Not even if your great-great-great-great grand-fucking-ancestor had been one of the First Benefactors themselves. If you talked, then you died.

Jett had already proven himself a waste of oxygen, so Reginald had made the smart choice and offered up his son without hesitation.

He'd come to Saint Vale convinced he'd easily become a Night Son and that his bloodline would secure his place, but he was severely mistaken.

Reginald tried to pull every string he could reach, but that wasn't enough. Becoming a Night Son required unanimous approval from all Current Sons, ones who still attended the university.

You had to pass the tests and prove your loyalty.

And none of us trusted Jett, so we all voted no.

Unfortunately, though, we couldn't kill him for shits and giggles, so we were forced to tolerate his existence and the way he seemed to always appear everywhere and annoy the shit out of us.

Finally, we had gotten permission to get rid of him. It'd felt like Christmas fucking morning.

Cassian returned from the bar with a bottle of vodka dangling from his bruised hand. He fell onto the couch beside Nico and dragged a hand through his dark hair before lifting the bottle to his mouth.

"And how's your new Fawn?" Brooks asked, licking the edge of the rolling paper as he finished the joint.

"Boring," Cassian said, taking a swig from the bottle. "She didn't shed a single tear tonight." He drank for a solid ten seconds and didn't lower the bottle until it was almost empty.

"Your last one was boring too," Brooks replied, fishing a lighter from his pocket. "She had the personality of a fucking squid. I'd jump out of a window if I were her too." He sparked the flame and lit the joint. The tip burned red as smoke curled in the air along with his words. "I was disappointed when you chose her."

"Money always talks," Nico muttered from behind his screen.

"You do know that's against the rules?" Brooks added, taking a long drag of the joint before passing it to me.

I leaned back and inhaled slowly.

"I piss on rules," I said as smoke slipped from my mouth, "and wipe my ass with their consequences."

After realizing Jett would never be a Son, Reginald had approached me last year with a request. He wanted me to choose Clarissa as my Fawn. He refused to let his bloodline be shut out completely.

At first, I'd laughed in his face at the nerve of asking me for a favor. I didn't take requests from politicians who smiled for the cameras and then fucked over their constituents.

I fucking hated politicians.

With two exceptions: Brooks and his father, the sitting president of the United States.

President Byron had done my family more favors than any senator or governor in the country. He'd helped my father bury his crimes, erase evidence, and quietly remove his name from half a dozen FBI watch lists.

Of course, the feds always added him back eventually.

It was a tedious little game we played with them.

Reginald, on the other hand, was a different breed. A wolf wrapped in wool. The kind of man who shook your hand while plotting against you.

I preferred working with men who were openly ruthless and conniving.

Still, I'd changed my mind when Reginald placed a million dollars on the table in exchange for my choosing Clarissa. He also threw in a Hamptons beach house and the keys to a shiny, brand-new red Porsche.

I didn't want the Porsche. I only liked red when it was blood, and I didn't trust gifts that could be tracked.

But I accepted the deal because taking things from people I disliked was deeply satisfying. And every government official under our thumb made my family stronger.

I gave the Porsche to a random homeless guy outside a gas station, signed the Hamptons property over to our housekeeper, and kept the cash for myself. It wasn't that I *needed* the money. I just liked taking it from people.

The problem was that the Night Sons' rules strictly prohibited payment for selecting a Fawn. I'd broken that rule, but I wasn't the one punished for it.

Reginald was now missing a middle finger for it. The Elders knew better than to touch me.

"Circling back to Jett," Cassian said, dragging me out of my thoughts. "We need to get rid of his body."

I cut a look at Nico. "That's on you."

Nico's fingers stilled over his keyboard. "Damn it, Enzo." He shoved his glasses higher on his nose and glared at me. "I just finished dealing with Marv's hand. Give me a break."

"Breaks are for the weak." I returned the joint to the ashtray before resting my elbows on my knees and leveling my stare at him. "Are you weak and need a break, Nico?"

Cassian snorted, finishing off the vodka in his bottle. "Yeah, what are you? A fucking Kit Kat?"

"Nico," I said, my tone carrying a clear warning, "dealing with bodies that aren't completely mutilated is child's play compared to what you'll be handling later."

On paper, in the Marchetti bloodline, Nico technically outranked me.

Benny—his father and my brother—stood next in line.

Then Benny's first son and Nico's brother, Cedric.

Then Nico.

Being the youngest son of the boss was a raw deal because every time my brother knocked his wife up and produced another heir, my place in the family hierarchy shifted down another notch.

It was like watching your inheritance get chipped away piece by piece.

But that hierarchy existed outside Saint Vale.

Here? I had more power and a higher rank, and Nico knew that.

But if we were being honest, my word was stronger than Nico's in the family. Nico still had growing up to do. He couldn't be a pussy-ass bitch and lead a Mafia family. In fact, last week, I'd told Benny that he was being too easy on him.

"Listen to your uncle, Nico," Brooks said with a chuckle, wiping sweat from his brow while grabbing the blunt. Ashes drifted from the burning tip and scattered across his lap.

Nico's jaw tightened, but he stayed quiet.

Brooks flicked the joint on the table and looked over at me. "Enzo, that makes you sound ancient, man."

I shrugged, hating that joke, indifferent to my father's choices. "That's what happens when your dad marries a woman half his age."

Twenty-three years ago, he'd married my mother, who also happened to be my older sister's best friend. Their marriage started a war between the Marchettis and Lombardis. A messy and bloody one.

But, as with all wars between powerful families, it eventually ended in negotiations and alliances.

Then my parents had me.

Despite the age difference, their marriage wasn't some fucked-up dynamic. They loved each other. My father killed for her, and he'd do it every day without blinking if he had to.

Had my father not done that, I wouldn't be here to make the world hell.

How tragic would that be?

Brooks stroked his chin, as if thinking of his next scheme, then snapped his attention to the girls on the couch across the room. "You planning to do anything about Daphne?" he asked. "You know she's whispering Sons stories to her new little roommate."

I cracked my neck slowly. "Daphne's harmless."

Brooks scoffed.

"I don't care if Daphne rambles bullshit to her." I stretched out and draped my arms along the back of the couch. "She's probably told Blair as much as Jett did. Daphne is scared of me, as she should be. I also have the problem of my sister. She'd complain to my parents if I tossed one of her best friends out a window." I pointed toward Brooks. "Same goes for your sister."

At the mention of my younger sister, Seraphina, I peered over my shoulder at her.

She was wedged onto the couch with Daphne, Gemma, and Adelina—Brooks's sister. All of them held glasses filled with different shades of alcohol and were deep in conversation.

They weren't supposed to be here tonight, but I guessed they'd had a change of plans.

I'd only agreed to let Daphne into Devil's Lair because Seraphina begged me to. Adelina had done the same thing to Brooks.

Daphne already knew about us, thanks to her family's connections.

Seraphina had also run to our parents, crying about how heartbroken she was that I was excluding her best friend.

Boo-fucking-hoo.

Seraphina had our father wrapped around her finger. He naively believed she was innocent.

When I clicked my tongue, Seraphina's brown eyes met mine. And since it was our dominant language around here, she raised her middle finger in my direction and kissed it.

"Admit it," Cassian, whose face was now flushed from most likely having alcohol poisoning, said to Brooks. "You're looking for any excuse to get rid of Daphne. She gets under your skin because you want to fuck her but can't."

Nico nodded absentmindedly, still typing away. "Pick her as your Fawn and move on."

"I'm not that fucking desperate," Brooks snapped, already rolling another joint. It was his stress response. Dude was higher than Willie Nelson most days but hid it well.

Like me—until yesterday, that was—every Son but Nico still hadn't chosen our Fawns.

We were being selective this year. Options were limited, and we didn't like making mistakes.

A Night Son didn't get his first Fawn until sophomore year. My first two had been careless choices. The first time, I thought with my dick. The second time, with money. Both had been equally stupid.

"My father would shit a brick if I selected Daphne," Brooks said. "Her dad tried to plot his fucking assassination. She shouldn't even be at Saint Vale. Who gives a shit who her mother is?"

"You could choose her, and no one would know," Cassian argued. "Nice try, though."

Brooks scoffed in irritation. "Every move I make is watched, in both public and private. If I want the presidency one day, I don't get the luxury you Mafia spawns do." His sluggish gaze bounced between Cassian and me. "We can't erase bodies and mistakes the way your families can."

"That's the plus of having us," I said. "We're excellent at cleaning up messes."

Brooks raised his joint in a silent salute.

We'd all killed. It was mandatory to be a Son.

The difference was why.

Brooks killed because he had to.

Those who came from Mafia families, like me, killed when we were bored or someone pissed us off.

Cassian tossed the empty vodka bottle behind him. It clattered across the floor and rolled under the couch. That reminded me I needed a new glass.

I pushed off the couch to return to the bar and pour myself another bourbon, letting the expensive amber liquid settle in the glass before taking a sip.

Then I turned and headed toward Seraphina.

She scooted over on the couch to make room for me, and I settled on the edge of the cushion beside her.

"You behaving?" I asked her.

My sister was the spitting image of my mother. Black hair and olive skin. A smile that could make both saints and criminals fall in love with her. And they did.

Her hair was braided into two neat French braids, each tied

with a ridiculous pink bow. The bows made her look younger than she was.

While Seraphina lived a privileged life, being a Mafia princess came with teeth. She was a walking target for every enemy my family had ever made. My father kept her protected at all times. Her dorm was in the restricted wing, and she never left the main building without an escort.

Marriage proposals for her came in faster than a trigger pull. My father rejected every single offer, saying Seraphina was in control of her own future.

I'd told him that was fucking idiotic. An arranged marriage meant leverage, influence, and money. Seraphina slapped me for that comment, right there in my father's office. He laughed and told me I deserved it. She gave me the silent treatment for a week after that.

That one was way too sensitive for her own good sometimes.

"Always," she hummed with the innocence of a black swan.

"Who'd you walk here with?" I asked.

"Adelina and Daphne."

"Good."

The Secret Service followed Adelina around like dogs, which meant my sister got the same protection. Several of those agents had once been Night Sons themselves, but we didn't allow them inside the Devil's Lair. We didn't want their old asses giving us advice.

Daphne leaned across Seraphina to get my attention. "Enzo, I have a question."

I ignored her. Daphne could be on fire, and I'd do the same.

She poked my arm. I slapped her hand away like she had rabies.

"Why are you tormenting her new roommate?" Seraphina groaned. "Wasn't one enough?"

"And who's her new roommate?" I asked.

"Blair."

"Oh." I took a sip of bourbon. "The girl we dumped in the woods."

"What?" Daphne screeched.

Seraphina punched my shoulder with the strength of a kitten, glaring at me.

"Relax," I said, calm in the way of a man who'd already ordered the hit. "We left her close enough to the main building. She'll find her way back." I took another drink. "Probably."

"Stop choosing her roommates," Seraphina complained. "Or I'll tell Dad to shoot you for my birthday."

I knew she'd be mad about Blair. Seraphina still blamed me for Daphne's *emotional trauma* over Clarissa. I cared about Daphne's emotional trauma as much as I cared about Jett's last breath.

"You're ruining my social life," Seraphina dragged on. "No one wants to be friends with the girl whose brother is a psycho."

Gemma, Adelina, and Daphne all nodded, as if they all weren't cut from the same corrupt cloth.

"You don't need friends," I told her. "They're overrated."

Adelina and Daphne both rolled their eyes.

Seraphina nudged me again. "You should seriously seek therapy."

"I did." I drained the rest of the glass. "Remember?"

"With a therapist you won't *fuck*."

"Boring," I groaned. "She fixed my issues the easy way."

Why bother with meds when you could come on your therapist instead?

I'd eventually lost interest in her, though.

She cried, which made me want to throw her out the window. That wasn't the worst part. She claimed to have fallen in love with me, which made me want to jump off a bridge. In revenge for sharing that disgusting emotion, I sent her husband a video of me fucking her from behind.

Last I'd heard, they'd revoked her license and committed her after she ran her car into a concrete wall.

I tapped Seraphina's arm. "Enough about me. Who among you troublemakers has black ribbon?"

"For what?" Seraphina asked with suspicion.

"I'm making care packages for the less fortunate," I replied with a fake, sarcastic grin. "I'd like to tie them with a bow to make them pretty."

"Swear to God, you're going to hell," Seraphina muttered.

I grinned wider, flashing my teeth. "Good. I look forward to ruling it with an iron fist." I pushed myself off the cushion. "I'll swing by your dorm later for the ribbons."

Just thinking about entering Seraphina's dorm room made me frown. Her dorm looked like Tinker Bell had vomited inside it with pink pillows, glitter, and fairy lights everywhere. She deserved to be disowned from the family just for that.

Blair would pay for me having to enter such a travesty.

"Because you have bad intentions for the ribbon, no," Seraphina argued like I cared.

"You know the word *no* doesn't exist in my vocabulary," I replied. "If there aren't at least fifteen ribbon options laid out for me, you're banned from the Devil's Lair. I'll also inform our parents that Adelina pierced your belly button with what I would assume was an unsterile needle. Fingers crossed you don't get hepatitis."

Seraphina shoved my shoulder. "Blackmail. How unoriginal."

I leaned down and kissed the top of her head anyway. "Love you too, little sister."

Daphne stood, slinging her Prada bag over her shoulder. "I need to go make sure my roommate made it back to our dorm."

"You're going alone," I said immediately, my voice turning hard as I rubbed my temple. "Neither of these girls will join you, *especially* Seraphina. I'll notify Secret Service."

Daphne crossed her arms, fiddling with her strap, biting back an argument. Before she could say anything, Brooks strode toward us, interrupting the conversation.

His jaw was tight, and his teeth were clenched.

"Enzo," he bit out, almost panicked, which was a rarity, "we've got a problem."

Brooks was the most levelheaded among us, meaning this was more than just a problem. This was something life or death.

And that was my cue.

I followed Brooks out of the Lair. Cassian and Nico were on our heels. We tore through the underground tunnels, headed straight for the Locker Hall.

As soon as the door shut behind us, Brooks hurled his phone across the room. It slammed into a locker and skidded across the floor while he paced like a caged animal.

Emeri looked up from his iPad in the same spot he'd been when we left. His knife was tucked into his shirt, the hilt peeking out while the blade's tip pressed against his heart. He rolled a toothpick between his teeth and lifted a brow at me.

I shrugged, waiting for Brooks to explain what the fuck was going on.

Brooks stopped pacing and stared at me, his Adam's apple bobbing in his throat. "You know the senator challenging my father's reelection bid?"

I scratched the back of my head. "The one who looks like the rat who raised the Teenage Mutant Ninja Turtles?"

Brooks's hands curled into fists, and he nodded. "His son, Hedgeford, just threatened to leak a video of me fucking a campaign intern in the Oval Office unless my father drops out."

He picked up his phone and shoved it toward me.

I took it, skimming the message.

The blackmail text was laughably amateur.

The idiot had sent it through a traceable number.

I rolled my shoulders, easing out the tension. "Emeri, you feel like riding with us?"

He cracked his knuckles. "Will there be blood?"

"Not immediately," I replied. "But we get to blow something up."

He shrugged. "I'm in."

"Nico." I turned my attention to him just as he unlocked his locker.

He shook his head. "I'm already in charge of dealing with Jett's body. Consider me tapped out for the night."

"Jett is a five-minute errand." I mimed a shove. "Up the steps and"—I flicked my hand—"out he goes." I reached around him into his locker and grabbed a spare laptop. "Hack into this Hedgeford kid's shit. Virus everything. Wipe anything tied to Brooks. If he has a girlfriend, dump her. And if there are any dick pics, send them to everyone working on his father's campaign and post them online. Bonus points if there's a video of him jacking off."

Nico saluted me.

I turned to Brooks. "Let's go make sure your dad wins."

Time to have some more fun.

It was sometime after four in the morning when I reached the cloister wall for my post-murder ritual.

The campus was dark and quiet as I stared up at the moon.

A two-hour drive had taken us off campus and straight to the frat house, where Hedgeford the Blackmailer was celebrating whatever pathetic milestone frat boys celebrated. Probably finding the latest roofie drug on the market.

I paid a drunk girl fifty bucks to steal his phone while Emeri slid under Hedgeford's Lamborghini and planted a bomb under the chassis.

When we got back to campus, I stopped by Seraphina's dorm and collected the ribbons she'd reluctantly laid out for me. From there, I made a quick detour to Blair's room.

She had made it back safely and was snoring in her little bed nook. I'd also left her a few gifts to wake up to.

I'm nothing if not thoughtful.

Now, I walked the narrow cloister ledge, kicking my boots

together as I moved along the stone and made a mental note to check the news in the morning.

Surely, the murder of a senator's son—even a rat-looking motherfucker like him—would earn at least one headline.

After another hour of pacing the wall, I hopped down onto the courtyard grass. Before calling it a night, I slipped my mask back on, crossed the courtyard, and stopped outside Blair's window.

I stood there for a moment, just in case she looked out.

My Fawn needed to know I was always watching.

NINE

BLAIR

"And here we go again."

Daphne's groggy voice dragged me out of my sleep.

I blinked, my eyes sluggishly adjusting to the morning light, as last night came crashing back into my head like a true crime documentary I'd never added to my watch list.

Enzo and his masked cult buddy dragged me through the woods, made me watch Enzo torture Jett, and then dumped me in the forest like discarded trash. I was barefoot, freezing, and my hand throbbed.

By the time I staggered back into the main building, my legs were shaking so badly that I could barely climb the steps. Head-master Arisono stood in the entrance hall when I finally stumbled through the doors.

She looked at my muddy feet in disgust and said three words. "Strike one, Blair." She turned and walked away without asking me if I was okay or needed help.

I ran upstairs to the dorms and burst into my room to find Daphne sitting on her bed, waiting for me. She pulled me into a hug, helped me clean the dirt and blood from my skin, wrapped my hand, and we went to bed without talking about what had happened.

She'd already known.

So had Arisono, which was why she hadn't asked if I needed help after coming back looking like I'd spent the night grave digging.

They had known Enzo was responsible.

I yawned, shifting under my comforter, and felt about as well rested as Enzo was sane.

The bitter cold nipped at my skin as goose bumps rose along my arms.

Something felt ... off.

My bed nook wasn't as dark as it had been yesterday.

Light spilled through the space in jagged streaks.

Groaning, I pushed myself upright, still foggy with sleep. Every muscle in my body hurt as I rested my elbow against my pillow.

Time suddenly seemed to slow when I saw what'd brought on Daphne's comment.

I swallowed, my throat dry, as I stared at the curtain hanging in front of my nook. The fabric was sliced into ribbons. Long, uneven strips dangled from the rod like an animal had tried to claw its way through during the night. Scraps of the shredded curtain littered my mattress and spilled across the rug.

My limbs still ached as I pushed through the torn fabric and climbed out of my nook.

Daphne was upright on her bed, snuggled into her pink comforter. She motioned toward the destroyed room. "Hurricane Enzo has made landfall."

I gaped at the destruction around me, realizing the curtains were just Enzo's warm-up. Every drawer in my dresser was open, its contents dumped across the floor like someone had violently searched them. My clothes were scattered everywhere. Half the items in my closet were missing.

My MacBook was gone from my desk.

Items were broken on the floor.

But just *my* things. Nothing on Daphne's side was touched.

I stood slowly, staring in disbelief between the wreckage, then at Daphne. "Did he do this while we were asleep?"

She nibbled on her lip and nodded.

"No way." I shook my head hard. My temples throbbed as I replayed the night in my mind. "I listened for *every* sound last night."

And I'd heard them all.

Our neighbors' voices floating through the wall. The creaks of the old building. The wisp of the wind brushing against my window. Even an owl hooting somewhere outside.

But I hadn't heard footsteps, or drawers pulled open, or someone shredding my curtains.

Daphne sleepily pushed her tangled hair away from her face. "You'd be amazed at what Enzo can do without making a sound. If I ever get diagnosed with a terminal illness, I'm spending my last few days kicking him in the balls. Maybe I'll just rip them clean off. I'd be doing a public service."

I laughed and slid off my bed. The floor was freezing against my feet as I shuffled to hers. She scooted over to make room, and I dropped down beside her, pulling the comforter over my legs.

"I'm texting Seraphina." She grabbed her phone from the shelf behind her. Her drowsy eyes studied her phone, and she gasped. "Holy fucking shit." She smacked a hand over her mouth.

"What?" I asked in a scratchy voice.

She turned her screen toward me. "Jett jumped out of the infirmary window last night."

Messages and notifications crowded her phone screen, so many that I couldn't focus on a single one.

Jett jumped, my ass.

He was tossed, courtesy of the Night Sons.

Daphne's shock about Jett's death was short-lived as she started typing, reading her text out loud. "*Your brother is a deranged lunatic who trashed my room.*" After hitting Send, she tossed the phone aside and collapsed on her back with a long, dramatic sigh.

My body was still sore when I flopped down beside her, staring up at the ceiling.

"Is Seraphina Enzo's sister?" I asked.

"She is."

"Poor thing."

She scoffed. "*Lucky* thing. Being Enzo's sister means protection. Seraphina will never be a Fawn."

I jerked upright, as if suddenly brought to life.

Daphne did the same, scooting to the corner of her bed and tucking her legs beneath her.

"Can you tell me about this Fawn thing?" I asked.

I wasn't sure if she'd answer. Everyone around her was so secretive.

"You're about to find out anyway, so screw it," she said, as though she'd finally tired of protecting the Night Sons' secrets. "If Enzo chooses you as his Fawn, which after ..." She gestured toward his mess. "I'm almost positive he will." Sympathy passed over her features. "He'll make your life a living hell, Blair."

She scooted closer and lowered her voice, as if Enzo were listening somewhere. "If there's any chance your parents will let you drop out, leave now."

My pulse roared as I squeezed my eyes shut. I was stuck here. My stepfather wouldn't allow me to drop out. And I had better odds of my mother ignoring my calls than answering them.

I buried my hands in my hair, bowing my head, remembering I didn't even have a phone. I must've lost it in the woods, or Enzo had stolen it while manhandling me.

Asking for a replacement would only add to my problems. I was already at the top of my stepfather's shit list, and it would hand my mother another excuse to unleash her favorite punishment—the silent treatment. Last time, she stretched it to eight months straight. I wouldn't be surprised if she tried to beat her record next time.

Enzo's words from last night clawed their way back into my head. *"I'll force you to bathe in their blood before I drown you in it."*

My insides went tight. I believed every word.

"I don't get it," I muttered. "Why do families send their daughters here, knowing this can happen?"

Daphne lifted a shoulder in a tired shrug. "Most people have no idea the Night Sons or Fawns even exist. To them, Saint Vale is just prestige and pedigree, a secure place where their nepo babies can screw up without the world watching."

"What about the ones who do know?"

"They're usually former Sons or former Fawns. And in those cases, the parents hope their daughters get chosen."

"What?" I shrieked. "They *want* this to happen?"

"Only the powerful become Sons. And sometimes those Sons end up marrying their Fawns. For certain families, being chosen can be a great opportunity ... or it can be hell. With Enzo, it's always hell." She rubbed her arms as her gaze traveled to the window behind my bed. "He's had two other Fawns. Clarissa last year. And the girl before her ended up institutionalized."

Oh great. So death or an insane asylum.

"Have you ever been a Fawn?" I asked.

She shook her head. "I like to believe I'm safe, but nothing is guaranteed."

"Safe?" I leaned forward. "How?" *And how the hell do I get on that list?*

"I'm friends with most of the Havens."

I blinked at her. "The ... who?"

"The Havens. Every Son can mark a girl as off-limits. Just one. They usually pick a sister or someone in their family. Those girls are called Havens. I'm friends with most of them and considered part of their group. If a Son were to choose me, it'd piss off their Haven. They don't want that drama."

I stared at her, then at the shredded curtain, then at my desk, where my MacBook once had been. "What the hell did I get myself into?"

"The underbelly of the rich and powerful," she said gently, climbing over me to hop off the bed. She squeezed my foot in a small, pitying gesture. "Saint Vale was built on secrets. I'm sure your parents didn't know this could happen."

"Why would Enzo choose me?"

She shoved her feet into her slippers and shrugged. "No one understands Enzo. His mind's warped, and his heart is dead. His Fawns have been different every year. There's no pattern. He has no preference. I heard that he wasn't taking a Fawn this year, but I guess he saw you and changed his mind."

What the hell did I do to catch his attention?

Whatever it was, I knew one thing for sure: I hadn't dragged myself through life, fighting to survive, only to kneel to Enzo Marchetti.

If he thought I'd submit, he was wrong.

I'd fight back.

My throat felt raw when I cleared it. Probably leftover damage from my screaming last night.

"They tortured Jett in front of me," I revealed.

Daphne rolled her eyes, shocking me with her lack of sympathy.

Maybe she was more like the Sons than she pretended.

"Jett was a manipulative asshole," she said. "No one here liked him. *I* hated him."

And Enzo isn't worse? He and his red-masked friend?

"Why?" I twisted a loose thread on her pillowcase. "He warned me about Enzo, and that's what he got for it. He was only trying to help."

Daphne sighed like I'd disappointed her. "Oh, sweet, naive Blair. If you're going to be a Fawn, we need to make you smarter."

I frowned, taking her words as an insult.

I wasn't naive. I'd witnessed things just as ugly as what they had done to Jett.

Daphne gave my foot another squeeze. "Trust me. Jett wasn't helping you. He was being petty. Don't you dare blame his little window dive on yourself."

I wrinkled my nose. "Then why—"

She cut me off. "Because Jett wanted to be a Night Son. And they never accepted him." Her tone stayed light, as if she were talking about someone who'd cut her off in traffic and not a murder victim. "He and his father paid Enzo to select Clarissa as his Fawn. I'll never forget the night Jett stormed in here and threatened her, saying if she didn't please Enzo, there'd be hell to pay."

My eyes widened, and I hugged the pillow to my body.

"Jett thought Clarissa could convince Enzo to reconsider and allow him to join the Night Sons, but his plan backfired, and Clarissa paid for it. Trust me, Jett didn't want to protect you. He did it out of spite."

She wandered over to the vanity, then suddenly stopped. "Oh." Turning to face me, she held a black envelope between two fingers. "Looks like your demon admirer left you a love note." She lifted a small box sitting beside it. "And a gift."

I slid off the bed and crossed the room to her. I plucked the envelope from her hand and tore it open. A single piece of paper was inside. As much as I didn't want to read it, I knew I had to.

The paper was black, and the words written in white.

His handwriting was sharp with restrained strokes. Too neat for such a violent man.

I only find red appealing when it's your blood.

From this moment forward, you only wear black bows and ribbons.

Failure to listen comes with punishment.

I clutched the note to my chest, took a deep breath as I let it fall from my fingers, and stomped on it. The note crinkled beneath my heel.

Daphne watched my little rebellion with a smile before handing over the gift box, and I took it from her.

It was lighter than I'd expected. I turned the box over in my hands, eyeing the trash can beside the vanity and seriously considering slam-dunking it inside and pretending it never existed.

The wrapping paper was black. So was the satin ribbon tied around it. A small name tag dangled from it.

My soon-to-be Fawn.

With shaking hands, I pulled the ribbon loose and peeled back the wrapping paper, bracing to find something horrifying inside.

A finger, an eyeball, someone's soul, a piece of Jett.

I let out a breath when I found none of those.

Instead, my ribbons were inside, lying neatly on black tissue paper. He'd cut each one clean through the middle. A clump of my hair sat on top of them.

Okay, maybe it wasn't horrifying, per se.

But it was still fucked up.

A gasp tore from my throat as my hand went to the back of my head, my fingers combing through my hair in search of a missing chunk.

No fresh damage, so it must've been what he'd cut yesterday.

Inside the box was also another smaller one. When I opened it, I found a stack of black ribbons folded inside.

These ones weren't shredded.

Daphne collected the note from the floor, read it, and peeked inside the box. "Saint Vale's own Mr. Darcy," she muttered.

I couldn't help but laugh.

I dumped the ribbons, the hair, and the entire stupid gift straight into the trash and got ready for the day.

And no, I didn't wear a black bow.

Enzo Marchetti would regret ever choosing me to be his Fawn.

I arrived at my American Gothic Lit class as early as possible.

Even before Professor Nelson.

I refused to have my back to Enzo again, choosing the same desk in the back row that he'd sat in yesterday.

Before leaving my dorm, I'd pulled my hair into a tight bun and tied a pink ribbon I'd borrowed from Daphne around it. The urge to pull it into a ponytail nagged at me, but I wouldn't risk Enzo chopping off any more inches.

Daphne warned me not to do it while she straightened her hair. I knew it was a bad idea, but desperate times called for desperate measures. All I'd thought about was convincing Enzo to choose another Fawn.

Guilt dripped inside my belly—if he did, that meant he'd torture another poor girl.

If only we could stop him from choosing anyone.

I smiled at the thought of breaking Enzo's legs. Pretty damn hard to terrorize someone if you couldn't walk. Then again, knowing him, he'd probably find a way. The man seemed plenty resourceful.

My brain felt like mush as I sat there. Enzo was already mentally defeating me, and he'd yet to officially choose me. If this was only the beginning, I couldn't imagine the nightmare waiting for me.

I pressed my palms against the desk and forced myself to control my breathing while giving myself a mental pep talk.

If you think it, you can believe it.
Manifesting and delusion are the same thing, right?

Goose bumps erupted on my skin as I looked around the lecture hall. I eyed the Gothic paintings on the walls, the heavy wooden furniture, and the dark wood paneling.

Yesterday, I'd considered it Gothic décor. Now, it felt like the Night Sons had chosen every detail.

Crafted by the same men who built the entire Fawn System.

Fuck, I detested those men.

My attention drifted back to the grotesque mural above the whiteboard. The one where angels were being sacrificed like livestock. I flipped it off just as a book slammed onto the desk beside mine.

I turned in my chair to find the guy who'd sat beside Enzo yesterday. The one who'd looked thoroughly entertained while Enzo tormented me.

He dropped into the seat. My pulse kicked hard when his dark brown eyes slid toward me, narrowing like I'd done something wrong.

The look made me contemplate skipping class.

I tightened my fingers along the edge of the desk as he leaned back in his chair with a smug half smile. He rolled his neck until it cracked, then pulled his phone from his pocket.

My brain started racing.

Is he Red Mask? Did he kill Jett?

Instead of the university uniform, he wore a black cashmere turtleneck, tucked into gray slacks. He leaned back in his chair, planting his leather loafers on the desk.

I turned away, shoving my hair behind my ear and forcing my focus anywhere but him. The windows. The clock. That weird-ass painting.

He popped his knuckles one by one. Then clicked his tongue. Whistling came next. Each sound he made crawled through my nerves.

He was doing Enzo's dirty work in his absence.

I bent to grab my bag strap, deciding to ditch class, but before I could stand, students began filing into the room.

Professor Nelson shuffled in seconds later with damp hair and a scowl. He dropped his briefcase onto the desk and set down his Saint Vale mug on a coaster.

Maybe I should've given him the benefit of the doubt.

That thought lasted for a second before I changed my mind. I had no respect for him after he watched a male student harass a female student in the middle of his classroom and did absolutely nothing about it.

I frowned when something landed near my desk.

A single matchstick rolled to a stop in front of me.

I chewed on my fingernail, peeking at the guy beside me.

He was still on his phone, aimlessly scrolling.

Faking calm, I flicked the matchstick on my desk aside and opened my notebook.

When I reached down for my pen, another matchstick appeared. This one had a symbol scrawled across the thin wooden splint.

I lowered my gaze and squinted, but couldn't make out the symbol. If I'd had my phone, I would've snapped a picture and Googled it.

With every move I made, I felt him watching me while pretending to focus on his phone.

I shoved the matchstick aside.

Since Enzo had stolen my MacBook, handwritten notes were my only option today.

Asking my stepfather for both a new phone and a laptop would be a headache. Money wasn't the issue. He had plenty of that. He just hated any inconvenience involving me. I was surprised he hadn't shipped me off to a school overseas. The farther away I was, the better.

The room grew crowded, but no one else sat in the back row.

By the time Professor Nelson started his lecture, Enzo still hadn't arrived.

Good. Hopefully, the police were questioning him about his role in Jett's murder.

Every clue led straight to him. If Jett had *jumped* out of the infirmary window, someone would have had to drag him up there first.

I anxiously tapped my pen against the desk, and out of habit, I wrote six words.

Six words that had lived inside me for years.

Six words stitched into my chest like another organ.

Words I'd tried to forget more times than I could count.

But they always came back.

Writing them now eased a nervous tic inside me. A strange comfort, like going home. An unhappy home but still familiar.

I will atone for my sins.

I wrote it again.

I will atone for my sins.
I will atone for my sins.
I will atone for my sins.

My pen flew across the page.

A clock ticked loudly in the background, but the chatter around me faded as I wrote, slipping back into my old world.

Nelson's nasally voice disappeared. Even the guy sitting beside me vanished from my thoughts.

"Boo!"

I jerked upright. The pen fell from my fingers and rolled across the desk. My teeth sank into the inside of my cheek as I slowly lifted my head.

Enzo stood in front of me. He invaded my space, blocking my view of the lecture hall. I curled my shoulders forward and glared at him.

While he wasn't wearing his neon mask, he still wore one. Only a different kind.

One that concealed how truly demented he was behind a cruelly beautiful face.

His knuckles were split open, and when he lifted his hand, I noticed dried blood on it. *Our blood.*

I couldn't stop myself from glancing at my own. My skin was raw and tender from scrubbing it last night.

My eyes returned to Enzo.

His black shirt stretched across his broad chest, the red stitching along the collar resembling blood. The top buttons were undone, revealing a sliver of tanned skin.

He reached down and plucked the notebook off my desk.

"No!" I lunged for it, the edge of the desk jamming painfully into my stomach.

He ignored me, flipping through the pages, wetting his finger before each one. His neck flushed as he read the same sentence repeated hundreds of times.

I will atone for my sins.

Over and over and over.

How stupid of me. I'd set myself up for that.

Sleep deprivation was a hell of a drug.

At the front of the room, Professor Nelson stopped mid-sentence.

Enzo ripped page after page from my notebook, letting them fall to the floor.

"That's my seat," he said between a tear. "Move."

I crossed my arms, forcing my spine as straight as it'd go. "This class doesn't have assigned seating."

"You're right," he said calmly. Too calmly. "Guess I'll find another one."

Something about the way he'd said that made my stomach churn.

He clutched my notebook to his chest like a lovesick teen protecting her diary at all costs and walked down the aisle. Two steps later, he reached my row.

My lungs stalled, and I expected him to sit in the empty seat beside me.

Instead, he stopped directly behind my chair.

My notebook suddenly sailed over my head, landing with a slap on my desk.

"What—"

My words cut off when he hooked his fingers into the back of my collar and yanked me upright. The fabric cinched tight around my throat, choking me. My feet barely scraped the floor as he dragged me back.

Heat flooded my face as my lungs fought for air.

I coughed the moment he released me, doubling over to suck in deep breaths. Before I could straighten, he wrapped an arm around my waist and sank into the chair, dragging me down with him.

Right on his freaking lap.

I squirmed, trying to slide off his legs, but his grip held me there like an anchor.

The classroom fell silent as everyone watched.

The guys who idolized Enzo smiled in awe, as though they were witnessing a legend unfold.

Some looked horrified.

Others turned away in guilt.

Enzo never looked at them. No one existed to him unless he chose to see them. And right now, he saw only me.

He kept one hand braced against my stomach, pinning me in place. With the other, he opened my notebook. I flinched when he slid a pen from behind his ear.

I leaned forward to read as he wrote.

I will submit to my sins with Enzo.
I will submit and suck Enzo's cock.
I will submit and bow down to Enzo.

The handwriting matched the note from this morning.

My pulse thundered as I clenched my fists. Rage simmered beneath my skin while I tried to decide what to do next.

Before I could move, the guy beside us dragged his desk closer, trapping me between two monsters.

"What the hell is your deal?" I asked. "Haven't you tortured me enough?"

He chuckled and kept writing. "I haven't even started."

I will submit to my sins and obey Enzo.

"I want my phone and laptop back," I bit out.

"You'll get them back," he said easily. "When I'm done going through them."

I hated the way my body betrayed me when he shifted. His hold loosened slightly, and before I could stop it, my muscles eased against him.

I blamed it on the soreness from last night. My poor body needed *any* relief it could get.

He paused mid-sentence, hovering the pen over the paper. "What are your passwords?"

"Fuck off," I snapped.

My body might've started relaxing, but my hate toward him was strong.

He tsked me. "The easier you make this, the sooner you'll get your belongings back." He raised the pen to tap it lightly against my head. "Unless I find something in there I don't like." The way he rested his chin on my shoulder and roughly whispered in my ear sent shivers through me. "Let's hope you've been a very boring girl and never spoken to any other guy on those devices."

"I'll report them stolen." I dug my nails into his pants, gripping hard enough to wrinkle the material.

"Do it," he challenged, sliding his hand up my thigh.

Before I could push it away, he slipped his fingers beneath the hem of my skirt.

"And I'll show you how much worse this can get," he added.

My spine went rigid, and I shifted instinctively, trying to move away from him.

That was when I felt it.

His cock jerked beneath me.

I didn't know if the hiss that left my lips was from fear or desire.

Fear. Definitely fear, right?

His lips brushed my ear, and I twisted in his lap, trying to create any distance I could.

"You want to fight me, Blair?" he asked quietly.

"I'll fight you every minute of my life," I whispered, surprised at how steady the words came out, given the war waging inside my chest.

He chuckled darkly. "Then maybe I should tell the class where my hand is right now. Tell them how soft your pussy is." He dragged his fingers upward, snapping the waistband of my tights against my skin. "Maybe I'll even force you to the front of the room to *show them*." He snapped the elastic again.

I froze as terror struck me. His every word burned into my skin like one of those stupid matches.

Enzo had already humiliated me enough, and after all I'd already witnessed, I wouldn't put it past him to make good on his threat.

He rolled his finger under my waistband as his breath brushed over my skin.

I stopped fighting and gave in.

For now. FOR FUCKING NOW.

He snapped my tights in approval.

For the rest of class, I remained trapped on his lap while he subtly tortured me.

A slow tug at my tights.

His thumb sliding over my core.

A quick flick of his finger against my clit that made my vision blur.

All of it through the fabric, yet the heat of his touch still lit up my skin.

Professor Nelson continued his lecture like nothing was happening, but others stole glances at us.

"What sins do you need to atone for, Blair?" he whispered in my ear. "I'll tell you if those sins are worse than mine." He brushed his lips along my neck before reaching up and untying the ribbon from my hair. "Let's trade. Sin for sin."

I squeezed my eyes shut to trap the memories that always came up like monsters in the night.

He slid the ribbon free from my hair, lifted it, and then looped it around my neck.

"Maybe, little Fawn, we can commit them together." He tied the ribbon around my neck. "Trust me, in the end, you'll enjoy the pleasure."

"I don't want any pleasure from you," I said with a tremble.

The ribbon shifted against my pulse when I swallowed.

"Does that mean you prefer pain?" he asked as class ended. "Even better."

I clawed at the ribbon around my throat. It wasn't tight enough to cut off air, but it still restricted my breathing.

People stared as they shoved their laptops and books into their bags and left the classroom. Professor Nelson simply gathered his belongings and walked out without a word.

When the room had fully cleared, the guy beside us stood and shoved his desk back. As he passed us, he flicked something toward me.

I winced as the heat from the lit matchstick singed my skin.

Enzo finally released his hold on me.

My body swayed with the sudden freedom as he untied the ribbon from around my neck and shoved it inside his pocket.

He grabbed my notebook from the desk and stood. His tongue traced along his lower lip before a sly smile crept across his face. "Until next time, Blair."

TEN

ENZO

"You wanted to see me?" I asked, walking straight into Headmaster Arisono's office without bothering to knock.

The room smelled faintly like old coins, layered with whatever cheap perfume she was wearing. It was a scent you'd expect from a hooker.

From her polished wood desk, Arisono glanced away from her computer and nudged the ergonomic mouse away from her. Releasing a breath, she gestured for me to shut the door and sit in one of the black leather chairs.

I stepped back and slammed the door hard enough that the framed degrees on the wall shook.

The only reason I'd *followed* that instruction was because I never risked witnesses.

What I didn't do was sit.

Instead, I crossed the room and kicked the chair she'd indicated out of my way. It skidded across the floor as I stopped in front of her desk.

She stared up at me, cautious but steady as I towered over her.

I was impressed at how she kept her composure.

Arisono had plenty of practice in dealing with men in powerful positions. Her history at Saint Vale went back to the

First Benefactors. She was also a former Fawn. She'd survived hell and remained resilient. I supposed she deserved a little credit for that.

But it didn't mean I liked her.

The truth was, I wasn't fond of anyone in authority. Except my father.

She folded her arms on the desk and cleared her throat. "Blair Dupont."

"What about her?" I picked up the statuette of the school crest from the desk. I pretended not to give a shit about this conversation as I tossed it from one hand to the other, debating whether it was worth keeping intact.

"I suggest you leave her alone."

I stilled the piece in my grip.

I held it there for a moment, giving her time to think about her words.

To play them back in her head and realize what a mistake they had been.

At my lack of response, she nodded slowly. Her shoulders slouched as regret slipped through the cracks in her composure.

Suggestions were only useful when the person listening actually gave a fuck. I didn't.

I had a long-standing policy against anyone questioning me. It explained most of my issues with authority figures.

Her *suggestion*—and those of others—was as important to me as learning how bad it hurt to run my cock through a cheese grater.

Just as fast as her shoulders sagged, they straightened.

I let the statuette fall from my hand. A subdued smirk spread across my lips when it hit the floor and shattered. Metal fragments scattered across the floor.

"Wow," I drawled, nudging a piece with the toe of my boot. "That looked old." I peered from the broken pieces back up to her. "Family heirloom? Passed down through generations, maybe?" I spread my arms, motioning around the office. "You should think about getting a rug in here. Wouldn't want anything valuable breaking."

Arisono remained indifferent, clearing her throat and tapping her knuckle to her lips like she wanted to restart this entire conversation.

When she spoke again, she chose her words carefully. "What I mean is, Blair has a history. I don't trust her. Please leave her alone. Pretend she doesn't exist."

"I don't trust you. *Especially* if you allowed Blair into this university, knowing she was a liability," I stated. "That goes against Saint Vale's policy." I tsked.

Her hand rose to the Chanel clip holding her hair in place, twisting it once between her fingers. "Blair's stepfather used his position as leverage."

"And what position would that be?"

Her attention slid briefly to the door before returning to me. "He was a Son. First Benefactor blood."

Something sharp tore through me.

That's not what Nico told me.

That's not what I found when I did my deep dive on her.

According to our research, her parents were losers who'd hit the lottery and made friends with someone who had plenty of pull here, allowing Blair admittance.

I'd be smashing Nico's fucking iPad for that bad information, along with whatever other tech bullshit he stashed in his dorm.

My gaze hardened as my thoughts shifted back to Blair.

Who is her stepfather, then?

I needed to know everything.

For all I knew, I'd met her stepfather, if he was an Elder Night Son.

I could've shaken his hand, shared a drink, plotted a murder with him.

Some Elder Night Sons kept their identities secret. Graduation freed you from showing your face. You only had to unmask while you were a Current Son.

After that, you could wear the mask whenever you wanted. Some Elder Sons never took theirs off.

Here, we were Sons.

Cruel men with no reason to pretend otherwise.

Later, they'd leave the tunnels and crawl back into their respectable lives aboveground. Well, they pretended to be respectable. None of us were.

Elder or Current Son.

Arisono watched me warily, concern tightening the lines around her mouth. She knew more. I could see it in the way she held herself too still. She knew who Blair's stepfather was but refused to tell me.

Her protecting him made sense. She knew the rules to stay in her place.

In exchange, she had become the headmaster. Saint Vale only allowed headmasters from First Benefactor bloodlines.

She was also the first woman to hold that title. Saint Vale didn't thrive in progressive ideals. Traditions here leaned heavily toward old-fashioned bullshit.

Personally, I didn't care if someone had a pussy, a cock, or a fucking Lego between their legs. I treated everyone the same. I was equal-opportunity cruel.

"You let her in, you're responsible for her," I said, my icy stare locking on to hers. "If she falls out of line, you know who pays for it."

Arisono lifted her chin. "Which is why I've decided to expel her."

Keeping my composure in check, I slowly straightened and turned my head, glancing at her framed accolades lining the wall.

So many credentials, yet no common sense.

My father always said education didn't equal intelligence.

"And go against a former Son?" I asked, tapping my chin. "Depending on his influence, you wouldn't only lose that vote, but you'd lose your position."

She went quiet, and silence grew as she looked past my shoulder at nothing.

When she finally spoke, her voice was steady but strained. "I'll risk it to get rid of her."

I moved before she could start whatever carefully worded bullshit she'd try to feed me. Leaning forward, I planted my palms flat on her desk, right over her meticulously stacked paperwork. The paper edges ripped under the force.

"You're not expelling her," I said, my tone harsh as I curled my upper lip.

Her chair rolled back as she pushed herself away to widen the distance between us.

Nice try.

I stepped away from the desk and circled it in two long strides.

Her breath hitched when I shoved her chair from it until I had enough room to stand in front of her. I set my hands over hers on the armrests, pinning them there, and dipped my head to put my face level with hers.

I kept my voice low and calm, but it carried enough venom to poison anything it touched. "If you do, losing your position will be the least of your worries."

She held my stare, her features tightening with more spite and less fear.

Arisono didn't just resent me. She resented *all* of us.

"She'll be the demise of this university," she said.

I lifted my hands from the chair, one at a time, and adjusted my collar.

Her gaze followed me as I moved back around the desk. I stopped, bending just enough to pick up a shard of broken metal.

"You should worry about yourself, Arisono." I flicked the shard at her.

It skidded across the desk. Her body jerked to the side to dodge it even though it clearly wouldn't hit her. Dramatics.

If I'd wanted to hit her, I would've. I never missed.

I stepped back, never breaking eye contact. "I'll make sure

Blair stays in line." My lips formed a derisive smile. "*I'll* be her demise."

Nico's dorm was the second room I barged into that day.

Unlike Arisono, he hadn't requested my presence. But I gave no fucks.

Who doesn't enjoy an unexpected visit from yours truly?

They should pay just to breathe the same air as me.

Crux Hall was buried in the west wing, in the back, and secured behind a gate.

I had a key to the gate *and* his door. I had a key to all gates and rooms in Saint Vale. One of the many perks of running the place.

That was how sneaking into Blair's dorm last night to *borrow* some of her belongings had been so easy.

But even without keys, I always found a way in. Lock picking was a skill I'd learned early. And if finesse failed, there was always the universal solution to kick the door down. I tried to avoid that, though. Didn't like drawing attention to myself if I could help it.

With Blair's MacBook tucked under my arm, I stalked farther into Nico's room and stopped.

Nico sat on the edge of his bed with his pants shoved down around his ankles. Between his knees, a shirtless blond knelt on the floor, her mouth wrapped around his cock.

She moaned against it while he gripped her hair, guiding her movement.

"Hey, asshole," I called out.

Nico's head snapped up. "Man, what the hell?"

I sighed, bored as if I were watching a PBS special on melting ice caps. "Relax. I've seen worse effort."

He loosened his hold on the girl's hair. She pulled back, out of breath. I caught the flash of irritation on Nico's face. The girl leaned back on her heels and wiped her mouth with the back of her hand. When her eyes lifted and landed on me, they widened.

Then she smiled.

"Did you come to join us?" she asked.

"Negative," I replied flatly. "I'd rather rip my fucking tongue out."

Her lips jutted into a pout. "Nico said I needed to practice. Apparently, my performance is subpar."

Nico patted her cheek. "We're working on that."

I shifted my attention to him. "Smart move, picking someone inexperienced. Less chance she'll be disappointed at how small your cock is."

He flipped me off over her head, reached for the bottle of vodka sitting on the shelf above his head, and took a long drink. Mid-sip, he crooked two fingers at the blond to come back.

She crawled closer.

He tipped the bottle, letting vodka spill down her face and over her chest.

"Squeeze them together," he instructed her. "I want to see your nipples touch."

She obeyed, pressing her small tits together, and moaned.

"Now, lick it off."

She bent forward and did just that.

I checked my watch and yawned.

Nico leaned down to close his mouth around one of her nipples. She gasped and pushed herself closer, pressing her tits into his face.

When he pulled back, he guided her back down, spreading his legs as his head tipped toward the ceiling while he pushed his cock back into her mouth.

The blond was his Fawn. I didn't know her name, nor did I care to.

Nico had chosen badly.

When you first joined the Sons, the excitement of finally getting a Fawn always made us too impulsive, too impatient to vet our options properly. He'd done exactly that and snatched up the first shiny thing that dropped to her knees for him.

His Fawn was aggressively average. Six out of ten on her best day.

And that wasn't just about looks. Appearance was a bonus. A true Fawn needed substance. She needed strength, resilience, and logic. Trust was big with your Fawn.

Blondie had none of that.

And now, I hated her.

She was distracting Nico. He'd half-assed my orders to get his dick sucked.

I crossed the room and dropped Blair's MacBook on his desk, right under his wall of glowing monitors.

Nico groaned and told her to take it deeper.

My irritation spiked.

They were so lost in themselves that they didn't notice me step behind her. I grabbed the back of her neck and shoved her forward until she choked on Nico's cock.

Nico flinched, but didn't pull away. Instead, he held her there.

I released her and stepped back.

She gagged, spit dripping down her chin, and tried to breathe through useless gasps.

Nico groaned again, not even bothering to hide that he liked it.

The girl? Not so much. Her long nails scraped across his bare thighs as she tried to pull herself free.

When reality finally snapped into Nico, he loosened his grip.

She collapsed back on her heels, coughing. Mascara streaked down her cheeks as she dragged in breaths. After a few seconds, she returned to sucking Nico's cock like nothing had happened.

I grabbed Nico's computer and ripped it straight off the desk so hard that the cord snapped. I threw it on the floor and drove my heel into it.

The screen shattered, and the plastic cracked.

That sure got Nico's attention.

He shoved the girl away.

"What the hell?" she shrieked, scrambling upright while Nico dragged his pants up, swearing under his breath.

She snatched up her clothes and bolted for the door.

"Pleasure seeing you suck cock terribly," I called after her.

The door slammed, and I grabbed Nico's iPad, smashing it against the edge of the desk. The screen cracked with a dull crunch.

That was when he finally moved.

He lunged at me and swung. His fist clipped my jaw.

I answered with one of my own. His head snapped to the side.

One punch. That was the Sons' rule.

If we were pissed at each other, that was how we handled it.

We always made sure to make *the one* count and then moved on.

"The fuck is your problem, Zo?" Nico yelled as I shook out my hand.

"I told you to dig up everything you could on Blair."

"Who?"

I shot him a cold glare.

"Ah, right. The girl ... your Fawn."

"Blow jobs don't come before work. They're a privilege, not a distraction," I said coldly. "You don't indulge until after. I told you I wanted *everything* on her."

"Did I not do that?"

"You failed to mention her stepfather was a Son."

He stiffened. "What?"

"That's called fucking slacking."

"How the fuck was I supposed to find that?" he shot back. "Someone created a fake file for her, then."

"No shit, Sherlock."

"Finding out Son information is difficult. You know that information is locked down." He rubbed at the back of his neck in frustration. "How'd *you* find out? Did Blair tell you?"

I shook my head. "Arisono."

Nico frowned. "She didn't give you any more information?"

I shook my head again.

"I hate that uptight cunt."

"You and me both."

He dragged a hand through his hair before grabbing his glasses from the desk. "They don't keep digital records on the Sons. There's nothing to hack. Anyone would've missed that, especially if the parents listed fake names." He looked down at the smashed computer at his feet. "So, congratulations. You owe me a new computer and iPad. Go to fucking anger management."

"Did you get into her phone?"

He opened a drawer and tossed it at me. "Reported stolen. Everything was erased from it."

"You were too slow."

I grabbed his phone from the desk and hurled it across the room.

It slammed against the wall.

Nico exhaled sharply. "How about you do your own hacking?"

"We all have our jobs." I gestured toward the mess of his electronics now scattered across the room. "Yours is information. If you can't handle that, we'll assign you another job. Cleanup duty. I'll have you scraping brain matter off walls until you beg to hack into *anything*."

He rubbed at his forehead. "I'll figure out her laptop, but I can't do anything about the phone. Once it's wiped, everything is gone."

I walked toward the door, stopping right before I lost sight of him. "If you don't figure the laptop out, remember what I said. I'll also slit your Fawn's throat and make her suck your cock while she's bleeding out. Don't let your distractions fuck up your Sons' status." I left his dorm.

My next stop was to punish the girl who'd reported the phone stolen.

I was really making my rounds today.

When I walked into Blair's dorm room, she and Daphne were both stretched out on their beds.

Their bed curtains hung open, the chandeliers dimmed low, and the air smelled faintly of vanilla.

Daphne sat with her laptop on her thighs, typing fast, headphones on, head bobbing to whatever she was listening to. She didn't notice my arrival.

Blair did immediately.

She wore no headphones. I'd taken every device she owned.

Her shoulders tensed when she saw me. She slammed her book shut and threw it aside before adjusting the thin strap of her tank.

I waited for her to scream, but she didn't.

Good. She's learning already.

As I passed Daphne without breaking stride, Blair's scowl grew deeper the closer I got to her.

She scooted backward across the bed to get away from me. I dropped to one knee, caught her ankle, and dragged her closer in one smooth pull.

Her mouth opened, most likely to scream, so I sealed my hand over it.

"Don't say a word." I angled my gaze toward the window. "Unless you want to test your ability to fly."

She snarled under my hand.

I eased my hand away, waiting to see if she'd try something stupid. "Come on. Let's take a walk."

She kicked at me. "I'm not going anywhere with you."

My gaze drifted to the window again, and I raised a brow.

"Push me then," she dared.

My chest tightened at the defiance in her tone.

I hated to admit it was cute.

Cute? Who the fuck am I?

The mattress sank under my weight as I climbed onto her bed.

She scrambled until her back hit the window. Elbows pressing into her sides, she closed herself off from me. I reached past her to crack the window open, and the chilly night air spilled into the room.

When I glanced back at her, I saw the veins in her neck pulsing.

Such a beautiful sight.

I loved how I made her nervous, but she still fought me.

That was what I wanted from a Fawn. I knew deep down that Blair was strong. I needed that.

My gaze left her neck, drifting down, and my pulse jolted. Along with the tank top, she wore black plaid pajama shorts. Her nipples hardened through the thin tank fabric, the tiny pebbles peeking through.

I studied her breasts like they were the only class I was interested in passing here. They moved with her breathing, faster with each shift in tempo.

Deep. Short. Long.

The pattern constantly breaking.

I slid my hand up her calves, my movement controlled and firm, anticipating another kick. She sucked in a quick breath, and goose bumps covered her skin. Suddenly, I had a craving to lick each one with my tongue.

What the fuck is going on with me?

These callous hands, which had committed more sins than any preacher could name, wanted to touch her everywhere.

Blair was delicate but powerful. And while I wanted to fuck her, I couldn't yet.

I hadn't come here for that tonight. I had come here to make a deal.

"I'll throw you out that window." I stopped at her thigh to squeeze it tight.

She recoiled, her head almost hitting the window at my sudden mood shift.

"And I won't lose a second of sleep over it," I continued. "Get up. We're leaving."

She crossed her arms, hiding those nipples I'd already grown obsessed with. "Last time I went on *a walk* with you, you took me to a place that smelled like death and made me watch you torture someone." She waggled her finger at me. "Oh! Then you ditched me alone in the woods."

"I was helping you learn your way around campus." I loosened my grip on her thigh before patting it. "Don't worry. I won't do that tonight."

She narrowed her eyes, untrusting. "Just tonight or ever again?"

I didn't answer and pulled myself to my feet.

"Come on, Blair." I held my hand out to her.

"No," she bit out stubbornly.

I grabbed her wrist, dragged her across the bed, and forced her to her feet. "It's in your best interest. We need to talk."

"We can talk here." She pointed down at her bed.

"We can do this the easy or the hard way. I enjoy the hard way, trust me, but I recommend you choose easy."

She peered over at Daphne, who had ripped off her headphones and was watching us like she wasn't sure whether to intervene.

Blair looked straight at her, her voice turning serious. "If I'm not back in an hour, call the police and tell them Enzo Clarissa-and-Jett'd me," Blair told Daphne.

"Will do." She brought two fingers to her eyes, holding them there, before pointing them at me.

Since I wanted Blair to behave, I decided to refrain from telling Daphne that the police would do nothing if she called them.

Blair dragged a coat over her pajamas and shoved her feet into a pair of sneakers without bothering with socks.

For Daphne's little stunt, I paused before passing her. "Brooks says to tell you to fuck yourself."

"Tell him I'd fuck myself with a pineapple before I fucked him," Daphne fired back. "So, that doesn't sting."

"A pineapple would, though," Blair commented while crouching to tie her sneakers.

Daphne bit into her cheek, lifting a finger at Blair. "'Tis true."

I whistled, signaling for Blair to get her ass out the door.

Blair gave Daphne one last anxious look before moving past me and into the hallway. Neither of us spoke as we left Poenas Dare Hall.

It was after curfew, so the hall was mostly deserted.

As we went down the stairs, I took two steps at a time, and she lagged. When we reached the main floor, her pace slowed further.

She trailed me like a naive little doe wandering into traffic.

What she didn't know was that I'd already started my engine, ready to plow right through her.

A few lingering classmates paused and stared at us. Unless it was Seraphina, I didn't make a habit of being seen with women.

Not many here knew the Night Sons existed. Blair only did because Jett had been too stupid to keep his mouth shut. Realistically, she should've been thanking me. I was about to save her life.

Jett telling her about us had been a death sentence for them both.

After her behavior and threats, my choosing her as a Fawn was risky.

Not as risky as Nico's Selection, but still not as logical as I'd planned.

For some reason, after I'd seen her, my gut stopped caring about logic. I wanted her to be mine.

My fists tightened as I walked, forcing down the urge to grab her by the hair and haul her forward.

To keep myself in check, I slid a hand into my pocket and brushed my thumb over the ribbon I'd taken from her hair in class.

I was still undecided on how I'd punish her for disobedience.

She was lucky I'd shown restraint in class. I was capable of far worse than ripping up her notes and planting her on my lap.

My restraint wasn't out of mercy. I believed in no such thing.

I just needed her to cooperate tonight.

When we reached the main entrance, she stopped and took two steps backward.

"Unlike you, I'm not allowed off campus after curfew." She shook her head and threw her hands through the air.

I grabbed her wrist, opened the door, and shoved her through it. "Looks like you've broken it now."

ELEVEN
BLAIR

The doors slammed shut behind us, and I flinched so hard that I felt it in my jaw.

Staring ahead, all I saw was the unwelcoming darkness, punctuated by the low lights surrounding the university's grand fountain. The stone steps looked steeper than they had when I climbed them days ago.

My gaze tracked the long drive stretching toward the steel gates.

The only way in.

The only way out.

I squeezed my eyes shut, my thoughts returning to the night I'd arrived at Saint Vale.

The chilly downpour. The gloom. That unsettling feeling.

I'd stood in this exact spot, soaked and alone, thinking I'd reached rock bottom. I had no idea that'd turn out to be the most peaceful night I'd have here.

Only a few days had passed since my stepfather's driver had dropped me off and left me here, but it felt like an eternity had gone by.

Taking in shallow breaths, I scanned the fountain and the

long drive beyond it, my gaze refusing to drift toward the devil behind me.

There was no need to look. I felt every inch of his suffocating presence.

His smell, his breathing, his nearness.

It all sent warning signals through my body.

I chewed on my bottom lip as I tried to decide which was worse—being trapped with Enzo inside the university or out here with him.

Both felt like different versions of the same slow death.

I hugged myself, shivering, and wished I'd changed out of my pajamas. But it wasn't like I'd known we were going outside when Enzo asked—no, *demanded*—I take a walk with him. I'd assumed we'd go to the hall or library.

How naive of me to forget what kind of devil I was dealing with.

The chances of Enzo dragging me into another underground torture chamber were higher than him taking me somewhere normal.

Enzo shoved me forward, nearly knocking me down a step. I lost my balance and tumbled forward. Just before I fell, he grabbed my elbow, steadying me.

I recoiled, my footing unsteady at the edge as my heel skimmed it. For a second, I teetered there, caught between controlling my balance and falling.

He released my elbow, and then, in a flash, his hand caught mine.

A single second passed. Then two. Silence hung between us like a ghost in the night.

His hold on me was different than in the woods.

No cold leather glove. Just his bare skin.

The devil's hand felt warm, rough, and disturbingly human.

As he led us down the stairs, our shoulders brushed with every step. He laced his fingers with mine, and my pulse jumped.

Enzo had ulterior motives for taking me out here.

He either planned to kill me or convince me to keep my mouth shut.

If killing me was his intention, then he'd get away with it. Arisono and the rest of the university would bury any evidence against him.

My shoes scraped against the stone as I stepped down to the ground. Enzo guided us along the winding path toward a cloister wall.

Once we stepped far enough from the lights, he stopped. My hand slipped from his as he turned me, reached for my waist, lifted me as if I weighed nothing, and sat me on the stone wall.

He jumped up beside me with a grunt, close enough that his shoulder brushed mine. His body heat seeped into me.

I breathed in his scent mingling with the night. I turned toward him, but the darkness hid most of his face.

All I could make out were the sharp angles and shadows across his cheekbone and jaw.

Goose bumps pebbled my skin as my attention drifted back to the steps. My throat tightened as memories of that first night returned.

Maybe I hadn't imagined someone watching me.

Maybe it had been him.

He slung his arm over my shoulders, drawing me closer, as if we were two close pals rather than the hunter and the hunted.

"Now, Blair," he said.

If I were stupid—and I could admit, coming out here with him *was* stupid—I might mistake this for something, dare I say, *gentle.*

But I knew better.

This was an impostor Enzo. Just another one of his masks.

No one sane flipped between warmth and cruelty that easily.

My eyes snapped shut as his fingers trailed up my neck, slow and deliberate, like a spider searching for the perfect spot to sink its fangs.

I didn't say a word. Didn't dare to make a move. Just waited for him to continue.

"I think we got off to a bad start," he said.

I choked back the scoff burning up my throat.

I am alone with a killer and need to keep my composure.

My sarcasm could come back later.

I swung my feet against the wall. "You think?" I raised a finger. "Our *start* was you cutting my hair." Another finger joined it. "You kidnapped me." A third finger. "And forced me to watch you torture Jett." I held up my entire hand, displaying my palm. "And then you cut me."

"Jett?" he asked, saying his name with confusion that'd make any sane person question whether they'd dreamed up the entire scene.

This devil. He was a master manipulator.

"Jett," I repeated slowly. "The guy you killed."

"The kid who unfortunately jumped out of a window?" He scratched his head, as if genuinely searching his memory. "I'll have my mother send flowers to the family. How tragic." He splayed his hand around my neck, his thumb finding my racing pulse.

I gulped. "A tragedy *you* caused." As soon as the words left my mouth, I regretted them.

Why would I remind him I was a witness?

If he did lure me out to murder me, I'd just reminded him of his reason.

He didn't react to what I'd said. Didn't even flinch.

"Are you going to kill me like you did him?" I whispered in a shaky voice.

His thumb stayed on my neck, resting on my pulse, but he didn't apply more pressure or move it.

It was like he wanted to *feel* how every word affected me.

"I didn't kill him," he said.

"I was there."

My truth was useless. What I'd seen meant nothing. It was his word against mine, and his was worth more. He knew it just as much as I did.

"Quit making up stories about me, Blair. It's not courteous."

I snorted softly, turning my neck to free it from his hand.

The loss of his warmth felt almost suffocating.

"Don't you think it'd be fair that you get to know me before passing judgment?" he asked. "I don't believe everything I hear about you."

I turned my head toward him in panic. "What have you heard about me?"

He smirked. "Nothing I'd judge you for."

"I don't want to know the real you," I said with more confidence than I felt. "I wish you'd never sat behind me. Wished you'd never cut my hair for whatever sick reason you justified in your head."

"This is where I first laid eyes on you," he muttered in a low voice.

"What?" My voice cracked.

His fingers slipped beneath the collar of my coat, lowering the fabric just enough to let his icy fingers brush the side of my neck. "When you first arrived at Saint Vale, I watched that asshole abandon you here and then watched you climb those steps in the rain." He leaned in, his mouth edging toward my ear. "That's when I decided you were mine."

"I don't want to be yours." I hated how frail my voice sounded. Hated how tight my gut knotted.

"Too late. You've already piqued my interest."

"Not my problem." I lifted my chin. "Find another interest."

A low chuckle slipped from him. The first one I'd heard leave his lips that wasn't frigid. "That'd actually create a bigger problem for you."

"What do you mean?"

"Your life depends on being my Fawn."

All air nearly left my lungs right then. "What?" I stuttered out that one word in three breaths.

"Jett fucked you over from the moment he opened his mouth. No one learns about the Night Sons and lives long enough to talk about it. You were never supposed to know. You're an outsider."

Everything suddenly felt colder and darker.

To stop myself from crying, I stared ahead, wishing the night would swallow me up.

"He handed you a death sentence," Enzo said. "So this is the time you stop pretending you have a choice, Blair."

My breath hitched. "And if I refuse?"

"You die." He didn't raise his voice. He didn't have to.

He was also done hiding the Night Sons' existence.

That was now the power he had over me.

Something inside me snapped, and I jumped off the wall, landing hard on the ground. My heart raced as I stomped away, finding my way back to the steps that led to the entrance.

My stomps broke into a run when I heard Enzo behind me.

The faster I could escape him, the better.

Neither he nor the damn Night Sons would determine my fate.

My lungs hurt, and the wind stung my cheeks as I raced for the steps, but it still wasn't enough.

Enzo caught up with me quickly, his large hand closing around my wrist, and yanked me around to face him.

I stared at him, hatred burning my bones, as he held me in place.

His nostrils flared as he clenched his jaw.

"You can never outrun me, Blair," he said, his cut and callous palm cupping my face, forcing me to look up at him. "You can never outsmart me." He dragged his thumb over my lip, inching closer. "I'll always win. I'll always find you."

Panic snapped through me, and I struggled to break free.

His grip turned stronger as he steered me away from the steps toward the fountain. I twisted, fought, and dug my heels into the ground—every move so similar to how I'd acted when he grabbed me in the woods.

If anyone else was outside, no one came to my rescue.

Enzo moved with smooth ease, with a madman's calmness, as if my resistance was no more than a mild wind drift.

With each step closer, the fountain grew louder.

Its lighting cast a glow over the carved, round basin of dark stone. Three tiers rose from its center, and water cascaded from one level to the next.

So beautiful, but also so cold.

Fitting this place perfectly.

He forced me down to my knees beside the basin and wrenched my hands behind my back, pinning me there as the stone edge painfully jabbed into my ribs.

"Last chance, Blair." He squeezed my wrists together. "Commit to being my Fawn."

The urge to shout, *Never!* rocked through my thoughts, but I held back.

Instead, I said, "Just let me go, Enzo. *Please.* I won't tell anyone what I saw."

I dropped my chin, staring down at the copper pennies shimmering at the bottom of the fountain.

What a waste of money.

Wishes weren't granted here. Only nightmares.

Then it happened so fast.

One second, I was *considering* pleading for a penniless wish, and the next, I was pulled forward.

Enzo released my wrists, and before I could even catch my breath, he plunged my head beneath the water. Ice-cold water smashed into my face, nearly swallowing it whole. Sound vanished as water rushed into my ears. I'd never felt such a sharp sting before.

For a split second, I froze.

Then instinct took over.

I thrashed my head wildly in all directions as I struggled to break loose. My hair unraveled in the water, floating around my face and blocking my vision. I tried to push myself up, palms scraping the stone lip, but they slipped off the slick edge and sent me deeper beneath the water instead.

Just like he'd said, he'd always win.

Water forced its way into my mouth as I struggled to breathe. The taste was metallic and stale, like old coins and moss.

This wasn't a fountain for wishes. It was one for sins and ruin.

A place to drown your secrets.

My arms flailed weakly as my fingers scratched at the stone. Time stretched like I was dealing with the slowest hourglass. With each passing second, my chest felt more constricted.

As I shut my eyes, my strength dissolved. My limbs felt heavy, useless, broken. Every part of me was on the verge of collapse.

My body was desperate for air, for relief, and ready to surrender to Enzo.

To let him win. To let him own me.

At the same time that thought hit, he lifted me from the water.

My face broke through the surface, and I dragged in air like I'd just discovered what it was. Heavy gasps tore from my lungs as I violently coughed and spat up water.

His massive hand gripped the back of my head to suspend me above the water. Water streamed off my face.

He fisted my wet strands to remind me who was in control.

"Now, I'll give you one more chance." He tugged my head back until our eyes met. "Either I kill you or you agree to be my Fawn."

At this point, I didn't understand why he needed my agreement.

He'd already made my decision for me.

I choked out more water, my lungs burning, and said, "No."

His gaze stayed glued to mine, so firm that he didn't blink once. "If you thought I was brutal with Jett, you don't want to find out what else I'm capable of. I'd advise you to reconsider your response with a three-letter word."

"If I say yes ..." I stopped, struggling to pull air into my lungs. "You won't kill me?"

He cocked his head, as if he was still debating whether to do just that. "Why would I kill you? I plan to use you."

Cold dread washed over me.

Use me.

"But you won't kill me after?" I pressed, needing to hear that answer.

"I won't kill you *now*."

A shiver ran down my spine. I felt so drained and cold.

"Fine." My chin shook as I wheezed out breaths.

Tears heated beneath my eyes at how easily I'd surrendered.

Enzo pulled me away from the water, making sure my face didn't strike the stone. When he finally released me, my legs gave out, and I collapsed onto the ground beside the fountain.

He sat on the fountain's ledge above me like some dark statue connected to it.

I shivered, staring at him as my teeth clattered.

"Good girl." He petted my drenched hair like I was a dog who'd just learned a new trick.

I didn't even have the energy to smack his hand away. That didn't stop me from glaring up at him. He watched me beneath the lights, his stare rattling my core, and stroked my hair.

His fingers worked through my wet hair as his focus locked on me.

That unblinking stare of his was back.

It made me think he had more words on the tip of his tongue, but was holding them back.

He licked his lips again before biting into the bottom one, as if stopping himself, before dropping his hand.

A gust of wind hit me, and my teeth chattered harder as he stood.

I watched him, confused and in awe, as he unbuttoned his black button-up. The fabric was as wet as mine, clinging to his muscles. I flinched when he knelt to drape the shirt over my shoulders.

Suddenly, I wasn't as cold as before. Eyeing him, I was the one biting into my lip now.

"Wear this tomorrow," he demanded. "Make sure it's dry and wrinkle-free."

With that, he turned and walked away toward the steps. He didn't look back at me as I sat there, drenched and humiliated.

My teeth rattled as I scrambled to my feet and hurried after him.

Not only did I not want to be out here alone, but I also needed heat and dry clothes before my body shut down.

We climbed the steps in silence, Enzo way ahead of me, but halfway up, I would swear he slowed so I didn't fall too far behind.

I hated that I clutched his shirt tight around my body for warmth.

By the time I reached the top step, I was positive I'd have a nasty case of pneumonia tomorrow.

Still ahead of me, he opened the door and allowed it to shut in my face.

My shoulders sagged as I opened it again.

Just when I thought my night couldn't get worse, it did.

When I walked inside, Headmaster Arisono stood mere feet away.

Enzo whistled and walked right past her, like her little strike rule didn't apply to him.

"Blair, that's strike two," she stated firmly.

Daphne dropped her phone on the bed when I returned to our dorm. "I hope the reason you're soaked is that you took a shower in someone else's dorm."

"I wish," I grumbled, kicking the door shut with my wet sneaker and flinging his shirt across the room. My body was already sore from what happened outside. "Enzo decided I needed to taste the fountain water."

Water slid down the sleeves of my coat and dripped from every inch of me. I unlaced my shoes and kicked them off. One hit the wall. The other landed on my bed.

Daphne sprang off her bed to grab the hair dryer from the vanity before I could even ask for it.

I peeled out of the wet clothes and changed into dry pajamas. My movements were so slow, as if the cold water had frozen my brain.

It was official. I was Enzo's Fawn.

The only other option had been death.

Headmaster Arisono's words brought another wave of nausea. *"Blair, that's strike two."*

Like last time, she hadn't asked if I was okay.

She also hadn't reprimanded Enzo. Just me.

That proved again that he'd always be in charge.

"Sit." She patted the chair in front of the vanity.

I sank into it, my body slouching.

As the warm air from the hair dryer touched my scalp, the muscles knotted under my skin loosened. I coughed, still feeling water lodged inside my chest.

When she was finished, Daphne sighed. "Someone really needs to kick Enzo's ass."

I met her gaze in the mirror. "Are you volunteering for the job?"

"Hell no." She yanked the cord from the outlet and wrapped it around the dryer. "I enjoy breathing. Plus, I need at least a few more years to have flings with royals."

"Royals?" I glanced up at her. "You've had flings with *royals*?"

"A few actually." Her smile nearly took over her entire face.

I smacked her arm. "You can't say that and not provide details."

She giggled, gently squeezed my shoulder, and flopped back on her bed. "What happened with Enzo tonight?"

My body ached as I stood, crossed the room, and climbed onto her bed. We both shifted until our backs rested against the wall, our knees angled toward each other. It seemed her bed had become my classroom for learning about the Night Sons.

"I agreed to be Enzo's Fawn," I said.

Her hand flew to her chest. "Blair, are you fucking nuts?"

"I was left with no choice! The asshole was literally drowning me and said he'd kill me if I didn't!" Rubbing my arms, I pulled my knees to my chest. "Enzo said anyone who knows about the Sons, outsiders, ends up dead." I turned to face her. "How do you know so much about them and are still breathing?"

I needed as much information as I could get.

Anything to help me stay alive.

With a sigh, Daphne tucked a strand of hair behind her ear. "I guess you're a Fawn now, so it's safe to tell you."

I scooted closer.

"My mom was a Fawn, and my dad was a Son."

My mouth hung open, but then relief trickled inside me.

Daphne could tell me how her mom had survived being a Fawn.

"Was your mom your dad's Fawn?" I asked her.

Her eyes glazed over as she nodded before looking away. "He's a disgraced Son now. Banished, but, hey, at least he wasn't killed for it." She shrugged as pain furrowed her face. "I grew up around the Night Sons. My father ranked high and was very involved, so information was spoken openly around me because they expected me to follow in my mother's footsteps. The Night Son who selected me would marry me, and I'd live out the legacy they'd planned." She peered away. "But it didn't work out that way."

Scooting closer, I rested my hand over hers, trying to provide the comfort she kept supplying me. "What happened?"

"Blair, babe, do you not follow politics?"

I shook my head. "I didn't see my first TV until I was seventeen. My reading choices were very limited, so no newspapers."

"Seriously? What about the internet?"

"Not until college."

"Jesus! How'd you entertain yourself?"

"I grew up with strict parents." I nibbled on my lip in guilt.

Daphne had told me so much about herself while I kept everything about me so hidden.

"My father was a senator and plotted to assassinate the president," she revealed with a grim expression on her face.

"What?" My jaw dropped.

"He didn't do it alone. Other government officials were involved. They paid someone to carry out the hit, but he failed and testified against them."

I struggled to find the most soothing words I could. Even though I felt emotionally drained, I was happy she trusted me. Few people did.

"I'm sorry, Daphne." That was what I came up with.

I wasn't the best with words. I preferred to listen because it was what I'd done all my life. In fact, when the court had ordered me to attend therapy, I'd ended up asking the therapist questions about her life. Even found out her husband was cheating.

Her smile was genuine. "Thanks, Blair."

"Is that why Enzo said the Brooks comment to you?"

"One of them, but there are several reasons I hate the fakest man in the country."

"How are you still friends with Adelina?" I hoped my question didn't come off too strong.

"It obviously put a strain on our relationship, but our moms had been best friends since they'd attended Saint Vale. My mom divorced my father after he went to prison, removed him from our lives, and life went on. My mother is a royal, so her position offered us protection from complete social isolation."

"A royal?"

"She's the princess of Calira."

Since I wasn't that great with geography, I made a note to look up that country. "That means you're a princess."

"Yes, but I only mention that to my grandparents when I want a new handbag. Otherwise, it feels ... weird."

"Whoa, I've never been in the presence of royalty."

She rolled her eyes playfully. "It's not as luxurious as it seems."

"Where's your father now?"

"A maximum-security federal prison in Arizona."

"Do you ever see him?"

"I'm not allowed to." Her face was unreadable, completely blank, so I couldn't tell if that affected her.

I felt that same pain, though. Deep down, I hated my father. Like hers, mine was harmful, a danger to society, while also influential in a completely different way. Those kinds of men left too much wreckage behind to ever clean up.

We pulled away at the knock on the door.

Daphne cleared her throat and smoothed a wrinkle from her Versace pajamas. "My guess is, that's for you."

I slipped off the bed, whispering, "Please don't be Enzo," and crossed my fingers on my walk to the door.

I wished the door had a peephole as I swung the door open and stumbled back a step. My head throbbed, as I already knew that whatever was about to happen might be worse than Enzo's version of waterboarding.

"Blair, come with me," Headmaster Arisono said, wearing another one of her pantsuits. This one was blue.

I peered over my shoulder at Daphne, who was now perched on the edge of her bed, trying to see who was there.

Arisono, I tried to mouth without her noticing.

She most definitely did, though.

Daphne pressed both hands to her cheeks, mouthing back, *What the actual fuck?*

I gulped, feeling spit slide down my throat. "Let me grab my shoes."

She nodded.

I grabbed my loafers, shot Daphne one more hysterical look, and followed Arisono into the hallway.

"Are we going outside?" I asked, unable to stop the question.

She stared at me as if I'd sprouted two extra heads. "Absolutely not. You're not allowed out after curfew."

Why did she act so shocked?

She had seen me come in soaking wet with Enzo.

It proved that her concern for her students was very limited.

As genuine as mine was over which color mac and cheese was best.

My hand smoothed over the banister as we walked downstairs, through the vestibule, and to an open door. She motioned for me to go inside, and I peeked in before entering.

She shut the door, trapping me in with her.

"I warned you about my *three strikes* policy." Her voice was surprisingly neutral as she positioned herself behind the desk.

"I know, and I'm so sorry," I replied. "It won't happen again. I promise."

She looked like she believed me as much as one would believe Enzo was on track to enter the pearly gates of heaven.

The headmaster was smart. She knew I wasn't some out-of-control student. She also knew that Enzo was tormenting me. I was positive she knew Enzo had taken me outside and was waiting for me to come back inside.

Her role was supposed to protect her students, not aid in their suffering. But alas, my stepfather had enrolled me in the school from hell.

"Do you want to be expelled?" she asked.

"No," I rushed out, though secretly hoping she would.

She clasped her hands in front of her. "Let me remind you *again,* then. I expect you to follow the university's rules. No going out after curfew."

I bowed my head. "Yes, ma'am."

She flinched, as if I'd called her old to her face.

"One more strike, Blair."

"One more strike won't happen. I swear it."

One more strike.

Two down, all because of Enzo.

"You are free to leave now." As if she was still pissed about my strikes and my calling her ma'am, she dismissively waved her hand through the air.

She didn't need to tell me twice. I fled the office and hurried back to my dorm.

Though I was confused about our conversation.

Does she want me to obey Enzo, or does she want me to stay away from him?

"Told you late-night Arisono visits are never good," Daphne said on my second return to our dorm that night.

Both times, I had been just as freaked out.

She was now cleansing the room with sage.

"What's her deal?" I asked, changing my socks.

Impeccably clean floors or not, I wasn't about to dirty up my bed with them on.

"She's a hypocrite. I've known her since I was ten. Our moms were in the same class and Fawns together." She blew air through her lips. "I haven't been a fan since she told my mother to throw out all my Barbies since they were against feminism. I looked her straight in the eye and told her she could drag Skipper and Ballerina Barbie out of my cold, dead hands."

Daphne rested the sage on an ashtray and pulled out a bag of Cheetos from her drawer stash. "Anyway, you look like hell, and we need to sleep. And please, I beg you, pray for no more unwanted guests. I'm waiting for the damn bogeyman to come next." She ate a Cheeto and licked cheese residue off her fingers. "If someone does come, they'd better have more snacks."

I frowned with apology. "I'm really sorry."

"Don't be, babe." She ate another Cheeto and swallowed it down. "This place is dull, and the entertainment you're providing is nice. That's probably where my issues stem from." She offered me a Cheeto. "I'm glad you're here, and I will help in any way I can. Just do as I say, and we'll survive the wrath of Enzo."

I swiped a Cheeto from her bag, and we tapped them together, like a secret cheesy handshake. "Good night. See you in the morning."

"See you in the morning," she sang out.

As I got into bed, I pulled the flimsy, ripped curtain shut. I kept the chandelier illuminated above me while staring out the window, expecting to see a neon mask.

When I didn't, I collapsed on my back, having no idea what tomorrow would bring.

Because now, I was officially a Fawn.

TWELVE

BLAIR

The day was off to a good start when Enzo didn't show up to class the following morning.

I didn't care why he wasn't there. Maybe he skipped, was sick, or was attending his weekly meeting in hell.

His absence eased my worries, especially since I hadn't worn his shirt. Violating the dress code could risk me earning another strike from Arisono.

It was Friday, so I hoped Enzo had left campus for the weekend. I also hoped to figure out a way to do that myself, since I needed a new laptop and phone. Handwritten notes weren't cutting it for me.

I ditched the library and decided to eat lunch in the cafeteria. Just like the rest of the university, the stone-lined passageway that led to the cafeteria had a curved ceiling. Brass sconces lit the way, and the light from the stained glass windows streamed distorted patterns across the polished marble floors.

When the hall opened up to the cafeteria, I halted.

Calling the room a cafeteria was like saying the stars at night weren't big and bright deep in the heart of Texas.

The space reminded me of a high-end European restaurant.

Not that I'd been to one, but I'd seen them on TV. Big fan of *House Hunters International* here.

The ceiling was painted gold, or possibly *was* gold, and stretched high overhead. Crystal chandeliers hung low from it.

Like this was a formal event, candles flickered from the white-clothed tables. This wasn't a simple lunch where we ordered crappy microwaved food or plucked items from a buffet table. Servers moved between tables, carrying trays.

Lingering near the edge, I backed up against the wall, feeling like I didn't belong.

This wasn't *me*. I'd grown up eating at tables my father had built with his bare hands. Tables that gave you splinters when you cleaned them. The cafeterias at my other schools had plastic furniture and flimsy trays.

"Blair!" Daphne's voice cut through the room.

I glanced up, searching for her, and stepped away from the wall in relief when she waved me over.

I beelined to her table in the center of the room, nearly colliding and apologizing five times to a server. Adelina scooted her chair over to make room for me.

For the first time here, I felt a sense of belonging.

Adelina's smile was friendly. "Hey, girl."

I returned her smile, all bubbly inside, and dropped my bag to the floor before sitting beside her. Mine was apparently the only bag cheap enough for the floor. The others hung from small hooks on the table, their expensive bags kept neatly in place.

The other girls, the same ones with judgy stares, introduced themselves.

They no longer looked at me with distrust, as if Daphne had put in a good word for me. Like me, they all wore the Saint Vale uniform, though they each showed their own style with it.

I tried to memorize their names and faces.

There was Alessia. Her long, thick, wavy hair was parted down the middle and pulled into tight French braids, and a ballet slipper necklace hung around her neck.

Then there was Livia, a petite girl sporting white pearls and a black bob.

Then *Seraphina*.

Enzo's sister.

I struggled not to stare at her longer than the others. But my curiosity about her was so strong.

Studying her, I searched for the resemblances she had with Enzo.

She was definitely younger. Her black hair, the same color as his, was held back with a sparkly pink band. She wore no makeup on her smooth, flawless face. Diamond earrings sparkled in her ears. The same with the tennis bracelet clasped around her wrist.

She was the only one not wearing the school's button-up. Instead, she wore a black polo.

I gnawed on my lower lip, grateful I hadn't worn lipstick today or I would've smeared it. For a second, I wondered if these girls knew what Enzo was doing to me.

Do they know about the Fawns?

Daphne had said she hung out with Havens, so these must be them. According to her, they were protected from being a Fawn.

A server, dressed in a full tuxedo and white gloves, stopped by our table and handed us menus.

My stomach rumbled embarrassingly too loud as I read the options.

Lobster. Crab. Filets. Pastas.

There was even a page for vegans and vegetarians.

And here I was, eating stale bars and chips in the library when I could've been here.

The menu didn't list any prices. For all I knew, a meal could range from ten dollars to hundreds. My stepfather could easily afford anything I ordered. That wasn't the issue. I was just always careful about what I spent.

The others ordered their food first, and I went with a simple spaghetti.

A girl needed carbs to keep up with being tormented, right?

"Question," I said when the server left.

All eyes shot to me.

"Do any of you have a car here by chance?"

They stared at me like Arisono had last night when I asked if we were going outside.

"Or does Uber come to campus?" I quickly added.

Livia leaned in closer. "Arisono banned Uber."

Seraphina bumped Adelina's shoulder with hers. "What was her name for them?"

Adelina raised her fingers in quotes, moving them as she said, "*Unapproved third-party carriers that could also be spies.*"

Seraphina rolled her eyes.

Daphne groaned, throwing her head back. "I swear, we need to get that woman laid. Even if it is by one of the third-party spies."

"How do you guys leave campus then?" I asked. "Does *no one* have a car?"

"A select few do," Seraphina said.

"What do you need a car for?" Daphne grabbed her water flute. "You ditching me already?"

I hesitated, unsure if I should tell her this in front of these girls.

How close is Seraphina with Enzo?

Deciding I had nothing to lose, I took a deep breath and said, "Enzo stole my laptop. My phone too. I reported my phone stolen—"

Alessia interrupted me with a whistle, "Yikes, bad move."

Adelina agreed with a nod. "It'd have been easier to let him just look through it."

"Hey!" Daphne said. "Would you guys want someone snooping through your things?"

I paid her a smile for the backup.

"Absolutely not," Seraphina said. The smile she sent me was similar to what I'd given Daphne. "But we're only trying to help her tame Enzo."

"Is there even any taming Enzo?" Adelina asked.

"My mom tried." Seraphina shook her head. "Failed. I gave her a gold star for the attempt." She made a simple clapping motion.

Adelina scooted closer. "Look, if you need a ride—"

She abruptly stopped talking.

So did everyone at my table.

And the rest of the room.

My heart wilted when someone tapped on my shoulder. I debated even turning around. When I didn't, they tapped again.

Slowly, so agonizingly slow, I turned my head to find Enzo behind me.

His stare swept over me as he worked his jaw, assessing every inch. It sharpened, as if deciding I didn't measure up to the others.

Then I realized that wasn't the problem.

"You broke my dress code," he said.

I nervously tugged on my sleeve. "Yes, but I'm wearing the school's."

"I override the school's."

Since everyone's attention was on us, I hushed my voice so only he could hear. "Arisono said I only have one more strike before I'm expelled."

Enzo gripped the back of my chair, yanking it back. "Up."

My knees hit the edge of the table. "What?"

"Up," he spat, throwing a clean shirt on my lap.

One of his black shirts.

I crossed my arms, refusing to be humiliated in front of my peers *again*.

But like always, I should've remembered who I was dealing with.

Enzo snatched the shirt from my lap, draped it over his shoulder, and reached past me. Someone at our table gasped when he grabbed the water flute and poured water over my head.

Cold water hit my face and stole my breath.

I choked on my spit, speechless, as ice cubes scattered across my lap. I blinked back tears as water streamed down my chin.

Everything in the room froze.

Every sound dulled.

Every movement slowed.

Students, teachers, servers—no one dared to move.

Enzo leaned in to brush his lips along my ear. "Uh-oh, Blair. Looks like you're in need of a dry shirt."

I wiped water from my forehead to hide my embarrassment.

His voice grew more menacing. "If you don't get up and follow me right fucking now, I'll make you strip out of that shirt in front of everyone and change into mine." He clicked his tongue. "You know I don't make empty threats."

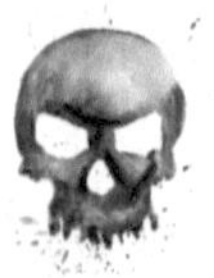

THIRTEEN

ENZO

Rituals were a beautiful thing.

I revered them with the same severity I reserved for threats.

Skipping classes on Fridays was another ritual of mine. Four days a week was more than enough time in academic hell.

Since I wouldn't see Blair in class, I'd texted Cedric to ask what she wore. To see if my little Fawn had followed my instructions. He'd replied with a photo of her *not* wearing my shirt.

It seemed her near-drowning experience hadn't been persuasive enough to teach her obedience. I had no tolerance for unruly Fawns.

They made me look weak. Lower-ranking Sons looked up to me. The Elders watched my every move to make sure I was fit to be in charge.

Blair's pathetic excuse of following Arisono's rules meant nothing to me.

My rules outweighed hers. Outweighed everyone's.

Everyone watched Blair stand, grab her bag, and leave the cafeteria with me. I loved the way her cheeks reddened. My cock twitched at how her soaked shirt clung to her body, and her nipples poked through the wet fabric.

I needed to see them in person before I lost it.

Needed to wrap my lips around them because it was all I'd thought about last night.

My pace was so quick that I was surprised my shoes didn't fly off my feet. Like last night, idiots stared.

Blair struggled to match my speed. "Where are we going?" she called out.

Since I owed her nothing, I didn't respond.

We climbed two flights of stairs, and when she veered toward the corridor that led to her dorm hall, I caught her bag and tugged her back.

"This way." I shoved her toward the next flight up.

She tore herself from my hold and stormed up the steps. When we reached the landing, she pivoted, planting her hands on her hips and waiting for my next direction with full attitude.

I wiped the side of my mouth, stepping into her space and settling my hands on her shoulders. Her bag dropped off one of her shoulders as I turned her to the right, steering her in that direction.

Only three halls existed on the third floor. Malum Hall claimed the east wing, and I was its only resident. I'd rather drink poison than share four walls with some loser.

We reached my gate, and I pulled the padlock key from my pocket to unlock it. The gate wasn't for my protection, per se.

It mostly existed to keep others out, especially those stupid enough to think rifling through my belongings would earn them leverage over me. I'd once found a professor trying to slide under the bottom.

He no longer worked here.

He was also no longer breathing.

When I had enrolled in Saint Vale, I demanded a private hall. I took the tour, decided I wanted Malum Hall, and kicked the current resident out.

The hall fit me, sitting on the far end. The light was limited, with only small sconces. Two of them were burned out. No windows or photos graced the walls. The door was as black as the night.

Before moving in, I had the space remodeled, ignoring Arisono's protests about defiling centuries-old architecture. I knew that wasn't her biggest problem. She had been pissed that *I* was the one doing it.

Those who had come from First Benefactors looked down on those who hadn't. We were new to the Night Sons, inferior in some eyes, but I found it to be the opposite.

Malum Hall was also personal to her. Her grandfather, father, and the Son she had served as a Fawn had resided here. In her eyes, it was sacred real estate I didn't deserve.

Blair followed me through the opening, and her body tensed when I locked it behind us. Her loafers squeaked against the floor as she dragged them along the corridor.

I opened my dorm room door and motioned for her to enter. She wasted time peeking inside, so I shoved her through the doorway and slammed the door shut behind us.

She stopped in the middle of the room, looking around, taking in the small details of my most personal space.

"Is this your dorm?" she asked, turning to me and furrowing her brows.

"No," I said. "It's a fucking dungeon."

It was a fair question. My dorm was nothing like hers. It was bigger. A king-size bed sat against one wall instead of being crammed into an alcove.

Three black-stained windows lined another wall, hidden behind curtains thick enough to choke out any light trying to get through.

So yes, if I closed them, it became a dungeon.

I'd left them open today. I didn't want to freak her out *too* much.

The rest of the room was dark wood and clean lines. I liked my space clean and simple. A kitchenette occupied one corner with a full espresso bar setup. A real bar was tucked into the cabinets below.

Blair narrowed her eyes at me.

"Sit, Blair." I gestured toward the cognac-colored leather sofa pressed against the wall.

She stayed where she was.

Fine. I crossed the room and shoved her down into the cushions myself.

Last night, she'd agreed to be my Fawn.

But agreement without understanding meant nothing.

I peeled off my jacket and draped it over my desk chair.

Her gaze shot to the door, as if thinking about running.

I gave her a smile that invited the attempt.

Technically, there were rules for selecting a Fawn.

We had to perform an Ask. It was a sacred tradition.

I could choose her, but she still had to accept. It had to be private. Both of us clearheaded. Consent had to be binding and free of fear.

Which meant not while I was shoving her head under water.

Personally, I gave no fucks about the Ask.

Blair had agreed to be my Fawn, and she would be my Fawn, whether she liked it or not.

But first, I'd try to play by the rules.

I pushed my hands into the pockets of my slacks. "Thanks for coming with me." The words sounded almost comical, coming from my lips.

"I was *forced* here," she shot back, folding her arms and leaning back on the couch. She tugged at her wet shirt's hem. "Stripping in front of my classmates wasn't how I wanted to start my weekend."

I inched closer, not enough to crowd her, and kept a careful distance. Still, I noticed her breath catch and her chest rise faster.

"Last night, you asked me what a Fawn was."

She gave a single nod.

I rotated the gold ring on my finger. "Fawns are made for Night Sons." I pressed a hand to my chest. "Made for *us*."

She didn't seem too surprised at my being a Night Son.

Not surprising since Jett had opened his big-ass mouth. I was sure Daphne had sprinkled pieces of information in there as well. For some reason, we left her alone. The Havens would probably poison us if we touched her.

"What do Night Sons do?" she asked. "What's the point of them?"

I decided to give her the simple version. The sanitized one.

"We make sure Saint Vale scandals don't surface and problems are corrected privately," I explained, hiding the grimness that went along with it—like that we made people vanish without noise, among other crimes.

She raised her chin, squinting up at me. "And a Fawn?"

"A Fawn is a woman placed under our protection."

Her face scrunched in displeasure. "That tells me nothing. Try again."

I enjoyed yet loathed the snark in her tone.

"What exactly do I need protection from?" she asked without giving me the opportunity to *try again*. "And what's the price of this *protection*? Hard pass on being some guy's fucktoy or whatever label you want to dress it up as."

"You wouldn't be a *fucktoy*. You'd be claimed."

Her jaw tightened. "Claimed by who?"

"Me."

She flinched at the answer.

When I sat down, she shoved herself as far away as the couch allowed. Unlike last night, I didn't stop her.

"If you're my Fawn, you're protected from the outside world and everyone here," I said. "Students. Professors. No one touches what's mine."

"Am I protected *from you*?"

I ignored her question. "That protection comes at a cost. As my Fawn, you're a reflection of me. Every move you make becomes mine. Your choices and mistakes are mine. It may sound scary, but trust me when I say, refusing will be worse for you."

I didn't waste my breath telling her how esteemed a Fawn's position was. Some families would go to great lengths to have a Son select their daughter.

Being a Fawn opened up more doors than any degree or title could.

Her voice dropped low. "Why me, Enzo?"

I shrugged. "You caught my interest."

She fiddled with her shirt button, looking everywhere but at me.

"You can refuse," I stated, since it was required.

But I was lying to her.

I'd never let her refuse me. I'd break the Ask rule if I had to.

Her body curled forward as she grumbled, "You didn't sound big on letting me refuse while attempting to drown me last night."

I paused, debating whether to apologize to her before deciding against it.

Apologies didn't exist to me. I couldn't remember the last time the words *I'm sorry* had left my lips. Probably never.

"You can refuse," I repeated. "But refusal doesn't mean that nothing will happen. Refusal means nothing protects you. Saint Vale—*this world*—can be a very dark place, Blair."

"The *choice* you're offering is no choice at all."

If Blair tried to bow out now, I'd ruin her life.

I'd spread rumors about her, and then I'd make Arisono expel her. And the people she cared about? Well, accidents happened.

"And if I say yes, you won't kill me?" she asked slowly.

I studied her for a long moment. "If you behave, I won't kill you." I twisted the ring around my finger. "We have rules. A Fawn cannot be killed without cause. And even then, not without process. Like I said, a claimed Fawn is protected."

That was the truth, though I never listed the full costs of becoming a Fawn during Asks.

Fawns didn't exist because we were lonely or desperate. They existed because a Son with nothing to lose became dangerous. Our Fawns and rank were always at stake, and losing either was worse than death.

Fawns were leashes crafted with care. Even if that care came wrapped in cruelty. We needed something visible, fragile, to remind us we didn't have to be monsters every second of the day.

They were there to tame us. To slow the violence inside us.

A Son who spilled blood recklessly was easy to notice. A Son who knew restraint was far deadlier. That was what we needed.

And while Blair had said she didn't want to be a *fucktoy*, I'd be fucking her. Being a Fawn wasn't sexual at its core. It was more strategic than anything.

I cracked my knuckles, locking my eyes on her, waiting until she finally looked at me. "And if anyone ever tries to hurt you, they'll have to go through me first. Which means they won't." I stood, walked over to my nightstand, opened a drawer, and withdrew a necklace.

Her gaze softened as it tracked my every step back to her. My dick stirred again when I realized her body wasn't as wound tight. Her pulse no longer fluttered beneath her skin.

With my free hand, I took hers. Her skin was smooth as I turned her palm upward, tracing the shallow cut I'd made the other night.

"Say yes," I said, almost in a daze.

One, two, three, four seconds passed.

I shut my eyes, inhaled a breath, and waited for longer than I wanted.

She didn't reply until I was no longer looking at her. "Yes."

My pulse exploded.

Blair officially belonged to me.

She was mine to touch. To command. To *own*.

Opening my eyes, I crooked my finger, motioning for her to stand. It took her a few seconds before she did.

We stood face-to-face.

Our lips, our eyes, our cheeks only inches from each other.

I clasped the necklace around her neck. "Now comes the rules." I dragged my finger along the chain, right along her neck. "You must behave, Blair. If I tell you to wear something, then you wear it."

A breath punched from her lungs as I started unbuttoning her shirt. I couldn't stop myself from dragging my thumb along her nipple, and my cock twitched when she shuddered.

When I hit the bottom button, reality hit her.

She smacked my hand away, and in response, I tore the shirt open. The remaining button flew across the room. The shirt slid open, revealing a lacy red bra.

I backed away, toward my closet, pulled a shirt off the hanger, and handed it to her. "This is what you wear from now on. Every week, a fresh supply will be delivered to your dorm."

She hurriedly slipped the shirt on while I wandered over to my desk and collected her MacBook from the top drawer.

I paused, admiring her in my clothes, and held up the MacBook. "Password. Now."

A brush of air hit my face when she lunged toward me in an attempt to snatch it back, but I was faster than she was.

"Aht, aht," I said in the most disapproving tone I'd ever delivered in my life. "Password first, and you'll get it back when I'm finished."

She jumped on her heels, trying to leap over me. "You're not getting my password."

"Then no laptop for you." I checked my watch. "I have to go now." I toyed with her necklace, placing a kiss along the antler pendant. "Be good. I have eyes everywhere."

Blair didn't yet know everything about her role.

She had to survive her Initiation next, and that was one of the hardest parts for Fawns.

After I was finished with Blair, I left her in her dorm, got in my car, and drove the hour to New York City.

The city where I'd lived my entire life. The place that would always be my home.

I headed straight to Lucky Kings Casino and parked in the private area before going to Julian Bellini's office.

Antonio, my brother-in-law and sister Gigi's husband, owned and ran the chain of casinos that stretched along the East Coast. Antonio was also the boss of the Lombardi family.

Julian helped him run the empire and was one of his capos. He also happened to be one of the best hackers I knew.

I needed him to get me into Blair's phone.

Someone had gone through a lot of trouble to create a fake family for her records. A perfectly polished backstory that covered up whatever she was hiding.

That alone pissed me off.

But now, there was another reason. Blair was my Fawn, which meant her secrets were now my business. I intended to find every single one of them.

She thought she was clever, putting her phone in stolen mode.

How fucking cute.

I sat in Julian's office for an hour while he struggled to hack into her phone. He did, however, manage to gain access to her cloud account. He used that information to sign her back into her phone.

Nico needed to learn a thing or two from him.

I paid him and returned to my Porsche Panamera before driving to the Marchetti mansion, the home I'd grown up in. My car rolled to a stop in front of the gates, and I lifted my hand, giving a quick salute to the armed guards.

The gates opened immediately, and I drove through, going deeper onto the property.

Our estate sat beyond the outer limits of New York City. The location was close enough for us to control everything that happened in the city, but far enough that we could disappear from it.

People claimed the Marchetti mansion was more secure than Fort Knox. They weren't wrong. If anything, the protection had doubled over the past few years. Our enemy list kept getting longer.

This home was where I had learned to walk, where my father had put my first gun in my hands, and the only place in the world where I didn't always feel like I had to watch my back.

It was a shelter of loyalty and a den of family secrets.

I parked in the circular drive, grabbed my bag, stepped out of my car, and headed for the front door. It was unlocked.

Inside, the foyer was quiet, except for the soft movements of the staff. I nodded toward a couple of housekeepers as I passed. Like the home, I'd grown up around them.

My footsteps resounded as I headed toward my father's office on the right side of the foyer.

"Hi, honey."

I stopped and turned to find my mother walking toward me. She wrapped me in a tight hug. I returned it automatically, kissing her cheek as we parted.

"I've missed you." She grinned brightly, like it'd been years since we'd talked, though it'd only been a day.

Every day, she texted Seraphina and me without fail, saying she loved us. Her mother had died when she was young, so she swore she'd never make us question how much we mattered to her.

Sometimes, because of who my father was, some people overlooked how beautiful and intelligent she was. They only saw her as the wife of a cruel man. But she was the softness that had helped shape him into the great father he was to us. She was also by his side when she knew he needed to show his teeth during tough times.

She helped him balance his control.

So similar to how the Fawn System worked.

Still smiling, she pointed at me, her tone turning serious. "Your father is upset with you about something, but he refuses to tell me what it is."

I shrugged, pretending I wasn't as nervous as I was. "Guess I should go find out what I did, then."

She nodded, kissed my cheek, and walked toward the staircase.

I knocked on my father's office door.

"Come in," his deep voice called from the other side.

I stepped inside, finding him sitting behind his massive oak desk with his posture relaxed in the black leather chair. Though I knew he was anything but.

My father lived in a constant state of tension.

That was the price of being a Mafia boss. Most men in his position died young.

I shut the door behind me, eyeing the family portrait hung behind him on the wall—the only thing in the office that had changed in decades. Everything else looked exactly the same since I was a kid. Dark wood, leather chairs, and the antique bar cart in the corner. The bar now held more liquor than the last time I was here.

This office would never belong to me.

Neither would the house.

That honor went to Benny.

The perks of being the firstborn son.

Right now, Benny had his own house on the Marchetti grounds. When the time came, I'd either move into his place or build something new somewhere on the property.

Either way, I'd always live here.

I'd graduate from Saint Vale, then spend the rest of my life doing what I had been raised to do—help run our family empire.

My father slid his reading glasses down his nose, then removed them completely before tossing them onto the desk. His hair, which had once been as dark as mine, was peppered with gray, but he still didn't look anywhere near his age.

He leaned back in his chair, his face rigid as he studied me. "Welcome home, Son. How's Saint Vale?"

"Good." I sank into a leather chair across from him. "Glad it's my last year."

He gave a slight nod, satisfied with my answer, and folded his hands together. "It's time we talk about your future."

"I think we both know what my future looks like after Saint Vale."

"The society you joined has rules, and you owe them loyalty."

I knew what he wasn't saying.

I'd sworn loyalty to the Night Sons, but my loyalty to my family ran deeper than that. And in the Marchetti bloodline, family always came first.

My blood boiled at how he stared at me, as if testing where my allegiance truly was.

I cleared my throat. "Attending Saint Vale was your idea. I wanted nothing to do with that place. You said it'd make our family stronger, so I went." My eyes held his. "Same with joining the Night Sons."

He worked his jaw, taking in my words.

"I swore an oath to them," I continued, my tone level. My stare remained locked on his. "But I had been born to protect this family."

Silence fell over the room, so I tapped my foot, hating it.

One. Two. Three.

Faster and faster.

For years, I'd always wished I could cut open my father's skull to see what he was thinking.

"The Night Sons are a network," I added. "I joined it to expand our reach. Not replace it." My tapping stopped, and I lifted my brow. "You questioning my loyalty pisses me off."

"Enzo," he snarled.

My father never raised his voice. He didn't have to.

"You're smart enough to understand my concern," he said. His chair snapped forward as he leaned toward the desk.

"I attended Saint Vale *for you*—"

He cut me off. "For our family." He steepled his fingers together. "My loyalty always supersedes."

His comment reminded me of what I'd told Blair earlier about Arisono's rules. So much of me was my father.

I rested my elbows on the arms of the chair. "That's always been clear. Why the interrogation about it?"

"You know this is far from a Marchetti interrogation."

True. Those usually ended with broken bones and someone bleeding.

He opened his drawer, grabbed a newspaper, and slid it across his desk to me.

Yes, he still read print.

My mom had once bought him a digital subscription to the *New York Times*. He responded by burning her credit card, claiming the purchase made him question her principles. She'd laughed in his face, pulled out twenty more cards, and spent the afternoon on a shopping spree at the Hermès store *for his attitude*.

I picked up the paper and scratched my head at the headline.

Senator's Son Killed in a Car Bombing.

Right. *That.*

"Your work?" my father asked.

I skimmed the article, looking for any clues that led to me, but there was nothing. My father just knew everything.

"He tried to extort Brooks," I explained.

That rigidness from earlier returned to his face. "You didn't think to consult me before murdering the son of a public official? A *very public* official, who has spent years speaking out against the president *and me*." He slammed his fist on the desk, rattling everything on it.

I folded the newspaper and set it back onto his desk. "This wasn't my first murder, and I don't consult with you before each one."

His fist opened, one finger stabbing toward me. "Don't get

cocky, Enzo. That's what gets men caught or killed." He lowered his hand and tapped the newspaper on his desk. "You stole the car you drove to the frat house in. Smart." His finger dragged back toward me. "What you failed to do was make sure no cameras caught you stealing it." He let the words settle between us before delivering the final blow. "They did."

I leaned back in the chair, dragging a hand over my forehead, rubbing at the pressure building from my fuckup. "Shit."

"President Byron and I cleaned up your mess. Paid the people we needed to pay." His shoulders tensed as he reclined in his chair. "Don't be sloppy and drag this family into a murder scandal. If you even *think* of doing something reckless like that again, you come to me first. I'll make sure it's handled properly. Got it?"

I pressed my thumbs into my eye sockets and massaged them.

"You and Brooks will be attending the dead son's funeral."

My hands stilled.

"President Byron and I will be there as well."

I dragged a hand down my face and groaned.

"Try to shed a tear."

"Such things don't exist in my body. I got that from you."

A crooked smile played on his lips.

For a moment, the room got lighter. My father was always intense, but I didn't tend to fuck up much, which meant we didn't have many conversations like this.

We looked at the door at the sound of a knock. He called for whoever it was to come in.

The door opened, and Benny strolled in, shutting it behind him.

"There's my college-educated, stupidly-blowing-up-people brother." He clapped a heavy hand on my shoulder when he passed.

I gave him the middle finger.

"Heard you blew up a frat house," he said, unimpressed. "Next time, don't get caught on camera."

I glared at him. "It was *a car* at a frat house."

He sank into the chair beside me, his attention shifting to our father. "You tell him yet?"

"Tell me what?" I asked, my back straightening.

Benny started humming "Here Comes the Bride" obnoxiously and off-key. My father shot him a sharp glare. My asshole brother might've been pushing fifty, but sometimes, he played too many fucking games.

"We're looking for a wife for you," my father said, snapping his fingers to stop Benny's singing.

My head started spinning. "Excuse me?" I choked out.

"Don't give him any details," Benny cut in, standing from his chair and walking toward the bar cart. "He might go blow up her house next."

This was a part of this world I hated. The one I'd prayed would skip me, even if I'd bitched about Seraphina getting out of it.

In this life, marriages weren't about love.

They were negotiations.

You married to secure power. Not happiness.

I shook my head as dread sank in my belly. "I'm not happy about this."

"None of us ever are," Benny fired back, pouring himself a glass of bourbon. He and my father were the ones who shaped my drink preferences. "But it'll work out eventually. I mean, look at Neomi and me."

The stories I'd heard about their engagement sounded less like romance and more like two sociopaths trying to drive the other insane. There were even rumors that at their engagement party, Neomi had dragged another guy into the billiards room where Benny was to provoke him. In response, Benny had blown his brains out.

I had zero interest in dealing with a wife who didn't like me.

"It also worked out for Gigi," my father added.

"Oh?" I asked with more attitude than was smart toward my

father. "Antonio didn't murder Gigi's first fiancé? The one selected for her?"

His nostrils flared. "A, your sister selected that fiancé. B, Antonio proved to be the better man. Not a coward who let himself get kidnapped and killed."

His dark glare stayed on me as he pushed out his chair and stood. He motioned for me to do the same.

"Don't mention this to your mother at dinner," he instructed me. "We don't need her upset."

I slipped my hands into my pockets, rocking back on my heels. "Don't arrange a marriage for me, and she won't be upset."

"Your mother never stays angry with me for long."

Dinner with my parents went exactly how it always did.

Seraphina wasted no time announcing that I was terrorizing a new girl at the university. I returned the favor by informing them she was sneaking out of her dorm at night with her little group of girlfriends.

She responded by throwing a dinner roll at me from across the table.

I smirked, lifted my drink in a mocking salute, and drained the glass.

At the head of the long table, my father remained composed. He also neglected to mention the small detail that he was currently shopping for a contract wife for me.

Out of respect, I didn't bring it up. My mom would find out eventually. Most likely after he made his choice.

I had until graduation to change his mind. Or at least negotiate having a say in the matter.

An arranged marriage might be inevitable, but that didn't mean I had to accept the first woman offered. He needed to give me choices.

After finishing the best apple pie ever made—courtesy of our chef, Miriam—I excused myself from the table and headed upstairs to my wing of the mansion.

The space was isolated and cold, just how I liked it.

A small sitting area opened into my bedroom. I'd remodeled my dorm to mirror it because no matter where I went, nothing felt right unless it resembled home.

The mansion version was more polished with dark mahogany crown molding wrapping around the ceiling. Black wainscoting climbed the walls beneath layers of gray paint.

I flicked the switch as I entered my bedroom. The black chandelier above my king-size bed came alive, casting a dim glow.

Dropping my bag, I unzipped it and pulled out Blair's MacBook and phone before collapsing on the mattress.

Time to see what Blair Dupont was hiding.

And what I found was ... interesting.

She had no friends listed and only three contacts saved.

Mom. SD. And SD's Driver.

No social media. No photos. No digital footprint.

When I dug into her financials, it got stranger. She had a modest bank account tied to an LLC with a vague name. Everything was filed under her mother's maiden name, as if her father didn't exist.

When I looked at her recent search history, it became even more interesting.

She'd searched for the number of a prison in Arizona.

I leaned back against the headboard, MacBook warm on my lap, and smirked.

Blair was hiding something. *A lot* of somethings.

I was going to drag every last secret into the light.

People were easier to control once you found out what they were desperate to keep buried. I'd do the same to Blair.

"Don't you think you're being a little too harsh on Blair?" Seraphina asked from my leather passenger seat as we drove back toward Saint Vale.

The road stretched ahead of us, trees blurring as we passed them.

We'd spent the weekend with our parents, and the entire time, I fought the urge to grab my keys and drive straight back to campus to Blair.

The girl occupied my thoughts through every meal.

She was on my mind during every conversation with my father and Benny about business and territories.

Half my weekend was spent locked in my wing, combing through her devices over and over. I'd searched every folder, convinced I'd overlooked something when I couldn't find all the answers I needed.

Blair was a puzzle with too many missing pieces, and it was getting under my skin.

I tapped my thumb against the leather steering wheel. "Keep your distance from her," I told Seraphina, sounding like our father. "Don't try to become friends with her."

I flicked on my turn signal and took a right without looking at her.

It always irritated me when Seraphina involved herself in Fawn business.

She slouched in her seat. "I have the freedom to choose my own friends."

My sister had been a pain in the ass since birth. I should've left her ten traffic lights back after she changed my music.

"Fine," I said. "Then I'll fuck Daphne."

She let out a snort. "Daphne wouldn't fuck you." She leaned across the console, her braid sliding over her shoulder, and flicked her fingers toward my ear as if swatting at a fly.

I nudged her back with the heel of my hand without taking my eyes off the road.

See? Fucking pain in the ass.

"Daphne would do whatever I told her to do," I replied.

"Hands off my friend, jerk."

"Blair isn't your friend. Nor will she ever be."

Seraphina kicked her boots up against the dash, knowing that always pissed me off, and crossed her arms. "I thought you were taking the year off from terrorizing anyone."

"Change of heart."

"You have no heart." Her tone turned playful as she leaned in, staring me down. "You like her, don't you? That's why you chose her."

I wouldn't look at her as I scoffed. "I chose Blair because she looked weak and pathetic the first time I saw her."

"Lies," she singsonged. "All lies, dear brother."

I flexed my fingers against the steering wheel.

There were only a few people I allowed to annoy me like this.

Seraphina was one of them.

She was a pain and always tested my patience, but she was also my little sister. Protecting her had been stitched into my bones the day she was born, when I was only three years old.

My sister knew about the Night Sons. Not everything, but enough to know she was protected as a Haven. She'd never be one of the ones we used.

"You saw something in her." She continued to irritate me. "I've known you my entire life—"

"Yes," I cut her off. "And for a significant portion of that life, you believed in Santa Claus. I don't exactly trust your judgments."

She grinned brightly. "Maybe you'll end up falling in love and marrying her."

My father's voice from his office echoed in my head. *We're looking for a wife for you.*

I needed to figure out a way to get out of an arranged marriage.

I'd spent my entire life making my own choices.

Who I fucked.

Who I used.

Who belonged to me.

I didn't like that power being stripped away.

Love or matrimony was never in my future.

I navigated through the tunnels with Cedric, Nico, Cassian, Emeri, and Brooks. All the Current Night Sons.

Four Elder Sons took the lead in front of us. Their movements were rigid as they walked in sync. Two others lagged behind us.

There were four ritual chambers within the tunnels. Each one had a specific purpose and sat at the end of a different corridor.

We stopped at the door that led to the Aula Cornuum.

Hall of Antlers.

The name was carved into the door in faded Latin. Massive stag antlers had been etched across its surface, and at their center sat a ring identical to the one on my finger. Every Son had one.

One by one, we stepped forward and scanned our fingerprints. A quiet beep followed each one.

With each confirmation, the small screen beside the door flashed the symbol tied to our locker. It registered every Son who walked through the doors.

Mine was a broken halo.

We filed into the circular room and spread into our assigned areas.

Aula Cornuum had been built like a tribunal. Stone tiers rose in a circle, each lined with benches for Elder Sons. The room could hold fifty men, though tonight barely half that number filled the seats.

The tiers curved inward, forcing every eye toward the center, where a long table of black oak waited below. Chairs had been arranged along one side, facing the tiers. Each bore the same antler crest carved into the door. The benches, the floor, even the iron railings dividing the tiers carried the mark.

The Elder Sons took their places, and the Current Sons claimed our seats at the table below. The chairs were narrow and stiff-backed, built for posture rather than comfort. But this wasn't a place for comfort.

The Aula Cornuum existed for Selections.

Two nights ago, I'd uploaded Blair's file into the Fawn System, a private network only Night Sons could access. Every prospective Fawn had a profile there—background, family ties, weaknesses, psychological notes. A catalog of the women we intended to claim.

Though most of Blair's file appeared to be fiction. I wasn't about to correct it.

Hers was already the smallest submission I'd ever filed. There was almost nothing on her. The moment I'd hit Submit, every Elder Son and Current Son received the alert.

Before any Fawn Initiation, we held a Selection Hearing.

A formal vote.

Any Son in the room had the right to challenge my Selection.

And if enough of them voted against Blair, she wouldn't become my Fawn.

It didn't happen often, but when a Son challenged a Selection, it was usually because he knew something ugly about the girl or her family. The wrong Fawn could be as dangerous as a traitor within our circle. We didn't allow threats inside our walls.

While we kept the deepest parts of our world hidden, the Fawns knew we existed. That alone made them a liability. Once a woman was brought into our system, she could never truly leave.

I lowered myself into my chair just as a faint light stirred in my peripheral vision. Lights along the tiers flickered on one by one.

I lifted my gaze toward the Elder Sons.

Some showed their faces. Others hid behind masks.

I hated the masks. Reading people was a skill I'd sharpened

early, thanks to my father. He'd taught me that faces revealed far more than mouths ever could.

Most of the men in the tiers wore masks because they had too much to lose if they were ever identified. They were judges, CEOs, politicians, men who held high positions in the world above us.

The ones who didn't bother hiding their faces were usually clinging to the glory of their old Night Sons days, desperate to be recognized for what they once were.

As a Current Night Son, I wasn't permitted to wear my mask during hearings. Only Elders had earned that privilege.

That rule always pissed me off. If you knew who I was, then I wanted to know exactly who the hell you were too.

Attendance wasn't mandatory for Selection Hearings.

To my left, a screen lit up with Blair's face. The photo was one I'd uploaded, taken from her previous university ID.

I shifted in my chair, studying it as if it were the first time I'd seen her. As if I hadn't already memorized every detail.

The curves of her plump lips. Eyes that had nearly transfixed me.

Slow heat writhed inside me.

I couldn't wait to corrupt her. To claim her.

And once she was mine, I'd no longer have to entertain as many bullshit rules.

I'd never wanted a Fawn the way I wanted Blair, and she wasn't even officially mine yet.

My previous Selection Hearings had always been routine. Another name, another girl to break.

This was the first time anticipation bit at me like an animal.

If any of these assholes tried to challenge her becoming my Fawn, there'd be hell to pay.

"This is the girl my son, Jett, died for?"

I looked up at the sound of Reginald's smug voice.

I slammed my hands onto the table, shoved my chair back,

and stood. "Would you like to lose another finger, Reginald?" I asked the room, not bothering to search for him in the tiers.

Most of the men hid behind pseudonyms, but not Reginald. He wanted to be known down here.

Even without seeing his face, I smiled. There wasn't a trace of humor in it.

Whispers rose from the Elders above, though I couldn't make out the words. One of our rules was to show respect to the Elder Sons.

Fuck that.

I rolled my shoulders back and straightened my hoodie before speaking. "I'm glad you brought that up." I pointed at Blair's face on the screen. "This is the woman your dipshit son ran his mouth to, spilling all our secrets."

A few Elders shifted on their benches.

I placed a hand over my chest. "So, yes, I made the decision to make this woman my Fawn." My gaze swept the room. "Wouldn't you all agree it's far less complicated to claim her than kill her?"

Every Night Son at the table nodded.

Some of the Elders from the tiers followed suit.

Others stayed silent and still.

Leaning forward, I braced my hands on the edge of the table. "This prospective Fawn has known about our existence for nearly a week. Yet she hasn't spoken a word about it." My eyes lifted toward the upper tiers, where Reginald usually sat. "Meanwhile, Reginald's son couldn't keep his mouth shut. He exposed us. The real question is how he learned enough to do it."

Conversation rippled through the chamber, and I flashed a shit-eating grin.

Reginald had really been fucking up lately.

Both of his children were dead. His reelection campaign was collapsing after news broke about several mistresses. I'd heard there were dick pics involved, but I had no interest in confirming it.

I preferred keeping my eyes intact, thank you.

"My son was supposed to be a Night Son!" Reginald shouted from his tier, every word laced with venom. "The problem was, none of you would approve him! Had it not been *this* group, we wouldn't have had an issue."

Chairs scraped against the floor as Cedric, Brooks, Emeri, Cassian, and Nico stood.

Every one of us had voted against Jett joining the Sons.

He'd been a bigger liability than if Benedict Arnold had become a Son.

I paid a glance to Brooks, crossed my arms, and waited—*prayed*—that Reginald would keep running his mouth, so I could punish him for it.

Unfortunately, he knew when to shut it.

We sat back down, and I scanned the room again, this time my target was Blair's stepfather. He had to be here. It was his step-daughter's Selection Hearing.

"Any other objections that have actual merit?" Brooks asked the room.

No one spoke.

Brooks struck the gavel down against the table. "Prospective Fawn approved. Prepare for Initiation."

FOURTEEN

ENZO

The Past
Initiation Day: Sophomore Year at Saint Vale University
Age Twenty

I pulled my hood over my head and stepped inside the Initiation Chamber.

Adrenaline moved steadily through my bloodstream as my eyes adjusted to the dark. The space was swallowed by darkness.

But I knew I wasn't alone.

The Night Sons were watching and waiting.

Flames sprang to life around the chamber, dozens of candles placed along the outer ring of stone. Their light revealed what the darkness had blocked.

Symbols carved deep into the walls and floor.

Only the men who had survived their Initiation knew what they meant.

Soon, I'd be one of them.

I rolled my neck slowly.

Whatever they had waiting for me, I was ready.

I had no idea what was coming, but I knew one thing: there'd be no hazing.

It made sense why they'd never incorporated it.

Humiliation was a weapon for insecure men. Men like us didn't tolerate that kind of weakness. I couldn't remember a single moment in my life when anyone had tried to humiliate or degrade me.

Let a motherfucker dare, and he'd be in the ground by nightfall.

Hell, I wouldn't even bury him. I'd leave his body in the open and let the animals pick him apart.

We'd swear allegiance to the Sons, but we weren't the kind of men who'd crawl on our knees to become one.

Men who begged for power looked weak.

And weakness had no place in the Night Sons.

Societies where superiors degraded others reminded me of frat houses, and no fucking thank you on that.

But this Initiation was far riskier than any humiliation ritual. If you failed, they killed you at the end.

The tiers above me slowly illuminated, masks emerging from the darkness. Each mask had glowing neon X's where their eyes should've been. A thin, horizontal slash marked each mouth.

It was showtime for the Night Sons.

Both Current Sons and the Elders.

More masks came to life on the chamber floor. These were the Current Sons, the ones I'd work beside and stand with.

Fuck the old bastards in the tiers. These men were the only brotherhood that mattered to me.

I stood alone at the center of the chamber, barefaced and unhidden, unlike them, as I felt each stare on me.

I popped my knuckles. Not one for patience, I threw my arms out in a *what's next* gesture. They had come here for a show, and I was going to fucking give them one.

I'd give them the best, bloodiest fucking Initiation they'd ever seen.

I was a Marchetti, and we were the kings of violence.

A spotlight came on overhead, flooding the center of the

chamber with harsh light. It illuminated what looked like a boxing ring, stripped to the bones, with no ropes or padding. Just a wide square of concrete.

The chamber door opened again, and a masked Night Son stepped inside, moving toward the ring with long strides.

Tape was wrapped around his knuckles, and he cracked his neck the same way I had minutes ago.

I knew the next step without needing any explanation.

Music suddenly blasted, an old Obie Trice song playing, flowing from hidden speakers above in the soundproof room as I strode toward the ring.

The masked Son ripped off his mask and tossed it aside. Him wearing a mask would've been a severe disadvantage for me, making it harder for me to bash his face in.

Paul's eyes met mine from across the ring. He was chosen to lead the society that year. He was also the Son who'd brought me in and the realest dude I knew.

This was his final year before he became an Elder and moved back to the UK to resume his normal life.

Neither of us waited for a signal. We moved fast, closing the distance as we collided. Paul swung first, his fist cutting through the air toward my jaw. I twisted to the side, sidestepping his strike, and immediately swung back. My fist slammed into his face, and I grinned at the sound of bones cracking.

Pain shot through my knuckles as I shook out my hand, unsure whether the cracks belonged to my bones or his face. Probably both.

I wouldn't know until later. The adrenaline canceled out any discomfort.

His next hit made contact, landing on the right side of my face. My head flung to the side at the blow. Before I could fully recover, his fist drove into my face again. My teeth clacked together. I groaned, driving my head forward and slamming my forehead into his. Paul staggered back but caught himself before he lost his balance.

We bounced on our toes as we fought, hitting each other, one strike after another. Paul was as violent as I was, so I wasn't dealing with an amateur.

Our fists flew through the air, delivering blow after blow.

Kick after kick.

Blood dripped from his nose. My lip was split open, warm blood sliding down my chin and trickling onto my hoodie.

I was positive that both of us would have mild concussions by the time this was over.

This wasn't torture to us. It wasn't hazing.

We thrived on this kind of violence. We could've kept fighting for hours, maybe days, until one of us finally dropped.

My next swing connected with his jaw, snapping his head sideways.

Here, we were showing our true strength.

How we refused to quit and were worthy of being a Night Son.

We stopped when the light above us cut off.

Paul's silhouette faded into the darkness, the sound of his footsteps retreating the only noise in the chamber. The door opened, and a thin beam of light seeped through the shadows, before it shut again.

I stood there, waiting for what was next.

A simple fight wouldn't cut it. Initiation wasn't that easy.

Another light clicked on, and the spotlight now focused on the far side of the chamber. As I walked toward it, a faint ache spread through my muscles. I'd feel that fight for the next week.

Even from across the chamber, I could make out the brass cage waiting for me. Weak cries spilled from inside it. Desperate, pleading sounds that annoyed me.

The closer I got, the louder they grew.

A man fell to his knees when he saw me approaching. His filthy fingers curled around the bars, as if he wished he could tear them apart.

He was tall with shaggy red hair, and his skin was slick with sweat and grime. His shirt was ripped in shreds, displaying offensive tattoos he needed to die for anyway, and he reeked of cheap liquor.

His voice was hoarse as he asked, "What the hell am I doing here?"

I stepped up to the cage and leaned forward until the cold bars brushed against my cheek. "You're my sacrifice."

His already-pale face went even whiter.

"What?" he whimpered, scrambling backward until he slipped and collapsed onto his ass.

I stepped back as the man hauled himself upright. His hands returned to the cage bars like he had to hold them to keep himself steady.

To my right, several racks held the tools meant for the job. Devices designed for one purpose only: death. Beside the rack stood a narrow metal table with a folder resting on it.

Before any of us had agreed to Initiation, we had been told one thing: if you wanted to prove yourself worthy of being a Night Son, you had to kill.

Unlike some new initiates, I wasn't new to murder. By nineteen, I'd already begun killing my fair share of men, all under my father's supervision. He treated those kills like training exercises, and afterward, he'd pointed out the mistakes I'd made and explained what I should've done differently.

My father was a killer. Benny was one too. Most of the men who surrounded me were.

Still, there was an art to it. One simply couldn't go around murdering people. I mean, you could, but you'd get caught.

Getting away with murder required precision, planning, and obsession over every detail. One mistake was all it took to lead to a lifetime of rotting in an orange jumpsuit and eating shitty food where fuckers pissed in your chili.

It was even harder in today's age. Technology had turned the world into one giant surveillance system.

This was required to join the Night Sons, to prove we could

handle violence and weren't merciful men. They wanted any innocence inside us eradicated. Not that I had any to begin with.

The victims for Initiations weren't chosen for entertainment or personal vendettas. The Elders only selected those who deserved to die, and they were always predators and abusers who poisoned society.

The man in the cage was one of those.

As I opened the folder, the man dropped to his knees in desperation, and he shoved his face between the bars.

"Please," he sobbed, sounding pathetic. "I have a wife. I have kids."

I ignored him, skimming the first page of his file.

"Marlow Sutton," I said, his name tasting rancid on my tongue.

He smashed his face harder against the bars, his cheeks flattening against them. "How ... how do you know who I am?"

My lips peeled back as I bared my teeth with each word I read while flipping through the pages.

One page of sins. Two pages. Three.

"You're a fucking rapist," I said.

Anger detonated inside me as the words left my mouth. Heat surged through my veins as every word of his file sank into my brain.

None of Paul's earlier punches had hit this nerve.

Marlow hurt women. According to his file, he hunted them on the streets and at bars near college campuses. He'd follow the women outside when they were too drunk to fight back, then rape and kill them.

The police hadn't connected the disappearances yet.

But the Sons had.

We always did.

I shut the folder, looking at him like the scum he was, and dropped it onto the ground. Whistling, I walked over to the rack, eyeing my weapon options.

Certain tools would give him a faster death, like a gun, knife, or machete. And then there were ones that'd offer a slower suffering, like the pear of anguish, a rusty tongue tearer, and a chappy chopper. A bottle of cloudy liquid sat with them, most likely poison.

I shoved a few knives into my hoodie pocket, grabbed the tongue tearer and chappy chopper from their hooks, and unlocked the cage.

The metal creaked as the door swung open. Taking one step inside, I waited for Marlow's reaction.

Would he try to rush me to escape?

Or beg me for his freedom?

Marlow chose the second. He scurried backward on his hands and knees, sobbing loudly. He slid his back down the bars and pulled himself into a tight ball.

I shut the door behind me.

Marlow tucked his head between his knees, shaking, while pleading at the ground.

I didn't rush, taking my sweet little time, giving everyone a show as I tortured him. I said the names of the women he'd killed with every different device I used on him.

By the time I was finished, blood covered nearly every inch of us both.

He could barely lift his head. I dragged the blade across his throat, stepping away as blood spilled down his neck. His hands clasped around his neck, fingers slick as he tried to stop the bleeding, stop the pain, stop his impending death. But it wouldn't.

I waited until he took his last breath.

That was it.

I was officially a Sworn Son.

I'd killed to become one.

And I'd die if I ever betrayed them.

FIFTEEN
BLAIR

"*P*ure evil!" *a man shouts.*

"The devil!" another screams.

I stand in the water, still, as rough hands wrench my arms behind my back. A burning pain crawls up my arms when old, scratchy rope digs into my wrists.

"Evil!" comes from someone else.

The moonlight shines down on us, and tears fall down my cheeks as I stare down at my wet dress.

I gasp when he dunks my head beneath the water's surface, never knowing how long he'll keep me under. It always depends on his mood. Shutting my eyes, I try to relax as water rushes over my face and into my ears.

I learned to stop fighting long ago because the more I struggle, the longer he holds me down.

When he pulls me up, my eyes meet his menacing ones. "Four hundred sentences, Blair," he says in a razor-edged voice. "You need to atone!"

"Atone! Atone! Atone!" men chant around me. "Atone!"

I jolted upright in my bed with a strangled breath. Air ripped from my lungs so hard it hurt like the dream had been real and I'd just been underwater.

But it wasn't real, Blair.

You're not there. You're here.

I clutched the sheets, anchoring myself to the cool cotton, and my throat felt so raw that I was certain I'd been screaming.

"Blair."

The word cut through my anxiety.

I clapped a hand over my mouth as a shadow moved between the torn curtains around my bed.

"It's just me," Daphne said quickly.

My hand slid from my mouth to my chest, pressing hard against my frantic heart. "You scared the shit out of me."

"Girl, you scared the shit out of me. I thought Enzo's crazy ass was in here, torturing you."

I reached blindly for the switch beside my headboard, and the chandelier above us brightened, casting a gentle glow around my space.

I couldn't hold in my laugh when I noticed Daphne holding a pink stun gun.

"Did you bring that here to defend me?"

"Sure did." She grinned and pressed the trigger.

The sharp crack of electricity echoed through the alcove, making my pulse jump all over again.

"The next time Enzo comes here, you need to let me borrow that," I told her.

"You got it." She zapped it again before climbing into my bed across from me. She wrinkled her nose with concern etched along her forehead. "You were screaming in your sleep. Like, really screaming." She folded her legs beneath her and smoothed out her nightgown. "Nightmare?"

I stared down at my comforter, debating on honesty, and nodded.

I knew it made me look crazy. Not many things could make

people scream like that in their sleep. You were either dying or remembering.

A sharp stab of guilt moved through me.

Daphne had shared so much about her life with me.

The ugly, raw parts.

And all I'd given her in return were half-truths and deflections.

Carefully chosen fragments of my life that kept the real story buried deep.

But my secrets weren't public like hers.

The only people who knew about them were the ones who'd been there. Who'd watched and done nothing.

For fourteen years, my father, along with those around him, had told me I was evil and bound for hell before I even knew what hell was. They'd said something inside me was rotten.

While those voices were gone, I sometimes still believed them.

"Was it a nightmare about Enzo?" Daphne asked.

"Yeah," I lied.

She reached across the space between us to wrap her hand around mine, squeezing it. "I wish I could tell you it'll get better, but it probably won't." She gave my hand another squeeze. "But I'm here for you."

My eyes widened. "It won't get better, even after I become a Fawn?"

"Honestly, I don't know."

"Did Clarissa's life get better once she agreed? Did she have nightmares too?"

"Clarissa had nightmares about a lot of things."

"What really happened to her?"

"I'm not sure." Daphne gave a small shrug, sadness spreading over her tired face. She looked like that question was the one that haunted her at night. "I wasn't in the room when she jumped."

"Did she really jump?"

Her voice lowered back to a whisper. "I don't know."

"Why do people suspect Enzo did it?"

"She was his Fawn, and he was making her life hell. That's also what Jett told anyone who'd listen to him rant about it."

"The first night, you said, 'Ugh, blame it on Enzo's crazy ass.'"

She took a second to run the sentence back in her mind. "I hold him responsible for the emotional hell he put her through. Deep down, do I think he pushed her out the window?" She shook her head slowly.

My shoulders suddenly felt a tiny bit less tense.

"I wouldn't be surprised if Jett was involved and then blamed Enzo." Her weary eyes slid to the window. "We'll never know, though." Her voice sounded distant, almost whimsical, like she was speaking to herself. "I do know one thing. If I had to deal with Jett and their father on a regular basis like Clarissa did, I'd want to jump out the window too. Clarissa was too nice for her own good." Her voice started breaking, and she cleared her throat. "I miss her."

I flung my comforter off my body to stretch out and hug her. "I'm so sorry, Daphne."

In that instant, I knew I needed to be a better roommate to her. A better friend.

"Go back to sleep," I told her with a tender smile. "No one likes Mondays, and we need our beauty sleep."

I was already awake when my alarm blared through the room, never having gone back to sleep after the nightmare. Too many thoughts wound through my head to allow me to shut my eyes and relax.

Not only did having another dream worry me, but so did the anxiety of seeing Enzo. He had been MIA all weekend, but that didn't mean I hadn't thought about him the entire time.

I had so many questions.

Like now that I was his Fawn, what the hell did that mean?

I swallowed as his words infiltrated my mind. *Be good. I have eyes everywhere.*

This place felt lonely without him.

Over the weekend, I couldn't stop myself from visiting his wing several times. I'd eyed that locked gate while wondering if he was on the other side in his room. Wondered if he was thinking of me or with another girl.

My jaw had tightened whenever I thought about the latter. My tension should've eased because that meant his attention couldn't be on me.

I pulled myself out of bed and showered, brainstorming as the water fell down my body on how I'd get a new phone and laptop. I doubted my mother and stepfather knew I was without a phone, since I got more calls about my yearly Pap smear reminder than I did from them.

When I left the bathroom, dressed in my *new* uniform—aka Enzo's shirt—Daphne stared up at me brightly. "I like the new look."

The shirt was too large, so I had to knot the loose fabric with a hair tie and tucked it under my skirt. I was also wearing the necklace he'd given me.

"Let's hope Arisono doesn't give me a third strike for it," I replied.

"Blair, you're about to be a Fawn. What Arisono thinks now is irrelevant." She scoffed. "If we're being honest, you'll be *her* superior. Fawns are pretty much exempt from university rules as well. They just have to follow the Sons' rules."

On our walk downstairs, Daphne rambled on about being pissed off at a professor. We split and went our separate ways, and when I got to American Gothic Lit, I took the same desk as before.

So far, no Enzo.

His friend sat beside me again, and I turned my back to him.

I was almost positive he'd taken a picture of me with his phone on Friday to show Enzo my outfit. *Asshole.*

Professor Nelson entered the room as other students began filing inside. To get my mind off Enzo, I started drawing in my notebook.

Drawing, not *writing* lines.

The moment Enzo walked in, I looked up. My pen stalled against the paper, mid-heart drawing.

It was as if my soul recognized his presence now.

Not that there was any love between us. Most definitely not.

I loathed Enzo Marchetti.

Everyone watched him cross the lecture hall and climb the steps toward me. They waited in anticipation for whatever cruel spectacle he'd put on today.

Our black shirts matched, though his clung perfectly to the lines of his hard chest, the fabric fitted like it'd been tailored to show off his every muscle. He paired it with black pants and black boots. A black bag I'd never seen him with was slung over his shoulder.

He reached our row and ran a hand across his jaw. My eyes zeroed in on his gold ring. As if they were connected, on instinct, I dragged a hand over my necklace pendant.

When our eyes met, he winked at me.

His steps were slow as he walked to my desk. My pulse stuttered as I readied myself for whatever humiliation he had planned this time.

Instead, he reached into his bag and quietly placed a brand-new MacBook and phone on my desk. He tapped the edge of my desk and dropped into the seat beside me.

Then *nothing.*

For the rest of class, he didn't say a word.

It almost—no, it *did* piss me off that he didn't glance my way once.

He simply scrolled on his phone and pretended to pay attention to Professor Nelson.

His silence should've been a relief, but instead, it irritated the shit out of me.

Out of stubbornness, I wrote all my class notes by hand and didn't open the MacBook once.

When class ended, he stood while looking over at me and said, "I'll be at your dorm at seven. Be ready."

Enzo telling me to go anywhere with him should've been an immediate hell no.

A million red flags waving at once.

A *run as far as you can* warning.

But it wasn't like saying no to him was a choice.

Deep down, I didn't want to refuse him either.

My dread of being a Fawn was matched by an almost-obsessive curiosity about it.

The word *Fawn* sounded so harmless and gentle. Innocent and vulnerable.

A small, fluffy creature, driven by instinct more than understanding. One who trusted the world before realizing how cruel it could be.

From what I'd heard about how the Sons treated their Fawns, why would anyone want this? *Why would families want this for their daughters?*

But society had always favored wealthy, powerful men.

Even if they were monsters.

Yet at what point does the cost stop being worth it?

Every time I tried to piece everything together, it made me dizzy.

"Did you open your new phone yet?" Daphne asked.

I held up the latest iPhone model. Enzo had transferred the few contacts I'd had, but everything else was gone. My apps. My playlists. My notes. Even the stupid trivia game I played when I couldn't sleep.

His name now sat at the top of my Contacts list.

And by name, it was *The Man Who Owns Me.*

He'd also saved himself as my emergency contact.

The new MacBook sat on my desk untouched.

It was a newer version of the one he'd stolen from me. I had to admit, the upgrade was nice. My old laptop was scratched and had started running slow. I'd put off asking my stepfather for a new one. I tried to keep my requests to him at a minimum.

I dropped my phone onto my bed. "Where do you think Enzo is taking me?"

She tipped a vodka bottle to her lips, took a long swallow, then chased it with Coke Zero. "Could be the library." She pointed the can at me. "Could be hell. Let's just pray it's not for another dip in the fountain."

I playfully narrowed my eyes at her.

She grinned and held out the vodka, but I shook my head.

"Doubt it's for a romantic date," she added. "Enzo doesn't seem like the dinner-and-a-movie type. Maybe a sacrifice or a murder. That feels more on brand for him."

I snagged a sock from the laundry and tossed it at her.

She laughed and leaned to the side to dodge it.

The door swung open, and Enzo walked in without bothering to knock. Of course.

His gaze swept the room and landed on Daphne. He glared at her before turning to me. The air seemed to crackle when our eyes met. My stomach twisted uneasily, but my heart almost ... welcomed him.

He'd traded his school uniform for a black hoodie and dark jeans tucked into boots.

Behind his back, Daphne flipped him off.

I bit back a snort. "Where are you taking me?" I asked as he strolled toward my alcove and settled himself on my bed.

Instead of answering, he grabbed my copy of *1984* from the

headboard and casually flipped through the pages. His eyes moved over the text without truly reading it.

He was watching me.

I slid my phone into the back pocket of my jeans and pulled on a sweater. His glare burned into the sweater as if it personally pissed him off.

"Not that one," he said. "It's fucking hideous."

I frowned and tugged at the hem.

It wasn't exactly fashionable, expensive, or designer. But it was one of the few belongings I still had from my old life.

Ignoring him, I started fastening the buttons.

He tossed the book over his shoulder, and my fingers slowed when he pushed off the bed and moved toward me.

I backed away to create distance, but he kept advancing until I was pinned against the wall. As my body stiffened, I drew in a slow breath, the smell of his cologne wrapping around me. Somehow, it steadied my heart.

He clamped his hands around my waist, and with a frustrated grunt, I swatted at them when one lowered to my ass. I squirmed when he lowered his hand to my pocket and pulled out my phone before stepping back.

"Put on something black," he ordered, tossing my phone onto my bed. "I'm not a fan of you in white."

Not wanting to argue over clothes, I quickly grabbed a black Ralph Lauren sweater from a drawer and pulled it snug over my body.

Enzo gave an approving nod. I answered with a glare.

"Where are we going?" I asked again.

"You'll find out when we get there."

Before reaching the door, I looked at Daphne.

Stun gun? she mouthed, her lips curving into a smile.

Shaking my head, I mouthed back, *He'd kill me.*

She dragged her thumb across her throat in a slicing motion.

"Daphne, would you like me to send someone to slit your

throat?" Enzo asked, as if having eyes in the back of his head. He spoke without looking back at her.

She lowered her hand and crossed her arms.

"Don't make me call Brooks," he threatened.

"Do it," Daphne challenged. "I'll push him out the window."

That seemed to be the preferred method of murder at Saint Vale.

Defenestration.

I couldn't see the look he gave her, but whatever it was made her glare at him before looking away.

Knowing Daphne, I could tell she was fighting the urge to mock his voice. Every day, I liked her more.

She had guts. No wonder no one chose her as their Fawn. She'd give them hell the entire time.

As I passed her, she offered me the vodka bottle, and I almost stopped for a drink. Liquid courage might've helped calm me, but it also could've dulled my instincts.

I needed my mind sharp around the devil.

I followed him out of the room and down Poenas Dare Hall. Just like last time, people stared.

Instead of heading for the staircase, Enzo veered right and led me down an unfamiliar corridor. He stopped in front of a door I would've mistaken for a janitor's closet if I'd passed it alone, then slid a card through the reader above the handle.

A second later, it clicked open.

I followed him through it, glancing around, and saw a faint light over a set of concrete stairs that disappeared downward. I flinched when the door slammed shut behind us.

Enzo charged down the stairs, and I struggled to keep up. After two flights, he shoved open another door.

Cold air rushed across my cheeks the moment we stepped outside in the pitch-black night. Only a thin crescent moon cut through the darkness, casting faint outlines across the grounds. The university loomed behind us, and he seized my wrist, pulling me farther away from it.

We passed the greenhouse and two more buildings. Buildings that I'd planned to explore but avoided since being kidnapped by him and his masked buddy the last time I was out here.

The closer we got to the woods, the harder my pulse pounded.

I stopped dead before we passed the tree line.

No way in hell was I following the devil into the woods.

Count me the hell out.

Before I could turn around and flee, Enzo yanked me back, holding me tight against his hard chest. He wrapped his elbow around my throat, a viselike grip holding me in place.

It did nothing to ease my mind. All it did was remind me of the first night in the woods, how he'd held me just like this.

"Don't try to run, Blair," he warned.

My brain swam with all the thoughts of his plans for me in that forest.

The rattle of our breathing felt almost in sync as he held me.

Something gentle brushed my cheek right before darkness covered my eyes.

Not just the night's darkness.

Straight black, even blocking the sway of tree shadows.

"Not again," I grumbled under my breath.

What else should I have expected though?

The men of a dangerous secret society kept everything secret.

Not a shocker.

I sighed and pleaded a simple, "Please."

"Trust me," was all he said in my ear.

It felt more like a demon saying it than someone I could *trust*.

"You're the last person I trust," I said with full honesty as shivers traveled down my spine.

"Walk, and I promise, I won't drag you."

How sweet of him for that.

He clasped my hand, and I winced at the scrape of his worn leather glove against my hand. I must've missed him slipping it on during our walk. That new small detail only tightened the pressure around my heart.

People only wore gloves if it was snowing or they didn't want to leave fingerprints. There wasn't one snowflake in the air.

My balance faltered as he tugged me along like he was a kid dragging his favorite blankie.

Coyote cries wailed through the air, and branches crunched under our feet as we walked. The wind's whistle harmonized with the sound of an owl hooting in the distance.

Are there deer in these woods?

Fawns?

"Can you explain what being your Fawn means?" I asked Enzo when he guided me toward the right.

Because he was a man of many words, he replied with, "You'll find out."

"Can you let me find out *now*?"

"Why do you ask so many questions?"

"I believe anyone wearing a blindfold and being led aimlessly through the woods would do the same. It's human nature. Wouldn't you?"

"I'd never allow someone to blindfold me."

"What if they did?"

"They wouldn't."

"Yes, but hypothetically—"

"I don't do hypotheticals."

"What if someone tried? What would you do?"

"Worse than what I did to Jett when he was tied to that chair."

"But not worse than killing him? Pushing him out of a window?"

"I didn't push Jett out of a window."

I scoffed.

"Cross my heart and hope to die."

"If you didn't, then someone did it for you. Your pal in the mask, probably."

He chuckled but didn't dispute my statement.

"Are you always this unhinged?"

"I'm not unhinged."

I scoffed again.

As we walked, I was grateful for the few times he caught me before I tripped and fell. He showed even more care guiding me down the stairs. The smell of damp earth and cold air told me we were underground.

Please not the torture room again.

A girl could only see so many rogue fingers before she barfed.

I heard two beeps before heavy music blasted through my eardrums.

I didn't recognize the music, though that was normal. Growing up, I hadn't been allowed to listen to it. Even humming had severe consequences.

Enzo held me in place while removing the blindfold. I blinked, adjusting my eyes to the dim light, and glanced around.

The first thing I saw was a bar with liquor bottles neatly arranged on the shelves. My lungs drew in the smell of the room. It smelled like furniture polish and deep leather.

Wherever we were, I was certain it wasn't open to most Saint Vale students and that I didn't belong here.

In the distance, I heard voices, but couldn't see anyone.

Enzo gripped my shoulders, turning me, and slid the blindfold back into place.

"What the actual fuck, Enzo?" a guy shouted.

"Shut up," Enzo growled in response.

"This won't look good, man," another deep voice added. "You know the rules."

Enzo tugged me away. "I'll keep her in the back." He checked the tightness on the blindfold and led me away.

The music faded into the background with each step we took.

He didn't remove the blindfold until he helped me into a seated position on a chair. I sucked in a breath, prepared for the worst, since the last time this had happened, it was in front of a bleeding Jett.

A sense of relief hit me that I was only staring at a maroon leather booth along a wall with a table in front of me. It was almost like a restaurant setup, with one person in a chair and the other on the opposite side.

My thoughts jumbled while Enzo tossed the blindfold on the table, then slid into the booth. I eyed the blindfold, catching faint traces of my mascara on it.

I craned my neck for a better look at the logo sewn into the blindfold's inner lining, but Enzo snatched it off the table and shoved it into his pocket. I drew a slow breath in through my nose as he peeled off his gloves and jammed them into the other pocket.

There wasn't much in the room. Stark cream walls with a Bluetooth speaker tucked into one corner.

Enzo snapped his fingers in my face. "Eyes on me, Blair."

My gaze collided with his.

His eyes were broody, a wild storm brewing inside them. They were a rich, deep brown with dots of green. My gaze lowered to his lips at the same time he licked them.

He cleared his throat, snapping me out of my staring. "Stay here." He squeezed out of the booth and stood. "You try to run, and plenty of people out there will make you pay for it. You'll never see the light of day again."

I pulled in another one of those deep breaths through my nose when he knelt and ran his cold finger across my cheek. My lips pressed together to stop me from running my mouth, and I tried to wrench my face free from his hold. His grip only tightened on my cheek as punishment.

"Good girl." He caressed my cheek once before releasing me.

He left the room, shutting the door behind him, and I kept my back stiff against the chair while looking around the room again. I squinted, seeing faint etchings on the walls. While I wanted to stand up and inspect them better, I kept my ass glued to the chair.

To ease my anxiety, I tapped my foot.

Dragged my nails against the table.

When Enzo returned, he was holding two crystal glasses filled with amber liquor. He set them on the table, then slid back into the booth.

He pushed a glass toward me. "Drink."

I shoved it away.

His voice turned a touch harder. "Drink." He nudged the glass closer until it almost fell off the edge and into my lap.

"I don't drink." Though the longer this night went on, the more I contemplated changing that.

He dipped his finger into his glass and splashed liquid at me. "Are you lying to me, Blair?"

I shook my head, meeting his eyes to show the truth in them.

"Have you ever had a drink?"

"Twice. My freshman year of college."

Growing up, I'd been taught by my father that anything other than water was toxic. Even juice and *especially* alcohol. As I got older and away from him, I realized that was complete bullshit. Nearly everything he'd spouted was.

I'd had my first drink when I went to college. I took it easy. The second time, I hadn't and spent the rest of the night hugging the toilet.

"Looks like tonight will be your third," he told me.

I still didn't take a drink.

He leaned in closer. "Unless you want me to pour it down your throat?"

I curled my fingers around the glass and raised it to my lips. My front teeth slid over the glass as I took a slow drink. I gagged at the taste of burned sugar and firewood as a wave of revulsion hit me. My throat burned as the liquid rolled down.

A low chuckle rumbled from Enzo. "It seems bourbon isn't your thing. I'll get you something different."

"Water?" I coughed, resting my hand on my chest. "Can I just have a water?"

He stood, finished his drink, took my glass, and left the room with both of them.

I tried to regulate my breathing while he was gone. To meditate. To manifest that I was anywhere but here.

He came back and dropped the glass in front of me again. Clear liquid splashed from the top.

Water? Or vodka? Or hell, poison?

"Your water," he said, motioning toward the glass while taking his seat again. "Figured you'd want a drink for this, but if you don't want liquor, that's your call."

His glass was full again with bourbon.

"A drink for what?" I asked.

His response to my question was to draw a knife from his pocket. I shrank back in my chair. He slammed it onto the table, and my gaze dropped to the handle, where something had been etched into it.

I blinked, seeing what resembled a broken halo.

His smirk was heartless while he ran the blade over the table. Tremors spilled through me. I'd never trust this man. Add a weapon, and he became ten times more dangerous.

This time, a pinch of ease settled inside me.

He said he couldn't kill me without permission. Since I didn't know how evil the men who gave that permission were, I'd never be perfectly relaxed with him.

"Why did you write *I will atone for my sins* in your notebook?" His question broke my train of thought.

My jaw dropped as I fumbled for words.

Any lie to blurt out.

Anxiety and dread crawled through my insides.

I was shocked I found words when I said, "It's something I do when I'm bored."

An unreadable expression crossed his face.

He caught my hand, turned it over, and skimmed his thick

finger over my palm. My neck hunched forward when he flipped it back. Curiosity pawed at me like an animal as I tried to figure out what the hell he was doing.

A gasp ripped from my throat when he pinned my hand down with his while using the other to spin the knife between his fingers.

With careful precision, he parted my fingers. My head spun when the cold steel of the knife's edge skimmed across my middle finger.

"Enzo," I huffed out. I wished my breath sounded like a warning, but it sounded more like a plea.

He ignored me and jabbed the sharp point between two of my fingers. I attempted to yank my elbow back to free my hand, but he held me in place.

I twisted my elbow, barely missing my drink. "Stop it!"

His laughter was sinister when I glanced over my shoulder at the door.

"Oh, Blair, do you think anyone will come to your rescue here?" He stared me down in a way a predator did before devouring their prey and jabbed the space between two more fingers without looking. "I could slit your throat in front of the entire student body and administration, and no one would bat an eye." He stabbed the knife into the table, so close to a finger. "They wouldn't even provide a simple tissue to stop the bleeding. I'm your only protection here."

"My protector or predator?" I gasped, my eyes fixed on the knife.

He shifted the knife to another gap between my fingers.

That started a rhythm for him as he slammed the knife's tip between my fingers, gap by gap, before starting over.

He played this as a game, and he wasn't gentle.

My eyes never left the knife. One wrong move, and he'd strike a finger. Blood rushed to my fingertips.

His hand moved faster as I gulped in breaths, waiting for him to slip.

My heart stammered in my chest when he looked up, focusing on my face and not his stabbing. His eyes didn't even glance at the knife now.

"You'd better start talking," he warned. "It'll be hard to write sentences in the future if you're short a finger." His next strike between the spaces of my hand landed harder. "When I hit one, I'll make you sit here and watch it bleed. No ride to the hospital for you."

I winced at the force of the knife driving into the table.

For a moment, I visualized the pain of metal crunching into my bone.

"It was how my father punished me!" I blurted out because he needed to get that fucking knife away from me.

He paused mid-strike, the knife tip hovering over a finger. "What sins did you need to atone for?"

"None," I whispered.

I was sure it sounded like a lie, like when you asked a child if they broke a rule and they said no.

But it was the truth. At least *my* truth.

"I don't believe you," Enzo said. "No one atones for sins if they didn't commit them."

Bold of him to think I'd had a choice.

He dragged the knife's tip across my middle finger, slightly breaking skin.

"I had no choice," I told him. "Not writing those sentences would have resulted in a worse punishment."

"What sins did he *think* you needed to atone for?"

My body relaxed when he lowered the knife, happy that I was answering questions, that I was spilling my secrets for him.

"Everything was a sin in my father's eyes." I motioned toward his glass. "A sin. If I backtalked, that was a sin. Me being left-handed was a sin. Anything he disapproved of, he deemed a sin."

I left out the biggest sin he'd blamed me for.

No one else needed to know that.

Enzo set the knife down. "Sounds like your father is fucked up in the head."

I nodded. "He is."

"Where's he now?"

I shrugged. "No clue. I cut off contact."

He eyed me like he didn't believe me. "Hmm."

"Is there a way for me to get out of this Fawn thing?" I quickly asked, in desperate need to change the subject to anything.

He brushed his fingers against the same knuckles he'd just threatened with a knife as disappointment clouded his features. "Do you want out, Blair? Do you want to go back on your word?"

My mouth felt suddenly dry, and I took a drink of water.

It was thankfully just water.

"Technically," I said, the words leaving me slowly, "I'm not a Fawn yet, right?"

He plucked the knife from the table and offered it to me. "Your turn to play. If you don't hit a finger, I'll consider letting you go. *Releasing you*."

I took the knife from him like I was making a pact with the devil.

Sacrificing my soul for peace.

Plenty of times, my father had told me that the Devil was an angel first. Later, it was how he described me to others. His little girl, who'd once been an angel, had turned into something evil.

Enzo splayed his hand out on the table in front of me.

Staring down, I eyed his gold ring. It had the symbol of a broken halo engraved against the gold.

He didn't have to ask me twice to use a knife on him. I carefully started driving the knife between his fingers.

While I didn't plan to stab him, thrill pinched my insides at me being the one holding the knife.

"You have to go faster than that," he snarled in irritation. "No pussyfooting around."

I stilled for a moment before upping my speed.

Just a little.

My brain thrashed against my skull.

"Faster, Blair!" He crashed his other hand onto the table, rattling my hold on the knife.

I upped my pace slightly more.

"I said, fucking faster!" He clamped his hand around my wrist, cuffing it, and controlled my speed.

My soul nearly drained from my body while he hammered the knife between his fingers. We got through one hand pass in mere seconds.

He did it again.

And again and again and again.

Until all the anger coiled inside me unraveled and snapped free.

I added force, helping him slam the knife into the table so violently that it rocked beneath us. My mind went blank as I lost control, releasing all my pent-up frustration.

My view grew fuzzy to the point where I could hardly make out his fingers. They became hazy shapes.

I froze, reality crashing in, when I heard a sharp crack.

I'd stabbed his finger, the knife connecting with bone. It wasn't all the way through his middle finger, but it'd broken through the skin. I yanked the knife out, and blood trickled from the wound.

It was a tiny spot at first, before crimson-red gushed out.

He grinned down at his hand. This was what he'd wanted. He knew I'd hit his finger, and I'd never get out of being his Fawn.

He grabbed the knife, slipping it back into his pocket, and leaned back in the booth to inspect his hand.

My blood boiled as I waited for his response.

He stared down at his finger, smearing the blood, and grinned. "You hit bone. Color me impressed. I'm shocked it didn't go deeper."

I didn't say a word because I couldn't form them.

His heavy gaze dragged from his finger to me. "How'd it feel, Blair?" He scooted closer, sliding his elbows across the table. Near enough that our lips almost brushed. "How'd it feel to finally release that anger built up inside you?" His alluring voice pulled me into his orbit.

Since the table was narrow, he didn't have to move much to lower his head and draw my lower lip between his teeth. The taste of that burned sugar returned to my mouth, now mixed with hints of Enzo.

"Tell me how it felt," he said with full fascination.

In a trance, I whispered, "Great. Empowering."

"That's my girl." He reared back a few inches. "That's my Fawn."

He pulled away, grabbed his glass, left the booth, and stood behind me.

I shifted in the chair, pretending to be more uneasy than I truly was, when he ran his fingers through my hair. I only hoped he wasn't using the bloody one.

His calmness was brief.

I winced in pain when he clutched a fistful of my hair and yanked my head back.

My stare crashed into his violently.

He smirked while using his hand holding the glass to open my mouth. Bourbon splashed onto my face before dripping down me.

My jaw fell slack, opening my mouth, and he poured the bourbon down my throat. From my position, I couldn't easily swallow. His grin twisted into something more sinister as I choked, fighting to drag my head back up.

He tapped my cheek condescendingly before releasing me.

I tipped my head forward, forcing down the liquor and gagging as I swallowed it.

His body still felt warm behind me as he trailed his fingers across my jaw. "Your Initiation is Friday night. You'll skip your classes, and someone will collect you in the morning."

I jerked back when he pulled my chair out, turning it, and dropped to his knees in front of me.

I whimpered when he skimmed his hand up my leg. I was suddenly grateful I'd swapped my skirt for pants earlier. He didn't stop until his hand rested over my mound. He made a petting motion, gently caressing me through my jeans.

A thousand sensations vibrated through me.

Some feelings I'd never experienced before.

A deep craving spread through my insides.

I suddenly felt hot. So hot.

As he massaged me between my legs, I'd never felt so full but empty down there.

This man was driving me to the brink of insanity.

It had to be the liquor he'd poured down my throat.

"Don't fail your Initiation," he told me, teasing my clit through my jeans.

I had to bite into my lip to stop myself from begging him to take off my jeans to feel his touch more intimately.

Enzo was the evil I'd been blamed for being all my life.

He suddenly stood, his face now serious, and offered me his hand. I took it and allowed him to lift me to my feet. The moment he had me in his grasp, he swung me around and shoved me against the wall.

My hand smacked into it, and I moaned at the feel of his hard cock pressing into my ass.

He swept my hair from my shoulder, his lips brushing my earlobe. "You either survive Initiation or you don't make it out alive." He sucked on the skin beneath my jaw. "You've learned too many of our secrets. Be strong to become my Fawn, Blair. Your life depends on it."

After leaving wherever the hell we had gone, Enzo led me back into the woods. This time, he at least waited as I walked away from him so I wasn't alone.

He propped his back against a tree and told me to go straight back to my dorm. At first, I thought it was another one of his games, like he'd try hunting me on my way back. He didn't.

During my walk back, I knew one thing for certain: I'd get through this year, stay strong, and not end up like Enzo's previous Fawns.

All I had to do was survive this year.

I entered the university and prayed Arisono wouldn't suddenly appear like a ghost to deliver another strike. My body loosened when she didn't.

My mind was still a cluttered mess, so I decided to stop at the library to clear it.

I turned the corner and collided with someone. That someone reached out as I stumbled backward and grabbed my elbow to stop me from falling to my knees.

His deep voice rumbled, "Blair."

I pulled from his grasp as my attention darted forward. Immediate distaste flooded my mouth as I locked eyes with someone I didn't trust.

"What are you doing here?" I asked my stepfather.

He stood tall in a black suit, looking around like he didn't want us to be seen together. It'd been months since I'd last seen him. I was happy his hairline was receding more.

I always hated the way he stared at me like he was now.

A nauseating blend of impassive but threatening.

You could fear this man without him actually doing anything to explain to anyone why you felt that way.

His eyes narrowed into cold slits. "Arisono asked me to come speak to her."

"About me?" I asked. My voice sounded too pathetic for my liking.

He nodded. "She said you have two strikes."

"Let me explain—"

"No need. As I explained to you before, this is *it*. Your mother is already disappointed about the two strikes. You don't want to make her feel worse, do you?"

"No, of course not."

"Good." He reached out to clap his hand over my shoulder. "Stay out of trouble." He shot me one last unnerving look before maneuvering around me and walking away.

I hunched forward, resting my hands on my knees.

That conversation with him had created just as much anxiety inside me as the knife game with Enzo. The quiet hum of the library no longer sounded inviting.

I made a U-turn and headed back to my dorm instead, praying that I didn't run into anyone else on my way there.

SIXTEEN

ENZO

I checked my watch, seeing the second hand nearing midnight, and stretched my neck from side to side. Every muscle in my neck tightened when I slammed the folder shut and tossed it aside.

Someone had dropped it off at my door two nights ago, and I still hadn't found out who it was. I'd reviewed video from the CCTV footage at my door countless times, but couldn't make out the person.

No one other than me—not even my parents—had a key to my wing.

At least, to the best of my knowledge, though it seemed I was wrong.

Information about Blair that I couldn't find online filled the folder.

Information that neither Julian nor Nico had found, hacking into everything they could, searching for Blair's secrets.

Inside the folder, they were laid bare, as if whoever had left it unlocked her brain and emptied it out for me. It still didn't answer all my questions. I had plenty more, *especially* after what I read.

Whoever left it knew Blair.

The real question was *why* they had done it.

They knew this information would make her Initiation harder. The more we knew, the worse we could make it on her.

I needed to find out who had played Folder Fairy and why they'd done it.

Cedric, Emeri, and Brooks had also received folders with the same information.

Initiations were to prove the woman we'd chosen as a Fawn was worthy. I hadn't been lying when I told Blair failing Initiation meant death. It wasn't us who killed them. They usually ended their own lives, not strong enough to withstand the mental torture we'd put them through. That didn't happen often.

Tonight was Blair's Initiation.

If she failed, it'd reflect badly on me.

She had to do well.

I tucked the folder inside my bag and left my dorm. No moon hung in the air as I walked through the pitch-black fog.

When I brought Blair to the Devil's Lair to play the knife game the other night, I had taken her the long way, leading her through the entrance in the back of the woods. We had a few other entrances that were closer to campus.

Tonight, I took the easier route through the secret entrance in the greenhouse.

Taking Blair to the Devil's Lair had broken the rules. I'd told myself it was okay since I led her to a secluded room and she didn't see anything.

I had taken her to one of our recreation rooms.

It was where we fucked, did drugs, and cleared our heads.

When I entered the Devil's Lair, I found Cedric, Nico, and Brooks on the couch. A pizza box was open on the table. Emeri sat at a secluded table in the corner, typing on his laptop. Probably working on his book. The one he wouldn't allow any of us to read.

Given his quiet nature, he needed an outlet for his crazy-ass thoughts.

I collapsed on the couch beside Brooks, following his attention to his father on the TV. President Byron replied to a journalist's question about attending the senator's son's funeral.

"Shit," I hissed, annoyance now rumbling inside me. "I forgot I have to attend that."

"We didn't miss it?" Brooks asked, glancing at me. "I hoped my father would forget he'd demanded I go."

"It's scheduled for next weekend," Cedric said.

"Why the fuck are they letting the body sit that long?" Nico asked. "It has to be rotten as fuck by now."

Brooks shook his head, shooting Nico an annoyed glare. "How did you pass the aptitude test to become a Son again? His body was blown to bits. There isn't anything to rot."

"He's right, actually," Emeri said from the corner.

Nico flipped Brooks off and puffed out his chest.

"They're piecing him back together," Emeri went on. "The mother refused to have an empty casket, so they're reassembling him Frankenstein-style."

"They're supergluing his parts together?" Nico asked.

"Not sure." Emeri shrugged. "It's for appearances, so my guess is, they're just arranging him to look pretty."

"Let's hope for an open casket," I said, grabbing a pizza slice and biting into it. "That's the kind of artwork I like to see."

All the guys nodded in agreement.

I chewed my bite while Brooks stared at me.

"How're you feeling about tonight?" he asked.

"Fan-fucking-tastic," I lied.

"She'd better not fail," Nico said, always giving his annoying-ass input. "You brought her here. We could get in trouble for not reporting you for that shit. You know, if someone isn't a Fawn, Haven, or fucking Daphne, they can't come to the Devil's Lair. It's too risky."

"Since when do you give a shit about playing by the book?" Cedric asked.

I shot Nico a frustrated glare.

All of us were close. We all knew he'd never rat my ass out. He just liked running his smart mouth.

Our loyalty to each other was what made us different from those who had come before us. Above all else, we were a brotherhood. Sons second.

Brooks rubbed the back of his neck. "Enzo knows what he's doing."

"Nah." Cedric shook his head. "This Fawn isn't like his others."

"True." Brooks took a sip of Coke.

Needing to prove them wrong, I kept my tone even and steady as I said, "She's a potential Fawn. That's it." I ran my hand over my face. When that didn't relieve the mounting tension, I rested my head back on the cushion, trying to loosen the strain there, and shut my eyes.

They were right. Blair was different. But I wouldn't admit that.

I'd never cared much about my Fawns. From my first year, I had known I'd never be one of those idiots who fell in love with theirs.

To me, Fawns only served as instruments.

To be used. Fucked. Controlled.

I didn't need a Fawn to help with my restraint.

I just had them for my own entertainment and to fulfill my Son duty.

Brooks discarded his pizza crust in the box and propped his feet up. "The Elders brought me in for a meeting last night. They said I have to choose a Fawn for the year."

"Same," Emeri and Cedric said simultaneously.

We were all seniors, and the allure of having a Fawn had faded. The rules mandated that we choose one. Everyone was dragging their feet.

"Just say fuck it and choose Daphne," Cedric told Brooks.

Brooks dropped his feet from the table, took a steady breath, and reached for the drawer beneath the table where he stored his weed. A deep crease appeared on his forehead as he took out and unfolded his rolling papers.

"He's right," I added. "Pick her. She knows the rules and will pass."

His eyes whipped to me, anger burning inside them. "I'd have to fuck her."

"You *want* to fuck her."

"My sister would hate me."

"Adelina would get over it," Nico added.

Brooks dropped the partially rolled joint and sank back onto the couch. "Like I've explained to you fucks before, my dad would lose his shit." His gaze pinged to me again. "Would you make a Fawn of the woman whose father tried to assassinate yours?"

The thought of someone trying to assassinate my father made me want to throw my fist through the wall.

Several men had been stupid enough to try and failed.

Each one was dead now.

Served them right. Fucking idiots.

But I got where Brooks was coming from. Assassination attempts in my world weren't out of the ordinary. They were in his.

Brooks went back to rolling his joint, and I knew we needed to change the subject. Initiations were long, and we needed to be focused today.

The seconds ticked agonizingly slowly.

Two hours later, I checked my watch again.

Once it struck three a.m., we'd begin.

SEVENTEEN

BLAIR

A violent tug ripped me from my bed.

My eyes flashed open in panic as I saw the low light filtering through my dorm. I cried out when rough hands seized me and dragged me across the floor.

I writhed in their hold as they jerked me upright.

I'd stupidly thought I'd prepared for this. I tried to stay awake, but my body betrayed me. Daphne had given me a heads-up that with Clarissa, the Sons hadn't waited until morning to *collect* her. They had come in the middle of the night.

That was why I was still dressed in my uniform and loafers and not in my pajamas.

When I started to scream for Daphne, a callous hand clamped over my mouth, forcing the words back down as someone stepped in front of me.

Enzo—my devil, my tormentor—stood tall, like the darkest omen that existed in the world.

A skull mask covered his face, and all I could see through the hollow circles around his eyes were two dark pinpoints.

The hand over my mouth disappeared when he stepped closer.

I dragged in air as I readied to scream, but my body relaxed when he reached forward and touched me.

His chilly hand cupped my chin to tilt it upward until I couldn't look at anything but him.

"It's time, Blair," he said, his voice almost sounding soulless.

Like there was no human behind that mask.

It's time.

The words settled over me like a death sentence.

My Initiation had started.

Someone moved behind me before I could react. I heard the sound of tape tearing before they smacked it against my mouth.

Before I could even attempt to fight, the person behind me grabbed my arms and hauled me backward.

Everything happened so fast that my mind could barely keep up.

They dragged me out of the room, their steps so rushed that they were nearly running. The walls and dorms blurred past me before they cut that view off by placing a cloth over my head.

Something slammed, and a frigid gust tore across my body. The sudden drop in temperature told me we were outside.

My mind snapped clear, jolting me fully awake, and I fought to awaken every survival instinct I had.

They stopped to bound my wrists and ankles together before moving me again. I heard a loud click, then the sound of scuffling broke through the silence.

My stomach dropped as they held me sideways to swing my body back, as if preparing to launch me across the damn state. I twisted, my muffled cries spilling into the tape across my mouth as I struggled to break myself free.

A second later, they let go.

I crashed down onto a solid surface. The slam reverberated through whatever space they'd thrown me into.

I smelled that new-car smell and chemical cleaner. My elbows brushed rough carpet. The bastards had put me in a goddamn trunk.

I curled myself tight into the fetal position, fighting against the bindings, but I couldn't break free.

All the air left my lungs when I heard the low rumble of an engine starting. The floor beneath me vibrated, the movement traveling through my bones as I felt the vehicle speed forward.

I rolled helplessly with the motion, landing on my back and trying to drive my knees into the trunk lid, but that didn't work. I was trapped, and I could do nothing but wait for their next act of torment.

The car whipped through turns so hard that my body slammed against the sides of the trunk. Nausea crept up my throat as the vehicle spun again.

Are they doing fucking doughnuts?

My head swirled, and I struggled to keep myself from vomiting.

The vehicle stopped, and my face slammed into something hard. I heard another click, then voices nearby, but couldn't make out their words or who they belonged to.

My head was still dizzy when they hauled me out of the trunk and dumped me onto the ground. I hit the soil hard, pain flaring through my arm as my elbow struck the dirt. Broken branches scraped against my skin.

Fear shot through me like a drug in my veins when someone hoisted me up and slung me over their shoulders, as if I were a bride on her wedding day, but instead of a honeymoon, they were carrying me to say my vows to the devil.

My body bounced with every step whoever was carrying me took before he stopped abruptly. When he dropped me, our heads knocked together before I hit the ground again.

Pain exploded through my body as I caught myself on my palms, feeling the cold, damp earth against my skin.

My world tilted, the vomit still threatening to come up.

I needed to see. To move.

Two large hands seized my arms and pulled me upright, but

my bound legs refused to cooperate, so they held most of my weight as my shoes sank into the dirt.

Something sharp and icy slowly traced along my clenched jaw.

The wind carried his evil chuckle through the trees, the sound bending around the branches before slamming into me like another warning.

"Try to run from us, little Fawn," a voice said in my ear.

Whoever it was cut my hands free and roughly shoved me back to my knees.

Trembling, I forced myself to my feet and ripped the blindfold from my eyes. The tape came off next, tearing painfully from my lips. My heart battered against my ribs as I shook out my stiff arms.

Somewhere in the distance, a fox screamed.

Before I could fully recover my senses, a shove knocked me back to the ground.

I looked up and around the woods they'd brought me to, but saw nothing but staggering trees and tangled branches. I heard nothing but the restless wind moving through them. Somehow, they'd all just, *poof*, disappeared.

Seconds ticked by as I spun in a circle, waiting, and stopped when I heard a crunch from somewhere.

My heart caved in, ready to hide itself in my chest, as I tried to find the source of the noise, but couldn't.

"You'll never escape us," a voice echoed from somewhere to my right.

Or was it my left? In front of me?

I spun in all directions, searching the darkness for them.

The trees towered above me, their branches like a canopy covering the stars. I had no idea where in the woods we were. The last time Enzo had left me out here, I could see the glow from the university in the distance.

This time, there was nothing that could lead the way.

"Over here, little Fawn."

I whipped around. My chest heaved as voices bounced through the woods.

"Over here, Blair!"

I pivoted again, only for another voice to call out from deeper in the trees, "Time to hunt us, little Fawn."

A faint glow flickered in the distance. At first, I thought it was the moon, but that light began moving.

Closer and brighter.

I froze, my feet rooted to the earth and unwilling to move, as the light approached me. Slowly, I saw the outline of a neon light.

The mask wasn't like the one Enzo had worn the night he forced me to watch him torture Jett or the one he had worn in my dorm earlier.

I jammed my hands beneath my arms, hugging myself against the cold, and hesitated.

Do I run?

Do I stay?

The wind whispered like it wanted to answer.

Or is that someone's voice?

I was so close to hyperventilating. If I didn't do something now, I'd pass out.

"Fuck this," I said to myself.

I turned and bolted in the opposite direction. My lungs burned like they'd been stung by a thousand bees as I sprinted as fast as I could.

My vision blurred, confusing my thoughts, and I hoped I was running in the right direction. Hoped that I was headed toward safety and not deeper trouble.

I didn't make it far.

A shadow with a ray of neon burst from behind a tree ahead of me. It slammed into me, kicking me sideways before disappearing just as fast. I hit the dirt hard, the impact rattling my entire body.

Heart pounding, I stood and ran in another direction.

Another masked man stepped in front of me. He didn't shove me down like the last one. He simply shoved my shoulder to send me off course before disappearing.

No matter which direction I turned or which way I tried to run, another masked figure appeared.

Sometimes there was one. Sometimes two or three circled me like coyotes pushing me toward a trap.

"Blair ... we see you."

Their fucking voices made everything just as creepy.

"Blair, we'll catch you."

My head whipped in every direction as I tried to track them, but they were everywhere, like a thousand demons spilled from the depths of hell for the sole reason to torture me.

All that surrounded me were trees, flickers of neon masks, and terror.

It was like the forest had come alive with its worst inhabitants.

Another shove struck me, sending me sprawling back.

Before I could fully stand, a hand gripped my collar from behind and forced me ahead. Then it released me.

Laughter circled me.

"Blair! We see you!"

"How long do you think you'll last?"

"Run, little Fawn!"

I staggered forward, my heart screaming for me to keep running. My legs trembled with exhaustion, telling me to do the opposite, but I ignored them and ran again.

I ran, almost feeling like I was moving in circles, until my legs failed on me. I collapsed onto my hands and knees. My lungs strained for air while I tried to keep my head up to search for them.

I crawled toward the closest tree and pressed my back against the trunk.

Something moved on the other side of the tree. I slammed my hand over my mouth to silence myself. My heart thumped so hard that I wouldn't be surprised if whoever was on the other side had heard it.

They hadn't just dropped me off in the woods.

They'd taken me to a hunting ground.

"Got you," was all I heard before someone grabbed me.

"Please," I whimpered, my fingers scraping desperately against the tree's rough bark as I tried to twist myself free.

Before another plea could escape my lips, something sharp pierced the side of my neck. Pain flared beneath my skin.

I gasped as the sting burned hot inside me.

Everything grew fuzzy, and my legs felt weaker as I collapsed to the dirt.

And that was when I saw her.

A lone doe stood in the distance, half hidden between the trees.

For a moment, she watched me.

I forced myself to blink *one more time*, seeing the white fur of her tail as she ran, before everything went black.

Cold air stirred me awake.

Still drowsy, I reached for my blanket to pull it higher up my body. My hand felt nothing but a hard, chilly surface.

A shrill tore from my throat as my eyes opened. I slapped my palms against the surface beneath me, not feeling the softness of my mattress. Instead, they met concrete.

My body shot up as I looked around in dread. Four concrete walls felt like they were closing in on me in the small space. I searched every inch for a door, a handle, a window, anything to get me out of here, but there was nothing.

Only gray walls and a low ceiling.

I turned toward the source of the chilliness, spotting a fan in the corner blasting cold air directly at me.

My body ached as I began crawling toward it, needing to unplug the damn thing. I only made it a few inches when something pulled me backward.

Metal clanked against the floor, bouncing off the bare walls.

I cried out, pounding at the floor, when I twisted around and found the heavy chain wrapped around my ankle. The other end was bolted to a hook drilled deep into the wall.

A strange haziness settled over my brain as I slumped back against the concrete, my head spinning. Everything felt slow, distant, like I couldn't form one coherent thought.

They'd drugged me.

Something had been in whatever they stabbed into my neck.

I tipped my head forward, noticing I was only wearing a black bra and a pair of panties. Someone had changed me out of my uniform. Assholes could've at least given me socks so I wasn't barefoot in this cold room.

My jaw clenched at the thought of any of them seeing me naked.

I did another scan of the room, noticing a small metal table was the only thing within my reach. I sucked in air through my teeth while scooting my ass against the rough ground toward the table.

A gun and a single bullet were intentionally resting on the table. A note sat next to it, along with a glass of water and a bottle of bourbon.

I picked up the note to read it. The handwriting matched the note Enzo had left after destroying my dorm room and cutting my ribbons.

If you hit your breaking point, that bullet is yours.

I snatched the note, ripping it into shreds, and threw them away from me. Salty tears trailed down my cheeks as I slouched against the wall. I sniffled, brushing them away, and rocked myself to get what little warmth I could.

How long did I sleep?

What time is it?

Hell, what day is it?

I clutched my arms around my knees, but that hold loosened when the fan shut off with a dramatic click. Rugged breaths left my lungs as I made another sweep of the room, looking for more clues, and spotted a camera in the upper-right corner.

My hands were stiff as I waved them toward the camera. "Hello!"

I wasn't prepared for the loud banging and screams that came from the walls. It was like a tornado, hurricane, and semi drove through them all at once.

When that stopped, I heard nothing but creepy whispers, like what they'd done in the woods.

"Let me out of here!" I screamed.

The crackle of static made me lift my chin. My heart lurched when it cut off, and music spilled out from speakers I couldn't find.

Not just music.

A certain song.

Ice, colder than the concrete, trickled down my spine.

"Hush, little baby, don't say a word. Mama's gonna buy you a mockingbird."

The volume wasn't blaring, but I recognized the lullaby. While it wasn't her voice, it was almost an exact replica.

I shook my head, attempting to distract myself from the lullaby, but it became louder.

"If that mockingbird don't sing, Mama's gonna buy you a diamond ring."

I wrapped my arms back around my knees again, this time rocking forward for another reason while staring at the wall.

Am I hallucinating this?

I am. This isn't real.

No way can it be.

They'd drugged me—I was sure of it.

Maybe my mind was playing tricks on me.

Maybe the lullaby was just a cruel hallucination.

The volume rose, and I sprang to my feet.

It went higher.

Higher.

Now blaring so loud that I couldn't even think.

Couldn't even feel myself breathe.

My eardrums burned, so close to bursting, as the one song I hated assaulted me.

"Turn it off!" I screamed at the top of my lungs while holding my hands to my ears. "Turn it fucking off!"

It paused for a moment, and I heard an evil chuckle before it played again.

Louder this time.

Then louder.

Louder.

Louder.

Louder.

My legs gave out, and I slid down the rough wall. Tears poured down my face as I cried uncontrollably. Snot pooled at my lips as I desperately pleaded for them to stop.

That fucking lullaby.

Fuck that fucking lullaby.

My mother had sung that lullaby to me once in my bedroom when I was five or six years old. We didn't celebrate birthdays, so I didn't know my real age until I was older.

Since I didn't know any better, I sang it that day while doing my daily chores. Someone overheard me and told my father. He stormed into the kitchen, yanked the mop from my hand, and cracked the handle across my face. I screamed for help as he dragged me out of the kitchen by my hair and tied me to a tree, telling everyone they needed to gather around.

They crowded around me and screamed.

Called me the devil.

Said I was evil.

I sobbed while begging my mother to help me.

When my father asked where I'd heard that song, I pointed at her. She shook her head and called me a liar.

She claimed I'd heard it from the Devil because the Devil lived inside me. With fake tears falling down her face, she told him she was scared to tell him all the evil things she'd witnessed me do, in fear he'd hurt me.

That day marked the moment my father believed I was evil.

That the Devil had sent me to ruin him.

To ruin everyone.

My punishment for the singing was confinement in a small, wooden shed for thirty days. He claimed it'd free me from the evil spirits within. Once a day, my mother would bring me food, a smile on her face, and then leave without saying a word.

Sometimes, I wondered if she was the one who had ratted me out for singing. If I'd known singing was forbidden, I'd never done it. I had been too young to know what I was doing.

I was just a little girl who'd heard music for the first time.

A small girl who'd learned how cruel the world could be that day.

And now, I was a grown woman who hated music.

The song repeated through the small room until I couldn't stand it any longer. I jumped to my feet, desperately banging on the walls, and screamed until my voice turned hoarse.

The space plunged into silence the second the music stopped.

I collapsed onto the concrete as a broken sob ripped from my body. Tears blurred my vision as anger burned inside me.

I hated that they were watching me.

Seeing me fall apart.

"Is this what you wanted?" I screamed into the emptiness. "Screw you!" My arms unwrapped from my body, and I flipped off the camera. "Fuck all of you, crazy fucks!"

My words came out weaker than I'd wanted.

Because every inch of my body felt too drained and too fragile.

How did they know about the lullaby?

I felt like I was wilting every second I was stuck in this place.

For a moment, the silence almost felt like mercy.

My shoulders sagged forward, and I massaged my temples, trying to dull the pounding inside my skull.

The reprieve vanished just as quickly as it came when a square panel in the wall opened. A monitor pushed through the opening.

I kicked my chained leg toward it, wishing I could reach far enough to smash the damn thing. "Goddamn psychos!"

Snot slid down my nose. I wiped it away with the back of my arm.

The need to hit something surged through me. I slammed my fist against the wall, panic rising about what the monitor was for.

I was sure they weren't about to give me TV time like a prisoner.

The monitor flickered to life, and my hand stilled mid-hit.

Someone on the other side was controlling it. I watched them flip through channels until they stopped on a preacher standing at a podium.

"Luke 11:24!" the preacher shouted, shoving his pudgy fist into the air. "When an unclean spirit returns with seven other spirits more wicked than itself."

The video paused, rewound, and replayed.

My hand flew back to my ears, trying to block out the preacher, but it wasn't his voice I heard inside my head.

It was my father's.

He'd spoken those words to me countless times, along with his accusations.

"When the Devil enters a body, it multiplies, Blair." I could hear the way he used to say it.

Like it was an undeniable fact.

To him, that was what I'd been to my mother.

She'd carried me in her womb, and I'd poisoned her.

"Please," I cried out, kicking my legs helplessly against the concrete.

The same scene *over and over and over*.

Just like with the music, the volume kept climbing, each time louder than the last.

Then, suddenly, silence again, and the screen went black.

Before I could even catch my breath, the nursery rhyme blasted through the speakers again. At the same time, the wall in front of me erupted with light. Neon colors flashed against the concrete in violent pulses.

Red. Blue. White. Orange. Yellow.

Red. Blue. White. Orange. Yellow.

The colors stabbed into my eyes so sharp that I slapped a hand over my face to shield them. Which meant my ears were no longer covered.

The nursery rhyme climbed its way back into my head.

My hands flew back to my ears.

But then the lights burned my eyelids, stars appearing in my vision.

Hands back to my eyes. Then back to my ears.

Back and forth, and back and forth, and back and forth.

The room spun as the mental agony unraveled me.

A deafening scream blasted from my throat as I jumped to my feet and slammed both fists against the wall.

I was ready to break.

The nursery rhyme cut off as I looked at the table.

At the gun. The bullet.

The lullaby didn't return. This time, a baby's cry replaced it.

A shrill, relentless, piercing wailing.

I teetered forward and dropped onto all fours, crawling toward the table. My fingers wrapped around the glass of water, and I tipped it back, gulping it down.

Cold liquid spilled down my chin, dripping across my chest as

I swallowed it. When the glass went empty, I snatched the bottle beside it.

The bourbon tasted repulsive, scorched its way down my throat, and landed in my belly.

I screamed when the monitor came back on.

This time, a cartoon version of the lullaby played on the screen. A mama bunny sang it to her babies as they hopped around her.

I clenched my hand around the bottle, wishing I could crush it, before screaming again and hurling the bottle at the screen.

The bottle shattered as liquid oozed down its surface.

My rage drained the last of my energy, and I collapsed to the ground. I pulled my knees against my chest and curled inward.

Every muscle in my body trembled while I begged them to stop.

Mentally, I believed I was stronger than this.

Nausea rolled through my belly, and I bent forward, dry-heaving and waiting for something—*anything*—to come up, but nothing did.

The sickness stayed trapped inside me, turning in my stomach like another punishment from them.

I was ready to crack.

Ready to grab that gun and end it.

But I couldn't.

Even if I didn't believe it at the moment, I was stronger than that.

I wouldn't let these men break me.

I wouldn't let *any* man break me.

"Focus, Blair," I whispered harshly to myself. "Forget about this. Go to your place."

I hadn't gone *there* since I was a child. When my father had locked me in the shed during my punishments, to stop the pain and boredom, I had learned how to disappear in my own mind.

Shutting my eyes, I tucked my face tight between my knees and imagined myself in a forest.

Everything was peaceful there. No parents were allowed. No other children. Just me and nature. In that world, rabbits hopped up to the door of my tiny cottage, waiting for me to feed them carrots.

A bird perched on my shoulder, chirping a song, while I sat in the sun, eating strawberries. A fawn slowly emerged from the trees, approaching me so carefully. Her soft brown eyes met mine.

When she sank to the ground at my feet, I ran my fingers through her thick, plush fur, feeling the soft texture between my fingers.

This softened me. Calmed me. Grounded me.

Somewhere in the background, the real room went silent, but I was too lost in my peaceful one to notice.

Not until I opened my eyes and noticed nothing but the dark.

The door opened, and a slender beam of light came through.

I held in a breath so deep that my cheeks stretched wide when I made out someone entering the room.

"Are you ready, Blair?" a masked man asked.

I wasn't, so I didn't reply.

He crouched down beside me to unlock my ankle, and I rolled it once it was loose. The chain dropped against the ground with a loud clank.

When he offered his hand, I didn't take it, so he thrust it closer.

Knowing I had no choice and not wanting to be in this room any longer, I grabbed it.

Another leather glove that felt rough against my palm.

He dropped my hand the moment I was on my feet, and I followed him out into a corridor that resembled a tunnel.

Crossing my arms, I tried my best to hide my cleavage while wishing I had an extra pair of hands to do the same with my ass, which was on full display.

The man walking alongside me wasn't Enzo.

He was shorter and didn't carry Enzo's scent.

The one that had become my favorite.

I knew Enzo more than I wanted to admit.

When I slept, he visited my dreams. When I was awake, he occupied my daydreams.

"Keep surviving, Blair," I whispered to myself, clueless as to what was coming next in this Initiation to hell.

EIGHTEEN

BLAIR

Please be over. Please be over. Please be over.

My limbs tingled with every step as I moved through the tunnel. I clung to the delusional hope that this was the end of the Initiation.

I suppressed an angry laugh.

From the hell these men had already put me through—not only today, but since the moment I'd arrived at Saint Vale—I knew better. They weren't done with me yet.

The corridor stretched on in the same dull gray. I kept my breathing steady and counted my steps. Anything to keep my mind from spiraling.

I stared at the guy in front of me, wondering if they had Initiations too. If they did, I hoped they were brutal.

The thought of them getting beaten up sparked satisfaction inside me. They deserved the pain.

I was at least thankful that, whoever this guy was, he wasn't manhandling me. He kept a careful distance as he walked ahead of me.

Is it Cedric?

He was the only one of Enzo's friends I could put a name to.

A pang of regret hit me for not grabbing the gun before I left.

I could've attempted to conceal it. Insurance, just in case I needed to save my life.

Though with the scraps they'd dressed me in, hiding a weapon would've been nearly impossible.

I was proud of myself for not breaking and using the gun.

Whatever was next, I'd keep staying strong.

We stopped at a door marked with a symbol I didn't recognize. The man opened it and stepped aside, gesturing for me to enter first.

Nausea burned through my belly as hot and fierce as my fear. Being alone with him in such a cramped space was the last thing I wanted.

Scratch that. Being chained to a wall, hearing that fucking lullaby, was worse. This was a close second.

The door clicked shut, and my mind instantly went to the worst-case scenario. I was nearly naked and alone with a masked man.

Without a word, he unhooked a black robe and tossed it toward me. "Put that on."

I caught it before it hit the ground.

I quickly slipped it on, clutching it around my body as if it were my only source of warmth in a blizzard.

He stood there silently, arms crossed, while I took my time fastening the robe. The robe was heavy and ceremonial.

Directly over the heart, a red heart had been stitched into the fabric. At the cuff, a single letter—*B*—was embroidered above a pair of antlers in silver thread.

"Lift the hood," he instructed.

I nodded, pulling the robe over my head.

He opened another door other than the one we'd entered through and pushed it open. "It's time."

When I stepped into the pitch-black room, my insides felt paralyzed. A chill settled in the air, something heavy with dread.

Wickedness clung to me with every step I took. Each one felt like it drained a little more of my spirit.

Eerie orchestra music vibrated against my eardrums.

The man guided me to what I assumed was the center of the room. I gasped, my gaze drawn to a flicker of light in the upper left.

I spun on my bare feet and saw a vibrant neon glow from that direction. A light beside it turned on, casting a faint glow. Then, one by one, tiers of masks came to life until the entire chamber was illuminated by rows of silent masks staring down at me.

The masks varied in color and style, though they all had the same *X* as eyes. Some displayed unsettling grins while others had scowls or thin lines.

Even at a distance, they felt looming, as if they were right above me.

A soft light shone a few feet away, drawing my attention toward it. I noticed another group of masked figures in robes seated around a long table.

The arrangement struck me immediately, as if they were mirroring Da Vinci's *Last Supper*. But instead of saints and apostles, they were devils.

Knelt before them was a line of other masked men, their heads bowed.

The door behind me creaked open. Another masked man entered the chamber, cloaked in the same robe as the others. He moved straight toward me.

By his height, broad shoulders, and the way he carried himself, I knew instantly it was Enzo.

I loathed myself for the small surge of relief that swept through me.

Stop it, Blair. This man is why you're here.

Why you just went through mental hell.

He nearly drowned you. Humiliated you. Cut your fucking hair.

Yet, in this moment, I craved to run to him for refuge.

To beg him to stop this.

Realization hit me. That was probably their strategy with us.

Break the Fawns down until we clung to the very men destroying us.

How profoundly fucked up.

These predators, the very creatures that hunted us, were now our saviors.

Enzo crossed the chamber in long, steady strides, and a light came on above me.

Glancing at my bare feet, I noticed symbols carved in the floor.

Intricate markings, like they were used during rituals.

My gaze lifted back to Enzo. The mask might've hidden his eyes, but I could still feel the weight of his intense stare.

My mind screamed for me to run. But my body only calmed when he came closer.

He towered over my smaller frame and bowed his head to look at me.

In what felt like slow motion, he reached out, his leather glove cupping my face beneath the hood.

I shivered, goose bumps rising along my skin, and I winced at the sudden intimacy when he brushed his thumb along my cheek.

My eyes slipped closed at his gentleness, as if he knew that single touch would force my body to surrender to him.

"Kneel," he ordered.

Before giving me a chance to obey, he placed his hand on the top of my head and forced me down.

Pissed off, I tried to stand, but he shoved me back down.

The man who'd escorted me to the room approached us.

"Who kneels before the Son?" he asked, his voice sounding monotone, as if deliberately disguised.

"*Electa mea*," Enzo replied.

My chosen in Latin.

"Is she unclaimed?"

"Yes."

"Mark her. Name her. Bind her."

A low chorus rose from the masked figures around the chamber.

"A Fawn claimed is a Fawn protected. With blood, she is chosen. From us, she shall be free. Stay loyal. Do not run."

The words vibrated through the room like a biblical prayer.

Enzo grasped my hand and pulled me to my feet before lowering my hood. My breath caught in my throat.

He turned my wrist in his grip, exposing my palm. For a moment, he studied it, his index finger tracing the line like he was reading a map and searching for his next stop.

When the man beside him handed over a knife, my fingers curled inward.

The blade caught the light, and I recognized it as the one he'd played that stupid knife game with.

My pulse pounded when he traced the same lines as before with the tip of the blade.

I squeezed my eyes tight when the blade pierced my skin, sharp pain shooting up my arm. A single tear slipped free before I could stop it.

"Eyes on me," Enzo snapped. "Do not fucking look away."

The command was quiet, meant for only me to hear.

My eyes flew open just as the blade dragged across my palm. Another sting burned through my wrist as it split my skin. Blood welled around the fresh cut.

"Electa mea," he said in a low rumble.

I wished I could see his face.

The mask hid every clue to what he felt in this moment.

I kept my cut hand still, afraid one wrong move would ruin the ritual.

Enzo freed his other hand from the robe and returned the knife back to the man beside him. Then he peeled off his glove and extended his palm.

Without hesitation, the man sliced into it.

The cut was deeper than the one Enzo had given me.

A sharp hiss escaped me before I could stop it, like I was reacting to the pain Enzo should've felt.

Blood spilled from the wound, but he didn't flinch.

His posture stayed loose, his body calm, as though pain meant nothing to him.

As though he welcomed it.

As blood dripped from his hand to the floor, Enzo reached for mine and pressed our wounded palms together.

His grip was firm.

Like he never wanted to let me go.

Warm blood slicked between our fingers.

He left it there for *one second, two seconds, three seconds.*

When he let go, it felt like I'd lost a vital organ.

His bloody palm rose to my cheek. He smeared our blood across my skin, his fingers dragging slowly over my face.

His grip tightened, as if he wanted the blood to seep beneath my skin, into my veins, to mark me as deeply as he could.

To infect me with himself so part of him would always live inside me.

The tension drained from my shoulders when he eased his hand away.

But the relief didn't last.

His hand moved to my other cheek and did the same before trailing to my lips, coating them with our blood.

I couldn't break eye contact when he gathered more from my cheek onto his finger and pressed it to my mouth.

I barely had time to react before he forced his finger past my lips.

I gagged, tasting the coppery tang of his blood mixed with mine.

He pushed it so deep I choked on it before slowly withdrawing it.

I watched in stunned silence as he tore off his mask and tossed it aside. It hit the floor with a quiet thud.

Our eyes met beneath the harsh lights.

In that moment, during the ritual that bound me to him, I'd never felt more exposed.

His eyes were like fire, the burn consuming me from the inside out.

Agonizingly slow, he lifted his blood-covered finger and slid it between his lips, sucking it clean.

He closed his eyes, his shoulders loosening, as if the taste soothed every muscle in his body.

Like it was the drug he needed to settle himself.

He opened his eyes and stared back at me.

"She is Chosen," the man standing beside us declared. "She is Sworn. The Fawn is claimed."

And just like that, with a little blood and a few words, I was officially a Fawn.

I belonged to Enzo ... though I had no idea what that meant.

I was stepping into a world I didn't understand, and I was fucking terrified.

Nineteen

Blair

I woke up in another unfamiliar room.

Relief washed over me when I realized I wasn't lying half naked on a concrete floor.

I was tucked beneath soft blankets on a large bed in a stark-white room. A mirror with a border resembling the stained glass windows in the university stretched across one wall. Knowing the Night Sons, that was probably a two-way mirror.

A sea of plush pillows was piled high around me like personal bodyguards. As I tried to burrow myself into the softness of the blankets, I felt a tight tug on my arm.

I gulped when I saw the IV line running from my arm to the pole beside the bed. A bag of clear fluid hung from it, dripping into my veins.

My fingers wrapped around the needle in my arm, and I tugged. A sharp pinch shot beneath my skin.

I started to rip the damn thing out but froze when the door opened.

Enzo stepped inside, his gaze drifting from my arm to the IV bag. "Stop that, Blair," he ordered as he closed the door behind him.

My face flushed when he crossed the room dressed in a black

suit. His hair was combed back and neat. He looked polished and proper, yet no less dangerous. Just dangerous in a different way.

Dangerous like the mafia heir he was.

The sight of him sent a shiver through me. I hated how attractive he was.

Ignoring the sting as the needle shifted in my arm, I tugged at it again.

"Go ahead, then." He sighed, loosening the buttons of his blazer. He shrugged out of the jacket and draped it over the leather chair across from the bed. "Rip it out. I'll make you drink that entire bag of fluid in one gulp."

My hand immediately dropped away from the IV.

He rolled the sleeves of his black button-up to his elbows while leaning against the wall, crossing his ankles while staring me down. My gaze jumped to his hand he'd cut last night.

There was no bandage.

Then it dropped to mine.

There wasn't one there either, but I did notice four neat, fresh stitches in the center of my palm.

I nodded toward the IV. "Are you drugging me?"

He started inspecting his nails. "You needed electrolytes."

"Are there drugs in this?"

"No."

"Then what's in it?"

"Potassium, magnesium, chloride, and sodium. No drugs." A smirk played at his wicked lips. "Promise."

"Well, thanks for not drugging me *this time*."

"Initiations tend to dehydrate Fawns. That will replenish your strength."

I had no idea how long I'd been asleep, what day it was, or when the last time I'd eaten or had anything to drink.

After Enzo had cut our hands and declared me his, everything had gone blurry.

Strangely, I'd expected a bloodier Initiation.

I'd imagined animal sacrifices or brutal violence. Instead, they had chosen another kind of torture. Psychological.

Their goal had been to ruin my sanity, strip me down to nothing, then rebuild me into whatever they wanted.

Military training for Fawns.

He pushed off the wall and walked to the IV stand, checking the bag. It was almost empty.

My eyes narrowed when he leaned across the bed and took hold of my arm. He stretched it out, and with practiced precision, removed the IV from my vein. Pain stung as the needle slid free.

A small bead of blood formed at the puncture site.

The way his breathing changed as he stared at it sent shivers through my bones. His throat bobbed with a swallow, and instead of bandaging the spot, he ran his thumb through the drop and gathered it onto his finger.

I stared at him, stunned, when he lifted that finger to his mouth the same way he'd tasted my blood last night.

I yanked my arm away before he could keep playing Dracula. "Is that some kind of fetish you have?"

He lifted a single brow, then gave his finger another slow lick.

I motioned toward my arm. "Blood."

The smile that touched his mouth looked rare. It lacked the cruelty of his usual one, making him seem almost normal. Almost like a man with an actual conscience.

"Why do you ask? Does blood turn you on?"

"No, because I'm not a fucking vampire."

"Nor am I."

"Right. Normal people"—I shoved my thumb against my chest—"*like me*, don't suck people's blood."

His smile grew. "You don't need to worry about sucking my blood, Blair. You'll focus more on sucking my cock."

"I think the hell not."

Any amusement vanished from his smile.

It settled back into his typical threatening shape.

I was paying too much attention to his face and not enough

to his hands. I yelped when he ripped the blankets off me, exposing the short black nightie clinging to my body.

One of the nighties he'd stolen from my drawer days ago.

In a single motion, he caught my ankle, turned me, and dragged me to the edge of the bed.

I kicked at him, but the difference in our strength was that of David and Goliath. When my hips hung halfway off the mattress, he forced my legs apart and stepped between them.

My eyes burned with hatred as his hands skimmed up my thighs, fingers slipping beneath my nightie.

I tried to slap them away, but one hand left my thigh to catch my wrist.

He shook his head in quiet disappointment, then warning, before releasing me. My breathing turned labored when he pressed his palms to my thighs, pinning me to the bed.

Our eyes locked, but neither of us spoke.

I waited, almost desperately, for his next move.

He dragged his tongue slowly across his lower lip, staring me down.

A warm heat rushed up my face. No matter how insane I thought he was, a traitorous part of me wanted to know what it'd feel like for Enzo to touch me in places he hadn't yet.

I'd never felt so exposed, but I was grateful that whoever had changed my clothes left my panties on.

But the way Enzo looked at me made me doubt they'd stay there long.

Just as that thought hit, he hooked his fingers into my panties, dragged them down my legs, and tossed them aside. He cupped his cut hand around my center and squeezed it tight in possession.

My knees pressed around his waist, locking him in place because I was just as batshit crazy for thinking any of this was a good idea.

His grip eased, and a second later, his fingers moved through the slick heat between my legs. His stare fixed there.

"Fuck, you're so wet," he muttered under his breath before pushing a finger inside me.

I sucked in a breath, arching my back against the mattress.

"And tight," he added, more to himself than to me.

I clutched the blanket in my fists when he added another finger, plunging them so deep inside me that I swore he was close to reaching my heart.

His eyes stayed on my face, watching my every reaction, watching the unbearable tension roll through me.

When he shifted lower, kneeling so his face was level with my hips, my pulse set on fire. I should've been embarrassed with his face *right there*, but for some reason, all I wanted was for him to give me more before I had to beg for it.

The veins in his neck pulsed, his face ticcing, as he parted my folds with pure focus.

"See," he muttered. "You're not the only one who kneels in this arrangement." His voice lowered, now rougher as he nuzzled his lips against my folds. "But don't take that kindness for weakness. This is still one-sided, but remember, I always take care of what belongs to me." He ran his tongue up my slit once, and his warm breath drifted along my skin. "I'll give you pleasure, my Fawn. So much of it that when this is over, you'll feel empty without me. You'll beg for me when I discard you. For the rest of my life, you'll ache for me everywhere."

Shoot, I'm aching for him now.

Burning from the inside out for him to touch me.

A sharp inhale left him and then a *ptui*.

I shot up, digging my elbows into the mattress, while staring at a madman.

Did he ... did he just spit inside me?

Before I could ask him what the actual hell, he shoved his finger inside me, swirling it in a circle, while inching his head closer.

I cried out at his first lick, the fire inside me intensifying with each one after.

My head lolled back, my body relaxing more than it had in years as he devoured me like his favorite meal.

I hadn't expected to surrender to Enzo like this.

I'd planned to make this hard on him, to give him hell, to show him that not all Fawns were obedient.

Damn, did he prove me wrong.

My knees shook around him, hitting the sides of his face, but he didn't seem to care.

He only kept licking, sucking, and pushing his fingers deep inside me. I slammed my eyes shut, and I gave in to the pleasure of his tongue.

With every heaving breath, I moaned, gasped, and begged him for more. It was the first time anyone had done this to me, and instead of feeling shy, I was nearly feeding myself to him.

My bottom dipped more off the bed as I tried to bring myself as close to his mouth as I could.

He lowered one hand there to hold me in place.

I was close. So close to *that moment,* the one you read in books and saw in movies, when someone fell apart.

He abruptly pulled away, straightening his back, and stood tall over me. "You want to come, Blair?" He licked his lips.

I glared at him, unable to form words.

He backed away until the wall caught him, then rested against it again. "Do you want to come, Blair?"

I only nodded.

He untucked his shirt from his pants. "Crawl to me then. I'll give you what you want."

"What?" I sputtered out.

He steepled his hands together. "You're probably feeling so empty right now, aren't you?" Mockery lined his tone. "You want my tongue back in your pussy, don't you? Come here to me, and I'll give you what you want."

"Please," I whimpered.

He didn't say another word.

He'd said his piece, given his demand, and now it was my turn to follow it.

My need for my pleasure outweighed my logic. I slid off the bed and dropped to my knees.

Our eyes met like a car crash as I crawled on all fours to him. The rug's texture was rough against my skin. It was better than concrete at least.

He unbuckled his pants when I reached him.

This time, I was the one at eye level with his waist.

"You want an orgasm, Blair?" he asked as he unzipped.

"Yes," I said in almost a desperate whimper.

"You'll suck my cock with those pretty lips first." His hips shifted as he pulled his pants down to his knees.

My jaw dropped open when his cock sprang forward.

Not because I was ready to take him in my mouth.

Because he was fucking huge.

In both length and thickness.

I doubted it'd fit in my mouth without causing jaw pain.

My gaze fixated on his cock, seeing the aching purple tip and the small bead of liquid seeping out. He didn't allow much time for my appraisal before sinking his fingers into my hair and holding me in place.

He reached down and touched my teeth with his free hand, running his finger across my sharp canine, as if craving to cut himself.

His cock twitched once. Twice.

He dropped his hand from my mouth to stroke himself once and groaned.

"Open wide, my sweet Fawn." He tightened his grip on his cock. "It's time you suck my cock. Then your Initiation will be complete."

He guided his cock to my mouth, running it across my lips. "Open wider for me, Blair."

I relaxed my jaw more before taking him in my throat.

He pushed himself deeper in, and I choked.

A near-praise grunt escaped him. "Has there ever been a cock inside this mouth before?"

I shook my head, though technically lying to him.

There had been one time, but it was only for a fraction of a second. In my freshman year of college, I'd attempted to give a guy a blow job. As soon as my teeth brushed his cock, he shoved me away and fled.

That was when I knew that intimacy and sex weren't for me. I had grown up hearing that it was evil. It seemed that Enzo was breaking that belief out of me.

"Suck me, Blair," he grunted, pumping his hips forward.

I pulled my head back, circling my tongue on his tip and in the narrow slit, causing his knees to buckle. Exciting him motivated me, and I sucked him harder.

When he pressed his stomach against my forehead, hard and rough, desire trickled through me like he was injecting something else into my veins.

The entire time I sucked him, he praised me.

Called me his good Fawn.

He tugged my hair, firm, then soft, guiding me how he wanted me to suck him.

A long moan left him when I raised my hand and jerked him off in sync with my mouth.

Every muscle in his legs tightened in front of me as his breathing became raspy. He stopped his talking, now just lengthy breaths leaving him.

The first trickle of his cum caught me off guard, and I hurriedly swallowed it down.

He patted my cheek in approval. "Swallow my cum, Blair, and I swear, it'll be the best damn electrolyte you've ever had."

I choked down the salty taste of him.

His entire body shook as he released himself, coating nearly my entire mouth. He held me by the hair, holding my head still, until I swallowed every last drop.

Still gripping my hair, he hauled me to my feet and spun us, forcing me against the wall now. He ripped my nightgown, tossed it aside, and with no bra on, I was completely bare to him.

There was the chance someone was watching us through the two-way mirror, but I didn't care. I was too turned on.

As I glanced down, that was when I noticed it.

The tattoo of a broken halo and antlers beside my navel.

"Did you—"

His mouth went between my legs, and the pleasure of his tongue and mouth inside me shut me up. He'd marked me without my permission, yet I still couldn't stand up to him, afraid he'd stop touching me exactly where I needed it most.

"Oh my God, yes," I cried out.

Enzo was reaching places inside me I never knew existed.

I'd never masturbated before. Though I was sure even if I had, the pleasure would never have come close to this.

The evil motherfucker had special orgasm powers.

The devil was great at oral, it seemed.

My fingers wove through his hair, and I tugged on his strands. I lost focus on everything as heat and butterflies washed over me.

So far, this Fawn thing wasn't so bad.

But I had a feeling this was the calm before the storm.

The pleasure before he destroyed me.

"Get dressed," Enzo ordered.

I'd just collapsed onto the floor, still coming down from the high of the orgasm he'd given me.

"We have a funeral to attend." He grabbed my ripped night-gown, tossing it in a small trash can in the corner, and motioned toward a door. "Bathroom. Everything you need is in there."

"Funeral?" I muttered, trying to collect my thoughts. "Whose funeral?"

He didn't answer me.

"Jett's funeral?"

A rush of selfishness hit me.

So much had happened with Enzo that I'd forgotten the Night Sons had murdered Jett.

I'd just sucked off and let a murderer go down on me.

Way to go, Blair.

Come to think of it, no one talked about Jett.

No one at the university had announced the death of a fellow student. The only mention came when Daphne saw the notifications on her phone that morning. Otherwise, silence. It was as if Jett had never existed.

Is Enzo really making me attend his funeral?

Is Enzo attending his funeral?

No one wanted their murderer going to their funeral.

Jett had died for telling me the truth.

Even if he was a shitty person, he'd be alive if he hadn't tried to warn me.

And this man in front of me, wiping my juices off his lips, was the reason.

"Chop-chop, Blair," he said with the snap of his fingers. "And, no, you don't have to see Jett's ugly-ass corpse. It's another loser's funeral."

TWENTY

ENZO

I'd never taken my Fawns off campus with me, but today, that changed.

If I had to endure the hell of fake grieving at the funeral of a man I'd killed, then Blair could suffer through it too.

My reluctance to attend the funeral for Hedgeford—the senator's son whose car we had blown up—wasn't from guilt. I felt none of that.

Guilt was a sign of weakness—something anyone with two fucking brain cells should know better than to feel.

Hedgeford had tried to blackmail Brooks. He should've seen his death coming.

But to save face, I'd go.

My father, who hated attending anything, was pissed at me for having to do the same. He typically forced Benny or me to go to events on behalf of the family.

When I heard Blair's shower water running, I pushed the bathroom door open to find her wrapped in a towel and checking the water's temperature.

"Keep that tattoo dry." I gestured to her stomach.

She pulled her hand from the water and flicked it at me. "You can't just mark people whenever you want."

I tapped my knuckles against the doorframe. "That's where you're mistaken, my sweet Fawn."

I stepped into the bathroom, trapping her against the shower's glass wall. My mouth curved into a cruel smirk when I tugged the towel from her body.

When she reached for it, I snatched her wrist to stop her.

Lowering my head, I whispered in her ear, "I can mark you, fuck you, do anything I want with this sweet body."

She shuddered as I crawled my fingers down the soft skin of her hips.

"Now, don't get that tattoo wet, or I'll make sure it's marked on your forehead next time." To emphasize my words, I tapped her forehead with one hand and smacked her ass with the other. "Come on. We don't have much time. Someone made me run late by making me eat her pussy."

As soon as I retreated a step, she quickly snatched the towel and wrapped it back around her. On my way out of the room, I grabbed my blazer and threw it over my shoulder.

I cracked my neck as I walked down the corridor toward a secret door hidden in a wall of stone around the corner.

After I scanned my fingerprint, the door slid open, revealing a dark tunnel. I stalked through it and made a beeline for Locker Hall.

"How's she doing?" Brooks asked when I walked in. He shrugged into his black blazer.

"Fine, given the circumstances," I replied.

"She seemed strong until we played that song."

I nodded.

"How fucked up that a lullaby was her weakness."

"I need to find out *why*, the significance of it all."

"The fact that someone had tipped us off on her trauma means they knew she'd been chosen, knew when her Initiation was." He kicked his foot up on a bench to tie his shoes.

"It had to have been her stepfather."

"Have you figured out who he is?"

"Not yet."

"I'll make sure the other Sons keep their ears open."

"Appreciate it."

"It's fucking bullshit we have to attend this funeral."

I pitied Brooks more than myself today. The funeral would be broadcast on TV and streamed live. The cameras would be on him and his family, so he had to pretend to mourn the pussy-ass bitch we'd killed. At least I could sit in the back with no cameras in my face.

Good thing I had been born to a mobster and not the president.

I could've never faked it like Brooks.

"You want to ride with me?" Brooks asked.

"Nah." I shook my head. "I'm taking Blair with me."

He dropped the Rolex he had been clasping around his wrist. "Seriously?"

"Yeah," I said as he stooped to pick it up.

"Since when do you do shit like that with Fawns?"

"Consider it another form of torture."

He grinned. "See you there then."

I left Locker Hall and headed back to Blair's room in her Fawn Quarters, hoping she didn't decide to drown herself in the shower. Or slit her wrists with the razor. Both had happened before.

Not to any of my Fawns.

My past Fawns had preferred to go crazy or jump out windows like they were in fucking *Peter Pan*.

After Initiation, Fawns were assigned a personal room within the tunnels. Sometimes, we'd instruct them to stay in those rooms for our convenience. Other times, if we wanted to avoid them, we'd make them stay in their dorms.

Everything depended on our moods.

Everything was always about us.

Like I'd told Blair, being a Fawn was hell, but I'd make sure she felt a little pleasure along with it.

To limit their knowledge about us and the tunnels, they had a private entrance. The hidden door I'd gone through was the only way to enter the rest of the tunnels. Most didn't even know there were more tunnels, chambers, or even the Devil's Lair.

While Blair had passed her Initiation, her work was far from over.

She still had plenty to prove.

She was a Fawn now and had taken an oath to me.

I needed to make sure she fulfilled that. We'd watch her every second of every day until we were comfortable giving her more freedom. I'd linked her phone and emails to my devices. When she got a call, text, or notification, I received it as well.

Not that she knew that. You never told someone you were tracking them.

I whistled as I walked, shocked and satisfied that Blair had surrendered so easily to me earlier. And, fuck, she'd tasted delicious.

The sweetest Fawn I'd ever had.

Though we needed to work on her oral skills.

While she had made me come—which I blamed on the fact that I'd been dreaming about her mouth on my cock since I'd fucking seen her—the blow job had been subpar. Her lack of cocksucking skills wasn't a problem for me. I preferred it because it usually meant she lacked the experience of having other cocks in her mouth.

I stopped my whistling, and my cock twitched in my slacks as I imagined how satisfying fucking her would feel.

Closing my eyes, I thought of all the positions I'd take her in.

All the ways I'd give her pleasure and pain.

When I returned to her room, I found her blow-drying her hair in the bathroom. The towel was knotted at her front, and her feet were bare, still dripping with water.

She turned off the blow dryer when she noticed me and gestured toward the items spread along the large vanity. "How did you know what products I use?"

When we gave Fawns rooms, we made sure everything they used daily was in there. We wanted them to feel comfortable here.

"I went through the bathroom in your dorm," I answered simply.

"Of course you did," she grumbled, rolling her eyes. "Speaking of invasion of privacy, who dressed and undressed me for this stupid Initiation thing?"

I clicked my tongue against the roof of my mouth in frustration.

Those electrolytes and my cum must've recharged her, restoring her attitude. They also must've given her the balls to disrespect the Initiation and me. She needed to be fucking grateful she was alive and not in the ground with Jett.

I inched into the bathroom, and she froze as I stood behind her.

My voice turned volatile as I pressed her body into the vanity. "Just because I ate your pussy doesn't mean I'll tolerate disrespect." I unplugged the blow dryer and took it from her.

She jumped when I smacked it against the vanity, breaking it. My heart skipped a beat in satisfaction when she pressed her palms against the vanity, trying to shove me off her as I loosely wrapped the cord around her neck.

I applied only a bit of pressure to remind her of her place.

Not tight enough to kill her.

Just enough to scare her.

I waited until I saw that fear deep in her eyes.

Until her mouth fell open, tiny gasps leaving her throat.

Snarling, I curled my upper lip and shoved her into the vanity, cord still wrapped around her throat. "Watch your tone and words when you speak to me, Fawn." I spat out the last word, not even bothering with pleasantries this time.

She released a single exaggerated gasp, and I rolled my eyes at her dramatics.

This wasn't even enough pressure to break a windpipe, let alone kill her.

Bored and short on time, I released one of her hands. That hand immediately went to her throat in an attempt to pull the cord away.

I snatched her wrist again, returned it to the vanity, and slid the cord up and down her throat. She choked again as I gave it one final tug and released her, pushing her forward until her ass was in the air.

As bad as I wanted to keep playing, I couldn't bring her to the funeral with strangulation marks around her neck.

People may think I'm not a great upstanding citizen.

With the blow dryer still in my hand, I retreated a step and hurled it toward the glass shower door. One crack formed before the entire thing shattered, shards flying across the room.

Blair recoiled from the sharp glass, careful around her bare feet, while holding her hands around her throat, massaging her fingers into the skin.

I crouched, picking up a shard, and pushed her back into the vanity. Her breathing shuddered as I pressed the shard point against her throat before lowering it to her stomach and circling the tattoo.

"Blair, I don't offer many warnings," I said. "And you saw me with Jett. You know the terror and violence I'm capable of." Raising my hand, I used the shard to scratch my neck, finding pleasure from it scraping my skin. "Be a good Fawn, and you won't get slaughtered."

I threw the shard in the sink and left the bathroom.

Let that be a fucking lesson to her.

Political figures, lobbyists, and opportunists crowded the cathedral for Hedgeford Mitchell's funeral. I was sure a few were genuinely mourning the idiot, but my money was not on many.

Maybe the group of frat boys in the corner, looking hungover and creepy.

From what I'd learned about Hedgeford, he didn't brighten rooms when he walked in. He was a lame-dick fucker who tried to blackmail Brooks on his father's behalf.

Like a duckling, Blair trailed me as I searched the cathedral for my father and Benny. I found them on the other side, having an in-depth conversation with New York City's mayor. Same as me, they both wore black suits with black ties.

It didn't surprise me that my mother wasn't here. My father hated her attending events that could put her in danger. Political gatherings were always risky.

When Benny glanced up, seeing us, he signaled for me to come over. They walked away from the mayor moments before we reached them.

"Who's this?" my father asked, his cold stare fixed on Blair.

I hadn't given them a heads-up that I was bringing her with me, for this very reason. He'd warned me not to.

Blair scooted closer to me, as if I was suddenly her protector.

That's right, sweet Fawn.

See me as that.

See me as all you have.

Because then it'll prove just how much I own you.

I didn't blame her. My father was fucking terrifying.

It was why I admired him so much.

His name instilled fear in people.

Even looking at him made them cower.

Benny carried that same stature, and when people looked at me when I entered the cathedral, I felt it too. The Marchettis were feared, no matter what age bracket you were in.

"Blair," I answered, offering no further explanation.

I wouldn't with Blair present or in public.

He nodded, but the displeasure was clear on his face.

Heat crept onto Blair's cheeks as she started to raise her hand to shake my father's, but quickly caught on that it wasn't a good idea. Her arm collapsed to her side as my father looked away from her. He left us and walked toward the New York governor, pulling him into the conversation that needed to be had.

We were trying to make a deal here.

Word was, the new city sheriff wanted to make trouble for us.

That meant the sheriff would be dead soon, and we needed to make sure no trace of evidence led back to us.

Benny, having some kind of fucking manners, nodded at Blair.

She tipped her head toward him timidly, bowing almost.

I led us to the end of the back pew. We sat there silently as I took in my surroundings. Brooks and Adelina stood at the nave of the cathedral with their parents, speaking to the senator and his wife.

Nothing in Brooks's demeanor suggested that he was responsible for Hedgeford lying cold inside that casket. Well, what was left of him.

Unfortunately, the family had chosen a closed casket. I'd already texted Brooks to ask because I wanted to see what they'd managed to do with the body. It turned out that piecing him back together had been too gruesome for public viewing.

I couldn't stop myself from smirking as I remembered the night we'd planted the bomb under the current corpse's car. While I usually preferred to stay and watch my work in action, we couldn't be caught in that area.

It seemed we hadn't been careful enough. Being caught on camera was embarrassing, and I'd never let it happen again. It wasn't only the Sons at risk if we were caught. My family was also on the line.

My gaze drifted to Adelina and the First Lady. Adelina hugged the senator's wife, who was weeping uncontrollably.

I smirked at Adelina flinching when a bit of snot from the senator's wife landed on the shoulder of her black dress.

All of us were so good at pretending.

As I glanced sideways, I found Blair also watching them.

She didn't seem surprised or awed by seeing the heads of our country. Cracking my neck, I wondered if she was around people like this often, and that was why she was so comfortable.

Fuck, I needed to find out who her stepfather was.

We slid over when my father and Benny approached our pew, making room for them to sit. Other people started taking their seats as the priest stepped to the podium, tapping the microphone to check it.

When he started speaking, I pulled out my phone. I caught up on emails, the latest news, and researched Hedgeford's sister. We needed dirt on Hedgeford to ruin his father's campaign, but if we couldn't find enough, we'd resort to his sister as backup.

My father and Benny were also on their phones.

Benny, next to me, tapped his foot, as bored as I was.

The priest babbled on about Hedgeford's life and mediocre accomplishments.

First off, who the fuck named their kid that?

It sounded like a fucking landscaping company.

When my phone started to bore me, I slipped my attention to Blair.

Her posture was perfect, like always, as she sat with her hands folded in her lap. She listened to the priest, taking in his words, not pretending like most of us.

I shifted in the pew, my dick getting hard as I stared at her.

I craved to feel those plump pink lips around my cock again.

Leaning in closer, I noticed a glimpse of a mark around her slim neck.

Just a tiny one.

I licked my lips, wishing I could trail my tongue along that mark.

Her hair was pulled back in a black bow. I had a feeling she'd done that because she wanted to get back on my good side after the little cord incident.

I'd had Seraphina order Blair's funeral dress. I was going to burn something in Seraphina's room for ordering something so bland and boring. The sleeves hit above Blair's elbows, and the length reached her knees.

It wasn't what I'd have chosen, but I had been too caught up in planning her Initiation to worry about funeral clothes.

Unable to stop myself, I lowered my hand and brushed it along her thigh.

Her attention left the priest, looking over at me, and when she attempted to scoot over, her hip hit the woman's beside her.

"Sorry," she grumbled to the woman, shooting me a dirty look.

I reached down and ran my thumb along the mark on her neck.

She bit into her bottom lip, but didn't pull away, not wanting to make a scene.

Benny's voice pulled my attention away from Blair.

"Since when do you bring women around?" he asked in a hushed voice beside me.

"Since Dad forced me to attend stupid shit like this," I remarked with a huff.

"I'm not happy about this either." He shoved his elbow into my side, causing me to grunt. "We're here because of you. Hopefully, you learned your fucking lesson."

My tone lowered so only he could hear my words. "I'll make sure my blowing-up skills get better." Tension built up in my neck as the words left me. I hated making mistakes.

The funeral dragged on for three fucking hours.

Three hours of my life wasted on this bullshit.

I almost stood and asked them to speed this shit up.

No way that idiot's life deserved three hours of mourning by strangers.

When the funeral finally ended, we followed my father and Benny outside. I led Blair down the sidewalk toward the corner, my hand plastered at the base of her back but wanting to venture lower.

"A word," my father said to me.

I nodded, giving Blair a glance that I hoped said, *Keep your ass there*, and walked along the edge of the grass. Benny joined us as my father stared at me sternly, a slight frown on his face.

"Do not bring a woman with you to something like this again." He jabbed his finger in my face, though still kept his composure. "I'm looking for a wife for you. Women don't want their potential husbands parading other women around. If you want to fuck her, fuck her, but keep it discreet."

I held back from telling him she was my Fawn.

My father wasn't a fan of the Fawn ordeal.

I shoved my hands into my pockets, annoyed but trying to conceal it. "Still on that arranged-marriage kick?"

Benny shook his head at my disrespect.

My father's face turned rigid. "Sure fucking am. And I will be until I find your wife and you say your fucking vows." He violently shook his head. "Make problems for me, and I won't be picky about my selection."

"Will you do the same with Seraphina?" I questioned.

Benny blew an upward breath.

"No, and watch your mouth." My father's finger was in my face again. "You know your role in this family. The male responsibilities are arranged marriages. Period. It won't change with you. With anyone. *Ever*." He scratched the side of his nose, gaining his composure. "And before you leave, the president wants to speak with you."

"You have no idea the amount of damage that you've caused."

A gleeful smirk spread across my face as I watched the president of the United States throw a baby-ass tantrum like someone had stolen his favorite binky.

He hurled a glass of whiskey across the makeshift office in the laundromat. It was a business through which Antonio laundered money.

He allowed us to hold meetings with the president here because it was too risky elsewhere.

The glass collided with the wall, shattering, and reminded me of breaking the shower glass earlier with Blair.

Seeing President Byron lose his shit over the senator was comical. Any sane man would've just killed the senator and gone about his day.

Well, any man in my world.

The rest of the world, if the men couldn't pull triggers easily, they paid us to do it.

President Byron slammed his hand on the rusted metal desk as he glued his eyes to Brooks and me seated in front of him. "Do you have any idea how this has hurt my campaign?" His face turned as red as a fucking tomato. "You saw how many people attended his funeral. His idiot fucking son's death resonated with voters and boosted his popularity. The margins have slimmed." His upper lip snarled. "The public feels bad for him."

"I don't feel bad for him," I said from my chair, shrugging.

To further show my disrespect toward everyone, I propped my foot up on the desk and examined a hangnail on my index finger.

President Byron shot me a sharp, disapproving glare.

He needed to correct his fucking attitude, or my little vote would go to the senator. Brooks shook his head before burying his face in his hands.

President Byron's glare intimidated me the same way Barney the dinosaur did. He grabbed another glass from the desk, poured himself a fresh whiskey, downed it in one gulp, and smashed the glass onto the desk.

Brooks dropped his hands. "Let's leak damaging stories about Hedgeford. We can easily make people turn on the senator if we make them believe the son brought his death on himself."

"His son did bring his death upon himself," I said in a bored tone. I was already collecting a list of information to use against Hedgeford.

President Byron turned his head toward my father and Benny standing in the corner, giving them a silent expression, like asking how they dealt with me.

Benny, who was only half paying attention in the first place, looked up from his phone and shrugged.

While Brooks—and most of the population—respected the president, I lacked that regard. I lacked respect for almost everyone.

"Enzo," my father warned, though his voice was laced with amusement, knowing I'd gotten that trait honestly. He turned toward the president, irritation of his disrespect toward me clear on his face.

No man but him could disrespect me.

It didn't matter who you were.

Even the president needed to watch his fucking mouth.

"I've already started working on the sympathy issue," I said. "I'm gathering whatever I can about Hedgeford. As well as his sister. I'll pay some idiot to ask for nudes or record himself fucking her and then release it if need be." My feet hit the dirty concrete ground, and I stood from the chair. "Now, unless you have anyone you'd like me to murder, I have other priorities to attend to."

President Byron's shoulders slumped as he bowed his head, staring down at the desk, as if wishing it had the answers he needed.

The possibility of him losing his reelection had to be stressful as fuck.

If he lost, he could no longer use his government power as a tool for his own advantage. Those not in power couldn't profit from a crooked government.

I cracked my neck as I headed toward the door, bored with this conversation. While I didn't like the president, I knew him having more power meant my family had more power.

We needed to make sure that continued.

"We'll be in touch, Byron," my father told him, following me out of the office.

We ducked out from the hidden entrance and stepped into a room filled with old washing machines. The laundromat was hidden in a neglected area of the city. An area the president had promised to bring back to life but lied about to obviously get votes.

I needed to get back to Blair. I'd left her in my car, locked the doors, and warned her if she tried to run off, the people in this neighborhood wouldn't hesitate to rob her for a penny before killing her.

The bell above the entrance door rang, announcing our exit to absolutely nobody, and the sun hit my skin as I headed straight to my Porsche in the parking lot.

All my blood pumped to my ears, and I charged toward the car. Some ugly, balding motherfucker was outside Blair's door, slamming his fist against her window.

"Give me your shit, bitch!" he yelled with another bang.

No one scared my fucking Fawn but me.

No one fucking called her a bitch without paying for it with their life.

I told Blair that Fawns received protection, and she was about to witness it firsthand.

While I didn't look back, I could feel the presence of my father and Benny behind me. The guy was too focused on getting to Blair, now tugging on the door handle and cursing, to pay attention to me coming.

I wasn't one to give warnings.

I didn't want to scare him off. I wanted him to *pay* for scaring my little Fawn. I dug my leather gloves from my pocket, thankful I'd brought them, and shoved them onto my hands.

Once they were secure, I collected my knife from my back pocket, gripping the handle tight, and crept behind the guy. "Time to meet your judgment day, you junkie motherfucker."

He hissed when I tugged him in a headlock, holding him in place. As he tried to fight back, Benny stepped to my side and stuck his Glock to the side of the guy's temple.

We couldn't pull the trigger. Neither of our guns had silencers. If Secret Service heard the sound of even a single bullet in the vicinity of the president, they'd lose their shit.

I grinned as I slit the man's throat, tugging on the loose skin as I dug my knife in deep. When I cut through enough for blood to burst from his neck, I shoved him onto the dirty concrete. He wriggled on the ground like a fish out of water, gripping his throat, beside dirty cigarette butts and used needles.

Blood seeped through his throat as he gasped for words.

I knelt to his level, my eyes meeting his bloodshot ones.

"Please," he gurgled out, reaching for me like I was some savior.

"Please what?" I asked.

"H ... he ..."

I could tell he was trying to say *help*, but couldn't form the words.

He wanted my help?

Sure thing, buddy.

I drew my arm back and rammed my knife through his eyeball. He howled in pain. Chuckling, I shoved it deeper into the organ until I felt the tip of the knife hit skull and then the ground.

The guy was pinned down by the face with my knife but managed to thrash his body from side to side.

I rotated my wrist, digging deeper into his eye socket. Once he gurgled blood from his mouth, I drew the knife out a few inches to cut the optic nerve with perfect precision.

I grunted in annoyance at the slight resistance and wiggled the knife a few times to break his eyeball loose from the socket. The muscle around the eyeball broke, and I pulled it clean out and held it up like it was a marshmallow on a skewer I was ready to make s'mores with.

Blair needed to behave, or I'd make her fucking eat it.

Speaking of Blair...

As I stood, I looked into the window, and she stared back, horrified.

"Get her back to the university," Benny said. "I wish we had something that could zap this from her fucking memory."

"*Men in Black* style?" I asked with a slight chuckle.

"If she says a word—" my father started.

"Don't worry," I assured. "She knows talking means her death."

My dad nodded, though I could tell he didn't fully believe me. He slammed the heel of his loafer onto the man's face to quiet his whimpers. I heard bones crack.

Blair beat her fists against the window as I saluted them and circled the car. I slid the man's eye in my pocket, removed my gloves, and tossed them to Benny, who was also wearing gloves, to dispose of them.

When my hands were clear, I unlocked my car via the key fob and swung open the driver's door.

She scooted as far away from me as she could get when I slid into the car. I chuckled when she tried to open the door, but my father slammed it back shut in her face. She shrank back in her seat at the stern expression he gave her.

I slowly started the engine while my father and Benny headed toward the front of the laundromat, where my father's driver was waiting in the black SUV. Benny was on the phone, and I knew he was giving directions for someone to come dispose of this loser's body.

No one would miss that man.

In fact, I'd done the world a favor.

You're welcome, civilization.

When my father and Benny were almost to the SUV, Blair opened her door.

"Go ahead," I said, my voice stopping her from doing something stupid.

She froze, staring at me from over her shoulder.

"Hang out with his dead body. I'm sure his friends will come over to finish the job he wanted to. And this time, I won't be there to protect you."

"All he wanted was my purse," she argued, slamming the door shut, then holding said purse against her chest.

I clicked my tongue. "Silly, Blair. He wanted your purse, that necklace around your neck, and to fuck your pussy before dismembering your clit and wearing it as a fucking earring."

She winced, her eyes widening, and pounded her pointer and middle finger against her skull. "What the fuck is wrong with your demented-ass brain?"

"Everything," I said with a giant smirk before winking. "If you haven't already established that I'm crazy as fuck, Blair, then I guess I severely doubted the smarts of the Fawn that I'd chosen." I shifted the car into reverse and pounded my foot on the gas.

We sped back so fast that we nearly backed into the laundromat.

I turned the wheel, speeding out of the parking lot, noticing my father and Benny. I waved to his driver, grateful they'd taken up the job of cleaning up the body. As much as I loved killing, disposing of the bodies was always a fucking drag.

It took the high out of it.

Blair sat on her knees to look out the back window. "You're just going to leave his body there?"

"No, someone will come take out the trash." I grabbed a napkin from the center console, plucked the eye from the pocket, careful not to smash it, and held it out to her with the napkin. "You want it?"

I refused to touch the eye with my bare hands. As a germaphobe who also messed with blood, I made sure to always have gloves with me. Who knew what was in this guy's bloodstream?

"What? No!" she shrieked.

"Fair enough." I tossed it out the window and drove over it.

Twenty-One

Blair

I'd sworn an oath to a madman.

To the damn devil.

Sitting in the passenger seat, I stared at him, jaw dropped, struggling to process how he'd casually tossed an eyeball out the window.

During the *removal*, shock had drowned out the voice in my head that kept telling me to look away. I hadn't thought he'd actually take out the man's eye.

As I shut my eyes, my belly knotted, and I regretted my agreement to be his Fawn. Though it wasn't like I'd had any say in the situation. My only options had been to accept his proposal or die. And I very much enjoyed breathing.

If only I'd followed Daphne's advice and fled Saint Vale when we found out Enzo had selected me as a Fawn. I'd feared my stepfather's threat of Saint Vale being my last chance, but his repercussions of me leaving yet another university would've been less traumatizing than being stuck with a man who enjoyed plucking out eyeballs.

Technically, Enzo hadn't done it for pleasure.

In a strange sense, he'd done it to protect me, but he didn't have to go to such extreme measures. Simply punching the guy and leaving would've sufficed. De-eyeballing him wasn't necessary.

I'd learned that simplicity wasn't Enzo's style. He liked to be batshit crazy at all times. After meeting his father and brother, I understood where he had gotten it from. His father had had no issue stomping that guy's face in.

Jett had been right. They were most definitely Mafia.

While the man had been banging on my window and I was terrified, I could never paint Enzo as my knight in shining armor.

He was a killer who had killed that guy. Who killed Jett. Who might've killed his last Fawn … and I was sure plenty of other people.

Enzo drove through the neighborhood, passing run-down, neglected houses. We drove by homeless people sleeping on the streets and in tents. He suddenly slammed on the brakes to let an elderly woman cross the road.

A hint of a smile touched my lips at the softness on his face when he gestured for her to go forward. She raised her hand in a silent *thank you* before pushing her shopping cart ahead.

My smile dropped into a frown as my eyes met her saggy ones steeped in sorrow. Her cart was filled with random bags and clothing, telling me she was also homeless.

With my chest caving in, I knew that could've been the reality of my mother and me if my stepfather hadn't stepped in.

When she was safely on the other side of the road, Enzo hit the gas. He maintained a normal speed until we left the residential area and reached the highway.

As if speed limits didn't exist and he possessed no patience, he weaved between cars and lanes, not caring if the line separating the lanes was solid or dotted.

I sat in the leather seat, staring at him and committing his features to memory. After the funeral, he'd shed his blazer, draped it on the hook over the back seat, and pushed his sleeves to his elbows.

Tiny droplets of blood dotted his sleeve. The tendons in his jaw moved as he swallowed. He was always tense. I doubted even the best day of his life had brought him peace.

He darted around an eighteen-wheeler. His mouth was slightly parted, as if he was lost in thought.

How could someone so demented inside be so utterly gorgeous?

Before the Devil's downfall, the Bible described him as being a creature of beauty and perfection, but that very beauty bred arrogance and corruption. The demon by my side was beautiful, too, but unlike the biblical Devil, Enzo's looks weren't marred by his sins.

Dark memories drifted into my thoughts, and I remembered how I'd been accused of something so similar. My father had claimed that my beauty meant I had been sent by the Devil to spread evil.

"Now, Blair," Enzo said, snapping me out of going to that dark place, "we need to have a little chat." He ran his finger over his ring.

"I'd rather we spend the car ride in silence," I replied, flicking my nail against the thick stitching in the leather console.

"You have no say in the matter."

"I can keep my mouth shut and not say anything." I crossed my arms with a heavy huff. "How about that? It's not like you can pry my mouth open."

A smile tugged on his lips, and I should've known that was a prologue to his violence. He jerked the wheel so hard that my head connected with the window. Pain shot through my skull.

I worked my jaw to each side.

That was his soft caution to me to check my attitude.

A threat that, yes, he could pry my mouth open if he wanted. With how demented he was, I wouldn't be surprised if he could crawl down my throat, collect all the words I'd swallowed for years, and drag them back up to answer his questions.

Frowning, I rubbed the side of my head, still not speaking.

"Tell me about your stepfather," he said.

"Why?" I snapped.

"I'm curious."

I tilted my head to the side, biting into my lip. "A question for a question."

"I don't do ultimatums, Blair." He stepped on the gas, passing two cars, and a semi honked when he cut it off.

My heart was beating at the same speed as the car's.

"What's his name?" he asked.

"Bill."

He scoffed, throwing me a dirty look. "That's not his name."

My brows furrowed as I tried to match his expression. "How do you know?"

"What's he do for work?"

"Finance."

"What's his last name?" He fired the questions fast, trying to trip me up.

"I don't know."

"Don't lie to me, Blair." His dark eyes stayed on the road as the sun set to our right.

"Seriously, I don't know. I've met him maybe a handful of times. They prefer me away, which is why I'm at Saint Vale. Since the day my mother met him, I've either been at some boarding school or university."

He drummed his hand against the steering wheel, thinking.

Of my punishment, probably. Or the next psychotic thing to do to terrify me.

He leveled his elbow on the center console, glaring at me. "Do you want me to take your eye next?"

"I'd prefer you not because I still won't have that answer for you."

"I believe those words would change if I had a scalpel to your eye." He mockingly winked at me before making a slice motion under his brow. "I think you'd tell me everything I wanted to know about what was in your pretty little head."

I raised a shoulder, a sarcastic expression on my face. "So you think I'm pretty."

"I wouldn't have had you on your knees, choking on my cock, if I didn't."

I coughed, suppressing any argument I had back.

"Why did the government seal your records?"

How did he know that?

That meant he was getting too close to things I didn't want him to know.

Things he wasn't allowed to know.

I tried to hide the fear sinking inside me. "I don't know what records you're referring to."

He lowered the window, and a rush of cold air smacked me in the face. I held in a breath as he veered sharply into the other lane. Since that was what he'd done the entire drive, I expected him to rejoin the correct lane.

He stomped on the gas pedal, and we sped ahead, driving straight toward incoming traffic. The semi barreling in our direction blared its horn.

"You won't do it," I said through gritted teeth as I tried to maintain my composure and not let him witness my fear. My hair flew in every direction, and I swatted it away to keep my eyes on the road ahead of us.

He gripped the steering wheel tight with both hands, as if he were a race-car driver on his final lap, and turned his head. His haunting eyes locked with mine, brimmed with challenge.

I looked away, my lip trembling as we got closer to the semi.

"Don't tell me I won't do something. It only makes me enjoy that challenge," he said. "I value no lives, Blair. Including my own."

I winced, cupping my hands over my ears at the semi's blaring horn in the background.

The tight knot in my throat dissolved as I screamed, "Okay! Okay! My stepfather had them sealed!"

The semi's blinding headlights pierced the car, and I squeezed my eyes shut as Enzo jerked the wheel back into our lane, narrowly missing a minivan. He didn't ease the gas once we were safely back in our lane, keeping his illegal speed as he continued driving toward the university.

I sat there, heart pounding, waiting for him to list off the rest of his questions about everything he wanted to know. I didn't blame him for his curiosity, especially for someone who had access to everything like he did.

It was why the records had been sealed to begin with.

That way, no one knew who I was or where I'd come from.

The rest of the traffic grew more distant, and we passed fewer cars the closer we got to returning to Saint Vale.

Enzo went quiet at the wheel, his lack of speaking pissing me off after he'd jeopardized my life for a question that he didn't even follow up with.

Staring out the window, I didn't say a word as my body shook. I rested my head against it and released deep sighs to relax.

I drew back when he turned onto a gravel path with a rusted sign that said *PRIVATE PROPERTY*.

He drove a few feet until we were completely hidden among tall trees, and the highway was no longer visible. My muscles tightened when he released his seat belt, and I balled my fist around the door handle.

I gasped as he climbed over the console and quickly straddled me in my seat.

It was a tight fit, and his weight kept me in place. I attempted to wriggle, lifting my hips to buck him off me, as he pinned my wrists above my head.

I writhed, terrified of what his next move would be, while breathing in the scent of him, mingled with the seat's fresh leather.

He rammed his hips into mine, pushing me more into the seat. "I want answers, Blair."

I hated that I groaned before crying out, "I don't know what you want from me. I don't have the answers you're looking for."

"You have secrets." He lowered his head to the crook of my neck and sucked on my skin. "You know why I love cracking open people's secrets?"

Goose bumps dotted my skin, and I trembled when he released one of my hands. His rough palm skimmed beneath my dress as I squirmed underneath him.

He trailed his lips up my ear. "Because I use those secrets against them. I turn them into their undoing."

My body throbbed, aching for more.

Finding a good angle, he shifted to stroke the skin that led between my legs. Instead of pushing him away, I relaxed my body, letting my weight sink into the soft leather. I turned my head in shame, refusing to meet the devil's eyes as I sinned with him.

As his lips brushed my skin, his face returned to my neck, and I felt the cruel curve of his smirk. A shiver ran through me, my nerves crackling, as his stiff cock grazed my leg through his pants.

It twitched once, twice, and I arched my hips, craving more, even though it was the opposite of what any sane person would do.

His wicked fingers danced over the delicate fabric of my panties as he freed my other hand. His grip loosened so much that he wasn't even holding my wrist anymore. The frigid air from the car vent stung my exposed thighs as he pushed my dress up.

His threatening to use my secrets against me should've had me slamming my thighs shut, but I opened them wider, silently begging for his touch. It was cramped and awkward, but of course the devil managed to slip his fingers under my panties.

"So wet for a man she wants to hide herself from," he muttered with a scoff, craning his neck to stare into my eyes. "I wonder if teasing your pussy and playing with this clit will have you singing your secrets out in any way I want." His thumb applied pressure to my clit before massaging it.

I arched my back as high as I could, his body blocking the

movement, as my lower lip quivered. To stop myself from begging him for more, I bit down on my tongue, feeling the sharp sting.

He repositioned himself again, the cramped space giving him limited room, and when that proved not enough, he tore my panties off. My knees buckled as he ripped them down my legs and threw them in the back seat.

There I was, fully bare to him.

His free hand rested on the seat, over my head, as his other ran a line down my slit.

A low moan escaped my lips as I whimpered, and my eyes fell on his gaze. It was full of concentration, completely emotionless.

His thumb returned to my clit as he whispered, "E," tracing a capital *E* with the pad. "N," he said, shaping the letter with his finger. "Z," he added, doing the same, and then finished with, "O." His lip curled, revealing his canine, and his words dripped with arrogance as he said, "Next time, I'll spell out my name with my tongue."

My body jerked up the seat, my muscles tensing, as he plunged two thick fingers inside me. An ache radiated through my core before my body eased as he slowly started pumping his fingers in and out of me.

He rolled to his side, moving his hand from over my head, and braced himself by digging his fingers into the skin of my hip. His eyes drank in the sight of the space between my thighs, to my most intimate part, as he sank his fingers inside me.

When he added another finger, an embarrassing moan left my lips. Like that turned him on, he increased his speed, pumping them into me faster.

His face contorted, as if touching me was injecting the same pleasure I felt inside him.

My entire core was burning up, my skin no longer sensitive to the air floating through the car.

I tilted my hips forward to meet his thrusts. My muscles tightened around his fingers, clenching in short spasms.

I'd never felt so desperate for something, for a *release*, my entire life.

As if knowing this, he slowed his pace, his fingers now lazily dragging in and out of me.

The fuck?

I thrust my hips, deciding to pick up the speed myself.

He moved his hand from my hip to push down on my belly to keep me in place. "Will you give me your secrets, Blair?"

I kept trying to gyrate my hips against him, wriggling as much as possible. He pressed down on my belly harder.

He traced my slit with a single finger. "All you have to do is say yes, and I'll put my fingers back inside your pretty little pussy and make you come all over them." He collected my wetness around a finger and smeared it down my thigh. "An orgasm is worth some secrets ..." His words lingered, unspoken in the air, and he met my eyes, raising a brow. "It's such a simple exchange."

At this moment, the bastard could demand I give him my eye to toss out the window, and I'd say yes. My body was desperate for *anything*.

My insides hummed, begging me to give him whatever he wanted.

The words hurt as they slid up my throat and fell out with a pleading moan, "Fine, yes, just ..." I jerked my chin toward my thighs in a silent demand.

"You just struck another deal with the devil," he muttered, shoving his fingers back inside me. He lowered himself off the seat, onto the floorboard, and his fingers continued their dance inside me.

My chest heaved forward when he lowered his head, latching his lips onto my clit and sucking.

That was it.

The final thing my body needed.

I fell apart, my knees colliding with his cheeks. As my muscles went limp, the sound of my moans filled the car.

Enzo kept his face between my legs, sliding his tongue through my slit to collect my juices.

When he lifted his gaze, he rested his chin on my belly. "For your homework tonight, you're going to write me fifteen sentences like you did in your notebook that day in class. But this time, each sentence will be a secret. If you don't have it ready for me by morning, you'll regret it." He gave my pussy a firm slap and climbed off my lap.

"Blair!" Daphne shrieked, springing off her bed when I walked into our dorm. "There you are! I was just about to organize a search party, not caring if I ended up on Enzo's murder list."

Her slippers scuffed against the floor as she walked toward me. I dropped my heels, and they landed with a soft thud, one of them turning over.

As I shut the door, my legs were still shaky from the car orgasm. It had taken me twice as long to climb the steps to get here.

Earlier, once Enzo had finished sucking the cum from between my legs—just thinking about it made my cheeks turn a crimson red—I expected him to say I had to return the favor.

It was what he'd done earlier before we left for the funeral.

That was what was expected from women most of the time. A quid pro quo with men whenever they gave pleasure.

Or anything at all, really.

At least in the world where I had grown up.

There, pleasure wasn't made for women.

Women who enjoyed it were evil.

Daphne held my shoulders when she reached me, keeping me at arm's length. As if examining me, she looked me up and down, keeping one eye closed. "Are you okay?"

"It depends on your definition of *okay*," I replied.

My eyes were intact, which was a luxury Enzo's other victim today hadn't had. I'd also had two orgasms, which increased my lifetime total to *two*.

I gently freed myself from her hold with a soft shrug. My dry mouth and rumbling stomach reminded me that I hadn't eaten.

All I'd had were the electrolytes Enzo had administered through the IV. *If that was what had truly been flowing through the IV.* I didn't trust him enough to take his word.

I padded toward my bed, seeing the sheets half torn off from when they'd dragged me out of bed.

My body ached as I collapsed face-first onto my mattress. The crisp sheets were cool against my skin.

Daphne climbed in behind me, making herself comfortable. She wasn't leaving until I provided her with details about the Initiation.

I'd most likely broken the rules when I told her that Enzo had said Friday was the night of my Initiation. I didn't care because I needed someone to know that if I vanished, he and the Sons were the ones to blame.

I'd asked if she knew anything about her mother's Initiation, but she shook her head, telling me no, *but* that she thought it varied for each Fawn so that they couldn't tell other prospective Fawns what to expect during theirs.

I craned my neck upward, my jaw popping as I stretched it, then situated myself to rest my back against the headboard.

Daphne drummed her pink-manicured nails against her cheek. "I've texted Seraphina *literally* all day to check on Enzo's location to make sure you were still alive. When she told me he'd taken you to a funeral, I nearly choked on my Coke Zero, worried it was *yours* and you hadn't made it through Initiation. *Thank God* it was just that senator's son's funeral."

She raised her finger, waggling it in the air. "Who, by the way, was a total douchebag. We went to private school together. He had a favorite date-rape drug." She leaned in closer, lowering her voice. "*So the rumors say.*"

My roomie rarely felt sorry for guys dying if she didn't like them.

Not going to lie, I liked her style. Even though I hadn't grown up in politics, I'd seen too many men in my life abuse their power.

She had a moment of hesitation, and her voice softened as she asked, "Are you okay?"

"Barely," I said honestly, stretching out my legs.

"That bad?"

With a silent curse, I nodded, and a tear slipped down my cheek. Since I'd been on alert with Enzo all day, my body hadn't processed what'd happened during the Initiation.

Now that I was finally safe in my dorm room, curled up in my cozy nook with Daphne, I could break down.

The lullaby had been the worst part.

Worse than the sheer trauma of the masked Sons terrorizing me in the woods.

Some people might never understand. A court-appointed therapist, though paid by my stepfather, had once told me I needed to get over those childhood memories.

That wouldn't happen.

Daphne carefully scooted closer, taking a moment to make sure I was comfortable before sitting next to me, wrapping her arm around my shoulders, and pulling me tight against her.

"Hey," she said. "We don't have to talk about it. Just know that I'm a listening ear if you want to vent, or cry, or scream. I'm here if you want to drink to numb it. I'm here if you want to tape Enzo's face to the wall and throw darts at it." She squeezed my shoulder. "In fact, I'll probably throw some darts at his face too."

A light giggle left me as I sniffled and wiped a tear off my cheek. "We definitely need a picture of Enzo to use for target practice."

"That's my girl. Also, if it makes you feel any better, Enzo has been ... *different* with you."

"A good different or bad different?"

"Good … *I think*."

I waited for her to continue.

"He's never taken a Fawn in public before. Most Sons don't."

"Really?"

She nodded. "They usually leave their Fawns tucked away here at the university, only going to them when they need something." She glanced away, us both knowing what that *something* was.

I'd already given the asshole that *something*.

Well, half of that something, I guess.

"The only times Fawns tend to make appearances with their Sons is if they end up marrying later," Daphne went on.

"That'll definitely never be Enzo and me," I said with a snort.

A playfulness glinted in her eyes. "You never know. You could be the Fawn who captures the heart of the cruelest Son of them all."

Fifteen sentences.

Fifteen sentences.

That repeated in my head as I lay on my stomach on my bed, an open notebook sprawled out in front of me. I tapped my pen against the lined paper.

I'd been here for two hours and not written a single word.

Fifteen sentences.

Writing them wasn't an issue. My father's punishment sentences had always been at least four hundred lines.

"I'll give you fifteen sentences," I muttered to myself. "Fifteen sentences that start with *fuck* and end with *off*."

A knot screwed in my belly as my thoughts rambled, and I started writing.

1. My mother gave birth at home.
2. My favorite color is purple.

I tapped my foot against the bed, brainstorming, deciding that my *secrets* didn't have to be the most personal. The definition of secrets was broad. I could give him boring ones.

I could keep my deepest, most sacred secrets hidden.

No one got those.

My phone vibrated on the shelf above my bed, nearly sliding off, and I hurriedly grabbed it before it whacked me in the face. My head hurt when I saw a notification from Enzo.

The Man Who Owns Me: Change of plans. I want your homework tonight.

I'd tried to change his contact name numerous times, and every time, it said *Permission Denied*.

I tossed my phone to the side, deciding to pretend I never saw his text, and go about my night.

My phone vibrated again.

Against my better judgment, I grabbed it, checking the screen. My heartbeat stuttered as I opened the photo Enzo had texted.

It was a photo of me on my knees.

His hand was fisted in my hair, and while you couldn't see my face, I knew it was me. He could tell everyone it was me.

When did he take that?

I'm going to kill him.

A knock on the door disrupted my thoughts. Daphne paused doing her homework and jumped off the bed to answer it.

Seraphina walked in, lightly shutting the door behind her.

I sucked in a long breath. Anyone related to Enzo at this point always made me nervous.

"Come on." She straightened her black headband that nearly blended in with her hair and snapped her fingers. "We're going to the Lair."

I closed my notebook, scooting closer to eavesdrop on what this *Lair* was.

"You too, Blair!" she called out. "Enzo said to bring your homework, whatever the hell that means."

I ripped the paper from the notebook and stuffed it inside my pocket. Daphne was talking to Seraphina as I grabbed my jacket. We left the room and headed for the Lair.

Twenty-Two

Blair

The harsh wind bit at my face as we stepped beneath a canopy of stars. Tonight's air felt heavier, like an unwelcome storm was brewing.

Before coming to Saint Vale, I'd never experienced weather that was constantly gray and overcast. It was like we were set in our own little dark world, where nothing happy was allowed.

After leaving our dorm room, I'd followed Daphne and Seraphina down hidden corridors and a narrow staircase instead of taking the normal route out of the university. I needed to start memorizing those secret exits. The fewer times I ran into Arisono, the less chance she had to give me my third strike.

My hair blew in every direction, sticking to my lips, and I paused to roll the hair tie off my wrist and secure my hair in a high ponytail.

I lagged behind Daphne and Seraphina as we walked the path toward the courtyard, passing gas streetlights and empty benches.

This Lair wasn't on the school map, telling me that it was a secret place only a select few knew about. Probably most of the *few* Daphne had said didn't have rules or curfews.

Since Enzo had instructed Seraphina to bring me here, I knew he'd be there, waiting for me. I gnawed on my lip, nervous about what that'd bring.

I trusted Daphne, but I was uncertain how I felt about Seraphina. Her veins held the same blood as the man tormenting me.

She was also the daughter of a Mafia boss they'd nicknamed Monster freaking Marchetti. Surely, some of that cruelty had seeped into her bloodstream.

I wondered what their mother was like. She hadn't attended the funeral. My thoughts drifted to whether Enzo and Seraphina had the same mother as Benny, given the significant age difference. Benny, though handsome, was a few decades older than they were.

I wanted to know Enzo's secrets as well.

To crack him open as much as he wanted to do to me.

My hand was clammy as I slipped it into my pocket, checking that the paper was still there. I knew Enzo wouldn't be happy when he read it.

I decided that I wouldn't be the only one expected to hand out their secrets. I wanted to know the secrets of the man who suddenly *owned* me.

Or at least *thought* he owned me.

"I can't believe he's letting her come to the Lair," Daphne muttered to Seraphina, though her tone was far from hushed. "Enzo could get in trouble for it."

"I was just as shocked as you," Seraphina said. "Me bringing her could get my ass in trouble."

"You're Cristian Marchetti's daughter," Daphne argued. "You can do whatever you want."

"You're wrong about that, dear friend," she muttered.

"And you're *positive* he said to bring her here?" Daphne asked with worry clear in her voice.

"I didn't dream him telling me that," Seraphina said before her voice turned into a low sigh. She hid her laugh as she said, "I dream about the brothers from *Vampire Diaries* taking off my clothes and sucking my blood. *Not* my brother bossing me around."

"Team Damon," they both said at the same time before high-fiving.

The antique light posts guided us as we turned right toward the greenhouse. No one else was outside.

"It's just ..." Daphne paused, her voice trailing off as we stopped at the greenhouse door. "You rarely see Fawns in the Lair. I don't know if I've *ever* seen one."

They spoke about me as if I were not there.

"Trust me, I know." Seraphina dug a key from her purse and jammed it into the greenhouse door's lock. "I had to ask twice if he was pranking me. When he swore he wasn't, I told him he owed me a new Rolex for my escorting duties."

I held in my snort of how she'd manipulated Enzo to buy her something for collecting me. My new goal was to reach Seraphina's level and win arguments with Enzo. I seemed to lose every single time with him.

Deep down, I knew I needed to start playing by his rules. If I wanted to survive this Fawn situation, I had to play the part and keep Enzo happy.

Daphne's words from earlier replayed in my head. *"You could be the Fawn who captures the heart of the cruelest Son of them all."*

A new idea sparked inside me. A new plan.

I could make Enzo like me. Maybe then he'd relax and lessen his cruelty. Maybe I wouldn't fear him killing me every damn five seconds.

We entered the greenhouse, and the hot, humid air smacked me in the face.

As I shut the door behind us, Daphne leaned toward Seraphina and whispered, "He's different with Blair."

My back straightened at her comment.

"Really?" Seraphina asked, locking the door behind us.

The rows of LED grow lights above the plants were our only source of light, bathing the greenhouse in a soft, artificial glow.

"Really," Daphne said.

"I mean, he did bring her around my father and Benny, which has *never* happened. But he could have also done it to piss off our father."

"What do you mean?" Daphne asked.

"He's setting up an arranged marriage for Enzo."

Daphne grasped Seraphina's elbow. "Oh shit. I already feel bad for whichever girl he chooses. I'd hate to marry Enzo."

"Bringing a girl around while also on the hunt for a potential wife is a bad look," Seraphina said. "One that'd make any father looking to marry his daughter off not happy."

So, Enzo brought me to the funeral to piss off his father.

The sounds of their words and footsteps echoed through the small building.

I followed them, breathing in the aroma of blooming flowers and green plants, while running my finger over a rose stem. I winced, jerking my hand away as a sharp thorn dug into my finger. I brought my finger to my lips, tasting the metallic flavor of the small drop of blood.

Hmm. I didn't get why Enzo was still obsessed with the taste. It wasn't anything special.

Realizing I no longer heard their voices, I turned in a circle, looking for them. My heartbeat blasted against my chest because I'd lost them.

It settled when I heard Daphne faintly call out my name. I hurried toward a small open door in the corner and squeezed through a narrow passage.

I blinked, adjusting to the dimmer light, and found them standing in front of a wall of shelves that hid another entrance.

Daphne vanished through the doorway first, and I trailed behind her. The moment I stepped off the main floor, I tripped on a step.

"Shit," I hissed just as Daphne turned, darting her arms out to keep me from falling.

"Are you nervous?" she asked as I steadied myself, wishing these concrete steps had a handrail.

I brushed dust off my sweater. "I mean, I am about to go to a place called the *Lair*," I said nervously as Seraphina pushed a button.

Behind us, the door swung shut, and the three of us descended the steps.

"It's actually the Devil's Lair," Seraphina explained when we landed in a long concrete hallway illuminated by wall sconces. "We just call it Lair for short."

The added *Devil's* at the beginning sure didn't make me feel any better.

Down in the earth again, I wondered how many places were underground here. I needed to research Saint Vale more because none of these underground areas were on the map Arisono had provided in my welcome packet.

As we walked, a sense of uneasiness settled over me, as if this were the calm before the storm.

Whatever I was about to step into would be a different world for me. Like Dorothy being whisked away, tumbling through the wind, and landing in the Land of Oz.

We didn't walk far until they stopped at a door eerily marked with a carved skull. As I inched closer, I noticed a snake slithering from the hollow eye socket.

This place keeps getting creepier.

"Welcome to the Devil's Lair," Daphne said. "A place few know exists, let alone are invited to."

Seraphina swiped a card through a scanner to the right. It gave a soft beep, blinked once, and the door swung open.

I followed them inside, my gaze sweeping the space. Unlike the cold corridor, this no longer felt underground.

The room matched the atmosphere of an upscale bar, built for billionaires to drown themselves in expensive liquor and cigars.

A sound from the right corner grabbed my attention. A

group of guys sprawled on the couch with their eyes glued to the TV.

At a pub table nearby, one sat alone. In the low light above him, I noticed a jagged scar on his right cheek. His gaze stayed on us as he repeatedly opened his Zippo, then snuffed the flame.

The room felt ... familiar. Goose bumps prickled my skin. I didn't know if it was the air or something deeper, but I had a strange sense of déjà vu.

Nausea swirled in my gut, telling me that this was where Enzo had taken me to play that ridiculous knife game.

"Come on," Daphne chirped, grabbing my hand and pulling me across the room toward Adelina and Livia, who were chatting on a plush leather sectional.

Insecurity surfaced inside me. I hadn't changed out of my black leggings, only thrown on a sweater, and I felt underdressed compared to the girls. The last time I'd looked in the mirror, dark circles ringed my eyes and exhaustion had been written all over my face.

Do any of these girls, other than Daphne, know I just endured my brutal Initiation?

Speaking of Sons ...

I suspected most of them were on the opposite side of the room, though it was hard to identify them when they weren't masked.

Cowards.

At least show your face when you're terrorizing women.

I didn't get a chance to pick the girls' brains before Brooks came toward us, swaying side to side with a glass of brown liquor in his hand.

As he joined us, he pointed the glass first at Daphne, then me. "Neither of you should be here."

With every sway, liquid sloshed over the rim.

I swallowed and tugged at my sweater, avoiding his gaze. Even though I so desperately wanted to leave, I had no idea *how to*. I was trapped here whether I liked it or not.

"Brooks," Adelina snapped, crossing her arms tight over her chest, "go back to your dorm and sober up."

"I will ..." His voice dropped to a slow growl as he stalked toward Daphne, towering over her like a predator closing in. The move reminded me too much of Enzo. "When *she* leaves."

Daphne didn't flinch. I couldn't tell whether he liked that or hated it. His hand tightened around the glass as he waited for her response.

She gestured toward the bar along the far wall. "Why don't you go drink yourself deeper into a stupor?" she asked flatly. "Or better yet, aim for alcohol poisoning. Maybe that'll prevent you from fucking random girls in the Oval Office."

Whoa.

I jerked back.

Definitely didn't expect that response from Daphne.

The air between them was thick with hatred.

"Okay, gross," Adelina muttered in the background. "Certain things are best kept private from sisters."

Whenever I saw Brooks on TV, he always looked like the perfect presidential son. His smile was polished and practiced. His words, tone, every gesture was flawless.

In public, he was a charming golden boy.

In private, he was the opposite.

Down here, people seemed to shed their fake skins and show what they really were. It was probably why he didn't want me down here.

The intense way he stared at Daphne, coupled with Enzo's pointed remarks about Brooks to her, made it obvious they had history.

Well, duh, Blair.

Her father did try to kill his.

But still, there had to be *more*.

As Brooks stared down at Daphne, I saw nothing but hatred in his eyes.

The same with hers.

The feeling was definitely mutual.

One thing I knew for sure was that the president's son was a fucking asshole. If he ever ran for president—which rumor was that he would someday—I was not checking his name on the ballot.

Daphne made a swatting motion. "Now, go away. I want to have a nice night without assholes interrupting it."

Anger flared in Brooks's eyes so hot it genuinely scared the shit out of me. He gave more Enzo vibes from that look alone.

He was a Night Son. I'd put everything on that.

I also knew, deep down, he'd been there alongside Enzo, torturing me in the woods. He'd also played a part in all the shit they did to me in that freezing room.

I shifted on the couch, silently urging Daphne to go on.

To berate him because men who thought they could do anything deserved it.

All of a sudden, I decided I hated the president's son.

He was no golden boy. He was another menace hiding in expensive clothes.

One thing I was learning about the Sons, other than they were fucking psychopaths, was that it was always about them. They showed no regard for the pain they inflicted upon others.

I chewed my lip, wondering if Brooks had had anything to do with the senator's son's death.

The kid of his father's political rival's car suddenly blown up?

I smelled murder, and it came from the drunk asshole standing across from me.

Brooks lowered his arm, snatching Daphne's elbow, and attempted to lift her.

"Jesus." Daphne planted her elbow on the armrest to keep herself in place. "At least let a girl get a drink first."

Rising, Adelina wedged herself between them as a barrier and shoved Brooks back. "Seriously, go to bed."

Brooks retreated a few steps, glaring at Daphne as she rubbed her elbow and glared back.

"Don't stick up for *her*," Brooks snapped, cold eyes slipping back to Daphne. "I can't believe you can even fucking look at her. She's nothing but ..." He paused his speech, sidestepping Adelina to get in Daphne's face. "A fucking snake."

Daphne reared back, and I swear to God, from the way she moved her arm, I was prepared for her to smack him across the face.

But instead, she calmly and gracefully brought her middle finger to her lips and made a kissing motion. "No snake here, Brooks. If anyone's a snake, it's *you*." She tapped her lip next. "You're not mad that my father tried to murder yours. We both know why you're really mad."

Seraphina leaned in closer. "Ohh, please tell the room why he's really mad. I'm *loving* this tea."

"Samesies," Livia said. "Air it out, Daphne. It's best to get everything out in the open."

"Jesus, fuck, Brooks."

The air left my lungs at the sound of the deep, masculine voice.

The one that haunted me.

While Daphne's devil stood in front of her, mine was walking toward me, looking every bit as dangerous as he was.

He looked freshly showered. The ends of his hair were still damp. His hoodie was black, and a gold chain hung at the open neckline.

Brooks stepped back and turned to face him.

I shuddered when he flung his arm in my direction, sending what remained of the liquor in his glass splashing out.

"Why the fuck is your Fawn here?" Brooks shook his head as if my presence here was an abomination to him.

Enzo remained unfazed by his attitude. "Because I invited her here."

"First Daphne, now *her*," he spat. "Let's just start letting anyone in."

"Stay mad, Brooks," Daphne said snidely.

Enzo strolled closer, walking around the couch to stand behind me. His hands dropped to my shoulders, pinning me against the couch.

"Can you please just fuck?" Enzo asked them, sounding almost bored at their little argument.

"Hell no," Brooks said at the same time Daphne shouted, "I'd rather poison myself."

Enzo lowered his hand to my heart, tapping it once. "Come on. Let's go."

I didn't want to go anywhere with him, so I made no attempt to move.

Let him act a fool in front of his sister and these other women.

Everyone went quiet at my disobeying him.

I'd forgotten one thing.

These women were protected Havens—minus Daphne, though she seemed to be protected *by* the Havens.

I wasn't.

I wasn't protected by anyone but Enzo, and only when he decided I was.

I was simply a Fawn. And from what I was learning, that put me at the very bottom of the food chain when it came to freedom.

A deep, slow chuckle left him as he dipped his head down, resting it on my shoulder, and whispered, "Trust me, you don't want me to make a scene. It'll only embarrass you. *Not me.*"

He pulled back, walking around the couch until he was in front of me, and held out his hand. "Time to do our homework."

Without waiting for me, he snatched my hand and tugged me up from my seat. Losing my balance, I fell into the wall of his chest, and he held me steady.

"Enzo," Seraphina said, "we wanted her to hang out with us tonight." She pouted out her lower lip.

"Yeah, while I love you, I'm not Dad," he told her. "That puppy-dog-face shit doesn't work with me."

She narrowed her eyes and flipped him off.

He smirked while turning my body, facing me away from them, and snagged my hand in his.

I knew this would happen, but I wished I'd been more prepared. Like Daphne had said, the Sons came to us only when they wanted something.

And Enzo wanted something.

This fucking list of secrets, for one.

He was about to be very disappointed.

TWENTY-THREE

ENZO

Although he was drunk and in a mood, Brooks was right. Technically, Blair wasn't allowed in the Devil's Lair.

We all had a silent understanding that Current Fawns didn't come here. They stayed in their own space.

The Devil's Lair was exclusively for Sons and Havens. We didn't want our Fawns to come crawling to us here when they were unwanted.

Before, most Havens hadn't known about Fawns. Immunity from becoming a Fawn didn't automatically grant them access to our secrets. We were still protecting them in that way as well.

But now that they'd let more of the Mafia families in, our Havens knew. They were smart, and quite frankly, we made it clear not to befriend them. It happened sometimes because our Havens tended to be stubborn as shit.

I'd debated whether to have Blair come here or go to her room in the Fawn Quarters, but I'd yet to show her the entry in there.

I also wanted her to be comfortable with the other girls. She was already close with Daphne. I'd never allowed Clarissa to hang out with them here, and look how that had turned out.

I didn't need to build a reputation for another Fawn ending up institutionalized or dead.

Plus, I wanted Blair *here*, in my element.

For some reason, being with her felt different. I couldn't put my finger on *why* that was.

A prideful smirk stretched across my face as I guided Blair, her palm slick with nervous sweat, toward the room I'd taken her the other night.

From the corner of my eye, I noticed Brooks charging away from the girls toward the exit that led to the tunnels.

Good. Hopefully, he was leaving to chill out.

While I personally didn't give two fucks about Daphne, I didn't want to deal with the other girls getting pissed if Brooks kicked her out of the Devil's Lair. Seraphina would start bitching, and I'd have to deal with that.

Plus, I didn't want to hear any more shit about Blair being here. The other guys were thankfully keeping their mouths shut.

Alcohol typically wasn't Brooks's vice, so I wondered what had happened. These past few weeks, I could tell something had been bugging him more than usual. I figured it was his father. He was always on Brooks's ass about everything. That pressure intensified as midterms approached.

When we landed in the room, I shut the door behind us and released Blair. Her shoulders slumped as she took the few steps toward the chair she'd sat in before, but I grabbed the back of her sweater, tugging her flush against me.

For a moment, I draped my arm around her neck, holding her in place.

I couldn't stop myself from pulling her hair free from its ponytail.

Unlike the horrid perfume she'd worn her first day in class, her scent had improved.

Tonight, she smelled like the roses my mom kept in the rose garden at the mansion. She'd taken over the garden from my father's first wife, who had passed away when Benny and Gigi were younger.

Even though my mom never knew her, she always tried to find ways to respect her in the home.

After three slow inhales, I shoved her toward the booth that ran along the wall. She fell onto her hands and knees on the crimson leather that suddenly reminded me so much of blood.

I climbed in behind her, and she scooted until her back was against the wall. I completely cornered her.

This time, I didn't want her across from me.

I needed her within arm's reach so I could do whatever was necessary to extract information from her.

I had to go a different route than I normally did in situations like this. Typically, if someone didn't tell me what I wanted, I'd torture the answers out of them.

Cut off fingers. Pull teeth. Saw off limbs. Bring their family in and do the same with them until they finally cracked.

Those were my typical means to get what I wanted.

But I couldn't do that to Blair. I *didn't* want to.

For the first time ever, not only was I taking it easy on someone, but there was a twinge of empathy for this girl.

Also, for the first time ever, I'd felt a pinch of guilt during an Initiation. But I couldn't say anything or ask to stop. It would've made me look weak.

Just as much as a Fawn had to prove herself during Initiation, so did we.

We had to prove our spines were strong enough to watch their torture. That we could watch our Fawn scream and plead to stop the Initiation. Normally, I had no problem. I'd grab a drink, kick my feet up, and enjoy the show.

But with Blair, it was different.

And I fucking hated that.

During her Initiation, as I watched, I wanted to tell them to shut that lullaby off. My fingers curled around the chair's armrests, and I hated that anyone else had seen her wearing only those bra and panties.

I wanted her for my eyes only.

Wanted her for *me* only.

There was more of a sense of ownership with her than I'd ever had with any Fawn.

I shook my head, bringing myself back to the present.

Us in this room.

We had several rooms like it in the Devil's Lair. They were like private rooms in a strip club.

Not all Havens were family members. Sometimes, they were girlfriends or just girls we wanted to fuck. So, occasionally, we'd bring them into these rooms and do just that.

I held out my hand, palm flat. "Your secrets."

She huffed out a laugh. "Seriously, that sounded ridiculous."

As I scooted closer, I noticed the poor Fawn had bags under her glazed eyes as she sagged against the wall.

She slowly pulled a folded note from her pocket and slid it toward me.

She watched me open it and read the few items listed.

The list was fucking pathetic.

She failed.

I gave no fucks about her favorite color.

The shit she'd put down was all surface-level. I hated surface-level. It meant you hadn't dug deep enough.

I wanted to dig my claws deep inside my Fawn and cut away everything that was her.

Not in the mood to play games, I pulled the revolver from my waistband and dropped it onto the table with a heavy thud. While I was normally a Glock guy, I needed a revolver for tonight.

Cracking my neck from side to side, I turned to meet her eyes.

Eyes that were now wide and fully alert as her gaze bounced between me and the gun.

I released a long, mocking sigh. "I had a feeling your list would be lacking. You disappoint me, Blair."

"Enzo—" she started, and I held up my hand, cutting off her words, not wanting to hear any worthless excuses.

She was given an assignment and failed.

I'd punish her for that.

I laced my fingers together, cracking my knuckles while keeping my eyes on her. "Let's play a game, Blair."

She tried to scoot away, but her back only rammed into the wall. "Pass on whatever that"—her eyes traveled back to the gun—"*game* is."

Weapon games were my favorite games. Hard pass on Twister or Monopoly.

When I played darts with people who refused to give me the answers I wanted, I used my knife and aimed for their eye. Darts were for pussies.

With bullets, I preferred a few shots first—places where the pain would spread until they gave me what I wanted. Then I'd press the barrel to their skull and pull the trigger.

Those were the only games I truly enjoyed.

Well, those, and the ones I played with Blair. Though I was sure she didn't share that enjoyment.

Blair quivered, practically flattening her back to the wall. I smirked at that.

I shifted to face her and pulled out a single bullet from my pocket.

"You ever play the game Russian roulette, Blair?" I asked, inserting the bullet into the revolver before spinning the cylinder. "This is *my* version. Each time I ask you a question, and you don't answer, I hold this gun to your head and pull the trigger. You have a one in six chance of that bullet being the one that tears into your temple, shattering your skull and splattering your brain matter around this room." I lifted the gun and ran the muzzle along her cheek.

She shuddered, her eyes darkening, and she flinched as the cold metal grazed her skin.

"Are your secrets worth your life, Blair?"

Her chin trembled as she whimpered out a word I didn't understand.

She gulped slowly. "You've got to be kidding me."

I shook my head, and her body relaxed an inch when I pulled the gun away from her face.

"Daphne ... your sister ... they'll hear the bullet," she said in urgency.

I motioned toward the room with the revolver. "Soundproof room."

"You can't kill me ..." she sputtered out. "Not without the other Sons' permission."

"There's no rule about playing deadly games with you. It was ..." I scratched my cheek with the revolver muzzle. "Simply an accident. I don't get in trouble for accidents, Blair." I cocked my head to the side, tapping the muzzle against my cheek now. "Come to think of it, I don't get in trouble for *anything*. Even when I don't follow rules."

I leaned in closer, lowering the gun, and she tried to push me away when I ran it along her thigh.

"As you learned with Jett, I have no consequences for the crimes that I commit." I rested my forehead against hers as the gun stayed in her lap. "I do whatever I want. I kill who I want. Fuck who I want." My lips met hers, and I bit down on her bottom lip. "Men like me don't suffer consequences for our sins. But Fawns like you, you not only suffer for your own, but for ours as well."

I lied to her.

I could absolutely get in trouble if I killed her. But it wasn't against our rules not to lie.

The Fawns really needed a handbook that explained their rights, but where was the fun in that?

She cleared her throat. "Move the gun from my lap, and I'll answer your questions."

I reared back a few inches. "Aw, you don't want to play my game with me?"

She shook her head, a single tear falling down her cheek, and I captured it with the revolver's muzzle.

See how kind I am?

Removing it from her lap.

This curiosity I had with Blair was something I'd never experienced before. Not only because I wanted the answers so damn desperately, but because she didn't open up.

My other Fawns would never shut the fuck up. I'd learned to tune them out, but it was still annoying. Blair knew how to keep secrets well, which was something I admired.

"Tell me everything I need to know, Blair," I said.

"Fine," she said shakily. "But I want the same from you."

I couldn't hold back my scoff. It was another first for me with a Fawn.

My first Fawn had just wanted to fuck, which was fine with me, and she liked it when I bought her designer bags. Well, *stole* her designer bags because I'd just go to the mansion and steal them from Seraphina's closet.

Seraphina had pissed me off that month, and the way to get my sister back for anything was to fuck with her bags and shoes. It used to be her Barbies, which I'd behead, but she'd grown out of that.

My parents had made me pay her back for that stunt.

For each handbag I gave that Fawn, she sucked my cock and told me her father's secrets. You see, my Fawn Selection wasn't always just purely about my cock or money.

My first Fawn, Ashley, had a father who owned a casino that rivaled my brother-in-law's. My family wanted information about him, so I got it while I was balls deep in pussy and giving her brand-name shit she could've easily bought herself.

Clarissa was really just because I wanted the cash from her father and was bored. She was hot, liked to fuck, and didn't talk as much as Ashley. During that time, that was all I wanted from a Fawn. Though she was rather boring.

The most exciting thing she'd done the entire time I knew her was jump from a damn window.

Her family tried blaming me for it, but my psychological

damage toward her hadn't been nearly as rough as from her family.

Shaking my head, I returned my thoughts back to now.

To more important things.

Like the Fawn beside me.

The one breaking my rules.

The one sending me into a spiral because I was constantly caught in the web of thinking about her.

Other than the scoff, I didn't reply to her little *I want the same from you* response.

She cleared her throat. "Ask your questions then."

I slammed the revolver on the table, causing her to jump. "Who's your stepfather?" I knew I'd already asked that question in the car, but I wanted to see if she'd give me the same name. Give me the same lie.

"His name is Bill."

"And what is Bill's last name?"

"Smith."

I snatched the gun and held it against her temple. "Don't fuck with me, Blair."

She squeezed her eyes shut. "That's the name my mother told me! I've only met him a handful of times."

"What's he do for a living?"

"I told you, finance." A gulp left her.

"What finance company?"

"I literally have no idea."

"Does your mother tell you nothing?"

"I hardly talk to my mother."

"Bullshit," I hissed, reminding myself to check her phone logs.

"My mother hates me, Enzo," she cried, panicked, and I saw the truth on her face. Heard the raw pain in her voice. "Maybe yours doesn't, so you wouldn't understand. In the past year, I've talked to her maybe three times. I don't spend holidays with her, and my birthdays are celebrated alone. When I tell you I know very little about him, I'm being honest. He's just as much of a secret to me as he is to you."

"Do you have a picture of him?"

She shook her head.

I wasn't sure whether I believed her.

Whether she had something fishy going on in that head of hers.

"Why did you get expelled from your last university?" I already knew that answer, but I wanted to see if she'd lie to me.

"My roommate was sleeping with one of my professors."

"And? People fuck. What's the problem?"

"He also tried to *fuck* me. When I reported him to the dean, she didn't believe me. So I had them call in my roommate, but my roommate lied. She claimed I was jealous that she was prettier than me."

I bit down on my tongue to stop myself from telling her no one was prettier than her. But my Fawn couldn't know how obsessed with her I was. That was for my knowledge only.

"After that, my roommate made my life hell in our dorm," Blair went on, shutting her eyes as if in pain again. Or maybe it was regret. "I shouldn't have said anything, but then I couldn't help it. A few weeks later, my roommate and professor went to the dean and said I was trying to seduce him. They'd even written fake love letters and everything. They expelled me."

Within the next few days, that professor would be dead. Possibly the roommate ... or I'd figure out a way to ruin her life. While I usually only killed men, her treating Blair like that made me grind my teeth.

I'd thought I'd be more pissed off when I heard the story come from Blair's mouth. From the beginning, I'd chosen her because word was, she was a snitch at her last university.

What I hadn't known was that it was toward a predatory professor. Nico was inching himself higher up my shit list with every day that passed. He'd failed to provide *that* little piece of information.

"And the universities before that?" I asked.

"The first one was because I couldn't sleep at night, so I'd fall asleep in class. I'd have nightmares and freak out. I'd also have panic attacks. That dean said I was too much of a disruption and expelled me."

"And the one before that?"

She looked away. "I kinda, sorta told a professor to go fuck himself." Her eyes dropped to her lap. "I also kneed him between the legs."

I'd never had a bigger smirk on my face.

"Why'd you do that?" My voice hardened. "And look at me when you tell me. When we talk, you meet my eyes."

I whistled, taking two fingers and pointing at my eyes, and doing the same when she glanced back at me.

"He tried to take my notebook and read it out loud to the class. He said I was paying too much attention to that rather than listening to his lecture."

"Your *I will atone for my sins* sentences?" I asked.

She flinched when I repeated the words, then nodded.

That professor had done the same thing as I did that day in class. Though I never threatened to read them to our fellow students.

That blackmail was for me and me alone.

I'd be the only one using those words against her.

She went on, as if needing to speak about something else. "Thankfully, my stepfather—"

"What was his name again?" I asked, still trying to trip her up.

"*Bill*."

I frowned that I hadn't.

"He told his assistant to pay the professor off so he wouldn't press charges."

"What was this professor's name? What were *all* those professors' names?"

She narrowed her eyes, as if knowing I wasn't asking to simply know. She'd seen me cause too much violence to think it was an innocent question.

"Blair," I said in amusement, flicking the revolver handle on the table.

Her eyes fluttered as she rattled off the names of the next men on my death list.

Look at that. All it took was a gun to get her to spill her secrets.

Now, it's time to get more.

"Speaking of those sentences," I said, "why do you write them?"

She winced at my change of subject.

"I told you, that was my father's punishment," she whispered.

"And I'll ask again, *what sins* were you atoning for?"

Her fear snapped into hatred quick, as if she suddenly remembered her Initiation. "You should know. You're the one who played that fucking lullaby."

I didn't know much about the lullaby.

Someone left a note in our folders that if we played it, it'd put her through hell. So, obviously, since that was our goal, we had.

"How did you know about it?" she pushed.

"Someone left a note for me about it."

"Someone left a note?" she asked, repeating my words slowly, as if sounding each one out and not believing me. "No one knows my past here."

"That's where you're wrong."

She cowered against the wall again.

Our conversation kept jumping, but that was what happened when you had enough secrets to weigh down the fucking planet like Blair did.

I thought I had secrets delved deep inside me, but Blair might've had me beat. They might not be as violent as mine, but I had a feeling they were just as dark.

Every answer she gave me led to more questions I wanted to ask.

"Tell me why that lullaby haunts you, Blair," I said.

She shook her head, her eyes turning away, and she tried to back up again, as if forgetting the wall was behind her.

Something stuttered from her mouth, but they weren't words that made sense. Her eyes darted around the room before she stared at the door distantly.

I grabbed the gun, and she froze. Her eyes grew glossy before tears poured down her cheeks as I spun the cylinder. I used the muzzle of the gun to brush one tear away before moving it to the side of her head.

Her body shook, and more tears fell.

I didn't sweep those ones away.

There were so many tears that I couldn't make out her pupils.

"Six chambers, one bullet," I warned. "Answer the question, or we'll see if the bullet is in this first chamber."

She shook her head violently, as if the words couldn't leave her mouth.

"Why, Blair?" I seethed. "Tell me so I don't have to pull this fucking trigger."

My heart rate sped as sweat built along my forehead. Tension grew in my neck, my shoulders, my hand holding the gun, my throat, everywhere in my body. I'd never had this feeling while holding a gun to someone's head.

Normally, it was satisfaction.

Not fear that I might regret this move.

She stilled, as if suddenly paralyzed, and focused somewhere on my shoulder. She didn't beg for mercy, didn't plead with me, only slammed her eyes shut, as if preparing for her death.

My finger slowly brushed the trigger.

She knew the rules of the game.

TWENTY-FOUR

BLAIR

I kept waking up somewhere new.

My bed. Cold concrete. A random room with an IV in my arm.

And now, *here*.

The moment I looked around, I knew exactly where I was.

Enzo's room.

A soft glow from the lamp on the desk against the back wall lit the space, and a kaleidoscopic beam of gray spilled across the opposite wall from the stained-glass windows.

Above me, dark depictions of Greek gods covered the ceiling. I'd missed that detail the last time I was here.

When I pushed myself up for a better look at the books stacked on his desk, a sharp tug stopped me. I looked down at the handcuff locked around my wrist. The metal bit into my skin when I pulled against it.

My arm fell limp in defeat. I shifted my hips and slid back against the headboard until I was propped upright.

Hardly comfortable, I read the spines of the books while I tried to learn more about Enzo.

The Castle of Otranto, The Fall of the House of Usher, Crime and Punishment, and *Macbeth.*

All very fitting for him.

My heart rate slowed as I pictured Enzo in this bed, lost in the pages of one of those books. The thought lingered, then twisted into a vision of both of us here, side by side, buried in separate stories.

I shook my head.

Stop it, Blair.

Whatever they'd drugged me with during Initiation had to still be in my system. It was the only explanation for such a stupid thought when the man had literally held a gun to my head the night before.

The click of a door broke my thoughts.

Enzo emerged through a doorway, hair dripping with water, chest bare, a white towel slung low around his waist.

My eyes betrayed me, lifting straight to his chest before tracing the hard lines of his muscles.

Why does he have to look like the Greek gods on that ceiling?

I snapped out of my daze, my attention shifting to the other door, the one that offered escape from him.

Surely, he wouldn't chase me down wearing only a towel, right?

"Morning, Blair," he greeted, his voice deep and calm.

My mind flashed back to last night.

The game. The revolver pressed to my temple. Me waiting to die. His finger grazing the trigger but never pulling it.

When he'd cornered me in that booth, my heart had been ready to burst from my chest. I'd silently prayed and braced for death, but after several seconds passed without the gun firing, I'd opened my eyes.

Pain had twisted across his face before he went rigid, frustrated he couldn't bring himself to pull the trigger.

Something he'd probably easily done dozens of times before without hesitation.

As much as Enzo hated to admit it, there was still some humanity left inside him.

Cruelty might've poisoned his blood, but it still ran through a heart. A damaged one. A working one. But a heart capable of compassion.

For me anyway.

The man staring me down might want to corrupt my soul, but at least he wanted it alive.

He dropped the towel. Tremors poured through my body as my gaze fell to his large cock. It was already hard and throbbing.

I yanked the handcuff when he joined me on the bed. He didn't slip under the blanket, just sat on the edge, staring at me while biting into the corner of his lip.

I stopped tugging when he opened his mouth and held out his tongue, where a tiny key sat. My brows furrowed when he spat it on the floor.

Frowning, I tried to free myself again.

"Quit wasting your energy," he said. "You need it for what we're about to do."

"And what's that?" I snapped, too tired for his games.

He rolled his neck. "I'm about to learn all your secrets, Blair."

I held back the urge to tell him he'd already tried. More than once. Even a gun hadn't worked.

"That needs to be done naked?" I asked.

"That towel was uncomfortable." He kicked it away from the bed.

"If I tell you my secrets, then I want to know yours," I said stubbornly.

He rolled his neck again before crawling closer. I smelled his mint toothpaste as he got in my face, and my back straightened against the headboard. I inhaled more of him, smelling fresh soap and citrus.

I gasped when he breathed my skin before his nose nudged mine. My body relaxed, briefly forgetting the jerk had me handcuffed.

Warmth spread through me, fogging my thoughts, as my free hand drifted to the tattoo on his right pec, directly over his heart.

His hand lowered to the matching mark on my stomach.

Both were broken halos.

"What does that mean?" I whispered, our mouths inches apart.

"Each Son has a symbol." He traced my tattoo with his finger. "I marked you with mine."

"Do you choose them yourself?"

He nodded. "We don't do names."

"A broken halo," I muttered. "How very devilish of you."

He smirked, his hand sliding lower to bunch my panties in his fist. My pulse kicked hard against my ribs.

All I wore was the T-shirt he'd given me the night before and a pair of panties.

I made no attempts to stop him.

Slowly shutting my eyes, I remembered the last time he'd touched me like this. How it'd lit up my body in ways I didn't know existed.

"Spread them for me, my sweet Fawn," he ordered.

My legs parted on command.

He dragged the blanket off me, then shoved the T-shirt up until it bunched beneath my breasts.

The sheets were soft against my skin as I writhed beneath him. I entered a different world when he shifted my panties to the side and slid his finger between my folds. As badly as I hated to admit it, nothing ever felt as good as when Enzo touched me.

It was like hearing music for the first time and not being punished for it.

My first taste of ice cream.

The day I was told I'd finally be free of my prison.

All of them belonged on the short list of things that would always mean happiness to me.

Enzo settled himself better between my legs, and his cock brushed my inner thighs. My muscles tensed as he gripped the base of his cock, slowly stroking himself.

I hadn't seen many cocks, but his was definitely the biggest.

When I'd first gained freedom and access to the internet, I'd looked up porn out of curiosity more than anything. In college, people talked about it constantly—Pornhub, OnlyFans, even videos they made in their dorms.

The bed shifted as he moved closer, putting his weight on one hand outside my thighs, and he brought his cock toward my core.

His grip was strong as he ran the head over my clit, nudging the tip against it. My knees shifted up, my heels digging into the bed, my body tingling.

I ran my tongue along the inside of my teeth at the way his mouth drifted open at the pleasure *I* was giving him.

I wanted to plead for more. To plead for less. My mind was playing whiplash with me, the need for pleasure overtaking any rationality.

The bedframe shook when I heaved forward, pulling the handcuff with me. I'd forgotten about the damn thing. It bit deep into my skin, and I knew it'd leave a mark.

"Fuck it," Enzo snapped, suddenly pulling away from me.

All the air escaped my lungs as I stared at him, confused, while he scooted away from me, taking that cock I was silently pleading for from where I needed it most. He bent down, his head disappearing, and when he returned, the key was in his hand.

His grip was tight when he snatched my arm and freed me from the cuff. My arm felt like Jell-O as it dropped.

With his head now only inches from mine, I stared at the man who was dragging me down to hell with him.

Cupping my hand around his chin, I held him there in place, waiting for his reaction as I took in the beauty of my tormentor.

His eyes shut as I ran my thumb along the rigid lines of his face.

Our breathing matched, pant for pant, and the weight of the devil weighing down my body felt like the very place he'd been kicked out of. I feathered my finger over his cheek to his lower lip.

That was when he jerked back, as if, for a moment, he'd broken out of his armor and suddenly needed to put it back on.

With a snarl, he wrenched himself away from me. Our eye contact fractured like the halo on his chest. I gasped as he snatched my wrists, pinned them to the bed, and flattened his body hard against mine.

His cock was caught between our bodies, rubbing against my center. I moaned when he rammed his hips against the mattress, nearly pushing me through it.

One of his hands left my wrist, and he flexed it around my jaw.

"Don't fucking touch me unless I tell you to," he said through a hiss.

He dug his fingers into my skin until I flinched, then inched back down my body, making himself comfortable between my legs.

He ripped my panties off and flung them behind him. They landed on his desk lamp.

His cock nudged against my clit again.

My back lifted from the mattress.

God, I want him to slip that hard cock inside me.

Want to feel full of him.

As if he could read my mind, Enzo inched the head of his cock inside me. My stomach coiled tight like a snake, wanting to unravel as waves of warmth flooded my veins.

"Please," I whimpered in shame.

Shame from how he'd treated me.

From the way he'd told me not to fucking touch him, but had no problem touching me whenever he felt like it.

"You want this cock inside you, Blair?" he asked, tilting his hips forward so his cock went deeper, but not enough.

I whimpered, a low, murmured, "Please," bursting from my lips.

He stared me down, as if contemplating whether I was worthy enough for him to fuck. Scooting back, he stepped off the bed.

I tugged my shirt down as low as it would go to cover myself.

He clamped his hands around my elbows and yanked me

down the bed until my back was flat against it. I hit my head on the headboard at the sudden movement.

Without a word or a glance, he rejoined me on the bed.

He cracked his neck again, as if he could never break the tension loose there. His predatory eyes zeroed in on my face as he straddled me, tightened his hand around my neck, and ran his nose along my cheek.

An eerie hum left his throat as he chuckled darkly against my skin.

He dropped his head, sucking hard on my neck, *marking me* like I was his prey.

After he was done sucking, he flicked his tongue against my skin, so much like he'd flicked it against my clit yesterday.

His mouth moved to my ear as his hand lowered to cup me tight between my legs.

"If I fuck you, Blair," he grunted into my ear, rotating his hips and nudging his cock against my clit, "you'd better fucking give me everything I want."

He reared back to stare me down. I clamped my front teeth over my lower lip and nodded in desperation.

"Good fucking girl." He patted my cheek. "That's my well-behaved Fawn."

My body nearly broke apart when he pulled back, yanked my legs apart farther, and thrust inside me.

I gasped as my head rammed into the headboard and pain ricocheted through me. I couldn't stop from squeezing my legs tight around his body.

That was a telltale sign.

I waited for him to stop and question *why* it hurt.

He stopped for a second, and I knew he knew.

A crooked smile passed over his lips, and he dug his fingers into my thighs as he slowly pulled himself out, then thrust deep again.

I cried out in pain, in pleasure, feeling so many emotions that I couldn't narrow them down to one. He wasn't patient, wasn't gentle, as he raised my legs over his shoulders and pounded into me.

The pain subsided into pure pleasure as his thumb played with my clit while he fucked me.

Fucked me hard and violent, like the devil he was.

My nails scratched at the sheets, at his hands on my thighs, at my own skin as I writhed beneath him, forgetting he'd told me not to touch him.

I gasped, moaned, cried out his name.

And I lost it.

Every thought in my head dissolved as pleasure overtook me. My body shook as my muscles twitched beneath my skin.

Heat surged from my pelvis, straight between my legs, and as the orgasm shattered through me, I felt ready for another one.

I was turning into a greedy Fawn.

His gaze rose from between my legs, where they'd been glued to since he thrust in me the first time, to mine. They were intense, narrowed, and I swore, for the first time, I saw an emotion that wasn't hatred.

The anger had melted into something else.

Something shifted between us as we stared at each other. He rotated his hips, changing his angle, and hit the perfect spot. His eyes stayed rooted to mine as he moved our bodies together.

"Shit." He stopped mid-thrust.

Before I could ask what the problem was, he muttered, "I don't fuck women while looking them in the eye."

"What?" I stuttered, staring at him in disbelief, but he only kept moving.

Kept fucking me and looking me in the eye.

It was as if the words meant nothing once they'd left his mouth.

I hated every time our eye contact broke as his grunts turned rougher. The bed slammed against the wall in heavy thuds, mixing with our moans and ragged breaths.

I admired every expression that crossed his face.

Each time he drove deeper, he bit down on his bottom lip.

Each time he pulled back, he released it.

Over and over and over.

His eyes would shut, then open.

His face would tighten, then ease.

"Fuck, you feel so fucking perfect, Blair," he groaned before pulling himself out of me.

I frowned at the sudden loss of him, as if I'd misplaced my favorite fucking teddy bear. This man would be my goddamn ruin. I knew it.

He inched back, his bottom hitting his shins, and he made a circle with his finger. "Turn around for me, Blair. Stick your ass in the air."

When I didn't move fast enough because I was still processing his demand, he slid away from me. I gasped when he grabbed my waist, flipped me to my knees, and slapped my ass before pointing it in the air. I held myself up with my elbows.

"So wet." He came up behind me and slid his finger through my warmth. "That's your sweet cum with my pre-cum, Blair." Another slap to my ass. "Put your hand between your legs. I want you to taste us."

When I didn't do that, he slapped the other cheek.

I dropped my hand, lowering it to do what he'd ordered, and brought the taste to my lips.

"Tastes good, doesn't it?" he asked as he situated himself and filled me back up with one thrust.

His thrusts were faster.

Harder.

His grunts louder.

And moans longer.

With each stroke, my elbows became softer, until they fell flat and he was holding me up.

"Such a perfect ass," he muttered, smacking my ass once more. "The best view in the goddamn world."

Needing to see him, hearing how close he was, I turned my head to look at him over my shoulder.

I froze when I saw his phone in his hand, aimed at where our bodies met.

"Enzo!" I shrieked. "What the—"

My words died when his other hand clamped onto my hip and he drove into me harder.

"Don't say a word," he hissed. "Or I'll pull my cock out right now and kick you out of this room and withhold an orgasm for a goddamn month. I'll make you sit in that hallway while your pussy fucking craves for this cock to fuck it."

I shut my eyes, dropping my head forward, and met him thrust for thrust.

Later.

I'll make him delete that later.

The fire lighting inside me burned out any rational thoughts.

"That's right. You let me do whatever I want with this body, don't you, Blair?" he asked, his voice now hoarse. "I knew this cunt would be perfection."

He kept fucking me, and I was beginning to think he had an unheard-of stamina when he flipped me over.

"Fuck it," he said again, as if those were his words anytime he broke his rules. "I need this."

I was flat on my back again with him inside me. He slung my thighs over his shoulders and fucked me hard.

I held his gaze as I moved with him.

His hair was slicked with sweat.

Beads of it dripped down his sleek chest.

Another orgasm stirred inside me, and when he hit *that spot*, it bloomed. It kept going and going and going and going, to the point that I felt like it was stuck inside my body.

"You're not coming on my cock again until you swear to give me the answers I want," he said, licking his bottom lip. He dropped my legs to get into my face and gave my neck another squeeze. "Tell me you'll give me all of you, Blair."

"Yes," I said around a long moan.

I breathed in deep breaths when his hand left my neck. He fell forward, his hands landing on each side of my body, and he thrust inside me.

"That's right," he muttered, moving our bodies up the bed with force. "Take that damn cock, Blair, and get fucking used to it."

My hands dragged across the sheets, so close to his. So close I almost covered them with mine, just to feel that connection.

But I was scared he'd pull away.

That he'd deprive me of the only thing I wanted right now.

I'd never felt so damn good.

So damn free.

And as I let myself go, as I cried out my moans while stopping myself from yelling his name, my body went limp.

He gave one, two, three more thrusts before releasing my legs. His body shuddered as he filled me with his cum. He collapsed on top of me while drawing in deep breaths.

We lay there, panting, trying to gather ourselves.

He said nothing as he pushed back up. While he climbed away from me toward the edge of the bed, I raised myself. My body had never felt so weak.

He wiped the sweat from his face and tipped his head, staring at the floor.

That was when I noticed the specks of blood.

Enzo glanced over his shoulder, following my gaze. His eyes flared, and his lips curved into a knowing smirk.

Go figure. The man loves blood.

I was surprised *Dracula* wasn't in that stack of books on his desk.

I rubbed my legs together, already feeling a sore ache, and whispered, "Can I go to the bathroom?"

He nodded, gesturing toward the door that he'd come through.

As I started climbing off the bed, he took my hand to help me.

My legs felt like they didn't belong to me as I walked toward the bathroom, like I was the Little Mermaid who'd just received them.

I flipped on the light, shut the door, and peed. After washing my hands, I looked inside his shower and ran my fingers over his hygiene products.

I whipped around when he opened the door and stood in the doorway, now dressed in gray sweats but still shirtless.

"Do you, uh ..." I started to ask. "Have a washcloth?"

He jerked his head toward a cabinet. "You need to shower?"

"No, I ..." I rubbed my thighs together as my gaze fell there.

He nodded in understanding and joined me in the room. While it was a decent-sized bathroom, his presence made it feel so tight.

He grabbed a cloth from the cabinet and motioned for me to leave the bathroom. I reached for it in his hand, but he pulled it back.

He turned on the sink water, allowing it to run until it met his temperature satisfaction, and wet the cloth.

"On the bed," he directed while following me out of the bathroom. "Sit on the edge."

Goose bumps covered my body, and I pulled the shirt down to hide them.

He knelt in front of me, resting one hand on my thigh. "Take off the shirt."

"Enzo—" I started.

"Take it off."

I did slowly, and he took it from me.

He opened my legs while at eye level with my pussy. "Spread them wider for me."

My cheeks warmed as I did, and I flinched as he started wiping me clean.

It felt too intimate for such a violent man.

"Such a beautiful pussy," he said almost in admiration. "Look how much I stretched you."

His words sent tingles through my body.

Enzo cleaned me up as if I were his latest crime scene. He stared at the blood he'd collected and then said, "I'm leaving my cum in there." The words were almost said to himself.

"You were a virgin, weren't you?" he asked, his voice sounding so casual for such a serious question.

I slowly nodded.

"I figured."

I scrunched my face. "What made you think that?"

"Just knew." He stroked the inside of my thigh. "I know you better than you think, Blair."

The warmth of the cloth eased my tenseness as he returned to cleaning me.

"Fuck," he hissed out of nowhere.

"What?" I suddenly worried I'd done something wrong.

Or that *something* was wrong with me down there.

I was fucking insecure, okay?

"Are you on birth control?" he asked.

I could tell by the way his face paled that he normally asked that question before he had sex with someone, but he'd forgotten with me.

I shook my head, bringing my hand to my forehead and rubbing it. *How stupid of me.*

"You'll go to the university doctor today," he instructed. "She'll give you birth control. Start the pills tonight—do you hear me?"

"We ..." My voice was weak. "We should've used a condom."

"No shit," he hissed. "I forgot to have you checked first too." He shook his head, looking away from me. "Why am I breaking all these rules with you, Blair?"

"Hey," I whispered, a faint softness overcoming me, "it's okay." I tucked my hand under his chin, pulling it up so our eyes met.

We held each other's gaze for a moment before he stood, tossed the cloth in a wastebasket, and opened a drawer.

He grabbed a pair of Ralph Lauren pajamas, shocking me as he brought me to my feet and helped me put them on.

Did he do this with all his Fawns?

Daphne had said everything Enzo was doing with me was different from what he'd done with Clarissa.

"Now"—he patted the bed for me to scoot back—"it's time to talk."

I rubbed my eyes, sliding across the bed as a headache started building. "I don't know how much I can tell you."

He sat across from me, stretching out his legs so they were on either side of me. "You'll tell me everything."

"You don't understand." I hated that there was a slight stutter in my voice. It was because of the panic. The fear. "I can get in a lot of trouble."

He rested his hand on my knee, giving it a squeeze. "You're my Fawn. What did I tell you before? I'll always protect you. You never have to worry about anyone hurting you now."

As much as I knew Enzo's protection carried a lot of weight, it didn't make me feel completely safe.

My body shook as I remembered that day in court.

Remembered the judge's gavel banging before my father was hauled out of the courtroom, making final promises to me.

Enzo's voice broke me out of my thoughts. "Your secrets are safe with me."

"That's not it," I whispered.

His brows snapped together, his voice suddenly accusatory. "Who are you protecting?"

"You wouldn't understand." Tears built in my eyes.

"Trust me, I understand." His voice lightened. "I understand fucked up. I've heard and seen things that'd give you nightmares for fucking weeks straight." He chuckled. "You saw me pluck out a man's eyeball, for fuck's sake, Blair. Nothing you say will surprise me."

I inhaled a deep breath.

Released it.

Did that again.

Again. And again.

Here I go.

I lowered my head, staring down at the blood on the sheets. "I grew up in a cult."

He reached out, gripping my face, and his movements were gentle as he lifted it.

"What kind of cult?" he asked, not looking shocked.

"What do you mean?"

"The word *cult* is often thrown around these days. My sister claims to be part of the Iced Coffee All Year-Round Cult." There was a slight playful roll of his eyes. "There are cults that believe in aliens. Charles Manson cults. Religious cults."

I kept my voice low. "Mine bordered on religion and were based on my father's beliefs." I only wished it were about iced coffee.

"What was the cult?"

"What?" I shook my head violently. "He didn't name it."

"Most cults have names." He cocked his head to the side. "I've killed a few cult leaders. They're usually losers who name their cult after them and use drugs to gain power over people."

He didn't know that drugs could only take cults so far.

The one that always stuck? That was religion.

Religion created so many cults. And it could be any religion. Sometimes even ones that the leaders had made up out of nowhere.

I swallowed down spit as he released my face. "You might have killed people in cults, but I lived in one. I've seen it from the inside. There's no cult handbook, Enzo. There wasn't a cutesy nickname. My father, the leader, didn't have time for that. We were a Follower of Abraham. That was the main rule of our cult. When he'd ask who we were, we said Follower of Abraham."

"Your father was the leader?"

I slowly nodded as more memories surged through my head.

"How long were you in this cult?"

"For as long as I can remember. I left when I was sixteen, maybe seventeen."

I hadn't known my real age. Still didn't know it now.

According to paperwork made after my father had been incarcerated, I was twenty-two. But since I had been born at home and no records had been kept, there was a chance we were off a year.

He scooted nearer, and that closeness eased me. "What did they do to you in that cult?"

While he tried to remain calm for me, I didn't miss how his nostrils had flared. He knew what happened in these kinds of cults.

His hand returned to my chin, fingers lightly brushing over my skin. "How bad did they hurt you, Blair?" And I swore I heard him say, "So I can hurt them ten times worse," under his breath.

Not wanting to sink deeper into my trauma, I shook my head. "They didn't ... it wasn't—"

He held my face still. "It was."

My shoulders relaxed, his touch working through me like my own personal Xanax.

"Those sins you wrote about atoning for. What were they? Why does that lullaby scare you?"

I let out a slow breath and squeezed my eyes shut. They opened again the moment I lost his touch.

He rose from the bed, crossed the room, opened the fridge in the corner, and came back with a bottle of water.

When he handed it to me, I drank half in one go.

I knew I had to tell him.

There was no way out of it.

He'd keep finding new ways to torture answers out of me until he learned everything about my past. And what he chose to do with that information was beyond my control.

Sooner or later, he'd probably get into the sealed records anyway. He had too many resources for me to believe otherwise.

Unless he wanted the truth to come from me.

I wasn't even sure if the truth was in those records. I'd never seen them myself. Nor did I ever want to.

I had no choice whether to share my past with Enzo. Just like becoming a Fawn, it wasn't my decision.

I decided to just let it all out.

Maybe I'd feel better after.

I told him the same thing I'd told the FBI when they'd locked me in a room for hours and asked the same questions again and again.

"My father started the cult before I was born. We lived on a compound with other families in the Arizona desert. In the middle of nowhere. We had no running water or electricity." I twisted the cap back on the water. "He built everything around religion. If he didn't like something, he said it'd been sent by the Devil."

I placed a hand against my chest. "Everything I did was proof I'd been sent by the Devil."

He flexed his shoulders forward as his jaw tightened.

I held up the bottle in my hand. "Being left-handed meant I was a witch, which made me evil."

Later, after my own research, I'd learned he'd pulled that from something he'd read about the Salem witch trials. They'd used left-handedness against the accused there too.

A sigh left me. "If a man on the compound looked at me too long, it was because I was evil and tempting him. He claimed I wanted people to sin." My throat tightened. "After giving birth to me, my mother struggled to carry a baby to full term. He said that was my fault. That in the womb, I'd filled her with darkness and stopped her from bringing more life into the world."

I looked away as a tear escaped my eye and fell down my cheek. "For those sins, he'd punish me. I'd have to write the sentences. Or he'd shave my head, beat me with a belt, or lock me in a tiny shed for weeks. After each punishment, he'd take me to the river on the property and dunk my head under water until I was close to drowning. He said he had to force the demons out of me."

Shutting my eyes again, I inhaled deep breaths, none of them feeling like enough to fill my lungs.

Enzo gave me that time, not pushing me to speak faster. I tensed when he reached out to brush my hair off my shoulder. My eyes opened just as he pressed a kiss against my cheek.

I used the back of my hand to wipe the tears as he pulled away. "The lullaby you guys played?" More tears welled in my eyes. "My mother sang that song to me in private one day. Not knowing any better, I sang it. I was punished for it." My head fell forward as I broke down in tears.

My father, I'd always known he was evil. But before that, I'd always cherished my mother. Loved her. Felt loved by her. That day was my reckoning.

I learned that no one loved me there.

No one cared about me.

I had been a little girl on her own.

Enzo grabbed my shoulder and pulled me across the bed until his arms locked around me so tight I could barely move. They felt like the most comforting blanket in the world.

I dug my chin into his shoulder as he held me.

Soothed me.

He ran his fingers over my neck. "I told you, my Fawn, you're now under my protection, and I will make every motherfucker burn and bleed in this world if they even think of laying a hand on you."

I felt so heavy in his arms.

Yet so weightless at the same time.

Like I'd handed him half my trauma, and for the first time, the pain didn't belong to me alone.

We sat there for a few seconds before I cleared my throat and inched away from him.

"What happened to your father?" Enzo asked. "Where is he?"

"He's in prison," I replied.

"What—"

Enzo's phone ringing interrupted his words.

He ignored it. "How did—"

It rang again.

He ignored it, waiting for me to continue over the loud, ear-grating ringtone.

"Shit," he finally cursed when it wouldn't stop, climbing off the bed and walking to his desk to pick up the phone beside his computer. He turned it off and tossed it across the room.

As he made his way back to me, he froze mid-step when someone pounded on the door.

"Enzo! We have a problem!"

He balled his hands into fists while stomping toward the door, swinging it open. Brooks came barreling inside, blood dripping off his hands.

I gasped, and his eyes widened when he noticed me. He turned on his heel and dashed to the bathroom, slamming the door shut.

Enzo hurriedly helped me off the bed and handed me his gate key. "Go straight to your room. Tell no one about this."

Twenty-Five

Enzo

I waited until Blair was gone before opening the bathroom door.

Brooks stood at the sink, head hung low, while he scrubbed his hands.

Bloody water swirled around the drain. I glanced down, seeing dribbles of blood on the gray tiled floor.

He was being messy *in my space.*

I clenched my fist to stop myself from driving it into the side of his face for being so reckless.

Who knew how much blood he had dripped on his walk here?

Speaking of that, how the fuck did he get through the gates?

I needed to get the locks changed.

"What the fuck happened?" I asked, sinking my fingers into the doorframe.

He turned toward me, keeping his hands under the running water. His eyes were dark and sleep-deprived. "I killed someone."

"Who?"

"Some asshole at a dorm party last night."

I dragged a hand through my hair, inching deeper into the

bathroom. "We told you to take your ass back to your dorm and sober up."

He turned off the water and pushed himself away from the sink. "That sounded too boring."

"Then you should've kept your ass at the Devil's Lair and ignored Daphne." I left the bathroom to ease my anger before I did something stupid, grabbed a tee from my dresser, and pulled it over my head.

When Brooks started to leave the bathroom, I charged at him and shoved him back inside.

"You're not tracking more blood through here," I hissed. "Shower, scrub yourself clean, and then we'll talk." I slammed the door shut in his face before dropping into the chair at my desk.

Groaning, I ran my hands through my hair.

This situation was the last thing I needed to deal with.

My plan for this morning had been simple. I was going to spend it cracking Blair open. She'd suck my cock as I watched it slide through those pretty lips of hers.

I hadn't planned on fucking her yet, but it'd happened. I wanted it to keep happening.

And between all that, I was going to make her tell me all the things I wanted to know.

Last night, I couldn't pull the trigger and decided to take a different route with her. I led her out of the Devil's Lair, brought her to my room, and told her to go to bed. She fell asleep fast, which was fine with me because I wanted her to have a fresh mind in the morning.

I'd decided to trade pain for pleasure to pull her secrets out of her. And it worked. Everyone was manipulated differently.

I did have one screwup. I'd fucked her without a condom without her being on the pill.

Normally, I waited to fuck my Fawn until the timing was perfect. I always had them checked for diseases and put on birth control. And I always fucked them with a condom. Never raw, like I'd just done with Blair.

I hadn't been lying when I said I'd ruin her for any other man. I'd make sweet Blair crave my dick with every move she made. I never wanted her to forget me, even after I kicked her to the curb when I was done having my fun.

Now, my entire day was fucked, and I couldn't learn more about her because Brooks had decided at the worst time to murder someone.

I grabbed my phone, uploaded the video of me fucking Blair into a password-protected folder, and closed out of it.

Later, I would need to upload it into our Fawn Database, along with the other video I'd taken of her sucking my cock.

Every Fawn had a file.

Only the Son to that Fawn had access to her file. If another Son wanted her for his year after we were finished with her, we'd give him access so he could decide if she was worth claiming.

We documented everything.

But every time I tried to upload it to the Database, I kept stopping myself. For some reason, I didn't want anyone else seeing Blair in intimate moments.

I wanted to keep everything to myself.

When Brooks exited the bathroom, he was dressed in my robe. I wanted to kick his ass for that, but I'd rather him wear that than his bloody clothes.

He paced in front of me, and I massaged my temples.

This was why we needed Fawns. To calm us.

That might've been why he said the others had been adamant about him choosing a Fawn soon. They had seen he was losing control.

A Fawn was meant to fix that.

To put a leash on him and distract him from whatever demons were tearing through his mind.

I wasn't sure if him losing his temper and killing the kid was about Daphne or something deeper, but he couldn't keep making these mistakes. We couldn't risk them. I wouldn't put my neck on the line for someone this reckless.

While I was loyal to Brooks, I was loyal to a *smart* Brooks.

Not this stupid-as-shit one.

If he kept making these mistakes, he'd be on his own. I wouldn't put my family's or my life on the line for someone being careless.

"What happened, man?" I asked him before looking at the door. "Where's your Secret Service?"

He stopped his pacing to look at me. "I told them to go home for the night."

I leaned back in the chair. "Tell me what happened."

He returned to his pacing, his hands clenched at his sides. "I killed someone."

"Who?"

"I don't remember his name. His dad is a prime minister." He stopped, turning to face me, and snapped his fingers. "From whatever country Daphne's mom is from."

Of course, Daphne was involved.

She always was when Brooks acted like a fucking fool.

I jumped up from the chair, rearing my fist, ready to punch him. Instead, I shoved him into the wall, trying to control my anger.

"You idiot," I sneered, stabbing my finger in his face. "Did you forget he and his brother are Prospects!"

I couldn't stop myself from kneeing him in the balls, and he fell to his knees.

"We all voted for them to be Sons!"

He deserved more for his fuckup, but I was being nice because Brooks was my boy.

"Which is why we have to keep this under wraps," he squeaked out, palming his dick through my robe.

"Where's the body?"

"His dorm."

"Does he have a single?"

He nodded, his face scrunched in pain as he rolled into the fetal position.

"You went to his room?" I eyed him warily.

Brooks never went to anyone else's room. He hardly even spoke to people who weren't affiliated with the Sons or Havens.

He sucked in a few heavy breaths to push through the pain before leveling his palm against the wall and dragging himself to his feet. When he was upright, he kept his hand there to keep his balance.

"Daphne came up in conversation, and he said he had a video of her in his room."

"And you went to see it?" I asked in pure annoyance.

He nodded. "When the guy showed it to me, I snapped."

I couldn't stop myself from charging toward him and driving my elbow into his face. He took the hit, choking as he pushed himself back up.

This was what happened when you did something stupid.

"Get up, pussy," I said as he dropped back down. I nudged him with my foot.

He glared up at me, wiping blood from his lip. "He said he was choosing her as his Fawn."

"And?"

"And she's not a fucking Haven."

"And?" I repeated. "You hate the fucking bitch. Why do you care?"

If Seraphina were here, she'd be kicking me in the balls. Blair too, probably, for calling Daphne a bitch. Calling her a bitch was more because I was mad at Brooks.

"Why are you suddenly fighting for her honor?" I added.

He shook his head, refusing to answer me.

I already knew why. He just needed to admit it.

"What do we do, Zo?" he croaked, and I'd never seen him look so mentally screwed up.

While he had made a stupid move, I couldn't turn my back on him. I had to help him. Had to protect the Sons.

I blew out a sharp breath, holding myself back from more violence. "Have you told anyone else?"

He shook his head again.

"Let's get Cedric and Emeri." I helped him to his feet. "This stays between us—do you hear me? No other Sons can know."

Not only was the kid a Prospect, which meant he'd be a Son soon, but his father was also an Elder.

I scrubbed my hands together. "I'll have Nico disable the cameras so we can get rid of the body."

I needed to see it first to figure out the best way to get rid of it.

Brooks was getting punched again if this took too much of my time.

"You owe me big time for this," Emeri told Brooks, snapping latex gloves on while sending him a glare.

This situation was why the Elder Sons had come to us.

Why they wanted us to join the Night Sons.

While they could pay their way out of problems, they were too pussy to clean up bloody crime scenes. The few who had tried were behind bars.

Brooks had done a number on the guy, Peter.

I'd actually liked Peter. He seemed cool, which was why I'd voted yes when his photo came up during Son Selection.

I counted at least fifteen stab wounds on the bloody body crumpled on a rug stained with red.

Nearly every stab wound was near the heart, but there were a few on his stomach and face.

Brooks's anger had gotten the best of him.

For someone who couldn't stand her, the idiot sure didn't like anyone else seeing Daphne naked.

We didn't want to risk his twin coming around, so I instructed Cedric to keep him busy. He'd dragged him off to some bullshit meeting in Nico's room.

I'd also told Arisono to clear the dorm floor. When she asked how, I reminded her she was the headmaster. Figuring that out was her job.

Twenty minutes later, she'd evacuated the floor, saying they needed to check on a gas leak.

We cleaned up the scene first, rolling the body off the blood-soaked rug and stuffing the rug into a plastic bag. After laying down a fresh tarp, we dumped him onto it.

The kid's skin had turned nearly purple by then. Brooks had taken a few hours to come to me.

Even with the floor empty, we still had to watch the noise we made. That meant Emeri had to use a handsaw to get through the bones. Power tools were always your friend in jobs like these, but it was too risky.

As Emeri started sawing through skin and bone, Brooks gagged and stumbled toward the corner.

"Nope." I grabbed him by the collar, dragged him back, shoved him down beside Emeri, and forced a saw into his hand. "You wanted to kill him. Now, you help clean it up."

It took hours to cut the guy into pieces small enough to fit inside the duffel bag.

I already had a plan in place, and Brooks would be in charge of cleaning up his own crime. He'd haul the bags to his car, drive them to the funeral home, and pay to have the limbs cremated.

We had a contact who owned a funeral home in the city, and for a large fee, he allowed us to bring in bodies to turn into ash.

I wasn't taking money out of my pocket because Brooks had gotten jealous that someone else was choosing Daphne as his Fawn while he was too much of a pussy to do it himself.

Brooks grunted as he slung the bags over each shoulder.

I stopped him before we left. "One more thing."

He dropped the bags and huffed out a breath.

"We do this, and you're choosing Daphne as your Fawn."

When he opened his mouth to argue, I kept talking. "If this kid didn't select her, someone else will. Maybe even his twin. You will select Daphne as your Fawn. Give me your word, or we're done, and you figure out how to get rid of that body yourself. Fix the problem on your own."

Brooks's lips flattened as he glared at me. The vein in his neck twitched as he stared at me like I was his worst enemy.

"You know my father—"

"Then you tell the president to fucking get here and clean your own mess up." I kicked one of the bags across the floor. "Yes or no, Brooks? Decide right now. You made the choice to kill this man. Now, we have to fix it."

Twenty-Six

Blair

I hurried back to my dorm in Enzo's pajamas, my bare feet hitting the floor.

I wasn't sure what time it was, but people were already heading to class. I upped my pace, wondering if Daphne had already left for the morning.

When I walked in, I found Daphne at the vanity.

Enzo told me not to say anything to anyone about Brooks, but can I hide this from Daphne?

She was about the only person I felt comfortable talking to anymore.

Is that breaking Fawn rules?

It seemed like everything was breaking Fawn rules.

She turned in her stool to look at me, mascara wand in hand. "Girl, it's about time you got here. I missed you last night." She waggled the wand at me. "Everything okay?"

I nodded, shutting the door behind me, and sounded out of breath. "Yeah."

She motioned toward my body. "I like the outfit choice."

I pulled at the edge of Enzo's pajama shirt. "Enzo's."

"Figured since you'd left with him last night. Did you sleep in your Fawn room?"

I shook my head, walking toward her. "How'd you know about those?"

"Clarissa stayed in the Fawn Quarters sometimes." She capped the mascara. "She'd hang out with other Fawns there."

"I've only been there once, but I didn't see any other Fawns."

In that area, I'd felt so alone.

Like I was a lonely fawn, lost in the woods, who had no one. If there were other Fawns, why wasn't Enzo introducing me to them?

I sat on the edge of her bed, staring up at her. "I stayed in Enzo's room."

"Holy shit!" Her eyes widened. "Clarissa definitely never stayed in Enzo's bedroom. I don't think she even knew where it was."

"Really?"

"Told you," she said, singing the words and swaying her shoulders. "He's being different with you than he was with her." She smirked while sliding a lip gloss wand over her lips. "Blair may be the Fawn who changes Enzo Marchetti." A dramatic sigh left her. "Who would've thought?"

Not only did I definitely not want to talk about that, but all that kept playing in my mind was a bloody Brooks storming inside Enzo's room.

"What happened with you and Brooks was crazy," I commented, trying to *casually* lean into the conversation.

"Brooks is an asshole." She dropped her lip gloss into the vanity drawer and slammed it shut. "Always has been. Always will be."

"Whenever I saw him on TV, he seemed like the total opposite."

"That's politics, baby." She stretched her legs to push the stool out from under the vanity and stood. "That's how so many of us here at Saint Vale are. Growing up, we have this image we have to fit in. We fake it because that's what's always expected of us."

I ran a hand through the knots in my hair. "Do you fake it?"

"Not as much as I used to. After my father was arrested, I started being myself more. I no longer had anyone to impress."

"Why do you and Brooks hate each other so much?"

"We've never exactly *liked* each other, but after the whole assassination thing—which, who can control what their parents do?—he pretty much wanted to kill me himself. But he also thought that Adelina would write me off, and he'd never have to see me again. I don't know if seeing me is a reminder of what happened to his father because he was there, standing right beside him, or if he's just an asshole. But I always tell myself it's just because he's an asshole." She shrugged, walking toward the closet to pull a blazer off the hanger and slip it on over her button-up.

The blazer had the school crest on the left pocket, just like our shirts. Which reminded me to make sure I wore Enzo's black shirt today. The other day, when I'd opened my closet, I'd found a few more that were now in my size.

She snapped her fingers, breaking me out of my wandering thoughts. "Come on, babes. You'd better get ready. You're going to be late for class."

I nodded and groaned while bringing myself to my feet. My legs still felt a little weak after everything.

While I showered, I thought about Enzo. Even with the risk of being late for class, I couldn't stop myself from dropping my hand between my legs to feel how sensitive I was there.

I slid my finger through the slit, seeing if I could collect any of his cum, and brought the tip to my lips.

I was no longer a virgin.

I'd literally given my soul to the devil.

I shut my eyes, remembering how my father would accuse me of being sent by the Devil to ruin people.

He was wrong.

So very wrong.

I had been sent *to* the devil.

Enzo didn't attend American Gothic Lit, and I didn't see him the rest of the day.

For the next class, Headmaster Arisono alerted everyone that classes would be held outside until she said otherwise.

Something about a gas leak and us needing fresh air.

Even Professor Nelson looked confused about the sudden change of classroom plans.

We sat outside, on the grass, as Arisono made sure no one went inside the university. She even had lunch delivered outside in plastic bags. I heard plenty of disgruntled grumbles about that.

Deep in my gut, I had a feeling that whatever had happened with Brooks was connected with us being banned from going inside.

As I sat outside on a blanket, with the sun peeking through the clouds, I admired the beauty of the campus.

Each building had character with thick stone and carvings. The ivy crawling over the walls looked like one more barrier keeping us from the outside world.

When I did try to listen to the professor, I struggled. I stared at the blank screen of my new MacBook, only thinking of Enzo.

My thoughts wouldn't stop drifting to earlier—when I had been in his bed, wriggling beneath the weight of him, practically suffocating from a pleasure that I'd never felt before.

I never considered myself a sexual person.

Losing my virginity had never held any importance to me. I wasn't sure if I'd ever marry or fall in love. My past had fucked my head up too much. Every marriage I'd seen was also dysfunctional.

I'd also never thought about intimacy, and as badly as I tried to convince myself otherwise, I felt that with Enzo. Really, every time we'd touched each other, there'd been a twinge of it.

Whether it was toxic intimacy was another matter.

It was toxic. More than toxic. I'd pay for that later. I knew it.

Enzo would ruin me, and I'd never be the same after this. My being a Fawn would mark me for the rest of my life.

All day, I couldn't stop checking my phone for any notifications from him. Couldn't stop looking around for any sight of him. Disappointment pinched inside me each time I found nothing.

He had taken my virginity and was now MIA.

How cliché of him.

When we were finally able to go back inside the university, Daphne declared we were having a girls' night in our dorm.

That was fine with me.

I needed something relaxing.

Maybe an Enzo-free night would help me stop thinking about him.

Now, Daphne and I were sprawled out in her nook, her laptop set up on the shelf that was eye level with us, as *John Tucker Must Die* played on the screen.

A plethora of snacks were scattered around us.

When the movie ended, I glanced over at Daphne. "Do you want to be a Fawn?"

Daphne paused mid-sip of her pina colada-flavored wine cooler, puckering her lips as she thought about it. "Honestly, not really. Before Clarissa, I did." She choked out a laugh. "Can you believe I was actually butthurt when she was chosen and I wasn't? How stupid was that?"

"Really?" I took a sip of my wine cooler. Mine was supposed to taste like a strawberry daiquiri.

"My mom made it seem like this wonderful thing, and maybe for her, it was. I think the Sons have changed from when she was a Fawn. Sure, they'd put her through mental and emotional hell, but Fawns weren't fucking dying." She took a long sip before pointing the glass bottle at me.

"Do you think you'll ever be chosen?" I rubbed my sock-covered feet together.

"Doubt it. Like I said before, people don't like me after what my father did. His stupid-ass behavior probably saved me from having to go through the mental turmoil of being a Fawn." She rolled her eyes before running a finger over her eyelashes. "At least that's one good thing he did for me, I guess." She smiled at me. "But I do think it was fate that you were placed as my roommate. At least I'm here to help you through it as much as I can."

I returned the smile, grateful for that. If she hadn't been here to walk me through some of the things that were happening, then I'd have been lost.

My phone beeped, and I snatched it from beside me.

I hated that my heart skipped a beat, hoping it was something from Enzo. My stomach coiled, and my hands felt clammy around the phone as I read the text.

Unknown Number: All Fawns must die.

I nearly dropped it when it vibrated again.

Unknown Number: All Fawns WILL die.

"What?" Daphne asked, dropping an M&M in her mouth.

I turned the phone to let her read the text. The M&M she was about to eat fell from her hand and onto the bed.

"Send that to Enzo," she said.

"What?" I asked, looking at the phone again, staring at the text, as if the sender's information would randomly pop up.

She grabbed the M&M and ate it. "Send that to him. If he doesn't already have your phone linked to his, he needs to know. That's fucking scary."

"Do you think it's Enzo?"

She shook her head. "If a Son ever said something like that, they'd be kicked out and probably dead. One rule that Sons have: No one fucks with their Fawns and lives to see the next day."

My eyelids felt heavy, and I struggled to keep them open during my Environmental Science class.

All night, I'd lain awake, unable to drift off to sleep.

I thought about how creepy Saint Vale was.

Thought about that text.

It wasn't sent to the wrong person.

It was meant for *me. Death to Fawns* meant death to *me.*

Each time I shut my eyes, I felt *something.*

Heard *something.*

Or maybe what I was hearing was the result of too many wine coolers.

Two wasn't that much, was it?

My tolerance couldn't be that pathetic.

Daphne had downed at least six, and she had been peppy as hell this morning.

Last night, I could've sworn I felt a touch in the middle of the night. I swatted at the air like I was batting away a mosquito before pulling back my new curtain—a gift from Daphne to replace the one Enzo had ruined.

I kept telling myself it was my imagination when a voice slithered through my mind and said, *"Take down the Sons."* The nausea wrenched tighter when I heard, *"Death to Fawns."*

It was like I had a chorus of demons chanting in my ears.

What had happened this morning did nothing to soothe my anxiousness.

When Daphne and I had walked to our classes, I'd heard the faint murmurs of classmates whispering about me.

They'd sneered, covering their mouths while talking shit.

Some of them had spoken a little too loud.

"I saw her with Enzo."

"She was wearing his pajamas, coming from his wing."

"Let's hope she doesn't push herself through a window."

"Don't let them bother you," Daphne had told me while flipping them off.

I wished her *I don't give a fuck* attitude was contagious and rubbed off on me.

Though, with every passing day here, I found myself speaking my mind more.

I felt a sense of peace and acceptance here.

Well, from some people. Not the whispering assholes.

From Daphne and the girls. Even from, dare I say, Enzo.

More than anywhere I'd lived, I felt the most comfortable here.

"Blair."

My gaze snapped to the professor at the front of the lecture hall. She was reading a note in her hand while a red-haired woman in black scrubs stood beside her.

"Will you come with me, Blair?" the woman in scrubs asked.

I crammed my notebook and laptop into my bag and bounced down each step of the room's rows, painfully aware of the stares coming from everyone.

The woman smiled when I reached her and motioned for me to follow her out of the lecture hall. She walked ahead of me without saying a word or checking if I was still behind her.

After swiping her badge to unlock a door, we stepped into what looked like a nurse's office.

A polished marble desk with a granite top sat in the middle of the room, with two leather chairs neatly placed in front of it. Framed degrees lined the wall behind it. Three doors were shut along the opposite side.

"Hello, Blair." She shut the door behind her. "I'm Dr. Everette. Saint Vale's private physician."

I nodded, giving her a polite smile.

She motioned for me to have a seat. My movements were slow as I did, and she sat behind the desk.

"First off, congrats on becoming a Fawn," she said. "Only the strong women become Fawns."

"You were one?" I asked.

She nodded.

My mind immediately went to who her Son had been and how he had treated her. Like Daphne had said, it seemed older Fawns saw becoming one as a great privilege.

Dr. Everette looked to be in her forties, but I had a feeling she was older, just someone who'd had work done that slowed down her physical aging. Whoever she'd gone to had done a good job. While she didn't have a wrinkle in sight, she also didn't have that plastic look.

Do all Fawns look good?

Is it like selling your soul to the Devil and you stay beautiful, youthful, and rich the rest of your life?

"Enzo said he told you I'd be coming to collect you." She opened a drawer and pulled out a plastic cup. "I'm going to have you pee in this, and I'll draw your blood."

I rubbed my arms together. The few times I'd had to give blood, I'd nearly passed out. It always made me lightheaded.

"Don't worry," she said, as if reading my mind. "I'll give you juice and crackers to make sure you feel comfortable the entire time."

And without any further questions, I did just as a Fawn was supposed to. I obeyed Enzo's orders.

After she finished, I played with the gauze wrapped around my arm. Then she handed me a packet of birth control and recited the instructions on how to take them.

"They take a while to kick in, but your Son should know to use a condom during the first month," she said before giving my shoulder a reassuring squeeze.

She walked me out of the office, and I checked the time on my phone, seeing that an hour had passed since I'd left class. The class was already over.

I started moving in the direction of my next class, but spun on my heel and headed back upstairs, deciding to skip the rest of the day.

When I returned to my dorm, I dropped my bag on my bed and found a note waiting on my pillow.

I opened it, seeing a typed message.

Death to all Fawns!
DIE, FAWN! DIE!

Gasping, I pressed the note to my chest.

Did Enzo leave this?

The Sons enjoyed playing mind games with their Fawns.

Is this part of his game?

I dropped the note on my bed and dragged my phone from my bag. My shoulders slumped when there were no notifications from Enzo. I plopped down, chewing on my lower lip, before a wave of nausea sent me rushing to our mini fridge for a juice.

As I drank, I asked myself why I wanted to talk to Enzo.

There should've been some relief that he'd left me alone.

But instead, I felt empty inside.

As I racked my brain, sipping on my juice, it hit me.

I tapped his name—well, the ridiculous name he'd saved himself as—and texted him.

> **Me:** Delete those videos you took!

Not only was that important, but it'd open up conversation for us.

My phone beeped seconds later.

> **The Man Who Owns Me:** You miss me, huh?
> Cute.

> **Me:** NO! I just remembered I needed to tell you that.

> The Man Who Owns Me: You miss me, Blair.
> You miss my bossing you around.

Before I could answer, my phone vibrated with a mass of texts from him.

> The Man Who Owns Me: You miss my cock
> inside you.

> The Man Who Owns Me: You miss your lips
> around my cock.

> The Man Who Owns Me: You miss my tongue
> in your tight pussy.

I shook my head as my cheeks warmed.

> Me: No, I want you to delete those videos you
> took.

> The Man Who Owns Me: Send me another,
> and I'll delete those.

Fine. He wants to play that game.
I closed out of our text, took a video of myself flipping him off, and then sent it to him.

> The Man Who Owns Me: Not good enough.
> Send me one with your fingers somewhere
> else.

> The Man Who Owns Me: That somewhere had
> better be between your slick pussy lips.

> The Man Who Owns Me: I'll be waiting for that
> video. Until then, keep missing me, Fawn.
> Don't worry. I'll be back soon.

I dropped my phone and sighed.

Why do I have an urge to send him a video of me touching myself?

To make him miss me while he's gone to ... wherever the hell he is.

I wanted him to think about me night and day, like I was about him.

And at that point, I decided not to mention the texts and note.

For now, I wanted to keep that to myself.

Wanted to pretend they weren't real and that another person didn't want to hurt me.

And if it was someone trying to taunt me, I knew they'd be another victim of Enzo's. I didn't want more blood on my hands.

TWENTY-SEVEN

ENZO

I peeled the bloody glove off my hand and stared into the dead professor's eyes. The woman across from him in the room had been dead for longer.

The woman's blood wasn't on my hands, per se. She'd been Blair's roommate at her previous university. The one who'd thrown her under the bus, lied, and made my precious Fawn sad.

Only I was allowed to make my Fawn sad.

Scanning the dining room, I eyed my work with pride. I always loved when a good plan came together.

The professor's home conveniently had two marble pillars dividing the dining room from the living area.

Earlier, after I'd walked in on him face-fucking her, I dragged their naked bodies out of bed and tied each one to a pillar so they faced each other. After handing them each a gun, I explained that only one of them would leave the house alive. If they wanted to live, they had to shoot the other person.

I gave them an hour, left the room, and ate a bowl of Cap'n Crunch in his kitchen while I waited. When I heard the gunshot, I grinned and dropped the spoon in the bowl.

The woman's body was slumped against the now-blood-smeared pillar. Blood dripped onto her hair and pooled beneath her.

I knew the professor would be the first to shoot. It was what pussies like him did.

"There," the professor had said, his hands shaking as he stared up at me. "Now, let me go."

I had laughed out loud—a rarity for me—and said, "Compliments of Blair, you creepy fucking bastard," before shooting him in the head, straight between his dimwitted eyes.

Afterward, I wiped down every surface I might've touched and staged the scene. Once I was certain there was no trace of me left behind, I dropped the suicide note I'd forced the professor to write before tying him and the woman up beside his body and left.

A private jet was waiting for me at the airport to take me back to New York.

I'd spent the past few days cleaning up the crimes I'd committed against those who'd hurt Blair. And by cleanup, I meant each person I'd found was either no longer breathing or lost everything when I unveiled their secrets.

Returning to New York didn't mean I was finished. More people were still on that list. I also was figuring out the identity of some of them.

And I would, no matter how much work it took.

I never left my business unfinished.

After stepping onto the private jet and making myself comfortable, I checked my phone and snarled in disappointment.

I'd hoped my last text to Blair would've tempted her to challenge me and send me a video of her playing with her pussy. It'd have been a satisfying way to end my day of murdering.

As the jet door closed and the pilot muttered bullshit through the speakers, I lowered my phone's volume and opened my private folder, typing in the password. My tongue dragged slowly across my lips as the video of me fucking Blair from behind filled the screen.

My cock twitched, and I lowered my free hand to my pants, squeezing my dick through the fabric as I listened to her moans and groans.

She's so fucking hot.

So perfect.

My foot tapped as I kept squeezing my erection, seeing the blood smears on my cock as it came out of her pussy. I loved the evidence that I was the first man to tear through her.

I frowned, pausing the video, and cursed myself for not recording while fucking her missionary. Jealous heat burned inside me as I wished I could see her face while I plunged inside her. I wanted the reminder of what her lips had looked like as they formed her perfect moans.

Why do I want to see her like that?

I'd never cared before.

There was always talk about the Night Sons falling for their Fawns. Becoming obsessed with them. While I knew a few who had, I'd never fallen victim to that particular curse.

I cared about very few, but not random women who meant nothing to me.

I shook my head and closed the video.

Four years at Saint Vale had made everything so predictable. Uneventful. My boredom was probably messing with my head, trying to convince me I liked this Fawn more than the others.

That she meant something to me.

To get my mind off Blair, I texted Brooks.

> Me: Did you talk to the Elders yet?

He needed to tell them he had chosen Daphne so her Initiation could start. And if he tried to go back on his word, we'd have problems.

I closed out of his message thread and texted Nico next.

> Me: Get your pussy ass up. I still need that information from you.

I closed out of that thread and texted the friend who'd loaned me the jet. He always owed me favors because, like Brooks, he didn't like to get his hands dirty. Fortunately, he had plenty of money to pay me to get mine a little bloody.

> Me: On the jet now. Thanks, man.

I glanced up when someone cleared their throat. The flight attendant stood there, unbuttoning her blouse and hiking up her skirt in a silent invitation.

As she licked her lips, I glared at her.

I'd fucked this one a few times. She gave decent head, but her moans grated on my nerves. The last time I'd fucked her, I'd shoved a napkin in her mouth to get her to shut the fuck up.

They were nothing like Blair's sweet whimpers.

They didn't make me want to fuck her into oblivion for the next fucking century.

"Button up your shirt and fetch me a drink," I said dismissively.

She stumbled back a step, confusion flashing across her face as she tilted her head.

I leaned forward, resting my elbows on my knees. "A drink. Bourbon. On the fucking rocks."

She turned and sauntered toward the bar, deliberately swaying her hips as she poured. When she glanced back, she even gave a slow little roll of her hips to get a reaction out of me.

She didn't, which only made her try harder.

When she returned with my drink, I muttered a simple, "Thanks," and waved her away.

She stepped closer, and I turned away, not giving her the attention she was looking for. My teeth clenched when she stepped closer, a smug smile on her face, and straddled my lap.

I took a slow gulp of bourbon before tossing the rest in her face.

"Get the fuck out of my lap," I ground out as she stared at me with wide eyes.

Liquor ran down her eyelashes and over her cheeks, but that didn't stop her from pressing down and grinding against my cock.

I shoved her off my lap. "Try that again, and I'll hit the emergency button and throw you out the window."

She hauled herself up and flipped me off with both hands. "Make your own drinks then, asshole."

She stormed off and slammed the door leading to the cockpit.

Give it ten minutes, and she'd be sucking off the pilot.

That was what had happened the last time I used her on this jet.

That was her role on this jet. She fucked whoever was on it, and that was why she was paid so well. Sometimes I participated, because why not?

But today, I couldn't even touch someone else without thinking about Blair.

It seemed the high altitude was fucking with my rationality because not only was I turning down pussy, but I couldn't stop myself from reopening the video of Blair.

I grabbed my AirPods and slipped them in. No one else deserved to hear those sounds from her.

For the rest of my flight, I watched the video on repeat.

I couldn't wait to get back to Saint Vale. Couldn't wait to get back to her.

I was ready to kill who texted me for interrupting my video, until I saw who it was from.

My Fawn was missing me—that much was clear.

I couldn't stop a grin from forming.

Beside her name, I had a little deer emoji. And, fuck, I never used emojis, except for the middle-finger one.

> Fawn: Still waiting for you to confirm you deleted that video.

I immediately replied.

> Me: Still waiting for you to send me a video to replace it with.

I winced, remembering *again* that I needed to upload the video into our Database, but I couldn't bring myself to do it.

No one else had to see it. I could withhold the password, but there was still a chance they could figure out a way to access it. I wouldn't risk any other motherfucker having their eyes on Blair's sweet pussy.

> Fawn: Where are you?

So curious.

I almost asked where she was, but stopped myself. She needed to believe I knew what she was doing every second of the day.

To further make her question and miss me, I tucked my phone into my pocket, hit the button to alert the flight attendant, and told her to stop sucking cock because I needed another drink.

No other woman compared to my Fawn.

And now, that was a fear I had.

If no one compared to her, how was I supposed to release her into the wild when it was time?

TWENTY-EIGHT
BLAIR

It seemed I slept better when Enzo was on campus.

Maybe the demon inside him kept all the others out.

As I stepped out of the shower, I could barely keep my eyes open.

Just like the night before, there had been this spine-chilling darkness that seemed to creep out at night.

As I lay in my alcove, I felt eyes on me.

Goose bumps pebbled across my skin, like finger pokes from someone annoying who was trying to get my attention.

Whether that someone was alive or dead, I wasn't sure.

My body tightened as I grabbed my lotion.

Is it Clarissa? Jett?

Are there spirits in the room with me?

Clarissa had died in this room.

Jumped to her death beside the very bed I slept in.

My father had raised me to believe that the spirits who stayed on Earth instead of passing to whatever other side they were destined for were here to spread evil among humans.

Snorting, I squeezed a dot of lotion into my palm, disbelief settling in that anyone believed him, let alone followed and committed to him. He'd ruled with fear, using it to keep his people obedient.

I wished I'd had a stronger voice back then. More of a backbone.

That voice would've told him to go fuck himself.

But got my day in court when I looked him in the eye and told the world what a terrible person he was.

And at that moment, that was when I saw evil.

But it wasn't from myself. It had been from *him*.

My limbs felt heavy as my shoulders sagged. I dropped the lotion and slowly slid down the wall, bowing my head as exhaustion got the better of me.

The sudden need for even a few minutes of sleep hit me hard.

Yawning, I rubbed my face as my eyes slowly drifted shut.

And when they did, I was pulled into my personal hell.

"Hi, Mama!" I say, racing toward her with the flowers I picked from the empty field. "I brought these for you. I even tied a string around them!" I hold up my other hand to show the smaller bouquet. "And these are for the baby!"

Finding fun out here, in the middle of nowhere, is hard, so I always have to be creative. I love picking flowers and making toys for the other children out of the sticks I find.

Mama rubs her belly where my baby sister is supposed to be.

Her eyes look cold. Empty. Almost dead-looking.

She snatches the flowers from my hands. "The baby is dead, Blair." She rips the flowers apart before shoving me away. "She's dead because of you."

"What?" I cry out, stuttering the word, grabbing the grass to help pull myself up. "How, Mama? I didn't do anything to the baby in your belly."

I look at my father standing beside her, with his usual stern expression.

"I didn't do anything," I say, my voice breaking. "I swear it, Papa. I didn't do anything to the baby."

Tears slide down my cheeks.

I wipe them with my dirty hands and pluck a tiny dandelion from the grass. I can't even see Mama's baby in her belly. How can I hurt her?

One time, while Mama was sleeping, I secretly sang the baby the lullaby I got in trouble for.

But that couldn't have hurt the baby, right?

Mama points her finger at me before grabbing the crushed flowers and ripping them apart again.

She looks over at my father. "I'm tired of you letting this evil thing live with us," she screams at him.

"But ..." I cry, my lips trembling. "I'm not evil, Mama. I didn't do anything to the baby. I love the baby!"

"Loved it so much that you killed it!" she shrieks, turning her back to me as she sobs. "Get her out of my sight."

Papa shoves two fingers in his mouth and whistles loudly toward the men across the field. "Fellas! Get over here!" he calls, waving them over.

I scramble back, crawling away from them in fear.

"Don't try to run now, Blair," my father warns. "Remember what happened last time you did that."

As soon as the two other men reach me, they latch their hands on my arms and drag me away. I beg, scream, and apologize for whatever I did wrong.

But I didn't kill my baby sister.

My father stalks behind us, allowing other men to do his dirty work, like he always does. When I see where they are taking me, I try to wrench myself free.

But they're stronger.

They're always stronger.

"Blair, this is for your own good," my father says when we reach the rickety old wooden shed. He grabs the makeshift handle and opens the door.

The men shove me inside and slam the door shut behind me. I hear the lock click and scream.

I throw myself at the door, pounding on it, but it doesn't budge.

For as weak as the shed looks, they made sure the lock worked well.

I fall onto the dirty ground and bang my fists against the door. Tears pour down my face so hard that they splash off my lips as I cry.

"Please!" I sob. "I'm so sorry! I never wanted to hurt the baby!"

My cheeks burn from the hot tears. They taste salty against my tongue when they reach my mouth.

I stare up at the small hole near the top of the shed. It's already getting dark. Nighttime is always the worst.

Still sobbing, I grab the small, tattered blanket from the corner and wrap it around my shaking body. I cry so loud, hoping Mama will hear and come help me.

That anyone will hear and help me.

As the night grows later, I hear the insects chirping and the animals moving outside. Bugs fly through the hole. Once, a bird came in and stayed with me for a while. It let me pet it before it flew back out.

But tonight, there's nothing.

No animal to soothe me.

No person to help me.

I curl the blanket tighter around my body and stare at the hole where a single star shines through.

Mama said I was evil, but I know one thing.

I'll never be a mama like her.

Bang! Bang! Bang!

The sound woke me from my nightmare.

My eyes opened, and my heart raced as the shed disappeared and the bathroom came into sharper focus. It took me a moment to fully return to the reality of where I was.

The door shook as Daphne knocked again.

"Blair! Are you ready to go?" she shouted from the other side.

I drew in a shaky breath while wiping tears from my face. "Yeah," I said, the word sounding hoarse as it left my mouth. Sniffling, I wiped my eyes and leveled my palm against the wall to lift myself.

As fast as I could, I dressed, shoved my feet into my shoes, and stepped out of the bathroom.

"You okay?" she asked when I came into her view.

"Yeah," I lied, sniffling as I tucked my chin into my neck. "Just allergies."

The look she gave me said she didn't believe me, but she nodded anyway, allowing me to get away with that excuse.

My stomach roiled, but I was grateful she didn't keep pushing.

We left the dorm, and I forced myself to make small talk as we walked to class.

I took my usual seat in American Gothic Lit, but ten minutes in, the grogginess crept back in. I rested my head on the desk before I could stop myself. My eyelids kept growing heavier, and I didn't mean to doze off.

The shed door busts open, waking me, and a flashlight shines straight in my face.

"Grab her legs!" a man shouts.

"No!" I scream, clutching my blanket as they drag me out. My dress lifts as branches and rocks scrape against my skin.

They carry me down the dirt trail we use when we gather our drinking water.

"No, no, no," I cry, fighting to free myself.

"Calm down, girl," a man warns. His breath reeks like rotten fish.

Papa waits by the river with two other men. Mama stands beside him, the only woman there.

"You know the drill," Papa says, puffing on a cigar.

They force me into the freezing water, gripping my waist on each side to keep me still, and I scream when they shove my head under.

Bubbles burst from my mouth as I struggle to breathe before they yank me back up.

I take in two gulps of air before they push me under again.

"May our lord reveal the truth," they chant. "May our lord reveal the truth. Save her soul! Demons be released!"

Their lord is my papa.

He's their religion.

But me? I know the truth.

He's no lord.

No god. Just a very bad man.

"All right, that's enough!" Papa shouts, waving them out of the water as I stand there, shivering.

This is what they do every time.

There's no real test for me to pass.

It's all theatrics.

"Take her back to the shed," Papa instructs. "Hopefully, that got the evil out of her."

The men bow their heads to him before carrying me back.

After they lock me back inside, I wrap the blanket around my shivering body. My teeth chatter as I curl tighter into myself.

I curse them, wishing I really were evil like they said. Then I can hurt them the same way they hurt me.

"Do you really believe the kid is evil?" one of the men asks outside the shed.

A lighter flicks.

They're probably smoking, breaking another one of Papa's rules. He's the only one allowed to smoke here. He says he gets certain privileges because he's special.

"Hell no," the other says with a rough laugh. "Her father is fucked up in the head, but hey, aren't we all?"

"Man, I think about leaving this place every day."

"Careful. You remember Ope?"

"Yeah ... come to think of it, I haven't seen Ope in a while."

"That's because he and his wife were planning to leave. People are starting to doubt Abraham's word. He's starving us here.

Making too many rules that are borderline cruel. And now, no one's seen Ope since." The man snorts. "Abraham is sleeping with Ope's wife now."

"Seriously?"

"Yeah. She told my wife that Abraham said not to tell anyone."

"What about this girl?"

"Her mom had a miscarriage. Happens all the time. My wife's had two. They just needed someone to blame."

"Damn. Even their own daughter?"

"Kids aren't always safe with their parents. They say the girl's evil because her mama's lost a few babies since she was born."

I gasp, clapping a hand over my mouth.

The man lets out a long breath. "Truth is, those things happen sometimes." He lowers his voice, almost like he's afraid someone might hear. "The universe probably just doesn't want that bastard raising any more kids."

"Careful," the other man warns.

For a moment, neither of them says anything.

Then the other man says something so low that I barely catch it. "One day, this place is going to burn to the ground."

Tears slide down my cheeks for a different reason now.

I don't know what a miscarriage is, but I know one thing.

It isn't my fault.

I didn't kill my baby sister. I loved her.

My parents are nothing but liars.

"You men sure have a lot to say."

I clamp my hands over my mouth at the sound of my father's voice.

A gunshot cracks through the night. Then another.

Then I don't hear the men anymore.

I jumped, nearly coming out of my seat, when a hand slammed on the desk. My lungs burned as if I were coming up for air after being dunked in the river.

One eye opened, then the other, and I stared up at Professor Nelson standing in front of me.

"Is my lecture boring you, Miss Dupont?" he asked, brows furrowed into an intimidating stare.

"No ... I'm so sorry," I rushed out, my head still spinning. "I just ..."

He cocked his head to the side. "You just what?"

"I don't blame her, Professor."

My chin lifted as I turned my attention to Cedric sitting at the desk beside mine.

His cold glare stayed locked on Professor Nelson. "Your lectures are boring as fuck, and your teaching style is subpar. I don't blame her for falling asleep."

I couldn't stop the grateful smile from spreading over my face.

Is this what they meant when they said Fawns were protected?

"Go teach, Professor," Cedric demanded, using his phone to motion for the professor to step away from my desk. "Let's see if you can do a better job this time."

Professor Nelson turned on his heel and walked back to the front of the lecture hall.

My throat felt dry, and I rummaged through my bag until I found my water bottle while he resumed his lecture. I lightly slapped my cheeks, trying to keep myself awake.

I couldn't let myself go there again.

Why am I suddenly going back to my past?

The nightmares had come and gone over the years and always returned when I was stressed.

Thankfully, I managed to stay awake for the rest of class, but when it ended, Professor Nelson said, "Blair, a word before you leave."

As the class cleared out, Cedric stayed at his desk, watching me approach Professor Nelson.

Professor Nelson ducked his head and kept his voice low. "Blair, you do not want to cause problems for yourself—"

"Speak louder, Professor!" Cedric shouted. "I'd like to hear whatever it is you need to say to Blair." He dropped his feet from the desk.

The steps seemed to vibrate as he stomped down them and cracked his neck as he came to Nelson's desk.

He ran his hand over the corner, sweeping everything there to the floor, including Nelson's coffee, and sat on the now-empty space. He rested his elbow on his knee, cradling his face with the palm, and stared Nelson down.

"Do go on," he told him. "Tell her whatever was so necessary that you made her stay after class."

Professor Nelson turned his back to us, circling his desk, and grabbed his bag from the back of his desk chair.

"I'm waiting." Cedric tapped his fingers against the desk.

Professor Nelson's mouth snapped shut.

"Exactly." Cedric slid off the desk, smashing his foot against the professor's glasses on the floor. "Come on, Blair."

I held my bag against my stomach as I scurried behind him, leaving the lecture hall. Cedric was already on his phone, texting, as we walked around the corner.

I was almost positive Professor Nelson would fail me in his class now. Even though I had a nearly perfect grade. I was used to shady professors who took it out on my grades when they didn't like me denying them.

"Stay here," Cedric told me. He held his phone to his ear and said, "Nelson was being a fucking asshole to her. Can someone please give me the go-ahead to skin that ugly motherfucker so I don't have to keep attending his classes?" He chuckled. "Yeah, got it."

He ended the call, and I wasn't sure what to do. So I started tiptoeing away.

"Don't move," he said to get me to freeze.

I stood there awkwardly as he typed on his phone.

Checking my watch, I muttered, "I, uh ... have my next class to get to."

"No, you don't," he replied, as if knowing that for a fact.

"Who do I need to kill for hurting my Fawn?"

I turned around to find Enzo only inches away from me.

He jerked his head toward Cedric. "Thanks, man."

Cedric nodded back and walked away.

"Let's go." Enzo made a *follow-me* motion.

I stood there, staring, as warmth spread through my blood. I hadn't seen him in so long that my body somehow ached to get closer to him.

Like he was the devil that could rid the demons that had come back to haunt me.

Someone shoved into my body, pushing me forward, and knocked sense into me.

"Watch where the fuck you're going," Enzo warned them.

The guy's eyes widened when he noticed Enzo, and he took off running.

I stood planted in place, shaking my head. "I have English."

He shook his head. "English can wait. You speak it plenty fine. You know your ABCs."

I crossed my arms, glaring at him.

"Come on, Blair." He clicked his tongue. "Don't make me ask again." He turned around and started walking, as if knowing that I wasn't stupid enough not to follow him.

As we walked up the steps, I made sure to stomp up them as loudly as possible. Deep down, there was relief that he'd rescued me. I didn't want to risk falling asleep in class again and suffering through another nightmare.

I planned to go to Dr. Everette and ask her for sleeping pills. She seemed to like fellow Fawns. Maybe she'd do that for me.

Enzo walked us to the gate that led to his dorm hall and unlocked it. When we were through, he locked it back, and I followed him into his room.

The air was thick with the smell of his cologne, and I inhaled it deep into my nostrils. It'd suddenly become one of my favorite smells. I glanced around, scanning the room for a bottle of it.

Maybe I'll just steal it on my way out of here.

"Why don't I ever go to my Fawn room?" I asked, dropping my bag on the floor.

"I don't care for that room." He collapsed onto the chair at his desk, doing a spin in it before facing me again.

"But isn't that where your other Fawns stayed?"

"Yes. It seems Daphne still has a big mouth." He shot me an unhappy glare.

I shrugged, happy she did. "She said that you never brought Clarissa here, to your dorm, and she always stayed in her Fawn room. She also said that other Fawns stay there."

I slapped a hand over my mouth, stupidity settling in that I'd ratted Daphne out. I'd just told him how much she knew about the Sons and Fawns.

"Don't worry about it," Enzo said, as if reading my mind. "Daphne already knew too much. It's why she's allowed in the Devil's Lair."

There was more he wasn't telling me. I knew it.

"If I sent you to your Fawn room, you'd be down there alone," he went on. "Plus, I like you here better." He opened a desk drawer, drew out a knife, and began sharpening it in front of me like the maniac he was.

Bending down, I collected my book and MacBook from my bag and walked toward the bed. Enzo dropped his knife, reached out, and snatched the book from my hand before I made it there.

I attempted to grab it back from him, but he held it out of my reach.

"Seriously?" I groaned, hating how annoying he was. "Just because I'm not going to class doesn't mean I don't have to do the work."

"*Rebecca*, huh?" he asked, reading the book title. Opening it, he fanned through the pages. "Let's make this a bit more interesting, shall we?"

I narrowed my eyes at him, already nervous about what that entailed. "What do you mean?"

He used the book to motion toward the bed. "You sit. I'll read to you."

"You can't be serious?" I asked around a scoff.

"Sit, Blair." He playfully smacked my stomach with the book.

With an annoyed sigh, I walked over to his bed and climbed onto it, my feet hanging over the sides. Running my fingers over the black comforter, I remembered what had happened the last time I was here.

Me losing my virginity.

Him panting behind me. Above me.

The heavenly sounds of his groans.

Enzo removed my purple bedazzled bookmark, flicking it across the room, and started reading from a random page. A page I'd already read yesterday, which did nothing for my progress.

His voice flowed through the room, and I shut my eyes, relaxing my shoulders like I was listening to my favorite audiobook. I took in the details of the words, reliving them better than when I'd read yesterday.

After a few pages, he stopped.

"I'm bored." He tossed the book aside. "Take off your clothes." He grabbed his knife and returned to sharpening it.

"Excuse me?" I huffed out before violently shaking my head. "No. I told you, I need to read that for class." I crossed my arms, as if safeguarding myself from not taking off my clothes.

The asshole was so fucking bossy.

So sure of himself that he thought he could simply tell me to get naked and I'd obey him.

It's what he's used to, Blair.

People obey and bow down to this man.

"Fine." He dropped the knife and sharpener on the desk.

I couldn't help my gaze from falling to the weapon.

"Blair, how I'd love for you to try that," he said around a chuckle, following my line of vision. "It'd make my day." He winked at me, keeping our eye contact strong as he grabbed the knife and tucked it inside his back pocket.

He kicked off his shoes and grabbed the book from the floor. "Now, what page was I on?" He pretended to actually search for the page, but when he started reading, it wasn't where he'd left off.

With the book in one hand, he walked over to me. I stared up, unsure what to do, and bit into my lower lip. My gaze was locked on his lips as the words left his mouth.

He grabbed a handful of my hair with his free hand as he grumbled the words and tugged my face toward his lap.

When he read the line about all of us having our own particular devil who rode and tormented us, I found it too personal in the moment.

He muttered another line about believing old demons had been conquered before releasing my hair and switching the book to his nondominant hand. He untucked his shirt from his pants, then unbuttoned and unzipped his black slacks. "People never conquer their demons."

He cupped himself, squeezing his erection tight, and undid the bottom buttons of his shirt.

I stared, jaw slack, as he dropped his pants and briefs to his ankles, freeing his stiff cock.

There it was.

Only inches from my face.

It pointed forward with a slight downward curve. The skin looked stretched, and the head was dark.

His skin was warm as I wrapped my hand around his cock, stroking it slowly. Veins protruded along the length.

The last time I had given him a blow job, I still felt half drugged. My anxiety had been on edge as I tried to process the Initiation.

But now, I took in every inch of his cock.

And there were plenty.

I hated that my tongue ran along my lower lip and my mouth watered.

"I'll keep reading, and you start sucking," he said, thrusting his hips forward.

I shot my hand out, resting it along his hip bone, and snorted. "You have such a way with words."

My gaze lifted, meeting his, and we both went silent.

He dropped his hand, resting it along my jawline, cupping my face as if it was something precious. "The devil in *our* story will always win, sweet Fawn."

I flinched when his fingers dug into my cheek before he plucked his thumb along my lower lip. As if on instinct, I opened my mouth as he guided his cock toward it.

My gaze stayed on his as I dragged in a slow breath before wrapping my lips around his wide length.

He hissed in a breath as I choked when the tip hit the back of my throat. He held me there, my forehead against his six-pack, while I struggled to breathe through my nose.

My eyes watered as he loosened his hold. I relaxed my jaw before pulling back, sucking him hard.

"Such a good Fawn," he said around a groan as he threw his head back. "That's my good girl."

He held the book with one hand while spreading his palm around the back of my head, keeping me at the pace he liked, and returned to reading the words aloud.

While he was in charge, I'd never felt so powerful as I worked him in my mouth. Reaching out, I wrapped my hand around his length, moving it in rhythm with how I sucked him.

He filled my mouth, and as I gained some courage, I lowered my hand to his balls, tugging on them.

"Yes," he said, his voice breaking at the end. "What a good girl, sucking this cock."

At this point, I didn't hear a word he read. All my focus was on sucking him, impressing him, and dragging myself into the dark world of the Sons.

Maybe his dark world would cancel out mine.

Maybe it'd stop my nightmares.

Saliva fell down my chin as he continued to stop after every sentence he read to praise me.

"Such a good Fawn."

"Oh, I'm training you well."

"You suck this cock so perfect, my Fawn."

Each praise felt like a new achievement.

His legs tensed, his hips tilting forward, and his words started to break up as his breathing grew heavier. I gagged when he pitched his hips forward and hollowed my cheeks as his cock swelled inside my mouth.

I kept sucking on the tip and taking long pulls of his cock as his breathing grew more erratic. His praises were accompanied by longer moans until I felt small drops of cum land on my tongue.

He dropped the book, using both hands to hold my head in place, and he filled my mouth. His eyes slammed shut while every limb in his body shook.

"See, I think we both learned something here," he said as he came down from his orgasm.

When he pulled out of my mouth, I moved my now-aching jaw to each side to ease the tension.

He patted my cheek before pulling up his pants. "You can go now. I have business to attend to."

"What?" I stuttered out in disbelief.

He grabbed my elbow, pulling me up from the bed, rested his hands on my shoulders, and guided me toward the door. One of his hands left me to open the door, and he shoved me out of the room.

Right as he was about to slam the door in my face, I pushed him back.

He grunted, falling back a step at my shove.

"You don't get to talk to or treat me like that." I pointed my finger in his face as anger spiraled inside me.

A slow smirk built across his face. "Or what?"

I stared him down.
He did the same, like a challenge.
Maybe it was the anger.
Or that I was sleep-deprived.
But I pushed him again ... and then I kissed him.

TWENTY-NINE

ENZO

I didn't fucking kiss my Fawns.

Never had. Never planned to.

I'd never kissed *anyone*.

Other than my mom and sister *on the cheek*, and that didn't count.

But for some reason, I couldn't drag my mouth away from Blair's.

How dare she think she could put her lips on mine?

She had more guts than I wanted her to have.

Blair's lips felt like what I imagined heaven might be like, though I'd never find out, of course. Maybe that was why I wanted another taste.

Everyone wanted what they couldn't have.

Blair was my little angel, my Fawn, and I was about to drag her straight into my hell.

I kissed her harder, stealing the breath from her lungs and loving the way it hitched when my hand curled around her neck.

I could taste myself on her tongue. I savored the flavor, mixed with mint.

My heartbeat thrashed like a monster in my chest as I stalked forward, guiding her into the hallway. She gasped when her back struck the wall.

I swallowed her shaky breaths, wishing I could inhale her completely and keep her there.

She moaned when I released her throat and shoved her skirt up, ripping her panties away and stuffing them into my pocket.

I quickly unbuckled my belt, already aching for her again.

All Blair had to do was breathe in my direction, and I was hard.

In seconds, I pulled out my cock, lined it up with her entrance, and thrust inside her.

She was soaked for me, and I loved that she'd probably been that way since her mouth had been wrapped around my cock.

"Yes," she moaned as I bent my knees slightly, adjusting my angle and moving faster.

Her legs locked around my waist, clinging to me like I was the only thing keeping her steady in a storm. Her fingers dug into my shirt collar as her lips attacked mine.

I pounded into her, catching her lower lip between my teeth to steady us. Her fingers slid to my shoulders, nails digging into my skin through my shirt, and she didn't even freeze when she heard voices coming from somewhere down the corridor.

I grinned against her lips, dragging my tongue across them before pulling back. "You hear them, Blair?" I asked, each stroke feeling better than the last. "Do you want them to see me fucking you like the little slut Fawn you are?"

She answered with a moan, pulling my mouth back to hers as a quiet, "Please," escaped her.

As the voices grew louder, the tension in my body wound tighter.

There was a chance they could see us, but right now? I didn't care. The electricity running through my veins felt like lightning under my skin. Nothing existed at this moment but Blair and me.

A switch turned on inside me, and I lost control as I fucked her.

Hard and fast and so fucking unforgiving that she'd be sore for days.

Her pussy swallowed my cock as if it was just as starved as I was for her.

I kept her facing me because I couldn't stop kissing her.

Couldn't stop tasting her.

And that was a problem for me.

It *terrified* me.

"*Fuuuck*," I groaned against her mouth when she rolled her hips, matching my rhythm. "That's right. Fuck me back, baby."

She panted, and I loved that she was so wet that I could hear my dick moving inside her.

My grip tightened on her waist as I rammed my hips forward, needing her as close to me as possible.

I also needed her to hurry up and come all over my cock because I wasn't sure how much longer I could last.

Her head tipped back, hitting the wall, as her legs trembled around me. I hated that I lost her mouth, so I dropped a hand from her waist to drag it back toward mine.

Relief hit me as our lips pressed back together. But now, it turned less into kissing and more like teeth colliding as our bodies moved together.

The voices got louder for a second before drifting away.

"Come on," I grunted against her lips, shifting my hips again to better hit her G-spot. My hand slid beneath her skirt, my thumb finding her clit, moving over it in small circles.

That was her undoing.

Her pussy clenched against my cock, so damn tight. A sharp moan escaped her lips as she pressed into the wall. I held her there, both hands back on her hips, and kept her steady as her orgasm rolled through her.

I kept her pinned to the wall, fucking her hard, and I knew if I released her, she'd slide straight to the floor.

It took me only three more thrusts before my body locked up.

I froze, a low groan falling from my throat, as the tension inside me snapped.

I held us there, not wanting a drop of my cum to leak out of her, as we fought to catch our breaths.

"Fuck," I panted out, forehead dropping to hers in the hallway.

My pulse thrummed through my body as her breath fanned against my face.

I'd never felt so connected with someone after sex.

Never felt the need to stay exactly where I was, like pulling out of her was losing a piece of myself.

She's mine. My Fawn. Mine.

That thought wouldn't leave my mind.

When I finally loosened my hold, her body sagged against me. I scooped her up, and she didn't fight me when I carried her back into my room.

My next order of business? Making sure my Fawn got some sleep.

THIRTY

BLAIR

I released a long yawn as I woke up.

I'd slept for who knows how long and hadn't had one nightmare in the safety of Enzo's bed.

The devil had become my protector.

But this moment of peace didn't trick me. I wondered how long I'd have it before Enzo dragged me into another version of hell.

Yawning again, I stretched my arms forward as I sat up, finding Enzo on the couch along the opposite wall with his laptop open on his lap. His feet were kicked up on the coffee table.

When he noticed I was awake, he dropped the laptop to his side and stood, walking toward me.

"You missed me while I was away," he stated matter-of-factly.

I furrowed my brows in a sleepy glare. "I did no such thing."

He sat on the edge of the bed. "It's okay. You can pretend you didn't." Grabbing my hand, he pulled us both to our feet. "Though how many times did you text me?"

"Always know where your predators are," I grumbled as he guided me toward the couch, dropping me onto an empty leather seat cushion. "Where were you?"

He strolled toward the fridge, pulling out two bottled waters. "Taking care of business."

"You're a college kid. What *business* do you need to take care of?"

"That's where you're wrong." He handed me a water. "A college kid is about number twenty on the list of who I am, Blair."

He plucked his laptop from the couch, setting it on the table, and the couch dipped as he sat back down.

I rolled my shoulders back as I took a sip of water. "What time is it?"

He checked his watch. "Four thirty."

"Shit," I hissed, slapping my hand against my forehead. "I've missed all my classes."

"And?"

"And? Unlike *you*, I have to pass my classes."

I didn't know why I thought he didn't need to pass. But I couldn't see Arisono expelling him as easily as she would me.

"They'll pass you," he said with that same certainty he always had.

I blew out an upward breath, rolling my eyes. "Oh, yes, Professor Nelson really appreciated me falling asleep in his class and then Cedric pretty much putting him in his place in front of the other students. He'll blame me for that and find a way to fail me."

"He won't fail you." Again, that fucking certainty.

"How do you know?"

"If he fails you, then he'll have to deal with me. Nelson doesn't want that. He tried that with my last Fawn and learned his lesson."

"What was his *lesson*?"

"None of your business."

"Speaking of Clarissa ..." I let my words trail off in hopes that he'd finish that sentence.

Unfortunately, he didn't.

He played these games better than I did and knew all the tricks.

"Did you push her out the window?" I finally asked when he didn't bite.

The corner of his mouth lifted. "Do I look like a man who'd push someone out a window?"

"Yes," I said with a heavy, certain nod. "You absolutely do."

He scrubbed a hand over his face. "I didn't push her out the window. She jumped. Suicide. The facts were clear as day. I wasn't even on campus that day."

"But Jett—"

"I thought we'd already established Jett was a liar."

"He didn't lie to me about the Night Sons." I gave him a pointed look.

"He didn't tell you the full truth." He took a long drink of his water, and his Adam's apple bobbed as he swallowed it down.

I raised one finger and started counting off on my hands. "Secret society." Another finger raised. "Fawns." Another finger. "Making my life hell."

He capped and dropped his water bottle, allowing it to roll across the couch and fall in a crack between the cushions.

I truly believed that Enzo hadn't killed Clarissa. There was something in my gut that told me he hadn't done it. Even Daphne, who wasn't his fan, hinted that Enzo hadn't physically pushed her.

But I *did* believe that he was a part of the pack that had driven her to jump. The people around us can be silent killers in ways they didn't know.

But there was always that chance that I was wrong too. I could've been dick hypnotized from all the orgasms he'd given me and ignoring the red flags.

That was all Enzo was. Red flags.

Though I kept following those flags straight to him.

Ss if they led the way to my happiness.

His voice turned deeper as he said, "Am I making your life hell, my Fawn?" He ran his hand beneath his lower lip. "I'm almost positive you were in heaven not too long ago when I was thrusting my cock inside your tight—"

Without thinking, I heaved forward, jumping on him to cover his mouth, shocking us both. Enzo caught me around the waist, pulling me onto his lap, and for a moment, neither of us moved.

My cheeks were red as reality hit me, and when I tried to climb off his lap, he slammed his palms against my thighs, holding me in place.

His hands splayed out along my bare thighs, slightly under my skirt, as my shins were pushed along each of his thighs. Lowering one hand, he played with the upper hem of my knee-length sock.

"Why aren't you sleeping?" he asked, focusing on my sock's lace.

I fidgeted in his lap. "Who says I haven't been?"

His chin rose, his eyes snapping to mine. "Your face." He tapped my cheek with his thumb. "You look like sleep-deprived shit."

"Thanks," I grumbled.

"I can't have my Fawn looking tired. Can't have her tired. You're supposed to be well rested for when I need you."

My shoulders rounded forward as my brain lost all words.

"You still have a lot to tell me about yourself, Blair," he added.

I gulped, remembering our unfinished conversation about my father and my past.

I'd spilled some of my secrets, but not all of them.

I'd never vomit all of them out.

Enzo slowly started unbuttoning my shirt. When I tried to grab his wrist, he used his other hand to drag my hand off his, finger by finger. My shirt opened, displaying my white bra.

"Very plain," he muttered, running his hand along the top of my breasts. "Very boring. My Fawn isn't boring. I want to see and learn about every version of you." He patted my thigh. "Get up. Time for us to go."

"Go where?" I asked.

When I didn't move fast enough, he kicked his leg over, depositing me on the floor as if I were a pillow he no longer wanted there.

"Fawns don't ask questions. Their blind loyalty causes them to simply follow," he replied.

THIRTY-ONE

ENZO

Blair carried her bag as she followed me outside and across the courtyard. The pinks and reds of the setting sun burned into the sky around us.

My jaw hurt from clenching it harder with every step.

I was breaking every rule I'd ever set for myself.

I'd kissed her. I was spending my free time with her. Hell, I was spending all my time thinking about her.

When I first saw Blair, she was alone and unprotected. I viewed that as a weakness.

But now? The thought of anyone else standing beside her created dark thoughts in my head. Because if someone was going to be by her side, it was going to be me.

Even in my first year, when having a Fawn felt like owning a shiny toy, I'd never become attached like this.

Truth was, deep down, I hadn't even liked those Fawns. They'd been nothing more than a convenience.

Blair was supposed to mean nothing to me, like them. Yet here I was, making sure she slept and taking her out in public with me.

I led her past the greenhouse and toward the edge of the woods.

The farther we walked from campus, the quieter everything

got. When the small cemetery came into view, that same lost look was on Blair's face.

While I'd managed to be a bit more patient with Blair, the girl was still so damn slow. I reached back, caught her hand, and tugged her forward beside me.

When she fell in step next to me, I should've dropped her hand, but I kept them interlaced as we walked between tall headstones, their polished surfaces just as meticulously cared for as the tunnels below us. Saint Vale's greatest contributors were buried there.

Gravel crunched below our feet, and we didn't stop until we reached the hidden garden. A small gate stood between two narrow stone columns at the entrance.

Saint Vale's crest was carved into each one with *Hortus Electae* beneath it.

The Garden of the Chosen One.

I pushed the gate open, and we entered the garden, where a building sat at its center.

Blair's innocence showed as she slowly turned in a circle, taking in the garden in awe.

I had to admit, the place was nice.

It was secluded from campus, and the most peaceful spot at Saint Vale. Small fountains bubbled between winding stone paths, iron benches, and flowers that stayed colorful all year-round.

We followed the path into the thick of the garden, passing a pair of doe statues standing watch along the walkway before we reached the First Benefactors Building.

According to Saint Vale's history, the First Benefactors Building was the first structure on campus, where the original four families had once lived.

Now, they claimed it served as a place to preserve the university's history and was always locked because that was a lie.

Only the Current Sons, Elders, and Fawns had access to this building.

The Elders and Current Sons' entrance sat on one side. It

connected to the underground parking lot. The Fawns' entrance was on the opposite end, the one facing the gardens.

Blair kept opening her mouth like she wanted to ask me something, but the question never came. Her hand squeezed mine when we neared a door.

I gave it a squeeze back, then let go and reached into my pocket to pull out her access card.

Back when there was no technology, they used skeleton keys, but we've progressed beyond that, thank God. Now, everyone had their own access cards.

"Here." I handed her the card. "This is yours. Don't lose it."

The same broken halo symbol etched on mine was stamped on hers.

She nervously took one last glance around the garden before looking at the door. "What is this building?"

"This is where you'll enter your Fawn Quarters."

I motioned for her to scan her card and go first when the door opened.

A steel staircase was the first thing you saw when walking in. Blair took a second to pull in a breath before following me down into the Fawn Quarters.

The space was large and had everything they needed, including a movie theater, gym, kitchen, library, and storage area.

"There are no other Fawns?" Blair asked me.

"One," I told her. "But she never hangs out here. Her Son likes to keep her to himself."

I didn't know if Nico had even bothered showing his Fawn her quarters. Most of the time, he fucked her and then sent her on her way.

No other Son had selected a Fawn.

According to the Elders, we were in a Fawn shortage, and they were pissed about it. That was probably why they kept insisting our generation of Sons was out of control.

But I couldn't blame the other Sons. Sometimes, having a

Fawn felt like owning a pet, and not everyone wanted that responsibility.

These days, it was easier to get a blow job or quick fuck from a random girl here at the university. We didn't have to swear them to secrecy and didn't have to protect them or answer their questions.

After passing three doors, I stopped us at the one with a broken halo. It was the same room I'd taken her to after her final phase of the Initiation, when we gave her electrolytes and let her sleep.

Also the room where I'd tasted her pussy for the first time.

"If you're ever in trouble, you come down here. It's the safest place you could ever go," I said.

The tunnels served as a form of protection against enemies. They were also so deep into the earth that they had served as bunkers during the Cold War.

We walked into her room, but since she'd already been in there, there was no need for a tour here.

"Why does everything look so virginal?" she asked, making a show of doing a twirl to emphasize the point that everything here was white.

White bedding, white walls, white furniture.

I shrugged. "It's been that way for as long as I've been here. In the library are old journals donated by past Fawns during their time down here. Feel free to browse through them. Maybe you'll learn some stuff."

Most of the time, when other Fawns were down here, we expected them to talk to the newer Fawns. But Blair didn't have anyone to learn from other than the limited information Daphne had.

Good thing I hadn't let Brooks strangle her all the times he wanted to.

Blair was quiet as I gave her the rest of the tour, and as I started to turn toward the stairs to leave, I stopped.

To get where I wanted to take Blair, we'd have to walk back through the graveyard, woods, and greenhouse. That sounded like a pain in the ass.

So I decided to break the rules because I might as well make it a damn habit.

"Come on." I led her to that secret door no Fawn was supposed to know about.

I scanned my card, and we walked into the tunnels.

"Pick up the pace," I called over my shoulder as we entered the restricted corridor and cut a right. "I feel like I'm saying that more than necessary."

She nearly tripped over herself as she walked faster. "Sorry, I don't have daddy long legs," she grumbled.

"Watch it," I warned with a smirk.

She rolled her eyes, and I considered taking her against this wall to punish her for her little attitude.

Our next stop was the Devil's Lair.

Blair needed to have some fun, release some of that tension, and I needed to speak with the guys while also keeping an eye on her.

An Evanescence song blared through the space, and I noticed a group of girls were in the corner.

Emeri and Brooks were seated at the bar, drinking.

I pushed Blair in the direction of the girls. "Go have fun."

"Yay!" Daphne called out as Blair walked over to them. "My girl is here!"

Brooks swiveled around in his stool to face me. "Dude, what the fuck?"

I snatched his drink and smelled what was inside, twitching my nose at the strong scent of vodka. "I told you to lay off the liquor."

He reached forward, attempting to grab it back, but I held it back out of his grasp. When he tried again, I gulped down the last sip and slid the glass across the bar.

Emeri only shook his head, taking a slow drink.

"You can't bring her through the main tunnels." Brooks propped one elbow on the bar and massaged his temples, as if my breaking the rules was his biggest stressor.

I glared at him. "You're the last person who should be questioning me right now. It was easier going that way than through the Fawn Quarters. If someone has a problem with it, they can take it up with me. She won't remember anyway." I took the stool beside him.

Brooks snorted. "You're getting stupid. Making stupid moves."

"*I'm* making stupid moves? Keep talking shit, and I'll make you take care of your own bodies when you're being fucking stupid."

"Both of you, chill out," Emeri said before settling his stare on Brooks. "We've all done stupid shit. Let's just enjoy the night because I'm sure we'll be dealing with another problem soon."

Nico strolled in, hands in the air, and interrupted our talk.

"Hey, bitches!" he yelled. "Party is fucking here!"

"See." Emeri shook his head. "We have to deal with the fucking toddler Sons who've yet to mature."

His patience for the younger generation was slim.

His patience for *everything* was slim.

"Sorry, Zo," Brooks said. "It's been a day."

Brooks stood, scrubbing a hand over his face, and stretched across the bar to grab a seltzer water.

"The fuck is going on with you, man?" I asked him.

"I don't know." He popped the cap open. "My father's reelection bid has been a fucking mess. He's acting like a nightmare. The pressure is on me because if he loses this election, then my chance of becoming president is gone."

I didn't know why anyone would want to be president. I'd rather slit my wrists and jump into a shark tank.

But that was Brooks's dream, and as his friend, I had to support that. Had to help make it happen.

"Don't worry." I patted his back a few times. "You'll get the gig, even if I have to kill someone to make it happen."

"Tonight, we're playing beer pong," Nico announced to the room, waving the girls over. "Havens, Daphne, and Fawn who isn't supposed to be here, bring your pretty little asses over here!"

Thirty-Two

Blair

Whenever Enzo dragged me somewhere, I felt like I was entering a new world.

Saint Vale existed in its own orbit.

I'd never seen anything like it.

And this was coming from a girl who had grown up in a religious sect that alienated its members from the real world. There were so many new things I experienced after my freedom.

None of them made me feel as alive as this university.

None of them gave me friends.

None of them gave me a sense of belonging.

Even if it was batshit crazy.

But I had been born and raised among madness. It was only fitting that it was where I fit in the best.

I supposed that was the hype around the place.

Why the rich and elite shipped their spawn here.

I stood beside Daphne, the blaring music making it hard for me to think as I took in everything that I could inside the Devil's Lair. What I'd established now was that this was the hangout for Saint Vale's most powerful.

While the real world had its divisions, so did the university.

And this right here? This was where only the select lucky few could come. And somehow, I'd found myself in the midst of it all.

Neither of my first two experiences down here had been pleasant. One of them was when Enzo shoved a knife between my fingers repeatedly, and the other when he held a gun to my head.

Fingers crossed tonight, there were no weapons near me.

When my gaze landed on Enzo, it stopped. He, Brooks, and another guy were speaking at the bar. Things looked heated between Enzo and Brooks, and I wished I could inch closer and listen to their conversation.

After a few minutes, Brooks stormed out, leaving the same way Enzo and I had come through.

That seemed to be a pattern with Brooks.

No wonder Daphne hated him.

My attention slid from Enzo to the guy who'd referred to me as *Fawn who isn't supposed to be here*. He and another guy carried a long table from a closet and began setting it up.

"Who are they?" I asked Daphne.

"Emeri is with Enzo at the bar," she said before pointing toward the guys setting up the table. "That's Nico and Cassian. They're Enzo's nephews. Both are also Night Sons."

I recognized Emeri as the guy who'd sat at the table, playing with the Zippo lighter, the last time I was here.

I'd seen Cassian on campus once before. He was taller than the other guys, which had made him stand out when I noticed him walking down the stairs near the vestibule. His thick brown hair was messy, pushed up into different directions.

Nico reminded me of a younger version of Enzo. Also a geekier version. His hair was lighter, longer, and he wore thick, black-rimmed glasses.

"Do they have Fawns yet?" I thought back to how Enzo had said one of them did.

"I think Nico does, but he's all hush-hush about it, and I'm pretty sure he keeps her chained in a closet somewhere."

She laughed at the horrified expression I gave her.

"Kidding. Nico is probably the most chill out of the Night Sons right now." She gestured to them. "As you can clearly see. Other than that, I don't know of any other Fawns, but I'm not exactly in on the intel." She smiled. "I just know enough to be dangerous."

I kept my eyes on Nico and Cassian as they dragged out a case of beer and dropped it onto the table. "What are they doing?"

"Girl, it's beer pong," she replied.

"Is beer pong a normal thing for them?"

In my head, I pictured them as always being creepy masked men who didn't do normal things.

"It's usually when the younger Sons come in, like Nico. The older ones act all disgruntled and pissed off at the world half the time. Letting loose a little is good for them."

"Pissed off at the world ... sounds like Enzo."

At the mention of him, my gaze returned to the bar.

He was now staring at me, his back resting against the bar and his arms spread along each side of it. As his eyes burned into mine, I swallowed hard, hurriedly looking away.

"All right, ladies, get your asses over here," Nico said again, popping open cans of beers.

Cassian arranged the cups as if they were pool balls going in a rack.

Nico turned on his heel to point at Emeri and Enzo. "You two fuckers." He moonwalked while beckoning them over with his hand.

Emeri pushed away from the bar. "I'm passing this time, Nic."

"Your loss," Nico replied with a half shrug before pouring beer into the cups.

Half of the liquid splashed onto the table instead of its destination.

Cassian moved to the opposite end of the table while Nico popped open another beer can. Beer fizzed onto the floor as he filled more cups.

When he was finished with his side, Nico walked behind the

bar, grabbed a bottle of champagne, and popped the cork before heading to the empty cups.

"Because you ladies always bitch about beer"—he poured the champagne into the cups—"I have something else for you."

"Good boy." Adelina tossed her phone to the side and stood. "At least one of you knows how to treat us well down here."

Nico fake bowed and winked at her.

"All right, everyone needs to release some stress tonight," Nico said as if he were an announcer speaking through a microphone.

He came over, handing a ball to Daphne, and looked at me. "You ever played?"

I shook my head.

He plunged two fingers in his mouth, whistling loud to get the guys' attention at the bar. "Enzo, get your ass over here and show this girl how to play. You brought her, which means you're responsible for her."

Enzo shook his head as he dragged himself away from the bar. His arms swung in the air as he walked our way. For some reason, the way he walked reminded me of all the dirty things I'd allowed him to do to me lately.

He scratched the back of his head, behind his ear, looking at me with that intense stare. "You've never played a simple game of beer pong, my Fawn?"

"I've heard of it," I said, suddenly feeling like an outcast. "Just never played."

I'd attended a few frat parties, but they grossed me out. Too many sweaty, bare-chested dudes, chest-bumping and bonging beers. It wasn't my scene. At the few I had attended, I'd always end up leaving early.

"Then you know the rules?" he asked.

"Throw the ball and hope to make it in a cup?" I formed a giant, cheesy grin on my face.

"Make it into a cup on the *opposite* end of the table."

"Obviously." I rolled my eyes in fake annoyance.

"Don't worry." Daphne slid over to us. "I'll be Blair's partner."

"I think the fuck not, blondie," Nico said. "Enzo is her partner."

"Nah." Enzo snatched the ball from Nico, threw it in the air, and caught it. "Let the girls play. I'll be the coach on the sidelines." He tossed the ball across the table, and it landed in one of the beer cups.

"Jackass," Nico said. "And you call yourself an uncle." He snatched the cup and chugged down the beer.

I shuddered when Enzo stepped in closer to lower his mouth to my ear.

"Just gave you an advantage," he said, his voice almost a low growl. "See the things I do for you?"

"Yes," I said as if I were a breathless damsel. "Such a gentleman you are."

His chuckle that rumbled through my ear made me squeeze my thighs together.

Daphne intertwined her fingers and popped them. "Come on, Blair. Stretch it out. We can't let them beat us."

Cassian stood at the end of the table, closing one eye, and lined his ball up with a cup. It landed in the cup in front of me.

Daphne immediately grabbed the cup and downed the champagne in one swig.

"All right, new Fawn, let's see you prove yourself again," Nico said.

"Prove yourself again."

He saw my Initiation.

Asshole.

For that, I didn't only want to hit his cup. I had another plan in mind.

I grabbed my ball, stood back as if I needed a special stance, and threw the ball. It didn't hit the table.

It headed straight for Nico's face.

I frowned when he caught it before it made contact.

"Nice try," he said with no animosity in his tone.

If I'd tried that with, say, Enzo or Emeri, their reactions would've been different.

Nico stared me down before looking at Enzo. "Bro, teach your girl how to aim."

I loved the amusement creeping onto Enzo's face, even though he tried to hide it.

He lowered his tone, his eyes on Nico when he said, "Next time, aim *lower*, Blair."

I couldn't stop my lips from forming a wide grin.

Nico took his turn.

His ball landed in the cup in front of me. I grabbed the cup and gagged while drinking the champagne.

I just wasn't an alcohol girlie.

Give me hot chocolate or lemonade any day.

Daphne took her next turn and sank the ball straight into a beer cup. Cassian winked before drinking.

When it was my turn, Enzo came up behind me.

Nico cupped his hand around his mouth. "Look at Coach Enzo, stepping into the game."

I loved the way my back felt against his warm chest.

"Now," he said, almost sounding flirtatious, "I can't have my Fawn making me look bad, can I?"

Tingles swept up my spine when he ran his fingers down my arm before lifting my hand with the ball.

"You want a good stance like this." He used his foot to spread mine farther apart and positioned me into a perfect stance.

But I wasn't pulling away from him.

I liked his touch too much.

I forgot what I was even doing as I inhaled the smell of him.

"Pay attention, Blair," he rasped. His face went into my neck. "Aim for the middle cup. You make that, and I'll reward you with my tongue later. Win this entire game, and I'll do it all night."

I felt his lips smirk against my skin before he inched away to draw my hand back. His hand stayed on my wrist as I threw the ball. It flew through the air and landed straight in the cup Enzo had instructed me.

He laid a gentle kiss on my neck and smacked my ass. "Good girl."

"Fucking cheaters." Cassian grabbed the cup and drank the beer.

"Damn." Adelina fanned herself from the side. "Am I watching a beer pong game or soft-core porn?"

Enzo gave my ass another playful slap before retreating to his sidelines. I frowned, wanting to beg him to come back and *coach me* again.

In fact, with how hot my blood was running, I'd be okay with him dragging me into one of those private rooms.

I didn't know what this man did to me.

But one touch, and my body was ready to be claimed by him again.

I had to drink another champagne when Nico made a shot.

Each time it was my turn, Enzo hyped me up.

I loved seeing this side of him. Liked seeing him act so human. So normal.

We played two rounds.

Each of us won a game.

Daphne, thankfully, drank most of the cups. She claimed she was a champagne queen and had no issue getting drunk tonight.

Enzo's phone ringing drew my attention away from the game. He pulled it out of his pocket, checked the screen, and put his hand to his ear while walking away to answer it.

I noticed the way his back went straight and the way his nostrils flared as he listened.

"Are you fucking kidding me?" he roared.

His hand holding the phone started shaking.

"I'll be right there," he snapped into the speaker. "You'd better keep me updated." He ended the call, looked up at the ceiling, and shouted, "Fuck!" before storming past us.

Without thinking, I took off after him.

"Anyone going to stop her?" Cassian said behind my back.

"She's his Fawn," Nico replied. "That's what she's there for."

Enzo left through the same way that we had come in, and I struggled to chase him.

I had no idea where he was going.

Might've been straight to hell.

But I was his Fawn, and I could tell he needed me.

THIRTY-THREE

ENZO

I ran through the tunnels, making the necessary twists and turns, and all I could think of were the words Benny had just told me over the phone.

I should've told Nico why I was leaving, but I had no patience for waiting for him to get his shit together. He was a big boy, and he'd find a way to the city.

I couldn't deal with his drunk ass right now.

Not when my father had been shot.

I heard Blair behind me but didn't slow down. Her loud breathing echoed through the tunnels. Poor thing was really struggling to keep up.

The words, *Go back, Blair,* were on the tip of my tongue, but they didn't leave my mouth.

My lungs hurt, but I didn't stop running. I figured Blair would eventually give up, but she didn't. I was impressed.

When I reached the door that led to the parking garage, I stalled. It was time to determine how the rest of the night would go.

I could shut the door and leave Blair, or I could wait for her.

She was a few feet away from me. Even in my panic, I couldn't help but think the way she ran was cute. Her face was flushed, and she looked ready to pass out.

But she didn't quit.

Like my own Little Engine That Could.

I told myself I'd give her five seconds, but when that passed, I pushed it to ten. Then twenty. She made it in seventeen.

I opened the door, and Blair followed me to my Porsche in the third spot from the front.

My hands were shaking so hard that I nearly dropped my key fob while unlocking the car. Blair hopped in the passenger seat without saying a word.

I glanced at her before starting the engine and backing out. All I could hear was her heavy breathing while she buckled her seat belt, and I drove up the ramp that led to the exit.

I should've dropped her off at her dorm, but I turned in the opposite direction. I drove and drove and drove until we couldn't even see the university behind us.

Gripping the steering wheel, I silently repeated, *Please don't be dead. Please don't be dead.*

Thirty-Four

Blair

The drive was silent as we left campus.

From the murderous expression on his face, I was almost too afraid to ask Enzo what was wrong.

I also needed some time to catch my breath well enough to form words.

Damn, he ran fast. I needed to hit the damn gym.

His phone rang, and he switched hands on the steering wheel to answer it.

"How is he?" he asked into the speaker. He nodded a few times. "Tell Nico to have Emeri drive him to the hospital." A few pauses. "No, I couldn't fucking wait." He cursed before speaking Italian, words I didn't understand, then ended the call.

His fingers flexed against the steering wheel. They did that about every ten seconds on the dot.

"Enzo?" I finally asked when I noticed his speed hit one hundred.

He didn't reply to me, just kept his focus on the road.

I stared out the window, regretting not grabbing my purse. It had been on instinct that I ran after him. Stupid instinct, but instinct nonetheless.

I saw the brokenness on Enzo's face and wanted to be there for him. I also wanted to know what had brought that pain on so suddenly.

Enzo rarely looked sad. The devil's usual facial expressions were those of anger and one that proved he was about to ruin your life. I'd never seen sorrow in those features. Never seen *fear* either.

And tonight, both of those had been clear on Enzo's face when he got that call.

"Enzo?" I repeated, unsure how much time had passed, but hoping enough that I'd get an answer out of him.

Silence.

"Can I, uh ..." I started, searching for words.

He turned to look at me, as if just now remembering I was in the passenger seat. Reaching out, he turned up the music, as if that was the answer to whatever my question was.

Groaning, I turned the volume down.

"Enzo," I said again.

"Blair," he fired back in a mocking tone.

"Can you tell me where we're going?"

"Should've asked that before you jumped into my car."

I paused. Good point, but still.

Things had been too hectic for me to ask *then*. I had only prayed my heart didn't give out while running.

But *now*, I could breathe, and we had the time.

Though if I pushed him too far, I wouldn't put it past him to drop me off on the side of the road.

"Let me have silence for a minute, Blair. You'll get the answers you want later."

I nodded, making myself comfortable in the seat and even turning on the seat warmer. I stayed silent, giving him that, as he drove.

When he pulled into a hospital parking lot, I had even more questions. He drove into an underground parking garage, swerved into the first available spot, and parked.

I followed him out of the car and toward an entrance where a man clad in a black suit stood guard. He jerked his chin up when he noticed Enzo, moving aside to allow us entry. It seemed these people had special entrances for everything.

We walked down a quiet hallway until reaching a small waiting room. Benny was pacing. Two women were seated, both crying, while a tall man stood behind one of the women, rubbing her shoulders.

Benny's pacing halted when he noticed us.

Well, when he noticed *me*.

His gaze tore into me as if I were an unwanted virus that'd just contaminated the entire hospital.

"What's she doing here?" he asked with fury in his eyes.

I was sure all his anger wasn't supposed to be directed at me. I was just getting the brunt of someone else's.

Since I didn't have the answer and didn't want to piss this man off, I didn't respond. The last thing I wanted to do was say I'd pretty much come uninvited.

His stare reminded me so much of Enzo.

I was labeling it the Marchetti stare. Cunning yet inviting, beckoning you into their darkness.

"She'd better not have a phone," Benny told Enzo.

"I don't," I said hurriedly, finding my voice to give him the assurance.

He gave me a dirty look in response, like how dare I reply to his question *about me*.

"Benny," Enzo warned, pulling me behind him.

My insides went fuzzy at the protectiveness in his tone.

"How's he doing?" Enzo asked.

Benny waved him over. The guy behind the woman dropped his hands from her shoulders, following Enzo, and they huddled in a corner while speaking in low voices.

The girl whose shoulders he'd been rubbing looked over at me. "Hi. I'm Gigi. Enzo's sister."

I shyly waved at her, and my voice was raspy when I said, "Hi. I'm Blair."

The older woman attempted to force a smile, but it almost seemed she was too weak to do so. "Hi, Blair. I'm Enzo's mother, Natalia." She motioned toward the chairs. "Have a seat. We'll probably be here for a while."

I walked over to them, taking a chair, leaving one between Natalia and me to give her space.

I was too nervous to ask them what had happened. It felt too invasive. My guess was that something had happened to Monster Marchetti.

As we sat there, I couldn't help but take in the women. They shared so many features with Enzo.

Gigi was older, looking nearly the same age as Enzo's mom. Her black hair was pulled into a messy ponytail.

Natalia's dark hair was down in long, thick curls, the color so similar to Seraphina's.

Both women were gorgeous—even as stressed as they looked at the moment with puffy eyes and swollen faces from their crying.

When my eyes traveled to Enzo, my gaze caught his. He gave me a subtle nod, and when the doors opened leading to the other side of the waiting room, the three men disappeared through them.

"Breaking news!"

The loud voice caused me to look up at the TV on the wall.

A reporter shouted into the microphone as she stood outside the White House. Breaking news text scrolled across the screen.

"President Byron has been shot," the reporter informed us. "There has been another assassination attempt on the president of the United States."

"Holy fucking shit," I muttered.

"Exactly the words I was thinking," Natalia said.

"Do you think Dad's shooting and his are related?" Gigi asked.

And there it was.

Enzo's father had been shot.

Thirty-Five

Enzo

The moment we stepped into the private hall, I looked at Benny. "I want every damn detail. How'd you let this happen?"

Benny fell back a step, fire burning in his eyes, and he balled up his fists. I waited for him to punch me. If he did, it was deserved.

He shoved me instead. "How did *I* let this happen? Someone shot Dad while he was in the back seat of the Escalade. I was at home, taking care of business, when I got the call."

"The SUV wasn't bulletproof?" I asked.

"That one wasn't."

"Why aren't *all* of them bulletproof?" This time, I shoved him. "He shouldn't even own a vehicle that isn't."

I wasn't even the family boss or underboss, and I knew that shit.

Benny ignored my shove. Just like with mine earlier, he knew he'd deserved that.

He massaged the back of his neck. "He hasn't had an assassination attempt since the Lombardi war."

I didn't miss the way his eyes drifted toward Antonio since

that was his brother who'd done it. Sometimes, I wondered how much Benny had truly forgiven Antonio. They acted like brothers now, but I could tell Benny considered digging up Antonio's father's grave and killing him again for what he'd done.

While Antonio hadn't been involved, his father had accidentally shot Neomi, Benny's wife, when Benny was the intended target.

We lived in one small, murderous, fucked-up world.

While they were common in Mafia circles, each assassination attempt needed to be taken seriously. Someone had been ballsy enough to try with our father. They knew if they failed, the repercussions would be deadly.

"He's currently in the OR with the best surgeon in the city," Benny explained, running the back of his hand over his sweaty, creased forehead. "He was shot twice. Luckily, only one of the bullets made contact and went through his chest. Barely missed the heart."

"Motherfuckers," I hissed through my teeth before blowing out an upward breath. "Any idea who's responsible?"

He shook his head. "We don't have any existing wars happening. We've been at peace for a while, everyone knowing their place."

"It was a black SUV," Antonio added. "I have my men pulling up all the city camera footage. Whoever was behind it, we'll find them. They won't live long."

He shook his head, fear and anger matching ours. Not only did he care about my father as a son-in-law, but he also didn't want his wife to lose her father.

I nodded in agreement, and we paused for a moment as a nurse passed us. Everyone on this floor was on our payroll, but that didn't mean we talked freely in front of them.

I cracked my knuckles, ready for violence and revenge.

Not only would the Marchettis be looking for whoever had shot my father but two other Mafia families—the Cavallaros and

Lombardis—would be searching as well. Not to mention, our connections in Chicago. We had also made friends with the head Bratva family who ran Boston.

Whoever had thought they were sly enough to cross us was royally fucked. If they hadn't acted alone—which I doubted they had—everyone in their organization would be dead by the end of the week.

I rested the sole of my shoe against the wall and released a long breath.

"Why'd you bring the girl?" Benny asked.

"She was already with me," I lied.

"Do you plan on taking her back to the university?"

I didn't reply.

"Jesus," he groaned, throwing his head back. "She can't fucking stay at the mansion. Not with all of this going on."

"I'm sure as hell not driving her back tonight." I thrusted my finger toward the ground. "I'm staying here, in the city, until we figure this shit out."

"One night." Benny bared his teeth, his face reddening more. "She can stay for one night, but you make sure she brings *nothing* into the mansion. I don't trust anyone right now."

I nodded in gratitude. That was him allowing something our father never would. It was a favor to me that I appreciated because we hardly ever let anyone, especially someone I knew very little about, stay in the mansion.

If Blair had had anything to do with this, which I refused to believe, I'd just fucked over my entire family.

Blair had no one. She never worried about her phone, and I never found her being sneaky. Surely, she wasn't involved. I'd never choose a Fawn who'd do something like that.

"Take her there now," Benny said. "We're still waiting on news from the surgeon. As soon as we get that, we'll be busy for the rest of the night."

"Got it." I pushed off the wall.

"And, Enzo?"

I turned my head to look at him.

"She stays in your wing, *period*. Lock her ass in there."

Benny and Antonio followed me out at the same time my phone vibrated in my pocket. I pulled it out, seeing Brooks's name on the screen, and I hit Ignore.

Seconds later, when we returned to the waiting room, I saw the TV headline.

"Shit." I moved in closer to watch the TV.

The guys did the same as we listened to the reporter update the public that someone had tried to shoot the president. Like our father, he was also currently in surgery.

"Do you think the two are connected?" Antonio asked as we watched video footage of the president going down.

It looked like a shot to the shoulder.

"It's real fucking suspicious," Benny said before snapping his attention to me. "Take the girl, Natalia, and Gigi home."

"I think not." Mom shook her head. "I'm not leaving here. As soon as they're finished with my husband's surgery, I'm at his side. I'm already pissed they wouldn't let me be in there *during* it. What was I going to do? Get in the way of someone handing the doctor a fucking scalpel?"

My mom could be a little hotheaded when it came to my father.

I noticed a sliver of a smile on Blair's face at my mom's response.

"Until then, I'm sitting in this waiting room." She stubbornly crossed her arms.

Knowing her, I knew we'd have to drag her out. She'd kick and scream, and then when she got home, she would figure out a way to come back here.

Nothing could make her leave my father right now.

Benny gestured toward Natalia and Gigi while looking at Antonio. "Get at least two of your men here to watch them. I want every entrance and exit secure in this place. Have Julian do a run-through of every person working on shift at this hospital."

"On it already." Antonio tugged his phone from his blazer pocket. "I'll also send some men around the mansion's perimeter to make sure no one tries to breach the walls."

"Appreciate it." Benny patted his back before mouthing, *Get the girl out of here now*, to me.

THIRTY-SIX

BLAIR

Sliding back into Enzo's car, I was undecided if chasing him in the tunnels had been the best decision.

In one sense, I had met his mom and sister. Just as much as he was trying to put my pieces together, I wanted to do the same with him.

In the other, I was entering an entirely new, dangerous world with him.

Will I even be able to leave when this ends?

Or will they make sure I disappear because I now know too much?

I sat in the passenger seat as Enzo sped out of the hospital's parking garage. Again, I wished I'd grabbed my purse so I had my phone. I seemed to be constantly without it lately.

I wanted to text Daphne about the president's assassination attempt. The news playing in the hospital had provided no updates on the president's condition or who the suspected shooter was.

The seat belt dug into my neck as I shifted in my seat to look over at Enzo.

"Can you tell me what happened?" I asked. I held back telling him that I knew his father had been shot because I wasn't sure if I was supposed to know. It might've slipped from Gigi's lips by accident.

From where I had come from, I knew that accidentally telling secrets could get people in trouble. Or killed.

The odds of Enzo being honest with me were slim, but a girl had to try.

Under a streetlight while he waited to turn, I noticed him working his jaw. It was so tight that I was surprised it hadn't snapped.

"My father was shot," he said, shocking me that he'd told me the truth.

I lost a breath before saying, "I'm so sorry, Enzo." Reaching out, I ran my hand along his arm. I *wanted* to take his hand but was worried about his reaction.

He didn't wince at my touch, though I'd expected him to. Some of his tension eased.

"Do you know who did it?" I was pushing it with another question I wasn't sure would get answered.

He shook his head, taking the turn, and we entered the heavy New York City traffic. It was night, but it was still bumper-to-bumper with other vehicles. I noticed a cab driver stick his hand out the window and scream at another cab.

Enzo hesitated, as if unsure if he could trust me. "Whoever it was, they won't be alive much longer." His jaw tension returned.

"What about your dad? Will he be okay?"

"He'll survive," he said with absolute certainty, like the man had a thousand lives. "He's strong."

I nodded, hopeful that was the truth.

How wild.

Hoping a homicidal Mafia boss wouldn't die was a new character trait for me, but it seemed Enzo was rubbing off on me.

"Are we going back to the university?" I asked him.

"No, I'm taking you to my home."

His home?

Holy freaking shit.

I slammed my mouth shut.

Worry and intrigue sank deep inside me.

He took phone calls back-to-back as he drove out of the city and through the suburbs, until we reached denser land. Most of his words were almost in code, so I didn't know what he was speaking about.

When I did get the hint that he was speaking with Brooks, I inched closer, not being subtle whatsoever, and tried to eavesdrop.

Enzo shot me a look and switched the phone to the other ear.

Well, that's rude.

While waiting for him to end the call, I made a mental list of all the questions I had for him. I wanted to know when we'd be back at the university so I could get my phone, but I didn't want to be rude.

He definitely wasn't worried about little ol' me not having a phone. His father had just been shot.

Plus, from the intense expression on Enzo's face, I was sure murdering whoever had shot his father was high on his priority list. Standing between that might not be the smartest choice for me.

When he ended the call and tossed his phone into the cupholder, I cleared my throat. "Is the president dead?"

His head turned slightly as he looked at me. "Why do you ask?"

I threw my arms up. "Uh, I don't know. He is also *my* president."

"Did you vote for him?"

I narrowed my eyes at him. "Actually, I did." I gave a *how about that* sneer. "Did *you*?"

He chose not to answer me. After making a right, he drove down a long road shaded by large pine trees, then stopped at a wrought-iron gate.

Four armed men stood there, weapons slung over their shoulders, and chills vibrated against my skin. The entrance reminded me so much of the entrance to Saint Vale.

I tore my gaze as different memories swarmed my thoughts. Not of the university gates, but of the ones I had grown up around.

My father hadn't had Marchetti money. He barely scraped by half the time—his only means of income was taking what his followers had—but near the end, he also had armed men at his entrance.

I hadn't been sure if it was to control who got in or who got out.

A guard approached us, and Enzo rolled down his window.

The guard dipped his head to speak to Enzo through the opening while hitching his gun farther down his back. "How's Boss doing?"

"Surgery went well," he said dryly. "He's in recovery."

The guard made the sign of the cross before tapping the car door. "Good to hear, Zo. Good to fucking hear."

The loyalty and concern on his face were also different from what I'd seen from my father's followers. This man truly liked and respected Monster Marchetti. He was genuinely relieved Cristian was alive and healthy.

While people had blindly followed my father, I saw that devotion start to crack, day by day, the longer they were with us. Those were the ones who disappeared.

The ones, by the time I got older, he'd made me help him with.

Unless you saw it up close, it was hard to grasp the power that words possessed. How easily they could manipulate and compel people. Sometimes, it didn't take violence, just bullshit lectures where someone used complicated wording to make others believe it was wisdom.

Words were what he'd started with. Violence had come later.

Enzo jerked his thumb toward me. "This is Blair. She's staying in the mansion. Keep an eye on her."

I chewed on my lip, not liking that instruction.

The guard's brows scrunched together as he stuck his head through the window to get a better look at me. "Benny okay with that?"

"Yeah," Enzo replied, not bothered by the guard's question, like I'd expected him to be. "As long as she doesn't leave, she's good. She has no phone, nothing to be traced back here."

"Do I need to pat her down?" The guard's eyes traveled back to me as if I was already distrustful in his eyes.

His boss had just been shot. I didn't blame him.

"Already did," Enzo said. "She's clean."

"All right, man." The guard stuck two fingers in his mouth, whistled loudly, and motioned to open the gates.

"Tell the boss man we're praying for him," he said before taking a step back.

Enzo nodded, giving a quick salute, and drove past him.

Since it was dark, I couldn't make out much as he drove down the long path, blocked by more massive trees. We passed a large home on the property, its porch and flood lights shining.

When we grew closer to a rounded driveway, lights swarmed around another house. No, it was insulting to call it a house.

Enzo parked in the horseshoe driveway as I gawked at it in awe. It reminded me of a castle you'd find in the UK, where royals had once resided, with a Gothic influence.

When the trees cleared, I noticed a stone perimeter wall, this one taller than the one at Saint Vale's.

I craned my neck to get a better look, noticing men standing along that wall every few feet.

Enzo didn't give me much time to admire the home before parking, killing the engine, and sliding out of the car. My butt immediately missed the heated seat when I did the same.

He met me at the door, walking beside me up the wide stone steps. He took my hand as soon as we entered the foyer, practically dragging me up the steps like he didn't want me to notice anything.

When we reached the top of the stairs, he yanked me right toward the end of a hallway, landing us right in a small space that resembled a living room.

"You'll hang out here until I return," Enzo said, then went on to almost sound like he was reading an instruction manual. "There's a mini fridge over there, stocked with plenty of drinks. I'll have the house manager check on you in case you get hungry. She'll make whatever you're in the mood for. If you get tired, that door"—he paused to point at the only other door—"leads to my bedroom. There's also a bathroom through there. Be good. Don't make me or my family regret allowing you to come here." He shot me a humorless look, spun on his heel, and left.

I heard the door lock behind him.

Being ditched here didn't sound like too much of a problem. I could snoop through his things. I rubbed my hands together almost villain-style at having the opportunity to find out more about him.

I eyed the living room, taking in signs of Enzo's personality through every inch of it. This must be his wing here.

As I walked past the cognac leather couch, I ran my hand over a black leather pillow. A Fender record player sat in the corner with a stack of vinyl records beside it.

I brushed my fingers over them next before flipping through the records, reading names of bands I'd never heard of.

Arctic Monkeys, Three Days Grace, Breaking Benjamin. Though I was hardly an expert in the music field. Over the past few years, I'd gotten over that fear to start enjoying it.

I wandered to the bedroom, and just like everything else, I felt like I'd walked into a royal's space. Dark wood spanned the entire room—from the molding on the walls to his massive bed with thick, ornate posts on each corner. The bedding was a deep black.

Bookshelves in that same color lined the walls beside his bed. I drifted toward them, noticing most of them had thick leather spines. A large walnut desk sat along a wall with a MacBook settled on top.

The space described my devil perfectly.

I plopped down on his bed, wishing I had my phone again.

Not to share this experience with someone, but to cure my boredom.

I *almost* worked myself up to look through Enzo's things, but the bed was too comfortable. I rested my head on his pillow, inhaling the faint scent of him, and wondered what wild turn my life with Enzo would take next.

I wasn't sure how long I lay there before I slid off his bed and returned to the sitting room to check the news on the TV.

There were reports of the president's shooting, but as I flipped through every news channel, both local and global, nothing was said about New York's notorious mob boss being shot.

I was sure that was on purpose.

People like the president, like Brooks, stayed in the public light. Everything in their lives was broadcast.

Some might like that.

But I was more like Enzo.

Like a Marchetti.

I liked to hide in my darkness and secrets.

I wanted solitude.

I wanted *freedom*.

And I wasn't sure if I'd ever get that.

Not only from Enzo, but from my past.

THIRTY-SEVEN

ENZO

On the drive back to the hospital, Benny told me our father was out of surgery, and everything went well.

Mom leaped from her chair and rushed into my arms when I returned to the waiting room.

"Everything is okay," she said between hitched sobs as her tears soaked through my shirt. "He's alive."

Before marrying my father, she had known the lifestyle and risks of being his wife. A mob wife had its perks and dangers.

My father's chance of dying young had always been higher than living to old age. When you were a killer surrounded by other killers, longevity wasn't common.

He'd already beaten those odds. He was the oldest among Mafia bosses. The rest from his generation had already croaked.

Mom pulled away and stared at me with watery eyes. "You'll find out who did this, right?"

I used my thumb to wipe a salty tear from her cheek. "Yes, and I'll kill them."

She gave a satisfied nod, then pressed a kiss to my cheek.

As soon as my father was brought to the private recovery room, we gathered inside and waited for him to wake from the anesthesia.

He was hooked to IVs, and a bandage covered his bullet wound. The imbeciles had aimed for his heart and missed. I wouldn't make the same mistake when I found them.

"Hey, son," he said when I stepped to his bedside after giving Mom the time she needed with him.

"Dad." I couldn't hold back my smile that he was alive.

His chest shifted, and he winced when a small laugh escaped him. "Fuckers really thought they could take me out with a single bullet." Without lifting his head, he shook it against the pillow.

According to Benny, a black SUV had swerved in front of our father's and shot through the window. The SUV sped off before the driver could catch a license plate. The driver had taken him straight to the hospital, which was less than ten minutes away.

My fingers closed around my father's tattooed hand. I breathed in a thick puff of air to hide my emotions. The love and respect I had for my parents were unmatched.

Each one for different ways and reasons.

My father had molded me into who I was. He kept our family safe, risking his own life at every turn.

Someone's desire for his demise meant a threat to *all* of us.

I looked up when the door opened. Nico squeezed through the doorway. In a line behind him was Cedric and Cassian. Their expressions were just as murderous as Benny's, Antonio's, and mine.

Seraphina almost knocked Cassian over when she charged toward our father and rushed him into a hug, not even thinking that the man had just been shot. Behind her were Livia and Benny's daughter, Gemma.

A stab of guilt struck me for not waiting for them so they could ride to the hospital with me. I knew they'd find a way here. All that had been on my mind was that my father needed me.

Livia hugged Mom tight before going to Seraphina. Gemma made a beeline for my father to hug him. The girls' sobbing made Gigi and my mom cry even harder. Their emotions all seemed to blend.

While Livia and Cassian might have the last name Lombardi, they still had Marchetti blood flowing through their veins. Dad was their grandfather.

I said goodbye to my father, thanked the guard at his door, and walked outside with the guys to Benny's SUV. Dad was alive. Now, it was time for revenge.

But first, we needed a motive. And a name.

"I can't believe you guys have nothing," Nico said from the third row of Benny's Escalade.

Benny twisted in the driver's seat to look at all of us. "You think it could be tied to your little secret society?"

Cedric coldly glared at his father from the captain's chair beside me. "It's not a *little secret society*."

That was a familiar argument when the Night Sons came up. My father and Benny never fully understood what the Sons were, even though joining them had been their idea. I figured they saw the extra power, extra money, and stopped thinking beyond that.

They'd only ever owed loyalty to the family. But our loyalty to the Sons strengthened the Marchettis, which meant it protected the family too.

"Has anyone checked on the whereabouts of the Bratva?" Cedric asked.

"What about the fucking Irish?" Nico cut in.

"I talked to Pippa's cousin," Antonio said from the passenger seat.

Pippa was the wife of his underboss, Damien. Her sister ran the Irish mob.

"We keep them in business," Antonio went on, dragging a hand down the back of his neck. "Hell, we helped Riona kill her father and take power. She wouldn't turn on us. She knows the consequences."

"All right, and the Bratva?" Cassian asked.

"We're working on them, but Liliya is saying no."

Liliya was another Lombardi capo's wife who also happened to be connected to the Russian Bratva.

We had connections everywhere—*good* ones.

The kind that had kept us safe for decades. I couldn't remember the last time my family had been at war.

Well, I could, actually.

It was with Antonio's ass.

"Circling back to the Sons," Benny said. "You don't find it suspicious that the president of the United States, who brought you into the society, was also shot on the same day?"

I nodded, my head pounding. "I do."

"Who would want the president and Grandfather dead?" Nico asked.

"Everyone," Benny, Antonio, and I said at the same time.

Nico scoffed. "That sure narrows it down."

"It's your job to narrow it down," Antonio said. "Anyone talk to the president's son?"

"I spoke with Secret Service earlier," Benny said. "The president was in emergency surgery then."

"Let's hope his shooter also had bad aim," Cassian said.

"I have people meeting us at Seven Seconds," Benny said, referring to the nightclub my family owned.

It had been named after my father's favorite game, which he'd invented. He used to give his enemies seven seconds to run before killing them.

Benny's voice turned grim. "Prepare for a long night, guys. We're not resting until every motherfucker involved in shooting my father stops breathing." His stare locked on me. "You keep in contact with the president's son. I want every single update."

I nodded.

"Let's keep in touch with Secret Service too," Antonio added. "We need to know everything they know. I bet my ass these events are connected."

"Someone is probably unhappy the president is working with us," Benny said matter-of-factly.

Benny and Antonio had fought through bloody wars over turf and control of the city. They'd survived kidnappings, shootings, and enemies no one saw coming. They had more experience than any of us. I trusted them, and I trusted that we'd find whoever was behind this.

"We should get the Sons involved," Nico said. "They have some of the best connections in New York. In the world. In every damn sector. That's why we're affiliated with them."

Every man in the SUV nodded in agreement.

Benny looked at his son. "I want you in charge of that, then, as well as going through footage." His attention slid to me. "Enzo, you keep in contact with Brooks and get all the information you can from the Secret Service." He looked at Antonio next. "You talk to Liliya and Pippa about the Bratva and Irish." Cassian was his next line of focus. "You and Cedric are coming with me."

We were all armed when we stepped out of the SUV and split off to our vehicles to handle our assignments.

"I'm flying back to Saint Vale with the VP," Brooks told me over a secure video chat from *Air Force Two*. "We're meeting with the Elders. They're traveling from every corner of the world. They're pissed off."

I offered a nod from my dad's office at Seven Seconds. I'd been in there for at least ten hours, making phone calls and digging for answers. Every hour or so, Benny came in to trade updates and ask what I'd found.

A few other Elders had also told Nico they were reaching out to contacts across the city for any clue who could be behind it.

These were the times when the value of being a Night Son shone through.

"Do you think it's wise for the vice president to leave DC?" I asked.

"He's meeting with the other Elders," Brooks said. "We're getting revenge on the fuckers who did this. Someone shot the *president of the fucking United States.* They all know if he stops being president, our power shrinks."

Vice President Kirkland stepped into view, filling the frame.

"Enzo," he said, "any new information to report?"

"We got intel on the car driven during the shooting. It was registered to a Miami car dealership."

"We traced the vehicle involved in the president's shooting to a Miami dealership too." He lifted his wrist and checked the time. "The FBI is headed there to conduct a raid right now."

"Who owns the dealership?"

"We haven't confirmed that yet. We suspect it was registered under an alias because the name ties to an account in Cuba. One of the Elders has connections to their dictator. He's meeting us tonight, and we'll have him put us in touch." He straightened the flag pen on his lapel. "I've spoken with every Elder. We'll find out who did this. Will you be joining us for the meetings?"

While Brooks's face didn't come onto the screen, I heard his voice.

"They're staying in the city," he told Kirkland.

The VP frowned. "And your Fawn? Have you made sure she's safe in her Quarters? An Elder Son and a Night Son's father were attacked. *Her Night Son's* father. She could be in danger."

Brooks's face returned to the screen as the VP moved aside. "Where's Blair?"

"My home," I replied.

Brooks let out a low whistle. "Monster Marchetti permitted that? Wow. I'm not even allowed there."

"Benny agreed to one night, but she needs to return to Saint Vale today." I arched a brow, an idea striking me. "If you're making any stops, think she could ride with you?"

Brooks glanced toward the VP.

"I wouldn't object," he said. "But we'd need her in the next fifteen minutes."

Shit.

That wasn't doable.

I checked my watch. "I'll ask Emeri to take her back. He's at the casino and headed to Saint Vale soon."

"You don't think she's involved, do you?" Brooks asked.

The snarl and anger on my face must've been pretty damn clear on the screen because he hurriedly kept talking. "Don't kill me, but our information on her was limited, and now, both of our dads have been shot."

"Our fathers have been on people's hit lists long before Blair showed up," I said defensively.

While it pissed me off, the suspicion made sense. She was the newest person in our circle, but we needed to remember *who* had been targeted.

It wasn't average Joes.

A mafia boss and the leader of the free fucking world.

"We need to look into her," he said. "People don't have their entire history erased when they're living innocent lives. That *looking into her* should've been done before the Selection, like I said then." He shot me a dirty look.

He'd asked me to dig deeper on her, but I'd sworn to the other Sons that she was safe.

I narrowed my eyes and returned the look.

"Let's all stay in contact," the VP said. "Let me know any updates on intel. Make sure your Fawn stays safe. If you don't trust her, put her in the Fawn Quarters. That way, she's safe but also confined, just in case she is trouble."

After ending the call, I yawned and checked the time again.

Everyone was right to ask questions about Blair. My feelings for her were making me reckless with my own family. I needed her out of the mansion.

Deep down, I wanted to believe she wasn't involved with this, but I wasn't certain.

I needed to get her back to the university.

Then I needed to find my dad's killers.

Then I'd go back to learning my Fawn's secrets.

THIRTY-EIGHT

BLAIR

I didn't know how much time had passed since I'd crawled into Enzo's bed last night. The sun's rays streaming through a gap in the curtains told me it was at least the next day.

I jerked up, stopping myself from admiring the mural on the ceiling. I hadn't noticed it until I dragged the blankets up my body last night and stared ahead with the lamp shining on the nightstand beside me.

It almost reminded me of the painting in Professor Nelson's lecture hall with angels and demons. The mural was divided into two sections—one that looked like the clouds of heaven and the other the darkness of hell.

The angels in the clouds had fluffy white wings and golden skin. The ones in the darkness were surrounded by storm clouds with black wings and broken halos.

My hand dropped to my tattoo.

A knock on the door interrupted my staring.

"Yoo-hoo!" a woman shouted from the other end. "Are you hungry, Miss Blair?"

I rolled out of bed, wearing a black tee and sweats that I'd thieved from Enzo's closet, and opened the door. A short, older woman with pink-streaked hair stood on the other side in the sitting room.

Her smile was as bright as the sun radiating through the blinds. "Good morning," she said, all chipper. "What would you like for breakfast this morning?"

"Uh," I muttered, still waking up as I raked a hand through the knots in my hair. "Good morning. What are my choices?"

I'd never had anyone come to my door for a breakfast order.

"Whatever you'd like, dear. Eggs, spinach omelet, cereal, croissant. Any of those sound appetizing to you?"

I smiled at her gratefully. "An omelet sounds amazing."

"Very well. And to drink? Juice? Coffee? Latte?"

"A latte?" I replied, though it sounded almost like a question.

She awarded me a quick nod. "I'll be back with an omelet and a latte."

I inched out of the bedroom, halfway out the doorway, when she started to leave. "Do I have to eat in here?" I called out to her.

She halted, staring at me over her shoulder. "That's what Mr. Marchetti directed." She lowered her head in a nod before departing from Enzo's wing.

Which Mr. Marchetti directed that?

Cristian, Benny, or Enzo?

I wished she'd been more specific.

Knowing I couldn't argue with her, I shuffled back to bed and collapsed onto it face-first.

I'd waited for hours for Enzo to return last night before saying screw it and going to bed. I didn't have a phone or the password to his MacBook. Therefore, any information I had was from the news.

They only reported on the president's condition. Not Cristian Marchetti's.

I returned to the sitting room and was watching my next round of news—the most I had in all my years of life—when the woman returned with my breakfast.

As she set the tray in front of me and spread out my food, I felt bad that I didn't have any money to tip her with.

Am I supposed to tip her?

I had no idea how this worked.

"What's your name?" I asked.

She was old, a grandmother's age, and I wondered how long she'd worked for the Marchettis.

"Miriam," she replied with a sweet, wrinkled smile.

I returned it. "Hi, Miriam. It's nice to meet you."

So many questions sat on the tip of my tongue.

Is it normal for her to bring Enzo's guests breakfast?

Does he have guests frequently?

I didn't want to interrogate her and make it awkward, so I kept those questions to myself. Then she left.

I devoured the best omelet of my life and drank the latte.

The news hadn't changed from last night.

The president was alive and recovering from surgery. The person who'd shot him was on the loose.

My posture straightened when the vice president stepped in front of a podium, surrounded by reporters. Brooks stood to his side. I set down my latte and rubbed my chin as the VP spoke, telling the American people to remain calm and that no terrorism was welcome in this country.

Brooks nodded with every word the VP said, but I could see it.

The crack in his armor this time.

That perfect, polished manner was dead. He didn't stare into the cameras with sadness. He stared into them with suspicion, like he knew whoever had done it was watching. His eyes screamed every warning that he'd get his revenge.

When I had enough of hearing the same stories repeated, I turned off the TV and looked around, unsure what to do next. I had no clothing here. No toothpaste, deodorant, or makeup. Literally nothing.

That meant it was time to return to Enzo's closet for today's outfit. The smell of him drifted through the air, and I couldn't stop myself from grabbing a bottle of his cologne and spraying my hair with it.

The walk-in closet was organized impeccably. Shirts and hoodies hung, organized by color and length. Same with trousers and jeans.

I pulled a shirt free from a hanger and brought it to my face, taking a deep sniff. I opened the drawers, finding boxer briefs and socks in one. Another with sweatpants and shorts. One with swim trunks, another with tees, and the last with trays of watches and jewelry.

I stripped out of his sweats and grabbed a fresh set and a shirt. Just as I was leaving, I stopped, backtracked, and stole a pair of fresh socks that I knew wouldn't fit.

My next stop was his bathroom for a shower.

Like everything else, the bathroom was yet another sign of their wealth. I opened the glass shower door to turn on the water, letting it warm up as I splashed water over my face. I searched through the bathroom drawers for a spare toothbrush.

"Jackpot," I muttered when finding a new one still in the packaging.

I used his charcoal toothpaste and checked the water temperature before snatching a fresh towel and setting it on the hook. The warm streams from the massive showerhead felt like heaven against my skin.

I'd grown up taking not only cold but timed showers, five minutes max. That never gave me enough time to even wash my hair. I often didn't have shampoo anyway. My mother had refused to share hers.

I shook my head, telling myself not to go back to that place. I was here, in *this* shower.

Tilting my head back, I shut my eyes as water splashed over my face.

When I lowered it, my eyes met bottomless brown ones.

THIRTY-NINE

ENZO

I stood across from a soaking wet Blair in the shower.

What a fucking sight.

She looked ethereal, standing there.

Like the mural on my ceiling, she was the good angel in the light. And I was the dark one, bathing in the darkness.

Suddenly shy, she wrapped her arms tight around her stomach.

I had planned on showering, so it was convenient that, when I returned to the mansion, that was where I found her.

The fogged-up glass had blocked my view of her when I stepped into the bathroom.

I'd wanted to see her hot and wet body.

So I figured I might as well join her.

I had driven here with the intention of questioning Blair to make sure nothing was connected, but at the moment, I wasn't sure if I wanted to.

If I found out I couldn't trust her, I was afraid to admit it'd hurt.

Not just because I hated traitors and liars, but because I liked my Fawn. I liked being around her, liked her voice, liked how I managed to get answers out of her she wouldn't tell anyone, liked how she made me feel.

I was becoming attached to her, and I didn't want to cut that cord.

My mind scrambled in endless directions, but one thing I couldn't do was take my eyes off her. My view roamed over her body as water poured down it.

I curled my toes as my cock twitched, already rock hard. I thought about all the ways I wanted to pound into her in this space.

Blair had the body of a goddess.

Her body would bring men to their knees in worship of it.

And me? I'd never been a man who got on his knees for any-fucking-one, but with her, I wanted to kneel and taste her everywhere.

My eyes stayed glued to her breasts that moved with every gasp she took. Gasps so intense that I heard them over the shower.

I was nearly salivating as I took in her nickel-sized nipples that begged for my mouth. I stepped closer on the tiles until my toes curled over hers. Those gasps turned more rapid when I ran my hand over her breast, running my thumb over the hard peak in the middle.

"Hello, my Fawn," I said, my voice sounding hoarser than I'd like.

She blinked water from her eyelashes as she looked up at me with an innocent expression. My cock twitched, and I lowered my hand to stroke it once.

I raised my hand from her breast to her face, pushing the wet hair from her eyes.

She whimpered, resting her cold hands on my arms. I clocked her gaze dropping down, stalling at my cock.

Grinning on the inside only, I took her hand to wrap it around where I desperately needed it, moving it once to stroke me before she took over.

I gave her a second to relax and jack me off.

Then two, three, four.

At five, I slid my hand into her hair and knew it was time to do what I had come here for.

I yanked her head back, and she winced, her hand falling from my cock.

Fuck, what a loss.

Her hand, her mouth, had been born to be there.

"Blair, tell me right now that you don't know anything about these shootings," I said with a tug of her wet hair.

Her teeth chattered, and I wasn't sure if it was because she was cold from us now sharing the water *or* terrified of me.

"I don't," she finally managed to squeak out.

I backed her up, water pelting our skin, until she collided with the tiled wall. Her hair stuck to her shoulders and face as she glanced up at me.

"Can I trust you?" I asked.

She licked water off her lips. "If you don't trust me, then leave me alone, Enzo."

Her words sent a fire burning inside me. All she needed to do was say yes.

I drove my hips forward. "You're my Fawn until I fucking release you."

Lowering my hand to her hip, I shoved her harder into the wall.

When that didn't seem like a harsh enough punishment for her little suggestion, I thrust my hips forward, pinning her to the wall with my body.

"Then release me," she shrieked. "No one asked you to choose me."

A spark of bravery flared in her eyes as she jabbed a finger in my chest. "If you think I had anything to do with your father getting shot, then release me! Lord knows my life was a lot calmer before you barged into it."

I scoffed, my lip snarling. "Was it calmer, Blair?"

My thighs nudged hers apart as I crowded her, until I was exactly where I belonged—between her legs.

She had no choice but to spread them wider so her bones wouldn't break.

If she thought for one damn second that I was releasing her, she'd lost her mind. That kind of talk needed to be corrected.

To punish her, I sank my hand between her legs, shoving four fingers deep inside her. Her back straightened against the wall as a long cry tore from her throat. I dragged my fingers out slowly before thrusting them back in again, harder and rougher this time.

There'd be no fucking talk of me releasing her into the wild to other wolves.

I realized I wasn't only here to question Blair.

I was here to break her open.

And if I happened to enjoy myself in the process? That was a bonus.

I lowered my head until my forehead brushed hers. "Don't ever say those words again," I grunted. My hand tightened as I finger-fucked her harder. "I own you, Blair." I withdrew my hand to grab my cock and slide it against her clit. With my free hand, I caught her chin between my fingers, holding her still to look at me. "You belong to me."

She moaned, her head tipping forward until it knocked lightly against mine as I massaged her clit with the head of my cock.

A series of short gasps escaped her when she started rocking her hips, moving them to the side, as if trying to force my cock inside her.

A giant smirk, one that belonged to the biggest villain in the world, spread across my face.

"If I make this pussy feel good, will you tell me everything I want to know, my Fawn?" I slid my tongue along the seam of her lips.

Her mouth parted immediately, welcoming my tongue, and I kissed her hard.

"Yes," she said in a pained plea.

My smirk widened at the desperation in her voice.

"That's my good little Fawn." I splayed my hand around her face, squeezing her cheeks together before sliding my grip down to her throat. "Now, you'll tell me everything I want to know. And if I hear one more word about me releasing you ..." I flexed my grip. "This throat won't work well enough to even mutter those words again."

I dropped my hand from her throat and bent my knees, ready to thrust my cock inside her, but stopped.

This wasn't how I wanted it today.

Not rushed against the shower wall.

If this was the last time I got to fuck my Fawn, I didn't want it here.

I wanted it somewhere the memory would live forever.

I stepped away long enough to shut off the shower, pulled her against me, and wrapped her legs around my body to lift her. I shoved the glass door open hard enough that I was surprised it didn't crack.

Water streamed off us as I carried her into the bedroom. I didn't give a damn about the trail we left behind or that my bed would be soaked by the time I was finished with her.

I dropped her on the unmade sheets and controlled my breathing as she stared up at me, sprawled across the bed.

She slowly drew her legs together, rubbing them, while biting down on her lower lip and waiting for my next move.

Dragging a hand through my wet hair, I drew my gaze down her gorgeous body.

Her scent had already taken over my bedroom, and I loved it. She was the only woman who'd ever been in my bed here. And if I had it my way, she might be the last.

I dropped onto the bed, and she pushed herself to her knees, crawling toward me.

"Ride me, Blair," I instructed, lifting my head and wrapping my hand around myself while holding her gaze.

My good little Fawn didn't hesitate. She climbed straight onto my lap and straddled my hips. Lifting my hand, I traced my index finger slowly along her jaw.

Her lips parted, and I stuck my finger between them.

"Suck," I ordered.

Her mouth closed around my finger instantly, and I pushed it deeper inside.

"Good girl." I watched her suck my finger. "Now, fuck me, Fawn."

An eager groan fell from my throat when she held on to my thighs and sank down on me. Her pussy fit around me perfectly.

I watched her face, tracking every change in expression as she rode me. The mattress shifted beneath us when her rhythm quickened, and she began losing herself in the pleasure my cock was giving her.

I leaned forward slightly, lowering my hand between us to tease her clit. Her breasts lifted with each thrust as she ground against me.

In one second, she flattened her body, trapping my hand while sliding her clit against me.

"Fuuuck," I groaned, the sensations of being inside her shooting straight through me.

She lifted herself, sank down on me, and then gyrated her hips.

I shut my eyes, taking in the feel of her pussy before grabbing her hips, holding her still. She groaned in protest when I pulled her off my cock and turned her around in one quick motion.

Without moving from my spot, I guided her back down, positioning her to ride me backward. The new angle allowed my cock to go deeper inside her. It felt so damn good that I was ready to come right then.

Her back arched as she rode me, sticking her ass right in my face, and I smacked it once, hoping to leave a mark. I did it again, watching her skin ripple.

Her back flattened at my strikes, and I clicked my tongue.

"Stay up," I said with another ass slap before gripping her hips and pulling her back into place. "Keep riding me. Don't let me down, Fawn."

"Okay," she moaned, settling back into her rhythm.

Her hips rolled as she rode me, that perfect ass still lifted while she grabbed on to my ankles to keep herself from collapsing forward while I controlled her pace.

Her pussy clenched against my cock.

I was ready to burst, and I needed her to fall apart first.

I smacked her ass. "Ride me harder."

She rode me harder.

Another ass smack.

"Fuck me faster."

She fucked me faster.

One more.

"Come all over my cock."

She lifted her hips, impaling herself on my cock like she owned it. And fucking hell, she did.

At that moment, I knew I had to make it official—Blair would never fuck another man like this. Heat stormed my veins as I thought about another motherfucker touching her.

About another man getting *this*, something so fucking precious.

I'd never felt lucky when fucking someone until her.

Never felt like I was getting something cherished that I needed to hold on to.

And I was royally fucked, especially if she didn't have the right answers to my questions.

But then my thoughts blurred as Blair fell apart on my cock.

FORTY

BLAIR

As my orgasm rocked through me, my body shook before going limp, and I collapsed on Enzo like dead weight.

Enzo lifted me off him, flipped me onto my back, and climbed over me. Within seconds, he was moving inside me again, his hands gripping the backs of my thighs as he drove into me.

The intensity didn't last long.

His body tensed, and he came apart. I watched his face, loving how it squeezed together before long breaths sputtered out of him in uneven bursts.

His weight settled over me as we struggled to catch our breath.

When he finally pulled out of me, it was slow, and I squeezed my eyes shut, a deep ache spreading through me at the sudden emptiness.

I rolled off the mattress, the sheet in tow, and went to the bathroom.

Enzo followed me. He grabbed a towel from the hook beside the shower, pulling it snugly around me, and squeezed it tight.

I held it there while he opened the linen closet, grabbed another towel, and tied it around his waist.

"Blair," he said, his voice thick as he pressed the heels of his hands against his eyes, "did you play any part in the assassination attempts against my father or the president?"

I snorted, and a frown creased his brow.

"You think *I* shot them?" I finished toweling off the last drops of water and reached for the vanity to get the clothes I'd taken from his closet.

"It's obvious *you* didn't shoot them."

I couldn't get dressed fast enough. The second his sweats were snug around my waist, I grabbed the shirt and threw it on as I walked out of the bathroom.

Enzo was behind me again.

He clamped his hand around my waist, stopping me in my tracks when I reached the sitting room. I'd planned to leave his wing, to leave the mansion, and get the hell out of here.

That plan went to hell when I allowed him to guide me away from the door to the couch. He sat beside me, leaving a cushion between us. The expression on his gorgeous face shifted from concern to dismay when he noticed my tear-streaked face.

Shit. I hadn't even realized I was crying.

The irritation in his voice dropped a decibel. "Blair," he said with a composed manner I'd never expected from him, "I need you to tell me everything about you." Desperation laced that sentence as he scooted closer. "This goes deeper than you simply being my Fawn." He shook his head, and a quick grimace flashed across his face, like this conversation was going to kill him as much as me if it didn't go well. "I chose you as my Fawn, yet you remain a complete enigma to me."

Sighing, I turned away, unable to look at him. *This* was why I'd never felt at home anywhere.

I kept too many secrets.

And secrets never led to trust.

Could I trust Enzo with my secrets?

He was manipulative and cunning.

But deep down, I felt like I trusted him more than I trusted anyone. But that was now.

What would happen when he got bored with me?

My secrets weren't safe with someone temporary. It was too risky.

He sighed again, like he'd tried the gentle approach, and now that it hadn't worked, he'd go with a harsher one.

And that was exactly what he did.

"Hush, little baby, don't—"

I lunged at him, scraping my nails against his skin to stop his singing. "Don't you fucking dare!"

His mouth clamped shut as I jabbed my finger in his face.

More salty tears streamed down my face, stinging my eyes and trickling down my nose and into my mouth.

"Then tell me, damn it!" he roared, temper flaring as his patience evaporated. "Why are you so scared to open up? How many of my secrets are you privy to, hmm, Blair?" He used his hand to indicate the room. "You're in my fucking house!" He pounded his palm against his chest. "That's against every fucking rule in not only *my* book but my family's! I give and give and give, but you offer me absolutely nothing!"

"I gave you myself!" I screamed, rising and charging toward the door.

Enzo was faster, sidestepping me to cut off my path, and blocked me from leaving. He pressed his hand against my chest, pushing me back until my spine met the wall.

His rough hands felt surprisingly gentle as he cradled my face, his expression softening again. "Blair, I'm begging you, to help us both. Please share your demons with me. I swear on my life, I'll take them down, one after another, until you're no longer in pain."

I squeezed my eyes shut, a desperate attempt to hold back more oncoming tears, and shook my head. "They're not pretty."

"Blair, pretty stories have never interested me. The morbid and dark have always held a certain allure for me, my Fawn. Give me your soul, and I swear to you, I'll always keep you safe."

"Until you're done with me. Until you're sick of me as your Fawn. Then I'll end up jumping out of a window or going to some insane asylum."

He flinched, the harsh truth of my words striking him. "Okay, first off, Ashley isn't in an insane asylum *now*. She became a nun."

I stilled. "Really?"

"Don't believe everything Daphne tells you. But something to believe from her is that, *yes*, I am different with you than I've ever been with any of my Fawns. *Yes*, you mean so much more to me than they did. Does it make me sound shitty? Probably. But if that's the worst shit I say all day, then so be it." His hands rested on my cheeks as he stared into my eyes. "You're so much more than a Fawn to me, Blair."

"Then who am I?" I whispered.

"You're the one I'd burn everything down for."

I looked away, speechless.

"But I'm only willing to do that if you tell me what I need to know."

He stepped back, offering me his hand, and I took it, allowing him to walk me back to the couch.

I tucked my legs under me, resting my back against the armrest, and closed my eyes. Drawing in a long breath, I was ready to spill my demons and surrender to the darkness haunting me.

"What do you want to know?" I asked in a shaky voice.

"How old are you?" His immediate question surprised me.

I'd expected it to be something more serious.

Something that cut me open deeper.

"I don't know," I said, embarrassed by my answer. "My *official* records say twenty-two, so that's what I use. I was born at home. How old are you?"

"Twenty-two. My public records and mother can corroborate this."

I cracked an easy smile.

"How'd you escape your father's cult?"

I glanced away, wishing I'd never agreed to this.

"Hey." Enzo kept his tone soft. "I promise, I'm the last person to judge you."

I didn't answer him.

"All right." He ran his hands through his still-damp hair. "Let's start at the beginning. Tell me about his cult."

Enzo was smart in his interrogation technique. This was easier to start with than what I'd done.

I cleared my throat once, twice, three times because the words felt glued there. "My father started the cult when I was a baby. Somehow, he and my mother convinced people through the power of my father's words that he was some holy prophet when, in fact, he was the opposite."

"How was he the opposite?" Enzo asked.

"He killed followers who tried to leave or those he suspected had become disloyal, then buried them on the compound." My gaze drifted away from him to the record player. "Sometimes he'd give me a shovel and force me to help him pile the dirt over them."

Enzo reached out to clamp my chin in his palm and slowly drew my gaze back to him.

"As I got older, he got worse," I continued. "More violent. A few members managed to escape and went to the police. Someone tipped him off that the feds were coming to raid the compound. And ..."

My mouth shut, and I could no longer speak.

Enzo grabbed both my hands in his, holding them together in front of us.

"And then what, Blair?" he asked lowly.

"And then we all had to burn."

And in an instant, my mind went back there.

"Into the chapel! Into the chapel!" my father yelled, waving his arms and rushing us toward the small building like we were cattle and a storm was brewing.

His followers crammed through the narrow entrance, and the old wood creaked under our feet. I stepped in with the others, near the back, where I always stayed, and watched him through a crack between standing bodies.

My father stood at the nave, barefoot, dressed in a white tunic and loose pants that brushed his ankles.

My mother stepped to his side, wearing a cream skirt and white blouse—her Sunday best, even though it was only Wednesday.

"Everyone," he said, spreading his arms wide in a welcoming gesture, "it's time for judgment day, time for you to prove your faith, to prove our devotion."

I didn't know what devotion they were proving. I tuned out most of my father's speeches. There were only so many times you could hear a man refer to himself as the Divine and Lord before wanting to scream out that it was all fake.

Instead of looking at him, my gaze drifted around the old chapel.

It was small with rows of narrow pews lined in front of the altar. The main entrance was behind us. The double wooden doors were the only way in and out unless you counted windows.

"Today is the day we die. We'll burn for our beliefs to take us to where our faith leads. You will stay in here, in the chapel, where we give ourselves to our faith." He peered over at my mother and rested his hand on her shoulder. "The Higher Beings have instructed me to go to my office and do this. My wife will be joining the Divine in our final moments while you stay here, my followers."

I rolled my eyes at how much he loved referring to himself in the third person.

My mother nodded, which led to others around me doing the same.

I scratched my head, staring at my father, unnerved, as a pain formed in my chest. Something about this felt wrong.

I heard something move behind me and looked over my shoulder to see the doors shut. When I heard a loud bang, I knew someone had dragged the wooden crossbar across the outside of the doors, locking us in.

My head spun in panic when my father grabbed a red kerosene container. He tipped it forward. Kerosene fell from the yellow nozzle, splashing onto the floor. He soaked the pews next, going row by row.

My chest suddenly seemed too tight as the sharp smell of oil filled the chapel. I wheezed out a breath when he struck a match and dropped it onto the floor.

At the sound of another match strike, I darted my gaze to my mother just as she tossed it onto a pew.

Then he flicked another while she did the same.

Small fires started near the front of the room, blocking anyone from moving toward them.

No one even tried to move anyway. No one screamed. No one did anything as my parents turned around and walked toward his small office.

For a moment, I didn't either.

The way they started the fires made sure no one could run to the office without going through the flames.

Kerosene fed the hungry flames, and they leaped from pew to pew, spreading fast.

Wood cracked and popped.

Within seconds, the fire had taken over the entire nave and was spreading toward us.

Heat spread through the room, and I fell back a step. Smoke covered the ceiling, caving in toward us, and people coughed.

Again, no one moved. I overheard a few people praying.

They wanted this. They were willing to die for the fraudster.

Children started crying, and smoke filled my lungs. The first cough that left me was my wake-up call.

I turned around, ran for the door, and pain shot down my arm when I rammed my shoulder against it.

It didn't budge.

I backed up again, hitting someone with my body, and slammed into the door harder this time.

Nothing.

The next time, I threw as much weight as I could against it, but again, I couldn't break that crossbar.

"What are you doing?" a woman yelled at me.

"Breaking out!" I screamed, waving them over so similar to how my father had. "Help me!"

More children were crying. Some parents clutched them close while others just stared at the fire, transfixed by the flames.

"We can't!" another woman cried out. "We have to go with the Divine!"

"You go ahead with the Divine then," I said, staring at her like she'd lost her damn mind. "Some of us don't want to do that."

"But you'll burn in hell."

I motioned toward the fire around us, hearing more people cough at the smoke. "We're burning right now!"

I slammed my shoulder into the door again, and this time, I felt a slight budge. Something had cracked in it.

Looking over my shoulder, I noticed the flames coming closer.

I wouldn't die here. Wouldn't die for him. Wouldn't let these people die for him.

My father might've been okay with these people's blood on his hands, but I wasn't.

More people struggled to breathe as the temperature spiked. The smoke made some of them realize they weren't ready to die for my father.

I coughed as I kept fighting the door until, finally, two teen boys grabbed a pew that hadn't caught fire yet.

"Here! Come help!" they called out to me.

I nearly tripped over my feet as I ran toward them.

Two more men helped us. When one follower tried to fight them, saying they were turning their backs on the Divine, another punched him in the face.

From behind me, I heard one follower whisper to another, asking why my father hadn't left his office when hearing this commotion.

"It's because he's probably not in there!" I screamed.

"Liar!" a man shrieked.

"Walk through the flames and check yourself, then!" I yelled back, refusing to give him any more attention because I needed to get us the hell out of here.

I ignored their fighting, ignored those pleading with me not to ruin what was right, while we kept ramming the pew against the door.

Splinters of wood came off, and we didn't stop until two boards busted open.

We kicked the weak boards down, creating enough space for us to escape the chapel. Smoke burned my lungs with every move, but I never gave up.

I grabbed the boy's and girl's hands, whose father had called me a liar, and ran out with them. The teen boys did the same, each grabbing the remaining children, even when their parents tried to pull them back into the burning building.

"Mama!" the little girl I pulled out wailed, trying to run back into the chapel, but I wouldn't allow it.

I hugged them tight, watching and smelling the fire take over the building with the people my father had betrayed.

And from the corner of my eye, while I held the crying children, I saw my parents running across the field.

My words were said through broken sobs, and by the time I was finished telling Enzo about the fire, his chest was soaked as he held me close. He stroked my shoulder, my back, my neck, all in an effort to comfort me as I broke down in his arms.

I'd only told the story two other times.

Once to the detectives and once to the jury that convicted my father.

Never in my life had someone held me like this. Let me cry out my nightmares without punishment. Made me feel like I actually mattered.

I sniffled, gulping in large bursts of air, then finally pulled away from Enzo. For a moment, I couldn't look him in the eyes.

There was too much shame inside me because I hadn't saved everyone.

Enzo stood, left the room, and returned with a box of tissues. I brought my knees to my chest as he wiped my eyes with one and then used another under my nose.

He squeezed my knee again while sitting. I immediately climbed back into his arms, turning so my back was against his chest.

"When the police arrived, I told them what had happened and pointed them in the direction of where my parents had gone." I went on because I wanted Enzo to know me, wanted him to know I was trustworthy. "They'd climbed through the window in the office. The police found them behind the shed they used to keep me in and arrested them."

Enzo stayed quiet, not asking any questions.

"Later, my father insisted my mother hadn't wanted to escape and he'd forced her against her will. Being his wife, she was shielded from testifying against him and refused to give a statement. The police needed someone to testify against him."

"And that someone was you," he said.

I nodded slowly. "That someone was me."

"What happened?"

"He received a life sentence."

"Should've gotten death," Enzo said under his breath.

"By the time sentencing was over, the judge gave him another life sentence."

"Why was that?"

"My father asked to read an apology letter to the victims, and the judge allowed it. In that statement, he stared at me the entire time. He said he regretted not drowning me in the river, and if he ever was freed, he'd find the nearest one and keep me underwater until he could no longer stand.

"The feds sealed my records in exchange for my testimony. For some reason, the federal prosecutor had instructed the police to withhold the details of what had happened from the media. They said it was to protect the other younger victims and me. Social media was practically nonexistent back then, so nothing about it ever went public."

"And your mom?"

"She quickly remarried a rich man, who paid off those who had survived to never breathe a word of it and then made them sign NDAs. Most of the people who'd died didn't even have families to report their deaths because my father had preyed on those who felt alone or were homeless."

"You still speak to your mother, though? And your stepfather?"

"We don't exactly speak. She called me a traitor for testifying, but she likes to keep me close and cared for. She's worried I'll tell people about what she did. That's how I ended up at Saint Vale. They still wanted to control where I was but not have me around."

My shoulders sagged as all the tension that'd been bottled up inside my body collapsed.

"That's my truth, Enzo," I whispered. "I'm everything you hate."

He wrapped his arms around my waist and squeezed me tight. "What do you mean?"

"I testified against my father. That first day I met you, you called me a rat. It was said as a threat. You also murdered Jett because he was one."

Why I'd been keeping this such a secret finally dawned on him.

He shook his head violently. "There's no comparison to you and Jett. And technically, I didn't kill Jett. He succumbed to his injuries."

I tipped my head back on his shoulder at that remark and shouldn't have found that devilish smile that formed on his lips to be adorable. But I did.

And at that moment, I was happy I'd told Enzo.

Happy I'd finally let it all out.

I had no one to speak to about this.

I tried to contact those who'd helped me break down the door on social media, but they always blocked me. No one wanted to speak about it. Not that I blamed them. Revisiting an ugly past was never easy.

Enzo's phone rang, and I jumped at the sudden noise.

"Shit," he said, climbing out from behind me. "Normally, I'd ignore this, but given—"

"No, take it."

He checked the caller and answered, "Yeah." He nodded a few times. "How far out? Okay. We'll be outside waiting."

After ending the call, he looked at me. "Emeri is driving you back to the university. I want you to go to the Fawn Quarters and stay there until I come get you."

"I can't stay here?"

He shook his head. "I'm sorry, but you'll be safe down there. I promise."

I'd created a bond with Enzo that I'd never had with anyone else.

A blood bond, one that couldn't be broken even if I tried to run.

I was done being a scared Fawn.

I was ready to embrace my role.

"Stay down here," Emeri said when he reached the Fawn Quarters. He started to leave, but then stopped suddenly. "And here's your phone. Enzo said to make sure you stay in touch with him."

His hand was cold when I took my phone from him.

He disappeared up the stairs and left.

During the drive here, he hadn't said a word to me. I sat in the passenger seat of his black Camaro, anxiety getting the worst of me. While I'd told Enzo my darkest secret, I hadn't told him *all* of them yet. I would eventually.

The other two times I'd been in the Fawn Quarters before I was with Enzo, and while he'd given me a tour, I hadn't had time to explore. I decided to do that now.

My first stop was the kitchen, which was fully stocked with food and drinks. I grabbed a yogurt and juice and sat at the table to eat.

After licking my spoon clean, I rinsed it off in the sink, stuck it in the dishwasher, and walked down the hall toward the library.

Enzo had said there were Fawn diaries down here. I'd spend my night reading them.

The library was at the end of the hall. Tall bookshelves lined the dark wood-paneled walls, filled with books about Saint Vale's history, about the men who had founded the university, and some classic literature.

I wandered over to a small shelf in the corner, settled beneath a large canvas painting of a young fawn standing alone in a snowy clearing. I ran my hand over the soft brushstrokes of the fawn's fur. My hand moved, tracing the painted pink blossoms on branches surrounding the fawn. The fawn's eyes were dark, as if it were watching me, as if warning me.

Lowering my gaze, I saw the worn leather journals lined across the shelf. I ran my fingers along the blank spines before pulling one free. I opened it and found a year written inside the front cover beside the Fawn's symbol.

I flipped through that one, and then another's, and another's.

Some of them even had pictures of the Fawn who owned it. Some with them with other Fawns. But none with pictures of the Sons.

I collected a stack of the diaries, headed back to my room, collapsed on my bed, and opened the top one.

With each diary I read, I felt like I was meeting the Fawns.

They were filled with pieces of their lives, advice for younger Fawns, and the different rules and Initiations.

The more I read, the more I felt as if I almost knew them.

I turned page after page, reaching for another diary each time I finished one.

Until one stopped me cold.

My breath caught as I stopped on a page, certain I was dreaming, as I stared at a photo of my mother.

FORTY-ONE

ENZO

"The girl is out of the mansion?" Benny asked before I even shut the door to his office in Seven Seconds.

I'd just come from the hospital after seeing my father. He was recovering well, better than the doctors expected, but that didn't mean he was behaving like someone who'd just survived being shot.

The first thing he said when I walked into his room was that he wanted out of that fucking hospital because he had mother-fuckers to kill.

I instructed him to relax, to which he glared at me like I'd said we were sticking him in a nursing home after this.

I'd told him we had it handled, but honestly, we didn't.

We still didn't know who the hell had shot him.

And that pissed me off more than anything.

Inside the office, Nico, Cedric, and Cassian were spread out, performing their designated jobs.

Cedric stood in front of the wall of monitors, watching security feeds. Cassian was on the couch, one ankle crossed over his knee, ending a call on his phone.

Nico was on his laptop, fingers flying over the keyboard as he remained focused, squinting at the screen. I could tell he was on a digital trail because he always made that same face.

Benny sat behind his massive desk in the center of the room.

"Yes." I gave him a dirty look.

I shoved my key fob into my pocket as I crossed the room.

Benny dropped his phone and leaned back in the leather chair. "You think I'm being a dick about her."

"I do," I answered.

Nico glanced up from his screen. "Dad doesn't get the whole Fawn thing."

"No, I *get it*," Benny corrected, waving his hand dismissively. "It's similar to arranged marriages. You're paired with someone. They serve a purpose, but in your *Fawn* case, you can cut them off whenever you want. That's what I find dangerous." He slowly shook his head. "Once someone knows your secrets, you make damn sure they're tied to you for life. You don't give them the opportunity to think they can turn on you."

I lifted my coffee cup, taking a slow sip before answering, "Just because someone isn't temporary doesn't mean they give you blind loyalty." I pointed the cup toward him. "Remember Dad's consigliere—"

"That son of a bitch, Rocky," Benny snapped immediately, tension clear on his face. Old anger carved deep into his features when he snarled.

Not that I blamed him.

I'd never met Rocky, but I knew what he'd done.

Years ago, before I was born, Rocky helped my mother's ex kidnap her. That betrayal had almost destroyed my father.

"He wasn't temporary," I said to Benny. "How long did his family work for ours?"

"Generations," Benny snarled.

"Yet he still betrayed us."

Silence settled over the room because we all knew the truth.

You could demand loyalty. Buy it. Threaten it.

But none of that meant people still wouldn't betray you the

moment it suited them. Power and money had a way of making people forget where they had come from.

Just as I was about to ask Benny if he had any updates since I'd asked him twenty minutes ago, my phone vibrated in my pocket.

I pulled it out to see Brooks's name flashing on the screen and answered it. "What's up?"

Brooks exhaled an annoyed breath on the other end. "Daphne is flipping out here. She's demanding I call you because it's an emergency."

I rubbed my temple in irritation.

"She won't tell me what it is until you're here."

"Look," I snapped, furrowing my brows. All eyes were on me. "I don't have time to play into your guys' dramatic bullshit."

"She said it's about Blair."

Unease crawled up my spine.

"Daphne found a note on her bed."

My grip tightened around the phone.

"The note says, *I can't wait to kill you.*"

"Fuck," I hissed. "I'll be right there."

I ended the call.

"What happened?" Benny asked.

"Someone left a threatening note on Blair's bed," I told them. Panic settled into my stomach like deadly acid. "It said, *I can't wait to kill you.*"

"Shit," Nico hissed. "Do you need us to go with you?"

I shook my head. "You stay here and handle this. I'll call you soon. Let me know if you get any updates."

As I left the club, so many thoughts raced through my brain.

The shootings, Blair's secrets, the notes.

Are they all connected to Blair?

FORTY-TWO

BLAIR

My head spun while I flipped through the pages of the diary.

The leather cover was delicate, and I was careful each time I turned to another entry. The paper was yellowed with age.

Whoever had owned it wrote nearly every day.

Sometimes her writing was confident. Other times, it was scribbled sloppily.

All of them were in my mother's handwriting.

At least, I was certain it was hers.

And unless she had a twin, that was her in the photo.

She had the same waves of dark hair. Same sharp cheekbones, slight dimples, and a proud lift of the chin.

On the commune, cameras hadn't been allowed, but I did find a photo stashed in one of my mother's drawers once. It was of her and my father. They posed for the photo while my father held a baby who I assumed was me. I never forgot it because in that photo, they looked like parents who loved their daughter.

In that photo was a younger version of her, and she looked identical to the one in the diary. She was even wearing the same yellow dress.

I flipped the page to read the next diary entry.

> *Dear Diary,*
>
> *Two Sons want me. I've never felt like such a lucky Fawn before. I know others are jealous of me. One day, I'll be married to the most powerful man in the world. I'll be the strongest Fawn ever and rule beside him.*

I swallowed, a bitter taste filling my mouth.

Her other entries were all similar to that one. Filled with pride, excitement, and a weird obsession with status and power.

I ran my thumb over the edge of the page, nausea and the yogurt gurgling in my belly.

Another entry caught my eye down the page. The ink was darker, like she'd pressed her pen into the paper so hard that it nearly tore it.

Scooting closer, I leaned in to read it, but froze when I heard a faint sound.

Footsteps.

Heavy ones.

I looked toward the doorway, expecting to see Enzo, but fell back, scurrying off the bed when I found two tall, broad-shouldered men dressed in black robes.

They wore masks I'd never seen before.

I screamed and ran toward the bathroom. One of the men lunged toward me, catching me around the waist before I made it. He clamped his gloved hand around my arm like a trap.

My screaming didn't stop when he yanked me around as I fought him.

"No!" I shrieked, thrusting against him. "Enzo! Enzo! Enzo!"

Before I could yell for Enzo again, the man pressed something soft against my mouth.

A sharp, chemical taste filled my lungs.

"No!" I wheezed out. "En ..."

I wasn't even sure those words left my throat.

I tried to fight, but they were stronger and carried me away.

My vision blurred, and my limbs felt like they weighed a million tons.

The last thing I saw before everything went black was the diary on the bed.

My head throbbed before my eyes even opened.

A dull, pulsing ache spread through my skull. Each beat of my heart pressed harder against my chest.

A chemical film coated my tongue. So thick that it clung to the back of my throat. It almost tasted like crushed pills, dissolved in rubbing alcohol.

I tried to lift my hands, but they wouldn't move.

My gaze was still half blurred and tilting sideways.

I could make out dark shapes. Flickering lights. Moving shadows.

Calm down, Blair. Take in your surroundings. Figure out where you are.

I was seated in a chair.

Wait, no.

I was *strapped* to one.

Rough rope dug into my wrists, bound to the arms of a wooden chair. My ankles were also tied. The fibers bit into my skin whenever I tried to break free.

The space looked similar to where I'd had my Initiation, but this one felt wickeder.

I was almost certain I was still in the tunnels.

And I was also almost certain these weren't the same Sons from before.

They gave off a different vibe and wore different masks.

What had happened in the Fawn Quarters rushed back to me.

The men, the cloth to my mouth, them dragging me away.

A bright light above me turned on, and I jerked against the ropes again, refusing to be a show to these psychos.

"Hello, Blair."

My entire body stilled at the distinct, chiding voice.

No, no, no-no-no-no-no.

Please, God, no.

I attempted to heave forward, but pain shot through my chest when a man stepped forward from the shadows. For a second, I refused to believe it was him.

He was the only one not wearing a mask.

He wanted me to see him.

When we came face-to-face, he dug his palms into my hands painfully. "Miss me?"

He inched back, studying me like I was an animal he'd just stuck in a cage, and he couldn't decide what to do with me.

"You're supposed to be in prison," I said with a cracking voice.

It was obvious that wasn't true, but those were the only words I could form at the moment.

My father smiled at me.

Not nicely. Not fatherly.

It was that same cold, demented smile I remembered from my childhood.

He had more wrinkles now, reminding me of old leather. He'd lost weight, and his eyes were more sunken in. His front tooth was decaying and chipped. But it was him.

Every feature of his face was burned into my memory.

He drew back, tapping his fingers together. "If you know the right people, you can get out of life sentences."

"But they said parole wasn't possible," I whispered.

"They were wrong." He pulled at the neckline of his robe. "You testified very well." He viciously smiled while giving me fake applause. "The jury believed your every word."

"Because it was the truth," I said around a tight throat. I spat, trying to clear the vile taste from my mouth, but also because I wanted to show him how much he repulsed me. "You murdered people."

He sighed. "When people turn their backs on us, they die." Another long, dramatic sigh from him. "I thought you knew that." His gaze lowered to the ropes binding me before returning to my face. "And I think, Blair, you turned your back on us."

Cold dread seeped into my veins.

"What do you want?" I asked him.

For a second, he didn't answer and just clicked his tongue to taunt me.

I squeezed my eyes shut, trying everything to stop the tears from rolling down my cheeks. But I couldn't. They fell like hot streams.

"Tell me something," he said.

I bared my teeth at him, curling my fingers around the arm of the chair.

"Do you regret testifying against your father? Your own flesh and blood?"

I pressed my lips together, at first deciding not to answer him.

But then, I changed my mind.

If he was going to kill me, which I knew he was, I'd say all the things I'd wanted to say to him for years.

I'd stand up to him. Speak my mind. Be the strong girl I was when I ran out of the burning chapel.

"No, I don't regret it." I raised my chin.

He cocked his head to the side, sneering at me.

"What I do regret is not slitting your throat all those years I witnessed you kill innocent people." I did my best to bring my face closer to his. "You deserved to rot in prison and then rot in hell, like the piece of shit you are."

It seemed I was not made for survival of the fittest games.

But I refused to plead for my life because I knew he wouldn't give it to me. When my father swore he was going to do something, he did it.

"Oh, she's now got a mouth on her," he said.

Pain stretched across my cheek and jaw when he slapped me across the face.

"It seemed leaving the commune made you falsely believe you could have a voice." Spit flew from his mouth as he spoke, hitting my aching cheek.

He sneered again before taking a step back. When he did, another person emerged, stopping at his side.

"Hello, Blair," she said in that angelic, manipulative voice.

It was the same one she'd used to drag people into my father's warped cult.

I glared at my mother as she waltzed forward in a long white dress, barefoot, with butterfly clips in her hair.

"It's time, my love," another masked figure said, joining them.

My mother took his hand, then my father's, as they came closer. She kissed each one before dropping their hands.

She stepped up to me, and I winced when she cupped my face.

"Hush, little baby, don't say a word—"

"Stop it!" I screamed over her, but this time, that song didn't strike the chord inside me it once had.

This time, it wasn't agony. It was anger.

"Fuck that song," I told her. "And fuck you!"

Her singing ceased, and she stared at me in shock at how I'd spoken to her.

"You chose strangers over your own blood." My father came forward, rubbing his hands together. "I've waited years to watch you die."

FORTY-THREE

ENZO

After the hour drive back to Saint Vale, the university building broke through the gray fog.

I parked my car at the circular entrance rather than the underground garage. The tunnels would've delayed my getting to the dorms.

As I entered the vestibule, I spotted Brooks hunched on the bottom step of the staircase, his elbows planted on his knees and his eyes glued to his phone.

His tie was crooked and loose. He looked exactly like a man whose father had just been shot. Furious and tired. Just like me.

"Dude, what the fuck?" I asked, stalking toward him. "Why aren't you in Daphne's room, already talking to her?"

He glanced up at me, a flash of irritation on his face, before pocketing his phone and getting to his feet. "She said she'd only talk to us together."

As we started up the staircase, he rambled, "She's in one of her moods, like always." He ran a hand through his hair. "Saying she doesn't trust me alone, which is fine with me because the less time I spend with my father's shooter's spawn, the better. I wouldn't be surprised if she was involved in yesterday's shootings."

I doubted that.

Daphne was dramatic and about a million other unpleasant things, but orchestrating an assassination attempt on the two most powerful men in the world was a stretch.

Still, like I'd told Benny, power had a funny way of changing people. I'd never rule anything out.

I had questions for Brooks. Whether he'd heard anything new about the car dealership or the shooters or where the VP was. But the hallway wasn't the place for that conversation.

Too many ears around here.

When we reached their room, I knocked. A first time for that.

The door swung open almost immediately, like Daphne had been standing there, waiting for us. She didn't smile or say a word, only stepped back and waved us inside before shutting the door and locking it.

"What's with all the theatrics?" I asked.

"Yeah," Brooks added, dropping onto her bed. He grabbed one of the stuffed animals piled against the pillows and tossed it aside. "What's the emergency?"

Daphne slid her hair over her shoulder. "First," she said, placing a manicured pink nail against her chest in sympathy, "I'm sorry your dads were shot."

My jaw tightened instantly.

Brooks's back straightened.

"I obviously had nothing to do with it," she added.

"The fact that you felt the need to say that is suspect," Brooks shot back.

I motioned between them. "You two argue later." Crossing my arms, I fixed my hard stare on Daphne. "How'd you know my father was shot?"

The president's shooting was on the news.

Only a handful of people knew my father had been shot. And Daphne wasn't one of them.

She shrugged. "I know everything."

Brooks let out a dry scoff.

I was already losing patience. "What was so important that I had to rush over here *right now*? Spit it out, Daphne. I'm a busy man."

"Yes, right," Daphne said, turning quickly and rushing to Blair's bed. She grabbed a small paper off the pillow and handed it to me.

The note Brooks had mentioned.

I can't wait to kill you, was typed across the center in black ink.

"Do you know who left it?" I asked.

Daphne shot me an offended look. "Don't you think I'd tell you if I did?"

"Did you ask Blair about the note?" I asked.

"I've tried texting her, but she isn't answering," she said. "Do you know where she is?"

"She's safe," I replied.

She raised a brow. "Is she, though?"

"The hell does that mean?" I snapped.

She strolled toward her bed, opened a drawer beneath it, and pulled out a locked safe. She slipped her hand into the front of her bra and fished out a tiny key.

"I've been doing some research." She dropped onto the rug in the center of the room, unlocked the safe, and pulled out a thick manila folder from it. "When Blair first got here, something felt *off*. Not bad *off*, just like she had a past she was hiding. After what happened with Clarissa, I decided I should probably know who I was rooming with, so I started digging."

"There's nothing out there," I said. "Trust me. I've searched, and so have people who can hack into a hell of a lot more shit than any of us."

Daphne smirked. "Sure, if you don't look in the right places or talk to the right people," she said before singing, "*Never have a man do a woman's job.*" She winked. "We're basically better than the FBI."

I made a *move on with it* gesture. "Tell us what you got then."

"First, I found out that Blair's mother was a Fawn." She

started flipping through her handwritten notes, as if going through bullets.

I winced, pissed that none of us had discovered that.

"Her father was also a Son," she continued. "So is her stepfather."

I frowned, further pissed at myself. "You figured out who her stepfather is?"

Daphne glanced at Brooks. "He's the vice president."

"Bullshit." Brooks stood from the bed and stalked toward us. "I know the Second Lady, and they don't have kids. She had infertility issues."

Daphne held up a hand. "Let me correct myself. Her mother is his mistress. For some reason, Blair refers to him as her stepfather. No one knows Blair exists. Her mother rarely leaves her home in Arizona."

Arizona.

That was where Blair had said the commune was.

Daphne had to be right about what she was telling us.

She kept going. "Blair's father was some crazy-ass cult leader who murdered members and went to prison."

"A cult leader?" Brooks asked. "Damn, Enzo."

I flicked my hand through the air. "I know about the cult and her dad."

"He and my father were at the same facility until hers was pardoned."

"Pardoned?" Brooks stiffened. "By who?"

Daphne rolled her eyes. "Who do you think signs the pardons in the United States, Brooks?"

"Hell no," Brooks said. "My father wouldn't ruin his image by pardoning a cult leader who murdered people."

"He would for a fellow Son," Daphne fired back. "They were all Sons at the same time. My dad, hers, the VP, President Byron. Blair's mom was a Fawn at that time. The same with my mother. She said that Blair's mom was, in her words, 'A power-hungry cunt who wanted influence over every Son.' She slept with a few to get that. Again, *cult shit*. It checks out."

"How did you figure all this out?" I asked her.

Daphne's gaze slid to Brooks. "You know the guy you killed, Brooks? The twin?"

Brooks scratched his cheek. "I didn't kill anyone."

She blew out a breath, rolling her eyes again. "He was feeding me information, and I lost that source when you killed him. The idiot would get drunk, I'd give him a little striptease, and he'd talk. I guess his father liked to brag about other Sons' secrets when he drank."

"So her dad was a Son, and the VP is banging her mom." Brooks spread out his arms. "What's the issue?"

Daphne frowned. "My father has been trying to get in touch with me, so I finally reached out to him."

"Why was your father trying to get in contact with you?" Brooks asked with suspicion in his voice.

"He heard that someone had chosen me as their Fawn."

Brooks's mouth slammed shut.

I wasn't sure if her father knew I'd told Brooks he had to choose Daphne or if he'd heard another Son wanted her, like the twin of the guy Brooks had killed. But right now, I didn't have time to hash that out. We needed to get to the bottom of what Daphne had just told us.

I rubbed at my forehead. "What else did you find out, Daphne, and what does your father have to do with this? With Blair?"

She held up a hand. "I don't know if what he told me has anything to do with Blair, but he did say that the current shooting with your dads? He thinks that the VP had something to do with it."

"Bullshit," Brooks hissed. "That's my father's best friend."

Daphne glared at him. "The VP thinks your father is a traitor for bringing the Mafia families inside the Sons and to Saint Vale. Before that, no outsiders were ever allowed. Some of the Elder

Sons, including the VP, believe he corrupted the Sons and spoiled the blood of the First Benefactors by bringing those not worthy."

If what Daphne had said was true, then we needed to find the vice president and question him. Right now, this Blair research would pause. I had a vice president to torture for information.

"Where is Blair?" Daphne asked, interrupting my thoughts.

"She's in the Fawn Quarters," I replied, knowing I shouldn't have told her that, but fuck it. She seemed to know more than us at this point anyway. "I texted her on the drive here. She texted back that she was going to take a nap and would call me when she woke up."

"Wait." Daphne scrunched her face. "She said she'd *call* you?"

I nodded.

"Are you serious?" she huffed out, jumping to her feet. "Do you not see any issue with that?"

I stared at her, unsure where she was going with this.

"When was the last time she called you?" Daphne grabbed her jacket. "We don't *call*. That's alarming." She pointed at my pocket, where I'd stashed the note. "We need to make sure she's okay."

"Wait," I said as something hit me. "You said her father was pardoned. When was that?"

"Last night," she replied.

My head started to pound. "He said that if he ever got out, he'd kill her."

I wanted to burn down the tunnels, the university, everything in my sight when I found Blair's bedroom in the Fawn Quarters empty.

My blood boiled as I took in the scene. Her disheveled bed, the half-empty water bottle on the small nightstand, and ... I inched farther, looking down at the sheets to find a small notebook.

I grabbed it, every muscle in my body tightening when I flipped through the pages of her mother's diary.

Daphne was right; she had been a Fawn.

Did Blair just find this out?

Or did she know before?

I'd told Brooks to call Nico and ask him to hack into the university camera footage to see everyone who entered and left the university. If Blair's father had come here, he'd have to be on camera.

I clenched my hand around the diary.

Unless...

Baring my teeth, I knew exactly what was happening when I called Brooks, who was still with Daphne.

"Blair's not here," I told him.

"Fuck," he said on the other line. "Nico is getting into the system right now." He paused for a second. "Whoever texted you wanted you to believe she was safe down there." He cleared his throat. "They think you're gone, in the city, with your family, Enzo."

"I know." I ground my teeth while refraining from smashing my phone through the goddamn wall. "They knew this was the perfect time to take her because she'd be unprotected."

A tightness formed in my chest, rough and hard, spreading until it hit my heart. "Where do you think they'd take her?"

"I have no idea," he replied. I heard him whispering to Daphne in the background but couldn't make out their words.

"Either a Son took her from the tunnels for himself *or* her father is down here. You keep having Nico check the footage."

I pressed my tooth into my lip until it drew blood, debating on asking Brooks to call the vice president. They were supposed to hold meetings down here today. I could ask him if he had seen Blair.

But right now, after what Daphne had told us, I didn't trust him.

If he had shot our fathers because he saw Brooks's father as a traitor, then I didn't want the fucker knowing my whereabouts *or* that my Fawn was in trouble.

I also didn't want him to know I was here.

A thousand thoughts ran through my mind like a movie I couldn't shut off.

Did they shoot my father to get me away from the university?

"You still there?" Brooks asked.

"Yeah. I'm going to search the tunnels."

Brooks let out a long breath. "You want me to come down there with you?"

"Keep looking outside and tell Daphne to wait in the dorm room, just in case Blair goes there. If you don't hear from me soon, come down and look for me."

"Be careful, man."

I ended the call, threw the diary across the room, and left to search the rest of the tunnels.

I needed to kill Blair's father if his plan was to hurt her.

Even if he wasn't responsible for her current disappearance, he was too much of a liability.

And if he did hurt her, if he had her now, I'd rip the mother-fucker apart limb by limb.

Then, for fun, I'd dump his dead body into the water, just like he said he'd do to my precious Fawn.

FORTY-FOUR

BLAIR

During my childhood, the fear that my father might kill me had been a constant companion.

He'd threatened to do it countless times.

His attempts to drown me outnumbered his hugs.

And he vowed in the courtroom that he'd do it if they ever freed him.

After his arrest, I'd tried to assure myself I was safe now. He was behind bars and across the country from me. But now, he was free, and I knew he'd fulfill that promise to himself.

No one crossed my father without paying for it.

The nasty taste was still in my mouth, so I tried to swallow as little as possible. My head still felt fuzzy and heavy, like I was wading through a thick fog as I tried to connect clues that didn't fit.

My father continued his incessant, irritating speaking, making my headache worse. The bastard couldn't simply take my life. He'd always been a fan of making people listen to his drawn-out rants.

Over it, I groaned. "Just kill me already," I spat at him, the chemical hitting my lips. "No one believes you're special. You're a loser and mad that your brainwashing didn't work on me."

My words were risky. Ballsy. But I knew there was no chance I'd leave here alive, so it was time I said my piece.

A wave of pain shot through my jaw again at the force of his second slap. The sharp edge of his wedding ring cut into my lip, breaking skin, and I could taste my blood.

He stepped behind me, grabbed a handful of my hair, and dug his fingers into my scalp as he tugged my head back so far that an aching throb ran down my neck. The scent of raw tuna wafted from his breath when he got in my face.

"You should be happy they forced me to keep you down here," he snarled. "I wanted to stay true to my word and drown you." He yanked my hair back again, and I couldn't stop myself from crying out in pain. "Every day in that prison cell, I fantasized about killing you. The only thing that kept me breathing there was knowing I'd get that someday."

He released my hair, but the pain didn't lessen. It came from everywhere. My cheek. My jaw. My head.

Closing my eyes, I struggled against the rope, and when I opened them, more men in masks formed a circle around me. They all wore robes like the Sons had during my Initiation.

The masked man who stood by my mother unmasked himself. He shook out his blond hair, but I wasn't surprised by him.

I always wondered why the Arizona senator—now vice president of the United States—had come to my mother's rescue after my father's arrest.

Always wondered why my father's arrest never made headlines or was talked about.

Especially because the public loved stories about cults.

They consumed documentaries and podcasts about people like him. Experts did interviews about the leaders' mental psyches.

But my father's name was never mentioned on those cult-leader lists. Deep down, I knew it wasn't in exchange for my testimony against him.

Now, it all made sense. The Sons had protected him. They

were more powerful than the police and had high government officials on their side. Given the vice president was here, I was certain both men were Sons.

These were men who had committed crimes and murder with impunity, and I came along and ruined that. I'd proven them wrong—that they could get penalized for their crimes—and now, I'd face the consequences for that.

I took a moment to look at each mask around me.

They were Sons. I knew it.

But which Sons?

Enzo? Brooks? Nico?

Goose bumps prickled across my skin at the thought of Enzo being here.

Was that their plan all along?

To make me a Fawn, get me down here, and kill me?

I hunched forward, nausea roiling in my stomach and up my throat, and spit out bile at the thought of Enzo turning on me.

No.

He was a man who'd kill for me. Not *kill* me.

Right?

I glared at my mother. Much like my father, the hatred had aged her.

Two years had passed since the last time I had seen her. That encounter was brief, and we didn't speak. She tended to ignore me while my stepfather handled all our communication.

I'd always wondered why they still took care of me. Everything made sense now. They wanted to keep me alive, waiting for the day my father could get revenge on me.

"How could you?" I cried out to her as tears rolled down my stinging cheeks. "You were—you *are*—supposed to protect me."

"Why?" she asked, as if genuinely confused.

"Because you're my mother!" I screamed at the top of my lungs, fighting against the restraints.

She jutted her hip out. "So?"

The men gave her space as she came closer. She maintained a

distance, as if worried she'd get some contagious disease if she came too close.

Her voice was as tender as the day she'd sung that lullaby to me. "I'm here to rid the world of evil, and you are evil." She rubbed her belly. "You robbed me of having another precious baby and then had my husband locked away to rot in prison because you're a selfish bitch."

My head snapped sideways when she hit me in the face.

It wasn't a slap like my father's. It was a full-on punch.

"Enough!" My father rubbed his hands and wet his dry lips. "No more speeches. No more letting her breathe for a second longer. It's time."

"It's time," the men in masks echoed.

My mother and stepfather stepped back.

A shrill gasp escaped me when my father tensed his shoulders and pulled a knife from his jeans. I held in a breath and accepted my fate, refusing to plead for my life. That'd only give him satisfaction.

I only hoped he'd make it quick, but given his personality, I didn't expect it. He'd prolong it for dramatic effect and because he was a hateful, violent asshole.

He'd give me the slow death that he truly deserved.

He came to my side and ran the knife's edge along my cheek. "This woman committed betrayal against a Son," he stated loudly. "What becomes of those who betray or deceive a Son?"

The masked men chanted, "Death."

I relaxed my body, rolling my shoulders back, as a silent prayer left my lips. Looking up, I stared my mother down. She tried to avert her gaze, but it kept finding its way back to mine.

My father pointed the knife at the men. "You sure we can't take her in the woods? There's a small river there. Just a little water is all I need."

"No," my stepfather stated, voice firm and final as he moved in closer. "We already risked too much by bringing you here. You have the girl. Kill her."

My father nodded, his brow creased in displeasure at that answer. I almost expected him to try to kill my stepfather so he could get what he wanted.

But he didn't. He only circled the chair to stand before me. His voice was a soft murmur as he said, "*Hush, little baby ...*"

I winced but didn't beg for mercy.

As he drew his arm back, the knife ready to plunge through my chest, the door opened.

FORTY-FIVE

ENZO

This chamber was where Sons punished those who'd crossed them. A Son could bring a victim here who'd wronged them and deliver their consequence.

It wasn't here for a killing free-for-all, and it had rules. Only those who had truly wronged us could be punished here. Four other Sons or Elders had to approve the punishment beforehand. Innocent people couldn't be brought down here for slaughter.

Each punishment had to mean something.

Had to correct a sin.

My Fawn didn't commit sins.

The robed men blocked my view from the center of the room, but that didn't stop my brain from spiraling, from knowing my Fawn was in danger. Surrounded by wolves I needed to slaughter.

The circle broke, and all eyes behind the masks turned toward me when I walked deeper into the chamber. Quickly, I counted eight masked men. My attention slid from them to the three unmasked people.

The vice president and two faces I didn't recognize.

Though I saw the similarities they shared with Blair.

I took calm strides toward the group, and they parted, but the three still obstructed my view of who was in the middle.

The vice president's back straightened, and he scooted closer to the woman. "Enzo. What are you doing here?"

I leveled my hateful stare on him. "I'm looking for my Fawn. Have you seen her?"

The fucker visibly gulped, and his false exterior of being a strong man cracked along with that.

My gaze slipped from him to the woman.

Her long black hair and that nose told me who she was.

A doe who didn't protect her Fawn.

She was a pathetic, low-grade version of my Fawn, who didn't deserve to breathe the same air as her.

And if she'd hurt my Fawn, her chances of doing that for long were slim. The same with all these fuckers.

"Your Fawn has betrayed one of us," the vice president had the nerve to say.

I rushed forward, toward the center, pushing past three masked men. They tried to hold me back, but I was stronger. Another masked Son tried to block me, and I punched him in the face. He tumbled to the ground.

Just as I reared my fist back to hit another, the vice president shoved a gun in my face.

"Enzo"—he gripped the handle tight—"you have to kill your Fawn."

I stared coldly into the barrel, close to ignoring it and ramming his face in for even suggesting that. But if I did and he shot me, then I couldn't save Blair.

"Excuse me," the man beside him said.

The man I knew in my gut was Blair's father.

He was short, reminding me of a little gnome. Short-man syndrome, I was sure. He also looked like hell, but I wanted him to look worse.

I ignored the gun in my face and turned to get a better look at Blair's dad. Then, quickly, before the vice president could even pull the trigger, I bashed my fist into her dad's face.

"What the hell?" he screamed, cupping his free hand over his nose. He gripped a knife in his other one. "This fucker just punched me."

I smiled in satisfaction, hoping there were broken bones beneath that hand.

With the vice president's attention on his idiot friend, I stormed around them to find Blair tied to a chair in the center. My eyes met her terrified ones, and I wanted to punch that fucker again. But first, I had to get her out of here.

I needed to rescue my Fawn, and then I could get my vengeance against them for hurting her.

I was only inches away from her when two arms pulled me back to restrain me.

"Did you not hear me correctly?" the vice president asked. "Your Fawn must die." He took the knife from Blair's father. "You pledged an oath to us, the Sons, Enzo. Not her. A Son must avenge his brothers. And tonight, you'll prove whether you're one of us or whether you'll be treated as a traitor."

"Wait a—" Blair's dad started to say, but the vice president raised his hand to shut him up.

"There's been a change of plans. You'll still get your revenge, but I'm questioning this Son's loyalty to us. We can't have a traitor among us."

Being a traitor meant death.

A disloyal Son was a dead Son.

What that meant was, every Son would come forth and stab you as you sat there and bled to death. That punishment was why Daphne's father had talked as much as he did to the feds and media because he knew if he wasn't behind bars, then he was a dead man.

I either had to turn on my Fawn or I had to die.

The chamber felt like it was closing in on me.

My eyes were on Blair, taking her in as she fought against the ropes. I noticed a bruise on her cheek as the vice president offered me the knife.

"Make your decision," he said, now in charge.

Blair's parents drew back a few steps before the masked Sons circled me. I eyed each mask, attempting to see if I recognized any of them.

"No!" Blair's father said, running over in an attempt to grab the knife back. "No one else gets this but me!"

"Aht, at," the vice president said in a patronizing tone, pulling it away too fast. "I got your pardon and the girl. You should be more grateful, Kevin. The circumstances have changed because her Son showed up—to rescue her, I'm sure." He rolled his eyes. "We have to test him now."

His attention came back to me as he came closer, attempting to cage me in. "Choose who you're loyal to. Prove to us that we were right for allowing outsiders into the Sons. Prove that you're just as worthy as First Benefactor Blood."

I took the knife from him, knowing that once I declared a loyalty to someone, I couldn't break it. Loyalty was woven into my bones, layered deep within me. Breaking it was never an option.

For years now, I'd told the Sons I had their backs.

Now, it was time that I proved it.

Blair was my Fawn—that was it—but she'd betrayed them, which meant she'd betrayed me. She'd lied and hidden that the vice president was her stepfather.

What else is she hiding?

The secrets kept piling up.

I didn't want a Fawn with secrets.

I stepped toward her as everyone closed in on us, waiting with anticipation. The men behind those masks had seen me kill before. They knew how bloody I made my murders.

Gripping the knife tight, I stood tall in front of her. She whimpered as I ran the knife between her lips.

My pulse sped as I dug the tip of the knife into her cheek. "Our time together was fun, but unfortunately for you, I'm a man of my word. You were nothing but a Fawn for me to use for my pleasure."

Tears dripped down her cheeks and onto my hand holding the knife, but she didn't look away from me.

FORTY-SIX

BLAIR

My heart beat in my chest like an animal trapped in a net as I sat there, waiting for Enzo's next move.

He brushed the tip of the blade against my skin.

It felt so rough yet gentle.

Like a tiny poke that was supposed to be more painful.

The skin bunched around his eyes when our gazes locked, and for a moment, everyone in the room who wanted me dead faded away.

Enzo's eyes softened as he dragged the blade against my cheek. Not deep enough to break skin.

Then everything happened so fast.

In one second, he dropped the knife from my face to my wrist. Swiftly, he cut it free, then did the same with the other.

"I told you to let me kill the cunt!" my father shouted when Enzo knelt to cut the rope around my ankles. "He's too weak to do it!"

My stepfather pointed his gun at Enzo's head. "Don't be stupid, Enzo. You know the rule. Sons before everything." He shook his head in disgust. "If you can't do it, which is a weakness we'll need to discuss later, then you let another one of us get the job done."

Enzo yanked me out of the chair like a rag doll when my father charged toward us. He shoved me off to the side to punch my father in the face, knocking me down. While doing that, his phone flew out of his pocket and skidded across the floor.

My stepfather pulled the trigger, and Enzo tackled me to the ground just as the bullet buzzed by my head.

Enzo hauled me to my feet and shoved the knife and his badge into my hands. "Run, Blair. Run like the Fawn you are. Find Brooks and Emeri in the university." He pushed me behind him, backing us up until I was closer to the door and making sure no Son got to me.

"No!" I screamed, grabbing his sleeve. "I'm not leaving you!"

For a moment, no Son made a move as they watched the scene play out in front of them.

A Son willing to die for his Fawn.

A Fawn willing to die for her Son.

This is how the power balance is meant to be.

This is the intention of their entire logic.

Why each of us has our roles.

He kept his eyes on those around us. "Go, Blair! No one is going to help us unless you get them! Go get help!"

I tried to hand him the knife back, but he wouldn't take it.

He shook his head as the Sons got closer. "Go!" he screamed as he pulled another knife from his pocket.

My stepfather shot at us again.

"Go!" Enzo yelled. "I can fight these bastards off for a minute, but I need you to get help!"

I knew I had to go.

To leave him.

My heart nearly shattered when I slid through the opening in the door. My bare feet pounded against the concrete, my heavy steps echoing through the tunnel walls, and I prayed I was running in the right direction.

Footsteps thumped behind me, but I didn't look back. I couldn't waste my energy or slow down my pace.

I needed to find Brooks or Emeri.

Needed to find a Son I could trust.

But right now, I wasn't sure who was on that list.

Somehow, as if God knew I wasn't evil and was on my side, I pushed open a door at the end of a corridor that led exactly where I needed it to.

Fresh air hit my face, and I took in my surroundings. Trees closed in around me, but through the fog, I saw the university standing tall.

I took off running, branches and roots cutting at my feet. My lungs ached as I weaved between trees. A voice shouted behind me, but I did my best to tune it out as I picked up speed.

I was close—so fucking close—when my foot caught on a root, and I crashed into the ground. Before I could pull myself up, something hard slammed into the back of my head.

A shot of pain exploded through my skull and spread across my shoulders. I rolled onto my side, staring up at my mother holding a heavy branch.

She drew her arm back, ready to strike me again, but when she moved, I kicked out my leg. The branch fell from her hand, rolling away as she lost her balance and fell to the ground.

I jumped to my feet at the same time she did.

We both went for the branch, but she was faster and snatched it up.

"*Hush, little baby,*" she taunted with that manic smirk, swinging the branch at me.

I needed to keep her away from me, but didn't have time to fight her and dispose of a damn branch so she couldn't grab it again.

When she swung again, I ducked and plunged the knife into her thigh. Her ugly smirk collapsed, morphing into a loud cry like an attacked animal, and she fell to the ground.

She crouched forward, staring at the knife in her thigh, and then back at me. I'd made sure to go deep enough to hit bone for a reason. She needed to stay put.

I shrugged, not about to waste any precious seconds helping her pull it out or explaining why I wouldn't do that anyway.

"Blair," she said as I took off running again.

I paused for a second to look at her over my shoulder.

That evil grin was back on her face as she made sure to fully articulate her words. "I wish you'd died during childbirth."

Disgust clenched inside me as I fastened my stare on her, mirroring her smirk. "And I wish I'd killed you during childbirth."

Her eyes widened, her mouth opening to spout more words, but I didn't waste my time hearing her response.

Nothing she could ever say could make me see her as a mother.

I had someone more important to save.

I picked up my speed, running as fast as I could, and ignored the pain in my lungs and head.

Unlike the last times, I wasn't a helpless Fawn running in the woods.

I was a Fawn on a mission.

Running to save myself and the Son who I realized meant everything to me.

I hurt everywhere when I made it to the edge of the woods. I cut to the right, moving faster, when my body collided with something hard. I fell back a step but managed to stay on my feet, thanks to two strong arms.

Emeri's emerald-green eyes met mine.

"Enzo!" I screamed at him, out of breath. "He's in the chamber and in trouble!" I thrust both my fists against his chest. "He needs help! Go!"

His hold dropped from my body, and he sped past me. Brooks came into view next, sprinting, with Daphne close behind him.

She wrapped me in a quick hug, mid-run, as we chased them.

"Stay here!" Brooks yelled over his shoulder.

Yeah fucking right.

Neither Daphne nor I listened.

As we ran past my mother, she cried out for help.
"Should we?" Daphne asked through heavy pants.
I shook my head and ran faster, needing to save Enzo.
I still needed my devil here with me.
Hell could have him later.

FORTY-SEVEN

ENZO

The chaos inside the chamber wrapped around me like an evil spirit.

What these fuckers didn't understand was that I became an entirely different animal when my adrenaline spiked or when someone I cared about was in danger.

Blood poured down my side when I limped across the floor, praying the bullet had made an exit and wasn't lodged somewhere inside me. I hadn't even felt the bullet hit me.

The vice president had managed to land the shot because I was distracted for two seconds when Blair's father charged at me with a knife.

The two old fuckers were slow and out of shape.

Two other masked men had tried to jump in earlier, both of them now bleeding in the corner. I'd slit Reginald's throat—because of course he was involved—when his mask fell off, and I'd buried my knife in the other man's groin.

The other Sons stood to the side wall of the chamber like frightened sheep, unsure whose side to choose. If they picked the wrong one, the consequence would be death.

And while Kevin was an Elder, he was still a risky bet. The idiot had already spent years in prison. If I walked out of this chamber breathing, they knew I'd kill each of them after for helping someone who had hurt my Fawn.

Elder or not, you couldn't kill someone's Fawn without permission. It didn't matter if you thought they were a traitor.

The vice president raised his gun again. I lunged sideways just as the shot fired. Concrete splintered when the bullet collided with it and lodged into the wall behind me.

"Shit!" he screamed, stomping his foot and lowering the gun. "Why don't you Mafia bastards die?"

I decided that I believed every word Daphne had said about him. He hated and resented the president for allowing us into the Sons.

Bringing us in was the smartest move they'd ever made.

Look at the morons I was dealing with now. The Sons would've fallen apart.

Kevin charged me again, his head lowered like a bull ready to attack. I dropped my arm, driving an uppercut into his jaw, and something cracked.

He staggered back, his body swaying, as if the tunnels were suddenly moving beneath us.

A cramp formed in my hand, and when I pulled it back, I found one of his rotten teeth embedded in the skin of my knuckles. I stared at it for half a second before flicking it off and crushing it beneath my shoe.

Before I could make another move, a fist slammed into my jaw from behind. My teeth snapped together when the vice president's weight crashed onto my back, his arms wrapping around my shoulders like an animal clinging to me.

Kevin wiped blood from his mouth, red streaking his chin as he spat another tooth onto the floor. "She must die!" he screamed.

Rage burned inside me, and my vision turned sideways at my blood loss, but I did my best to control it. I had to.

I roared and grabbed the vice president's arm before hurling him over my shoulder. His scrawny body slammed into the ground. I drove my foot into his ribs as the gun slipped from his hand.

He scrambled for it, his fingers clawing into the ground, but I kicked it away. The gun slid across the floor. Kevin and I both ran toward it.

Since he was closer, instead of diving for it, I stormed toward him. He dropped to his knees to grab the gun, and I drove mine upward, using the same uppercut motion as I had before.

My knee crashed into his jaw, and I grinned in satisfaction at the loud pop.

Kevin crumpled to the floor, clutching his face, and a strangled noise forced its way past his broken jaw. Blood poured from his mouth, spraying across the ground as he tried to slur out words.

Behind me, the vice president groaned while dragging himself to his feet.

The world swayed again.

My head spun as I grabbed the gun.

My shirt was soaked with blood, the liquid warm and sticky against my skin. But again, I ignored it.

I hunched forward, nearly stumbling, and aimed the gun at the vice president's head. He froze when I pulled the trigger.

His head snapped back violently, and his body staggered for a moment before he fell backward. I grinned when I heard the crack of his skull connect with the ground.

I popped the gun's magazine free and checked the remaining rounds. A single bullet.

Standing over Kevin, I stared down at the despicable excuse for a father sprawled across the floor. A coward who had tried to destroy the one person I'd burn this entire society down for.

His mouth hung crooked from his shattered jaw, the teeth he had left red with blood.

"She ..." he gasped, choking on the word—or maybe that was his blood. Either way, I didn't care. "Must ..."

"She'll never die," I said with ease as I made it a point to look at the other Elders watching from the wall. "All of you mother-fuckers will have to go through me first. And spoiler alert: until the fucking day I die, I'll protect my Fawn over *everyone*."

And because I couldn't stand looking at the face of the man who'd wanted to hurt my precious Fawn, I raised the gun and pulled the trigger.

The final bullet tore through the center of his face.

I admired my work for a moment, wishing I had another bullet to do it again, and then turned around, realizing Blair's mother was gone.

The hallway became a blur when I ran out of the chamber. My blood trailed like a path behind me. As I rounded the corner, I slammed straight into Emeri.

"Dude, you good?" he asked as we steadied ourselves.

"Blair!" I shouted. "Where's Blair?"

"Down here!" Blair screamed, and I saw her waving her arms.

Relief punched the air out of my lungs. I couldn't see the rest of her yet, but hearing her voice was enough to steady the violent storm inside me.

"Give me your gun," I told Emeri.

He didn't hesitate before handing over the Glock in his hand. I stalked back into the chamber and emptied the magazine into the remaining Sons. Bodies dropped before they could even run.

There. That handled it.

I released a long breath.

"Let that be a lesson," I said to the empty room. "Touch my Fawn, and it'll be the last thing you touch on this earth."

I eyed the chamber one last time, making sure no bodies were moving, and limped out. The moment I turned the corner, someone else crashed into me.

"Enzo!" Blair gasped as I dragged her tight into my chest.

Her body trembled, and she buried her face against me. Her shoulders shook as she quietly sobbed, and my arms tightened around her, never wanting to let her go.

"You're safe," I whispered into her hair. "You're safe."

She was my Fawn.

Mine.

And I had no intention of ever letting her go.

Across the corridor, Daphne stood a few feet away, pretending she wasn't gawking, while Brooks and Emeri slipped past us toward the chamber to take in the aftermath.

I had a lot of explaining to do.

Killing that many Elder Sons wasn't exactly something you could easily walk away from.

But every life I had taken was worth saving Blair's.

"You okay?" I asked, pulling back just enough to grip her shoulders and look her over.

I checked her arms, her sides, her legs, searching for any blood or injuries. Just a bruise blooming along her cheek that made me want to go shoot all those fuckers again.

"I'm fine." She caught my arm as I swayed. "But you're not." Her gaze fell to the blood soaking my shirt. "Let's get you help."

Daphne yanked her sweater over her head and rushed toward us. She pressed the fabric hard against my bullet wound while the guys moved in, lifting me as we made our way out of the tunnels.

Blair was okay.

I was okay.

At that moment, that was all that mattered.

FORTY-EIGHT

BLAIR

I curled into Enzo's uninjured side in his bed as we watched the scandal unravel across the TV, our backs propped up against the headboard. Every headline that rolled across the screen was more shocking than the last.

My father's disappearance had been easy to bury, but the vice president couldn't simply vanish without the world demanding answers.

Even though I hadn't been in the meeting, I knew Enzo, his father, Brooks, and Benny had sat down with President Byron to decide what version of the truth the public would get.

They gave the media just enough to keep them satisfied. And enough fuel to keep the headlines burning for months.

The reporter on the screen spoke in that practiced urgent tone as she delivered the story. According to the official version, the vice president had secretly convinced the president to pardon a cult leader who'd been blackmailing him. The cult leader supposedly had proof that the vice president had been involved in the original plot to assassinate the president years ago. And again recently.

She went on to say that after the vice president picked the cult leader up from prison, the two got into an altercation. The cult leader shot the vice president, then turned the gun on himself.

A murder-suicide.

I was fine with that explanation.

The man who had wanted me dead was gone.

Enzo had killed him for me, and I felt no guilt over it.

My father was a horrible man who deserved it.

The reporter continued, explaining that the cult leader's wife —who also happened to be the vice president's mistress—had been part of the plan. My mother's mug shot appeared on the screen. She'd taken a deal to repeat the same story in exchange for less prison time.

She'd begged Enzo and the president to let her speak with me, most likely hoping I'd ask them to spare her. I gave her the silent treatment she'd given me for years. She also admitted that Reginald and the vice president had been the ones leaving me notes. They'd found a way to intercept the texts from reaching Enzo. All at my father's request.

Enzo and Brooks were now trying to find out whether any other Elders had been involved in the attempts on their fathers' lives. I'd overheard Enzo say he regretted shooting them all and wished he'd tortured them first for answers, but he'd been too enraged to think past revenge.

Fortunately, the bullet that had hit Enzo tore through muscle and missed anything vital. It passed clean through his side, so the doctor cleaned his wounds and stitched him up. He tried to keep Enzo overnight for observation, but Enzo refused. His mother had only laughed and said he was a typical Marchetti.

"Let's watch something more positive." I changed the channel, only to land on another reporter recycling the same story, and sighed.

Enzo stole the remote, turned off the TV, and tossed it aside. "How about we *do* something more positive?" A wicked grin tugged at his mouth.

I laughed and smacked his shoulder when his hand slipped up

my bare leg. "You're supposed to be resting. You're injured, remember?"

Goose bumps rippled across my skin. Every time Enzo touched me, my body reacted instantly. His touch was my own personal heaven.

"Yes," he said, voice threaded with amusement. "But you're not."

The higher his hand traveled, the warmer my body grew.

I caught his wrist before he reached my core.

He frowned, giving me a stubborn look.

"I don't want to hurt you," I said softly, sliding my fingers along his arm. "It's only been two days since you were shot."

That stubborn look didn't fade.

"Right, and I know exactly what'll make me feel better." He shifted on the bed, the movement tugging at the stitches along his side. His jaw tightened for a split second before his familiar arrogance slipped back into place. "Get up here and ride me, my Fawn."

Being his Fawn felt so different now.

Like a privilege.

A smile tilted my lips.

I guess I have to make him feel better.

I mean, the man had killed a handful of Sons to protect me.

He had been shot so I could run.

My body was panting for him like he was water and I'd been stuck in the desert for weeks.

Geesh, why do I want this man all the damn time?

I swung one leg over his hips, careful of the bandage along his ribs, and climbed onto his lap.

"Careful," he grunted, settling his hands on my waist to anchor me in place, as if worried I might change my mind and slide off him. "The doctor said I should avoid all sudden movements."

"I think what I'm about to do involves a lot of *sudden move-*

ments." I brushed my lips to his and rolled my hips. "You're the one who started this, mister."

Even sitting on him, I tried to keep most of my weight off his injured side.

"That may be true, and I'll never be sorry for wanting to touch you and fuck you," he admitted, tugging me closer to keep sliding my core against his hard cock through our clothes.

His gaze dropped to my mouth, and as he kissed me, his eyes lifted to meet mine.

A groan left him as I swiveled my hips. He held my face and kissed me hard, catching my bottom lip with his teeth and biting into it.

"Take this shirt off," he muttered against my lips, tugging on the hem of his tee that I was wearing. "I want to see your tits."

I pulled the shirt over my head and tossed it aside.

He leaned forward with a brief wince, then cupped them in his hands. He squeezed them and pinched my nipples before drawing one in his mouth.

"Now, the panties," he demanded in a rough voice.

I carefully shifted to drag my panties down my legs while he pushed his boxer briefs down. His massive cock sprang out. I rubbed my legs together, so ready to feel him inside me.

Enzo had definitely turned me into a sex fiend.

I was a big fan of his cock and what he did when it was inside me.

"Don't slow down, Blair," he said with a tortured groan as I eyed his cock. "I need to feel your pussy against my cock right damn now." He groaned again, stroking himself once.

To further fuck with him, I took the head of his cock inside my mouth, sucking on the tip and parting the slit with my tongue. His body jerked forward, his legs straightening.

"That'll do as well, baby." He pumped his hips forward to feed me more of his cock.

I did one, two, three deep-throats before drawing his cock out of my mouth and straddling him again. Reaching down, he sank two fingers into my pussy before I slid myself all the way down.

I squeezed my eyes shut, moaning at the pleasure.

"So soaked for me," he said around another groan. "Always so wet for me, baby. I can't wait to spell my name with my tongue in this pussy, like I promised, as soon as I feel better."

"As your Fawn, I think I'm supposed to be wet for you," I said around a breathy moan.

His hand left the space between my legs, and I rocked against him, spreading my wetness along the length of his hard cock.

"Please bury my cock inside your pussy before I die," he said, out of patience, and rotated his hips, as if trying to get his cock in that way. His hands went to my waist again as he started to lift me. "I'll pop as many fucking stitches as I need to hold you down and fuck you hard if you don't start riding me in the next five seconds, Blair."

Not wanting to push an injured man too far, I lifted myself before slowly settling back down onto his cock.

When he fully filled me, a soft groan escaped both of us.

I started riding him slow, taking my time, and our eyes met. Our blinking was limited, as if neither of us wanted to look away.

He smoothed his hand over my cheek, his thumb brushing my hair from my face. The tenderness of that gesture made me clench my thighs.

With every rock of my hips, he lifted his gaze to meet mine, each motion keeping a rhythm between us while I allowed myself to get lost in the pleasure of Enzo.

It didn't take long before his thrusts beneath me grew faster, harder, more urgent. I lost a breath, two, then lost count as I fell forward, bracing my elbows against the bed as he pounded his hips into mine.

An explosion of pleasure rocked through me.

Thank God he had his own wing because not only were our moans and gasps loud, but so was his bed frame, bumping into the wall with each of our thrusts.

Our skin was sweaty and our breathing erratic as we grew closer. His hand squeezed between us, and he started playing with my clit while still fucking me.

Tension built tighter and tighter, knotting into my belly as my blood shot to my core.

The way this man could do all that while recovering from a gunshot wound made Enzo even hotter. The butterflies inside me fluttered harder. Enzo could probably lose both hands, and he'd still find a way to unravel me.

I raised myself before my hips crashed against his, and all the knots inside me snapped as I cried out when pleasure rushed through me.

Enzo kept pumping beneath me until his knees locked and he groaned my name. His cock got harder, and I smiled, knowing that he'd just filled me with his cum.

I loved the way this man made me feel so good inside and out.

He made me feel so comfortable in my body.

He made me feel loved for the first time in my entire life.

"My favorite color is purple," I told Enzo while we got dressed in his dorm room.

"Knew that already," he replied.

"My favorite foods are warm toast with cinnamon butter and cherry cheesecake." I wrapped my arm around his neck and pressed a light kiss to his lips.

"And I have absolutely no idea what I want to do after I graduate from college," I added. "I never really thought I'd have much of a future."

Enzo lifted my hand from around his neck and kissed my palm before doing the same to the other. "I'll buy you anything purple I see. I'll make sure you're fed those favorites whenever you want them." His thumb brushed along my jawline. "And the only plan you need after graduation is that you'll be with me." He studied me for a moment. "Now, what's with the sudden random facts?"

I looked away, biting the inside of my cheek.

"Tell me, my Fawn," he said, his voice thick and rough.

It always sounded like that after sex, and I loved it.

When I looked back at him, I swallowed and spoke softly. "I just want you to know everything about me. Because I want you to keep me as your Fawn."

His expression darkened, and he hooked a finger under my chin, lifting it until our eyes met.

"You think that's something you need to convince me of?" His lips curved into a smile. "You're mine, Blair. You'd have to run pretty far and fast to escape me. I'm never letting you go now."

His words settled the anxiety inside me. I hadn't realized how badly I needed to hear him say those words.

My fingers slid into the front of his hoodie as I leaned closer.

"Good," I whispered. "I wasn't going to make it easy for you to get rid of me."

He caught my hand in his hoodie and led me toward the couch, moving carefully, like he'd been standing a little too long.

"I've become the Son who fell in love with his Fawn and is going to marry her." He grinned.

Not his usual irritated or smug grin.

But one that made him look genuinely happy.

That grin made me fall deeper for him.

But I was still too scared to say those words. Afraid they'd push him away, and he'd change his mind.

"I know I said I don't like you in white," Enzo continued, stretching his hand out before taking it in mine, intertwining our fingers while he scooted in closer. "But one day, you're going to wear it when you walk down the aisle before we say our *I do*'s and you become my wife."

A tiny laugh left me. "What if I don't want to wear white?"

"Honestly, I don't care if you wear black or fucking puppy

pajamas. Just know that you'll be my wife. You won't just be my Fawn anymore. You'll be a Marchetti."

Those words felt like heaven.

"And what does your family think about that?"

"My mother asked what color invitations we want."

I smiled, thinking of the woman I'd had a two-hour conversation with after she came to the hospital when Enzo was shot. I'd told her about my past, about my truths, about everything because, for once, I felt a maternal warmth from someone.

I had known at that moment that I wanted her to be my mother-in-law.

That no matter how dangerous the Marchettis were, I wanted to be a part of it. I wanted to be in their son's life and have a future with him.

"And the arranged marriage?" I asked because not only had I overheard that conversation, but I'd asked his mother about it, not knowing it was a secret.

I could tell she wasn't very happy about it.

"She said that since her son was shot, he deserved to select his own wife," Enzo told me. "Good job on blurting that out."

I smiled. "I had to make sure I don't have to fight for you."

"Never, my Fawn. I'm yours and only yours."

We sat there for another two hours, trading random facts. With each one, I fell deeper in love with him and never wanted to leave his side.

When it was over, Enzo looked me in the eye, and I loved the way his lips moved when he said, "Blair, even with every fact you gave me, light and dark, good and bad, you only proved something I never thought would wake inside me." The next words left his mouth slowly, as if he wanted me to hear each one and never forget them. "I'm in love with you, my Fawn. I want all of you forever."

Hope, love, and happiness spread through me.

Just like that emotion had climbed out of him, a feeling just as powerful surged through me. No one had ever protected me like he had. I'd never looked forward to waking up beside someone, telling them about my day, or hearing their voice.

A moment passed, and for the first time, I saw fear on Enzo's face as he waited for me to speak.

No bullet scared him.

No knife. No weapon. No threats.

Only the thought that I might not love him back.

That I didn't want him as much as he wanted me.

I pressed my lips to his and said, "I love you," into his mouth, like I wanted the words to fall down his throat and rest on his heart.

So they'd linger inside, like a new organ he needed to live, because I would be with him until he took his last breath.

# FORTY-NINE

ENZO

I t was official.

I was a Son down bad for his Fawn.

It was like my heart had cracked open and spilled every feeling I had for Blair.

For years, I'd mocked the Sons who fell for their Fawns.

Called them desperate fuckers who couldn't control their emotions.

But I learned that was what love was. An uncontrollable emotion.

It sucked that for once—and it was limited with us Marchettis —I was wrong. Tragic, if it wasn't for a good reason.

I watched Blair shrug her black Saint Vale blazer on over my button-up shirt. Every time she wore my clothes, my mouth watered. Hell, every time I looked at her, it did.

"Are you sure you're ready to go out?" she asked as I pulled on my boots. "You can rest for a few more days."

I stood from the couch and kissed the top of her head. "My Fawn needs to get out and have some fun."

She waggled her finger at me, looking cute as fuck. "You'd better take it easy down there then. No guns, fighting, or any of that wild stuff you Sons like to do."

I pressed a hand to my chest as my lips tried and failed to form an innocent smile. "Who, me? Never."

Her cheeks blushed as she grinned. I took her hand as we left the room and walked downstairs to the vestibule.

This time, I wanted everyone to see Blair was mine.

Not just at Saint Vale. Every-fucking-where.

We passed Arisono, and it took every bit of self control not to flip her off. She could've saved me a lot of time and a bullet wound if she'd just told me that Blair's *stepfather* was the vice president.

When I'd asked Blair why she called him that, she'd said that was what he'd instructed her to do. It was also less embarrassing than admitting her mom was screwing a married man.

Outside, a trace of the sun hit our skin. She chatted on our walk to the greenhouse, sharing more about her life.

I'd never cared for small talk before, but I liked it with Blair. Every new thing I learned about her hit me like a shot of adrenaline.

Learning about someone you truly cared about, about someone you loved, was its own personal drug. I wanted to pry her brain open to see all her loves, so I could give them to her. Then I wanted to find her fears and destroy them.

We entered the greenhouse, and I saluted Dr. Melro, the university's botany professor. He was one of the few chill professors here. A former Son, he'd been given the job to watch those who came and went through the Devil's Lair and the tunnels.

On our way to the back, I plucked a rose and caught Blair's hand to twirl her around. I tucked the stem behind her ear, pushing her hair back as I did.

She clasped her hand over mine, and her smile was a comfort I never knew I needed.

I motioned for her to go inside. "After you."

She glanced at me, still smiling, and I scanned my badge. Any argument that Fawns weren't allowed in the Devil's Lair was gone. Blair could come and go whenever she pleased.

In fact, I was making it a new rule that any Fawn could.

Look at me. A champion for Fawn rights.

She tried to stop me from taking the stairs first, but I gently nudged her ahead before dropping down after her and skipping the last three steps.

I immediately realized that was a mistake. I'd probably broken a stitch.

Oh well.

When Blair came down, I watched her ass, of course, and when she reached the bottom, I offered my hand.

"Hey!" She grabbed my hand and hopped off the last step. "You're the one recovering from a gunshot wound. I should be helping you."

I shook my head. "But you're the one I never want to break. I'll take the scars, the falls, and the bullets, so you'll never have to."

The lighting in the tunnels sucked, but there was no missing the heat that rose on her cheeks. I loved when she blushed.

When we stepped into the Devil's Lair, the smell of pizza and booze wafted through the air. Everyone jumped up to greet us, shouting both my name and Blair's.

I faked not feeling any pain as I moved toward them. Tonight was Nico's birthday, and all of us needed something to celebrate.

The girls had decorated the Devil's Lair for the occasion, and it looked absolutely atrocious.

Seraphina skipped over and hugged Blair tight. I smiled, happy about how easily they got along. I couldn't wait to bring Blair to family dinners and watch everyone welcome her with open arms. She was one of us now.

Daphne and the other girls hugged her next.

I tipped my head toward Daphne. While I still found her annoying as a gnat discovering sugar for the first time, I appreciated her helping me with Blair and sharing all her research.

She was a true friend to Blair, and I was glad Blair had that. I'd still need to limit my time around her, though, because I knew Blair would constantly tell me to be nice.

Unfortunately for her, she'd be telling me that a lot. What my Fawn needed to understand was that she was one of the very few people I'd ever be nice to.

Getting shot hadn't changed me.

If anything, it only made me hate everyone else more.

I glanced at the Havens and my fellow Sons. Every Son had helped me dispose of the Elder Sons' bodies and stood by me when questions came.

Each one had sworn they'd kill the Elders before ever turning on me. We'd also decided that from now on, we'd be the ones making the rules.

I watched Brooks pass Daphne without one smart-ass remark. That was a first.

Something Blair had said came back to me. She told me she finally felt safe now that her father was dead and she knew the Sons had her back. I liked that she felt safe not only with me, but with all of us.

Daphne and Seraphina started to pull Blair toward their space, but I caught her hand first and stole a quick kiss before letting them take her.

"Oh my God, *swoon*," Daphne gushed.

"Please no," Seraphina said. "I cannot watch my brother be romantic." She paused, squeezing one eye shut as if reconsidering. "Actually, I'd rather see him romantic than be a freaking menace."

Blair laughed, kissed me again, then disappeared with them.

I stole a pizza slice from an open box on the bar, dropped it onto a plate, and headed for the sectional where the guys were.

"And the devil fell for his Fawn," Emeri said.

Him being here surprised me. Him showing up for anything that wasn't strictly Sons related was rare.

What happened with me seemed to bring us all closer.

"The predator for his prey," Brooks added from beside me, kicking his feet onto the table and staring at me with a shit-eating grin.

I stole the cup from his hand and drained the rest of the bourbon. "Just wait until it happens to you." I made a refreshing *ahh* sound before sliding the empty cup across the table. "Feels even better than the rumors, I promise you, fuckers."

Emeri shook his head.

Brooks snorted.

Nico said he'd rather rip off his left nutsack.

Cedric acted like he hadn't heard me, and Cassian only shrugged.

My attention landed on Brooks. "You're not getting out of it, you know."

He turned fully toward me. "Getting out of what?"

"Don't bullshit me." I lowered my voice, knowing some of those women had the ears of a hawk. "You need to tell Daphne she'll be your Fawn."

"About that ..."

"*About that* is that she'll be your Fawn."

"I changed my mind—"

"There's no changing your mind." I set my plate to the side to rest my elbows on my knees and moved in closer. "I'll go grab that guy's ashes, glue them back to-fucking-gether and rebuild his body if I have to. You made a promise, and we keep our promises here."

The cold gaze he gave me could freeze hell.

"You don't tell her, I'll put a new announcement out." I took a bite of pizza, chewed, then added, "I'll also let your father know."

He flipped me off and slumped deeper into the couch. His father was going to flip his shit when he found out he'd chosen Daphne, and he would once Selection started. But the president would have to get over it.

She was the one who had figured out the VP wanted him dead. He owed her father a pardon for that alone. Her father was also helping to lead us to every Elder Son who'd conspired to shoot the president and my father in retaliation for us joining the Sons.

I belonged here. We all did. More than they ever had.

We were the souls of the Sons, and there was no getting rid of us.

"You don't tell her tonight, then I'm *accidentally* telling Blair, and you know she tells Daphne everything," I added to further force him.

He was still out of control and needed a Fawn now more than ever. Daphne would calm him. I was sure of it.

Sure, she'd drive him insane, but I doubted he'd be out killing motherfuckers. And I knew other eyes were already on her. We'd just taken in new Prospect Sons, and soon, they'd be joining us and choosing their Fawns. It'd be one hell of a year if I had to deal with a jealous Brooks realizing too late what he wanted.

"Since we're making our own rules now, how about we no longer need permission to ask them to be our Fawns?" he suggested. "We grab Daphne in the middle of the night, drag her straight into Initiation, and bam! She's a Fawn."

Cassian nodded. "I like that idea."

"How many of those girls would have a heart attack?" Emeri asked. "They need a warning. Otherwise, they won't know what's happening."

"It'll show us if they're strong," Brooks said.

"Sounds like someone's worried Daphne will reject him." I raised a brow. "Tell her, or we'll start a new rule where we share that news in the Devil's Lair during birthday parties."

Brooks flipped me off. "Give me a week."

I smirked, loving when a good plan came together, and headed to the bar for beers.

When I returned, I tossed one to each of them and lifted mine while keeping my voice low. "To Brooks telling Daphne she'll be his Fawn in a week." I raised it higher. "And to Nico terrorizing the world for another year."

The others kept their voices low as they repeated my words, and everyone toasted except Brooks, who only chugged his beer.

If he didn't tell Daphne, I'd do it myself.

I wanted this newer version of the Sons to be calmer. Smarter.

"This motherfucker is going to make us all choose Fawns because he fell in love with his," Cassian said in frustration. "Some of us need to take our sweet time."

"Why?" I asked. "They may end up being the best thing that ever happens to you."

After celebrating Nico's birthday, it was late when I headed back to the university with Blair. We'd left before everyone else.

I told them it was because I needed to change the bandage over my stitches, but the truth was, I just wanted to be alone with Blair.

Her voice alone calmed me, and that was what I needed.

We walked along the cloister wall, and I ran my hand over the stone before stopping her. I turned her around, lifted her by the hips, and set her on top of it.

The sudden movement the doctor had warned me about?

Yeah, I just felt that pain. But it was worth it.

What kind of fucking gentleman doesn't lift his girl?

Only a lame dick would make her do that work herself.

The cloister wall no longer meant my quiet time after killing someone. Now, it held the memory of seeing Blair for the first time.

I hopped up, ignoring the pain, and settled beside her.

"Remember when I told you this was where I saw you for the first time?" I draped my arm over her shoulders and pulled her close.

"Mm-hmm," she muttered.

"I watched you from this exact spot. You looked so lost."

Shutting my eyes, I breathed in her perfume mixed with fresh-cut grass and the rain starting to sprinkle over us. Neither of us complained about it.

She scooted closer to rest her head against my shoulder. I lowered my chin to the top of her head, then pulled back long enough to kiss her hair that smelled like my shampoo.

"I did feel lost," she said with a lighthearted laugh. "But I was wrong. Being at Saint Vale, being with you, being your Fawn is exactly where I belong."

I grinned, staring at the moonlight, and ran my fingers through her hair. We sat there, talking, laughing, and at times, just letting the silent air fall around us, until her yawning took over most of her words.

I hopped off the wall and helped her down. The moment our feet hit the ground, thunder rumbled, and the sprinkles turned into a downpour.

We headed toward the steps, and this time, while the rain poured over us, she wasn't alone as she walked them.

I was beside her, and with each step we conquered, I felt like we were climbing higher together, on top of the world.

Blair had changed who I was. She made me question my entire being. She showed me the light when I only enjoyed the darkness.

Blair, my precious Fawn, wasn't alone anymore.

And she never would be again.

Stay in Charity's Mafia World

Marchetti Mafia Series
Gorgeous Monster
Gorgeous Prince
Gorgeous Villain

Lucky Kings Series
Sinful Sacrifice
Sinful Ruin
Sinful Hearts

OTHER TITLES BY CHARITY FERRELL

Saint Vale Series

Heartless Devil

Marchetti Mafia Series

Gorgeous Monster

Gorgeous Prince

Gorgeous Villain

Lucky Kings Series

Sinful Sacrifice

Sinful Ruin

Sinful Hearts

Blue Beech Series

Just A Fling

Just One Night

Just Exes

Just Neighbors

Just Roommates

Just Friends

Twisted Fox Series

Stirred

Shaken

Straight Up

ABOUT THE AUTHOR

Charity Ferrell is a Wall Street Journal, USA Today, #1 Amazon, and #1 Apple bestselling author.

She resides in Indianapolis, Indiana. When she's not writing, she's hanging out with her dog, on a Starbucks run, shopping online, or spending time with her family.